Ben Retallick

BEN RETALLICK

E.V. Thompson

ISBN: 0 333 30611 2

First published 1980 by
Macmillan London Limited
London and Basingstoke

Associated companies in Delhi, Dublin,
Hong Kong, Johannesburg, Lagos, Melbourne,
New York, Singapore and Tokyo

Printed in Great Britain by
St Edmunsbury Press Limited
Bury St. Edmunds, Suffolk

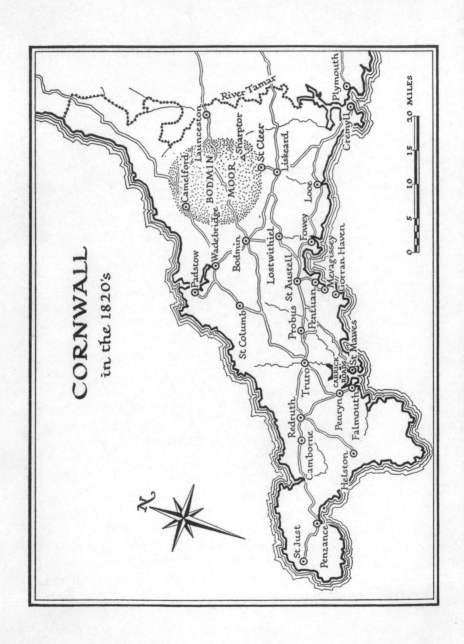

CORNWALL
in the 1820's

N

River Tamar

Camelford
Launceston
BODMIN
Sharptor
MOOR
St Cleer
Liskeard
Padstow
Wadebridge
Looe
Bodmin
Fowey
Lostwithiel
St Austell
Mevagissey
St Columb
Gorran Haven
Probus
Pentuan
Truro
St Mawes
CARRICK
ROADS
Redruth
Penryn
Camborne
Falmouth
Helston
Plymouth
Cremyll

St Just
Penzance

0   5   10   15   20 MILES

Chapter One

It was bitterly cold at the surface of the cliff-edge Money Box mine. The night wind blew from the sea with an icy ferocity, and the waiting miners about the shaft huddled closer together, cursing those ahead of them for their tardiness in descending the creaking ladders to the underground levels.

The wind carried spray from the rocks at the foot of the cliff, and young Ben Retallick tasted salt on his lips as he stood shivering in a threadbare thin shirt and cheap serge trousers.

'How's your dad, boy?'

The question came from one of the men pressing close behind him. Ben could not see his face in the poor light.

'Not so good, but he says he'll be back to work as soon as he can breathe easier.'

'He'll not be working underground again. I've yet to know a man with tin dust in his lungs get better. Tell your ma to take him right away from the mines if she wants him with her for a few more years. There's many a place in Cornwall where he'll be able to breathe air as pure as the Lord made it. Hereabouts, the dust clings like a disease.'

Ben frowned in the darkness. His mother had been saying the same thing to his father for as long as he could remember.

Martha Retallick came from the south coast fishing-village of Mevagissey and desperately wanted to return there. Pearson Retallick would have none of it. He was a tinner, at home only amongst the engine-houses and mountains of mine waste in the far west of Cornwall.

All the same, Pearson Retallick's health had been deteriorating rapidly of late, and the time would soon be at hand when he would have to do what he was told. This latest bout of lung sickness could hardly have come at a worse time. Working a poor tin lode on a high rate of tribute – or commission – Pearson Retallick and his partner had unexpectedly struck it rich: the poor-quality lode had suddenly opened out into a wide seam of ore. The two men needed to take out as much of it as they could before the next bidding-day. At that time the pitch they were working would be reassessed by the mine captain and auctioned off to the miner who was prepared to work it at the lowest rate of tribute.

The fire-doors in the engine-house of the nearby Botallack mine opened momentarily, throwing a red glow to the sky. In the unnatural light Ben saw the empty shaft of the Money Box mine yawning below him. Swinging on to the wooden-runged ladder, he began the climb down.

It was warmer in here, heat rising up the shaft from the lowest levels of the mine a hundred fathoms below, the cold night wind cut off by the rough-hewn walls.

Ben had only to descend to the thirty-fathom level. The tunnel where he worked sloped gently away from the shaft, extending beneath the rocks at the foot of the cliffs and under the bed of the Atlantic Ocean. It was here that Pearson Retallick and his partner mined the most ancient of all metals – tin.

Pausing at the mouth of the narrow tunnel, Ben lit a candle from the spitting, jumping flame of the half-inch butt he found wedged in a crevice there. He stuck the newly lit candle on his hard-brimmed hat and entered the tunnel. He had gone only a few yards when he heard the protesting squeal of an ungreased wheelbarrow, and a flickering light advanced along the tunnel towards him.

A short broad-shouldered youth, stripped to the waist, brought the heavily laden wooden wheelbarrow to a halt. Flexing the fingers of his hands, he rubbed the back of one of them across his glistening dirt-streaked face.

'Your pa still bad ?'

Dick Hooper spoke with the thick soft accent of Cornwall's far west.

Ben nodded wordlessly.

'Josiah ain't going to take kindly to that. If he had his way, we'd all be working non-stop until bidding-day.'

Josiah Clamp was Pearson Retallick's partner. The brunt of the additional work caused by the illness of Ben's father was falling on his shoulders.

'Pa says if he's no better tomorrow he'll get someone to

come in and work for him.'

'You'd best get along and tell the bad news to Josiah. I've got to get down to the sixty-fathom level. My brother should be down there working but he's sick, too. I've promised to help out for half a shift.'

Ben looked at the older boy in sympathy. At sixteen years of age, Dick Hooper was the head of his family, and its only permanent breadwinner. His father had died of lung sickness a year before, leaving Dick to support a mother crippled with rheumatism, and a consumptive brother. He would now work a half-shift at the lower level of the mine, then go home for a couple of hour's sleep. Returning to the mine at dawn, he would work a full day shift with the energetic Josiah Clamp.

'Leave everything just as it is, Dick. I'll tip the barrow after I've spoken to Josiah.'

'Thanks. I'll do the same for you some day.'

Dick Hooper lifted his crumpled shirt from the wheelbarrow. Tying the sleeves about his waist as he went, he hurried off in the direction of the main shaft.

In less of a hurry, Ben set off to find Josiah Clamp. Walking along the narrow rough-walled tunnel, Ben could hear the rumble of the storm on the sea-bed above him as hundreds of tons of shingle moved with the waves. The sound of stones grating one upon the other was a nerve-racking din in the confined space of the tunnel. Occasionally, an extra-powerful undersea current would dislodge a giant boulder and send it bouncing along the sea-bed in a terrifying game of underwater bowls. Echoing through the thirty-fathom level, the noise set every nerve in Ben's young body tingling. It gave him a feeling of raw exhilaration he had never experienced above grass. Ben was a natural miner. He had an instinct for his work, bred into him by countless centuries of Cornish tinners.

Josiah Clamp lay full length in a narrow fissure between two masses of granite, checking on the lode that opened out again beyond the rock.

Ben had to tap the miner's boot-clad foot three times before he wriggled his way backwards towards him.

When Josiah Clamp's head came into sight, he turned and glared at Ben, then looked beyond him.

'Where's your pa?'

'He's still sick. He'll get someone else in tomorrow.'

'That's no help to me tonight,' Josiah Clamp snapped. 'Damn! Why couldn't your pa have hung on for another week? Well, there's nothing else for it; I'll have to use black powder to bring this lot down. That should give you enough ore to carry away tonight. We'll have to take tomorrow as it comes.'

Josiah Clamp's statement dismayed Ben. His father would never allow gunpowder to be used on this level. He said that the sea-bed was too close above them – proof of which was the salt water oozing down the walls of the tunnel. When Ben reminded Josiah Clamp of this, the miner turned on him angrily.

'Do you think I don't know it for myself? But your pa isn't here to give us the benefit of his opinion, so I must do what I think is best. That means I'll blast. That idler Dick Hooper has left plenty of ore lying about here. You get to moving it while I set the powder and prepare the fuse.'

Ben's father was often saying that Josiah Clamp took too many chances in his eagerness to make money, but there was little that Ben could do to prevent him tonight. He could even understand the miner's reasoning. With one man trying to do the work of two, there was need for desperate measures. All the same, Ben felt a deep uneasiness about this operation.

Ben emptied the wheelbarrow left behind by Dick Hooper, then trundled it back to the work-face to pick up more ore. The Money Box was a small mine. It was a single shaft, used by the men to reach their working levels and also for hoisting ore to the surface. A horse-whim raised the ore. The same source of power operated the rag-and-chain pumps bringing up water from the lower levels of the mine.

Because of the limited means available for raising ore, each pair of miners was allocated a very short period of 'lifting-time'. In order that this should not be wasted, Ben needed to have enough ore at the shaft to fill the huge iron buckets or 'kibbles'.

He had been working for an hour and was trundling an overloaded wheelbarrow towards the shaft when Josiah

Clamp overtook him.

'Quick! The fuse is lit. Take cover.'

Hurriedly dropping the wheelbarrow to the ground, Ben followed the older miner and flung himself down behind a stacked pile of waste rock. Putting his hands over his ears, he remained tensed for almost two minutes, anticipating the explosion.

Nothing happened.

Ben uncovered his ears as Josiah Clamp cursed and scrambled to his feet.

'I thought the powder felt damp. It must have gone out. It's that bloody storeman at the Botallack mine. I pay him with good money and he palms me off with old powder that won't light.'

Ben grinned knowingly. Josiah Clamp had not paid over the counter of the Botallack mine store, of that he was quite sure. The storeman there was one of Josiah's cousins. He would have stolen the gunpowder and passed it on to Josiah in a gin-parlour for no more than the price of a drink or two.

As Josiah Clamp hurried back along the tunnel, Ben took up the shafts of the wheelbarrow again, leaning against the weight of the load.

He had taken no more than five unsteady paces when it seemed that the whole tunnel erupted about him with a terrifying roar. Ben was thrown forward over the top of the overturned wheelbarrow, an agonising pain in his head. It felt as though his brain had been crushed.

Josiah Clamp had been only partially correct about the gunpowder. It *was* old – but not damp. The straw-and-gunpowder fuse had merely been reluctant to burn. Spluttering and spitting, it burned a spasmodic course towards the gunpowder packed in a deep hole at the end of the tunnel. Not until Josiah was examining its burned-out trail did the powder suddenly flare up and take a leap forward. It had less than a foot to travel. Before the horrified miner could turn and run, he was blown into eternity.

Josiah Clamp was not to die alone on this stormy March night. As Ben picked himself up, gasping for the oxygen that had been burned up by the explosion, the ground beneath his feet began to tremble. Ben reeled about the tunnel for what seemed an age. In fact, it was seconds only before he realised that the thunderous roaring was not in his tormented head. It came from the tunnel behind him – and Ben knew what it was.

The explosion had blown a hole in the sea-bed!

The level was in darkness, every candle blown out by the force of the explosion, but Ben ran for his life, oblivious of the jagged edges of rock that grazed his head and outstretched hands. In his panic-driven flight he would have plunged to his death down the mine shaft had he not fallen headlong over the pile of tin ore waiting at the mouth of the tunnel.

Ben scrambled over the ore and his hands located the ladder leading to the surface – and safety. He climbed on to the ladder just as tons of sea-water and dislodged rock spewed from the tunnel mouth and thundered into the shaft.

The ladder began to vibrate dangerously and, although Ben was now above the level of the tunnel, the water soaked the lower part of his legs. He had begun to climb higher when his ankle was grasped from below and a hoarse scream for help reached him above the deafening roar of the water.

For a long terrifying moment Ben imagined that Josiah Clamp was trying to drag him down with him to a watery grave. He kicked out violently in an effort to break free. Then, as quickly as it had left him, reason returned. Ben realised that the hand holding his ankle belonged to another human, trying to escape from the tunnel that led inland from the thirty-fathom level.

The ladder was shaking in a frightening fashion as tons of water pounded at its lower sections. All the ladders were linked together, and it would not be long before the steel pins attaching it to the wall of the shaft were wrenched free.

This was not the moment to be thinking about what *might* happen. Gingerly, Ben lowered himself until he could reach down and grip the hand of the unknown miner below him.

As Ben secured his grip, the fingers released his ankle and closed about his wrist. With his legs twisted securely about the ladder, Ben heaved with all the desperate strength that was in him. Slowly, the unseen miner struggled clear of the thundering water pouring unceasingly from the ruptured tunnel – and then he was crouched, panting, on the rung below Ben's feet.

Disentangling his legs from the wildly juddering ladder, Ben shouted, 'Climb! The ladder will go at any moment.'

With these words, Ben began climbing as fast as his shaking legs would allow. He had made ten rungs when the ladder swung wildly to one side, with a suddenness that nearly dislodged him. He knew that the ladders below him had been swept away, leaving the one on which he was standing hanging by only one pin.

Slowly and fearfully, he climbed the last few feet to the ladder above. Behind him, the man he had rescued did the same.

Now they were both safe, Ben had to rest for a few seconds. His legs felt weak and were trembling so violently that he was afraid they would take him no farther.

'Are you all right?' The voice from the ladder below him was not that of a man, but of a boy, like himself.

'Yes. At least, I think so. And you?'

'Yes, but I have lost my boots. The water must have torn them off while I clung to the ladder. They were new only last week!'

It was such a ridiculous thing to worry about after coming so close to death that Ben felt an overpowering urge to giggle. The sound caught in his throat and came out as a choked sob. Ben gulped in air noisily until he knew he had control of himself once more.

'We had better get up top and tell them what has happened.'

Ben resumed the upward climb. This time he did not stop until he stepped off the ladder on to the ground at the top of the shaft.

Immediately, he was surrounded by the men who worked the whim, and off-duty miners brought from their beds in nearby houses when the water burst into the Money Box mine with a boom that was heard for a mile around.

'What's happening down there? What level are you from?'

Questions came at Ben from all sides.

'Thirty fathoms.'

No one worked above this level. The played-out tunnels of the ten- and twenty-fathom levels were now utilised as draining-adits.

'How many of you got out?'

A lamp was held up to Ben's face and in its light he saw the mine captain. Fresh from his bed, he tucked a nightshirt inside his trousers as he spoke.

'Two of us.'

Looking about him for his companion from the shaft, Ben saw only the faces of the anxious miners.

'Get a rescue team together. We'll go down to see what can be done.'

'Nothing can be done now.' The choking feeling in Ben's throat had returned. 'Josiah Clamp blew the top off the thirty-fathom level. The sea is in, the ladders swept away. You can't get down there – and no one will ever get out.'

For long moments the only sounds were the booming of the sea emptying into the mine and the mournful dirge of the wind as it plucked at the taut ropes of the shafthead whim.

'There are more than thirty men down there!' one of the miners whispered in horror.

'Thirty-four, and every one of them as dead as the Money Box mine,' corrected the mine captain grimly. To Ben, he asked, 'What is your name, boy?'

'Ben. Ben Retallick.'

'You will remember this day, Ben Retallick. It is the day the Lord has seen fit to take the lives of thirty-four men – and hand yours back to you. Make sure it is not wasted.'

The mine captain rested a hand heavily on Ben's shoulder, then turned away before any man could see his face.

Ben was left shivering in the darkness. Then he, too, turned and headed for home. Wednesday, 18 March 1818, was barely half an hour old. It was Ben Retallick's fifteenth birthday.

Chapter Two

In the cold grey light of early dawn, the last piece of furniture was carried from the Retallick cottage by a surly wagoner and dumped unceremoniously on the farm-wagon that stood outside the door.

'That's the lot. If you don't hurry up and climb on the wagon, we'll still be on the road when night falls.'

'If we are, then you'll need to find Mevagissey in the dark,' declared Martha Retallick. 'You'll not get paid for another day. You've been given your guinea. How long it takes you to earn it is your own business. Now, save your breath for helping with my husband.'

Pearson Retallick looked ill and frail as Ben and the wagoner helped him from the house and lifted him carefully on to the back of the wagon. He sat on a straw mattress, propped against the high driving-box seat. There was little meat on him, and he would never again earn his living digging tin beneath the ground in a mine.

Ben knew it, and so did his mother. Armed with this knowledge she had been able to get her way after many years of trying in vain to win her husband and son from the mines.

Martha Retallick hated mines and everything that went with them as deeply as her son loved them. The dust; the noise of the stamp-hammers and machinery; the ugly tall chimneys – even the miners themselves. Once above ground they had little interest in anything but brawling and drinking – and raising new generations of miners and bal-maidens to follow their unhappy example.

Martha Retallick's brothers and cousins were fishermen. Her father and his father before him had been fishermen, too. It was a permanent way of life, a healthy living. In Mevagissey old men might be seen standing on the jetty at dusk, sucking contentedly on their pipes as they talked and waited for the fishing-boats to return to harbour.

There were no old men in the mining areas. Those who miraculously survived the ladders, the roof falls and the hundred other daily hazards to be found below ground ended up like Pearson Retallick, dying of lung sickness, with half of their allotted lifespan unfulfilled. Few miners found contentment in their work – and Martha Retallick firmly believed they never would. They attacked and violated the land, taking what they wanted and discarding the remainder, leaving deep scars for all to see. She was convinced this was the reason they were paid back a hundredfold by the land. It took from them their health and happiness – even life itself.

Such was Martha Retallick's deep-rooted belief. Because of it, she used the disaster at the Money Box mine to force her husband to abandon mining once and for all. The mine would never be worked again, and Pearson Retallick's career came to an end with it. He would never again be able to find employment as a miner. The family's future now depended upon what she and Ben were able to earn. Ben was still classed as a boy. He might earn twenty shillings a month – if he were lucky enough to find a generous and sympathetic mine captain. For the surface work she was able to do, Martha Retallick would bring in another twelve shillings. Neither job would provide them with a house.

Martha Retallick argued that, if they returned to Mevagissey, Ben could go fishing with her family while she worked in the family's fish-cellar. Together they would earn twice as much and could live in the house occupied by Ben's grandfather and grandmother until they found somewhere of their own.

Supported by Ben, Pearson Retallick held out for as long as he could, but had finally been forced to give way to the logic of his wife's argument. He had agreed to leave the St Just mining area and move to Mevagissey.

Ben protested in vain that *he* was a miner and not a fisherman. His mother would not be thwarted now. She told Ben he was lucky to be alive. He should accept the disaster at the mine as a warning and turn to something else. To go down a mine and risk his life again would be flying in the face of providence.

As Martha Retallick closed the door of the tiny mining-cottage for the last time, she had not a single twinge of regret.

She had arrived at this cottage as a young bride. Ben, her only son, had been born here. But that was the only good thing to which she would admit during the whole of her life at the Money Box mine.

Climbing up to the high wagon-seat, she nodded to the wagoner. Flicking the reins, he shouted unintelligible orders to the horse. The beast leaned into its padded collar, and the Retallick family was on its way.

There was no one to see them leave the Money Box mine. No friends to wave, or wish them well in their new lives. The out-of-work miners had already moved away to seek work elsewhere. Only the families of the men who had died remained. There was nowhere for them to go. They would stay on at the derelict mine until hunger and desperation drove them out to join the scores of beggars and discharged veterans of Wellington's great and victorious army, roaming the lanes of Cornwall.

The journey along half the length of Cornwall passed without incident, although Pearson Retallick was shaken up badly by the pot-holed road. By the time they began the steep descent of the hill leading down to Mevagissey village he was in a state of exhaustion.

The horse, too, was tired. Head hanging low, it slipped and slid on a road wet and muddy after the storms of recent weeks. Halfway down the hill, on a sharp and narrow bend, they overtook a young girl. Across one of her shoulders was balanced a long pole, at each end of which was a large and cumbersome basket.

As the wagon passed, the tired horse slipped – recovered – then slipped again. The wagoner was so busy braking the wagon and cursing the horse that he hardly noticed the girl.

She stood as far back from the road as was possible, balancing on the very edge of a short but steep bank that fell away to a half-filled ditch. Unfortunately, there was little room at this particular spot, and as the wagon slid to one side it clipped one of the baskets.

Ben watched in awed fascination as the baskets and pole swung lazily in a wide arc, twisting the girl around. She lost her footing, stepped backwards and tumbled down the bank, the baskets falling with her. As the girl landed in the ditch they crashed to the ground and burst open, releasing a number of indignant, noisy and wildly flapping ducks.

Martha Retallick had not seen the accident occur, and she was startled when Ben leaped from the wagon to the ground. He slid down the bank to the unfortunate girl's aid while the wagoner continued to curse his horse, working all the time to keep the wagon on the road.

When Ben reached her the girl lay half-submerged in mud, her thin legs protruding from a froth of petticoats and dress. reaching down he grasped the neck of her dress and pulled her to her feet.

She came out of the mud like a cork from a bottle, but she showed very little gratitude to her rescuer. Flailing wildly, her fists caught Ben two substantial blows in the face. He immediately released his grip on her dress, and she slipped on the wet grass and fell back into the ditch.

This time Ben made no attempt to help her. Looking up at the road he saw the wagon disappearing around the next bend. His father waved to him, a wide grin on his pale face.

'Well! Don't just stand there. Help me!'

The girl was on her hands and knees in the ditch, glaring up at Ben.

'Why? So you can hit me again?'

Clamping her mouth tight shut, the girl hoisted her skirt above her knees with one hand and used the other to pull herself from the ditch.

'It was your cart that knocked me off the road. Look at my ducks! They are everywhere.'

She grabbed at one of the birds, which was head down in the ditch, worrying at the mud. The duck complained vociferously, but she unceremoniously dumped it in one of the baskets and went in pursuit of another at the edge of the water.

Ben helped her to recapture the remainder of the ducks. It was not an easy task, and by the time the last one was safely back in its basket he was almost as wet and muddy as she was.

'Look at the time!' complained the girl, glancing up at the

sky. 'The boats will have been in for ages. The best of the fish will be gone long before I get to the quay.'

'I'll help you carry the baskets.'

'No, you won't! You've caused me enough trouble.'

The girl's dark eyes warned Ben off as she shouldered the pole and baskets, but she did allow him to help her up the steep bank to the road.

As he walked beside her down the hill, he said, 'I'm sorry you've got all muddied up. The wagoner has never been to Mevagissey before. He didn't know how steep the hill is.'

The girl snorted derisively and they walked together in silence for a while. Then her mouth twitched in a sudden mischievous smile, and she gave him a sidelong glance.

'I don't suppose it was your fault really. Besides, you are as muddy as me now. I haven't seen you before. Do you come from Mevagissey?'

'No, from St Just.'

'Isn't that where all the mines are?'

'Yes, I'm a miner.'

Seeing her incredulous look, Ben's chin went up. 'Well . . . my pa was a miner. I worked with him. Now we've come to live in Mevagissey.'

'Why? There are no mines here – none worth mentioning, anyway. A good thing, too. Miners are digging farmers' graves, that's what my dad used to say. What are you going to do here?'

'My pa is ill. He can't work any more. So, when the mine flooded, Ma said we should come here for me to learn fishing with her folks.'

Ben lapsed into a deep silence as he remembered the Money Box mine.

The girl looked at him with sudden renewed interest. 'The mine you worked in . . . was that the one where all the men were drowned?'

'Yes.'

Ben clenched his fists tightly, and she could see the tension in him.

'I heard that only one miner, a boy, escaped. Was that you?'

'There were two of us, but I don't know what happened to the other one.'

'That must have been an awful experience.' She looked at him with a new respect. 'What's your name?'

'Ben Retallick.'

'I'm Jesse Henna. Me and my ma have a small farm up the hill at Pengrugla. Just a couple of fields really. But we get by.'

They had almost reached the small harbour now. Ben stopped at the entrance to a lane that was so narrow that the upper storeys of the houses on either side were only inches away from each other.

'This is where my grandpa lives.'

She nodded. 'Then you had better go. They will be wondering what has happened to you.'

Ben had turned to walk away when Jesse Henna called out to him.

'What is the name of your mother's kin?'

'Dunn.'

'I know them. They are good fishermen. I'll look out for you when I next come to Mevagissey and trade for any fish you've caught.'

Ben raised his hand in acknowledgement and made his way to Grandpa Dunn's house.

The little fishing-cottage had always fascinated him on his infrequent visits here as a small boy. Cosy and lacking light' it tucked tight into the hillside. The back door actually opened out of the roof on to a narrow terrace that descended in a series of elongated cobble steps to the harbour.

Ben let himself in through the front entrance and walked into an atmosphere that was as chilly as winter rain. Grandpa Dunn was leaning well back in his rocking-chair, watching the smoke from his clay pipe drift upwards towards the low beamed ceiling of the kitchen. In front of the fire Grandma Dunn busied herself with pots and skillets, arranging them noisily on the black foundry-made range. The old lady's bristling disapproval was held in check only by the smug satisfaction of being proved right – after sixteen years of waiting.

Grandma Dunn had never approved of her daughter

Martha's marriage to a miner. She had given it her reluctant blessing in a moment of uncharacteristic weakness, upon learning that Pearson was a Methodist – as were the Dunn family. But she had warned her daughter that no good would come from such a union. Mining, she had declared, was the Devil's work. The Prince of Darkness had his kingdom in the bowels of the earth. Men who invaded his domain either paid tribute to him or suffered the consequences. As a small girl, Grandma Dunn had listened to the fire-and-brimstone sermons of the aged John Wesley. His words had burned into her soul, allowing of no argument. Hell was in the darkness beneath the ground. Heaven was above; it came down to meet at the sea where a fisherman earned his living. It stood to reason, therefore, that a fisherman was closer to the Good Lord than any other man alive.

Grandma Dunn did not hear Ben arrive, so busy was she with her own thoughts. When she turned round and saw him for the first time, her hands found her hips and she glared at him in disapproval.

'Goodness gracious, boy! What *have* you been doing to get yourself in such a state? Whatever will the neighbours think? Away with you. Get out of those clothes before you dirty up my kitchen. You'll not sit down at this table in filthy trousers like those.'

'These are my best clothes! I've only got my working-trousers—'

'Don't argue with your grandmother, Ben,' Martha Retallick interrupted quickly. She wanted to avoid an argument at all costs. 'Your working-trousers are clean; they will do fine. You'll find them in the old trunk, upstairs in the back bedroom. Go on, now.'

When Ben left the room, Martha Retallick tried to explain why Ben was in such a mess.

'Hah!' The lines about Grandma Dunn's mouth deepened and her mouth clamped shut for a moment. 'There is no need for any boy to get into such a state. You are my daughter, Martha, and are welcome to stay here, but I'll have no miner's ways in this house.'

Still grumbling, the old lady turned back to her cooking,

and Martha Retallick breathed a sigh of relief. Family dissension had been averted – for a while. She would need to talk to Ben. To tell him to tread lightly in this house. Martha had succeeded in bringing her family to Mevagissey after many years of trying. She wanted nothing to go wrong now.

When Ben returned to the kitchen, an appetising meal of fish and potatoes was placed upon the table in front of him. Grandma Dunn, her feelings aired, was in a better mood.

Martha Retallick asked why places were not being set for her three brothers and received a look of surprise from her mother.

'Why, bless you, girl, I keep forgetting how long it is since you were last here. Your brother Mark has been married these four years, and Billy for three. Between the two of them they have given me five grandchildren.'

'And Walter? Is he not married yet?'

Grandma Dunn's jaw snapped shut as fiercely as a gin-trap. 'There is more than one girl's mother with reason enough to wish Walter had married years ago; but you had best be asking your father about Walter and his goings-on.'

'He is off at a parliamentary reform meeting,' said Samuel Dunn. He spoke through his fingers as he dislodged a fish bone, caught between two of his remaining teeth. 'Very strong for reform is our Walter.'

'Does Walter think we should all have the vote?' asked Pearson Retallick, speaking for the first time since Ben had entered the house.

'Walter thinks all manner of nonsense,' interjected Grandma Dunn. 'Unless he can learn to hold his tongue about some of it he will find himself in serious trouble. Sir John Vincent up at Lamorrack House has already warned him about preaching sedition to the estate workers. He told Walter that Parliament in London intends bringing in laws aimed at those who put foolish ideas into other folks' heads. Walter ought to listen to him. I've told him many times that no fisherman will benefit from all this "reform". It is a squabble between gentlemen. It won't put more fish into the nets, or sail a boat home at the end of the day. Instead of tramping around the countryside talking about things that don't concern him,

Walter should spend more time down on the quay, repairing his nets.'

Pearson Retallick would have pursued the subject, but his wife silenced him with a look. For a while the meal continued in silence. Then Samuel Dunn spoke to Ben.

'I hear you want to become a fisherman?'

'No . . . but Ma wants me to become one.'

Spoons stopped scraping on plates as everyone looked at Ben. For a moment he wished he had thought before speaking out, then his grandfather laughed.

'That's the same thing. We'll send you out with Walter tomorrow. He'll teach you all you need to know about fishing. Whatever your grandma might think, there is no better fisherman along this part of the coast. This time next year you'll be catching as many fish as a Mevagissey-born boy, you wait and see.'

Ben doubted whether he would ever fulfil his grandfather's hopes, but he said nothing of his thoughts.

As soon as the meal was over, Ben went to bed in the small dark back-bedroom he would share with his mother and father. That night he dreamed of fishing-boats being washed through flooded mine tunnels by wild sea currents, while a dark-eyed girl with black hair called for him to come with her and rescue some ducks.

Chapter Three

Early the following morning, Ben was shaken into wakefulness before the sun had risen. Bleary-eyed, he made his way downstairs to the kitchen. A tall bearded young man was dipping his head repeatedly into an iron-banded bucket that stood on a slate-topped table in a corner.

Raising his head and blowing hard, Walter Dunn grinned at Ben. 'Come on, youngster. Mevagissey fish don't wait around for those who lie in bed all day. Here, wake yourself up with this.'

Shaking water from his hair, he reached for a rough towel and rubbed the excess water from his face as he backed away from the bucket.

Ben was more cautious than his exuberant uncle. Cupping his hands, he brought the water up to his face. It was breathtakingly cold. Had Walter not been watching him, Ben would have forgone the unnecessary luxury of this early-morning wash altogether.

Breakfast became a hectic affair as the rest of the household rose and crowded into the tiny kitchen. Ben was glad when it was over and he was able to set off with Walter, followed by the good wishes of the family.

As he strode briskly beside Walter Dunn, men nodded to them. One or two called out to Walter, asking him about the previous evening's reform meeting. It was a subject about which Ben knew nothing, and he listened carefully as Walter spoke about 'rotten boroughs', 'purchased votes' and 'potboiling franchises'. It did not take him long to realise that Walter Dunn believed passionately in parliamentary reform, and the right of every man to vote for a Member of Parliament to represent him in the House of Commons in London.

But Ben's main interest was in the work that lay ahead of him. As he and Walter made their way along the edge of the quay, he asked Walter about the day's fishing.

'Are we going after pilchards?'

'We are going out after any fish that might be about,' declared Walter. 'If we catch pilchards, then so much the better, but I doubt if we will find any at this time of the year.'

Walter stopped suddenly, and Ben looked up at him questioningly.

'Look, Ben, times are not good for anyone – fishermen in particular. We have to make a living any way we can. Some of the things we do have very little to do with fishing. Ask no questions and keep your mouth shut about anything you see and hear. You do that and no Mevagissey man will be able to fault you. Is that clear?'

It was not, but Ben expected he would find out soon enough. He nodded.

'Good! Now, come and meet the fishermen you'll be working with.'

Walter led the way down a flight of green-stained stone steps that disappeared into the water of the harbour. Bumping against them were two twenty-foot-long wooden boats into which five men were loading nets and baskets.

Walter's introduction was brief. 'This is Ben, my sister Martha's son. He's been mining down-country until now, but the mine has closed and his father is sick. He'll be fishing with us in future. Mark . . . Billy, Ma says she expects you up at the house to meet Martha when we get back tonight.'

Mark, the eldest of Samuel Dunn's sons, was not happy with Ben's presence.

'I'm sorry to hear about Pearson, but do you think it's wise to bring the boy out with us? The Frenchie is expected any day now . . .'

'I have told Ben there's more to earning a living at sea than shooting a net and tucking fish. He'll learn, the same as we had to.'

Mark Dunn shrugged and turned back to his work. Walter told Ben to take his place in the bow of the boat crewed by Walter and two other fishermen. It was not long before they were ready to put to sea, and they left the small harbour in company with the other boat, in which were Mark, Billy and a third fisherman.

It was the first time Ben had been in a boat. He did not

enjoy the novel experience. Although it was by no means a stormy day, there was a fresh south-easterly wind blowing, and a fairly heavy swell. Within minutes of leaving harbour Ben began to feel ill. He kept his queasiness to himself for as long as he was able. Then, without warning, he was forced to make a dive for the gunwale. Hanging with his head only inches above the undulating water, Ben lost his breakfast.

His discomfiture brought a cheer from the following boat. When Ben raised his head miserably, he saw Walter and the two fishermen in his own boat grinning at him, greatly amused.

'Never mind, Ben.' Walter leaned back on an oar, sending the boat sliding over the crest of a long round-topped roller and tilting into the trough beyond. 'You'll feel better when we give you some work to do. Mevagissey has never yet lost a man or boy from seasickness. I doubt if you will be the first.'

Huddled in the bow of the boat, Ben could only nod miserably. He wished his stomach would keep time with the rise and fall of the vessel.

About a mile from the shore, the men in the two Dunn boats began casting their long seine-nets. Fastened at each end to one of the boats, the net was cast in a wide circle. When both ends were brought together the net was tightened until the fish were trapped inside its diminished circle and the fishermen were able to scoop the fish into their boats. Ben found this movement of the boat even more upsetting than being under way, but Walter set him to tucking fish and kept him busy.

The shooting out and drawing in of the net was repeated many times during the day. In between, Ben continued to suffer seasickness. By the time the day's work was over and the boats returned to Mevagissey, he was close to exhaustion.

It did not help his misery when he saw Jesse Henna waiting at the quayside. Clean and cheerful, she was the last person Ben wished to meet in his present dejected and sick state.

'Hello, Ben. How did your first day's fishing go?'

The pale and drawn face he turned to her told his story better than any words.

'Oh! You were seasick, then?'

'You might say that, missie,' one of the grinning fishermen answered her question. 'Young Ben was hung over the side for so long we might have mistook him for a long-line if he hadn't twitched once in a while.'

The laughter of the men in the boat was echoed by the fishermen standing on the quay. Brought up to feel equally at home on sea or land, few of them had ever suffered from seasickness. It was an amusing affliction from which only landsmen suffered.

Ben felt too wretched to take offence at the laughter of the fishermen. He had been longing desperately for his return to the land. Now, standing on the steps of the quay, it seemed the land, too, was swimming about him. He reached out to steady himself against the stone wall.

Jesse was highly indignant at the jeers of the fishermen. 'Being ill is nothing to laugh about. I would like to see your faces if you were to stand at the top of a deep mine shaft. The thought of climbing down in the dark would set your knees knocking so hard you wouldn't stay on the ladder for two minutes. It wouldn't worry Ben.'

'You'm probably right, missie. That's why fishermen go out in boats and miners should stay at their diggings.'

Jesse had done Ben no favour by reminding the listeners that he had worked in a mine. Miners and fishermen were different breeds of men, each scornful of the other's way of life.

But Jesse used the fisherman's retort to come to the main reason for her visit to the quayside. 'As a fisherman you'll likely have caught something worth trading for three dozen eggs. They were laid this very day.'

From the basket resting on the ground at her feet she took a clean brown egg.

All differences were forgotten, and swift bartering began. When the eggs and a dozen and a half fat mackerel had changed hands, Jesse asked Ben, 'Are you going home now? I'll walk a way with you.'

Ben wanted desperately to turn his back on the boat and the harbour, but he knew there was more work to be done.

'I have to help bring the fish ashore before I go.'

Jesse shrugged, putting on an air of indifference to hide the unexpected disappointment she felt. 'It doesn't matter. Here, have these . . . I saved them for you. They are to thank you for helping me with the ducks last night.'

She reached a hand into a pocket of the apron she wore. Pulling out two eggs, she thrust them at Ben. When he had taken them she turned away abruptly, ignoring the thanks he called after her.

'Well, I don't know!' exclaimed Walter, scratching his thick black beard. 'You've been in Mevagissey for hardly a day and already you've found yourself a pretty young maid. Tell me, Ben. How come you know young Jesse Henna?'

Ben told Walter the story of the wagon and the ducks. By the time he ended every one of the fishermen was chuckling.

'You got off lightly, young Ben,' commented Walter Dunn. 'Had I been a wagon that upset her I would have legged it away from there as fast as I could go. Jesse Henna was as likely to have hit you with the pole she carried, as look at you. She is a wild one, and no mistake.'

Ben remembered how Jesse had come out of the ditch swinging at him with her fists, but he kept the memory to himself. As they worked he asked Walter what he knew of Jesse Henna.

'Not much more than I have told you already. She and her mother have a place up at the head of the valley, at Pengrugla. They keep some livestock and mind their own business. What more is there to say?'

'What happened to her father?'

'Ah! Now, that's a question that might have more than one answer. Jesse's mother used to work up at the big house, at Lamorrack. She's a handsome woman – and was an even prettier maid. She married Tom Henna in something of a hurry. Folk said Jesse's birth came as more of a surprise to poor Tom than it did to Sir John's son, Colman. Whatever the truth of it, the Vincent family allowed Tom to get away with a great many things that might have hanged another man.'

Ben was intrigued. 'What sort of things?'

As they talked, they stood in line with the other fishermen, passing baskets of fish from the boats to the quay. Walter called down to one of his brothers, who was in a boat.

'Billy! You knew Tom Henna well enough. What would you say about him?'

'Tom Henna? He was a clever poacher and no respecter of other folks' livestock or property. There was talk of him taking part in more than one highway robbery on the old toll road. Such talk apart, he was a likeable enough chap – if you didn't fall foul of his quick temper.'

'What happened to him?'

'He fled the county and joined the Army after almost killing a man in a fight at Pentuan. It seemed he was as good at fighting Frenchmen as Cornishmen, and he died a hero's death at Waterloo. Sir John Vincent let Jesse and her mother stay on at Pengrugla – "in recognition of Tom's sacrifice for King and country", so 'twas said.'

'Does Jesse know about the talk?'

'Who knows? I certainly wouldn't ask her. If you have any intentions towards her, then neither will you,' Walter said. 'That's the last basket, Ben. We'll finish off here now. You get on home and tell your grandma we'll be there within the hour. Don't forget to take your present with you. I would lay you a wager that young Jesse came to Mevagissey especially to give them to you. Bringing the other eggs was no more than an excuse. She's a nice young maid, Ben. You could do a lot worse . . . But away with you now.'

Slipping the eggs into separate pockets, Ben set out for his grandmother's house, wishing the world would stop swinging about him.

It was almost dark now, the tangle of fishermen's cottages effectively blocking the last light of the setting sun from the narrow streets of the village. Ben was so deep in thought about Jesse, and of what Walter and the others had said, that he did not see the faint glow of a pipe in the shadows beside the door of the Dunn cottage.

'Is that you, Ben?' It was Pearson Retallick.

'Yes, Pa. You shouldn't be sitting outside now. It's coming in cold.'

'I've been waiting for you to get home. They've had you

working a long shift out there today. How did you enjoy the fishing?'

'It was all right. A bit new to me, that was all.'

Ben was glad it was dark, he had never been able to lie to his father.

Pearson Retallick was not taken in by Ben's words.

'You are bound to find the work difficult at first, Ben. It's very different to working below ground – but a sight healthier! I wish I had taken to fishing. I could have been out there with you today. A father likes to teach his own son to make his way in life. All I seem to have done is to lead you along a short path to nowhere.'

'You taught me mining, Pa – and you taught me well. That's what you know about – and what I enjoy doing. I always will. Fishing might be healthier, but I am no fisherman. I know it, and so do those I have been out with today. Sooner or later Ma will have to know it, too . . .'

'And what is it I am to know?'

Martha Retallick had gone upstairs to shut the windows of the bedrooms against the cool night air. She had heard Ben's last few words.

Looking up, Ben could just see the white of her face against the dark shadow of the window. 'We are talking about fishing, Ma. I am no more a fisherman than Walter is a miner. He'll tell you the same thing when he comes home. I spent most of the day being sick over the side of the boat. I was no help to him at all.'

'Then you'll need to keep going back to sea until you *stop* being sick, won't you? You are as much a Dunn as a Retallick, and the Dunns have been fishermen for as far back as anyone in Mevagissey can remember. There is no reason in the world why you shouldn't be one if you set your mind to it.'

Martha Retallick's face disappeared, and the window was slammed shut with a crash that set the small glass panes shivering.

'Your ma is right, Ben.' Pearson Retallick's quiet voice pricked the bubble of Ben's anger. 'Give fishing a chance – just to please her. She's had little enough pleasure from life so far. I'll have a chat with Walter in a week or so. If he

30

agrees with you that you'll never become a fisherman, I will take the matter up with your ma then.'

Ben dreaded the thought of going to sea for another few weeks, but he knew his father would keep his word. For his part, Ben would do what was expected of him until then.

As it happened, Pearson Retallick's intercession would not be necessary. The stage was already set for a drama that would shake Martha Retallick's faith in the permanency and respectability of fishing.

Chapter Four

Ben's second day at sea began in much the same way as had the first. No sooner had the two Dunn boats nosed out of the smooth waters of the harbour into St Austell Bay than Ben's stomach began rebelling against the alien combination of wind and sea.

True, his nausea subsided to some extent when they began working the nets, but towards mid-afternoon the wind freshened from the east and the feeling returned. The boat bounced and lurched beneath him, and when Ben was not helping with the catch he stayed huddled miserably in the bow of the boat. He did his best to keep out of the way of the fishermen, but they cursed him soundly when the unpredictable movement of the sea caused them to stumble against him.

Then the dark-blue sails of a three-masted barquentine appeared on the horizon, and the three men in the boat forgot all about Ben. They called to the fishermen in the second boat, and they, too, became inexplicably excited. From that moment, they fished in a desultory manner, seeming not to care whether or not they caught any fish.

By now, Ben was thoroughly ill and miserable. He wanted only to return to harbour. He was relieved when, one by one, the other Mevagissey boats stowed their fishing-gear and headed for home. Soon the two Dunn boats were the only ones still fishing. Ben looked eagerly towards Walter, waiting for him to give the order to stow their fishing-gear and return to Mevagissey.

The order never came. The fishermen sat at their oars, smoking their foul-smelling clay pipes and giving an occasional half-hearted pull on their oars to bring the bow of the boat into the sea.

They stayed out until the sun was sinking beneath the horizon into a fiery sea and Mevagissey was no more than a distant sprinkling of lighted windows. Only then did Walter give his order. It had the fishermen in the two boats moving with an alacrity that astonished Ben. The long net was hauled onboard, and the men strained on their oars with a vigour that made light of the long day's work behind them.

But they did not head for Mevagissey. Instead the two fishing-boats headed out into the waters of the English Channel. They were going to meet the barquentine, now bearing down upon them with every inch of her blue sails spread to catch the wind.

Minutes later the two fishing-boats bumped against the heavy timbers of the barquentine and a voice carrying a strong French accent called for Mark and Walter to come on board.

His indisposition temporarily forgotten, Ben watched with great interest as the two Dunn brothers swarmed up ropes let down from the sailing craft. His excitement quickened when, seconds later, a cargo that had little to do with fishing was handed down to the waiting fishermen. Casks and barrels were stowed in the boats beneath the day's catch. Others were lowered into the water and secured to the stern of the fishing-boats by long stout lines.

The operation was carried out with well-practised efficiency. By the time Walter and Mark returned to their respective boats the oars were already being run out. Moments later the two boats were heading for the distant harbour of Mevagissey.

The clandestine operation had taken less than ten minutes. Looking back into the Channel, Ben saw the shadow of the French barquentine heeling over under full sail. Turning westward, she headed along the Cornish coast to another illicit rendezvous.

In that short time, Ben had become a 'freebooter'. A smuggler.

Walter had brought a bottle of fine-quality brandy with him from the French ship and it now passed from man to man as they pulled for the shore. The bottle was handed to Ben, but the first whiff of the pungent brandy fumes made his stomach rebel again. He gave it back to the nearest oarsman, untasted.

As the fishermen laughed and joked amongst themselves, Ben looked ahead over the bow of the boat. He hoped that if he took huge gulps of the cold air blowing on his face his stomach might settle down again.

Sliding through the water, side by side, the two boats were no more than two hundred yards from the sea-wall of Mevagissey harbour when Ben saw an indistinct movement between the fishing-boats and the cottage lights, visible through the harbour entrance.

'There's a boat ahead of us!' he called to Walter.

At his words, the fishermen stopped rowing instantly. Leaning on their oars, they listened, straining their ears into the darkness. The only sound was of the incoming waves rushing through the crevices of the nearby rocks, and the squeaking of oars in the rowlocks of the other Dunn boat as it forged ahead.

Walter sent a long low whistle across the water in an attempt to attract the attention of his brothers. It was doubtful if they heard him – and it was already too late.

A flame spluttered hesitantly to life ahead of them. It was joined by another. Suddenly there were half a dozen torches flaring, the flames from them blowing in long irregular streamers.

'It's the Revenue men!' whispered one of the fishermen in Walter's boat. Walter waved the man into silence. A large Revenue boat was heading towards Mark and Billy Dunn's boat, driven through the water by eight of the King's men, one to an oar. More of them crowded in the stern, eager for the action to come.

'Mark and Billy will need help . . .' Even as Walter made the observation, the Revenue boat went alongside the other fishing-boat with a splintering of oars and a great cheer from the King's men. Then the dull crack of a musket-shot echoed across the water.

One of the men in the boat with Ben uttered a startled oath. 'I'm not tackling armed Revenue men, Walter. Pull for the harbour – and be damned quick about it!'

'But . . . Mark and Billy . . . ?'

'It's too late to help them. Unless you want the Revenue men to take all your father's sons, we'll need to get in fast as we can. Hurry, man! You're helping no one by dithering out here.'

Crouched in the bow of the fishing-boat, Ben's heart beat as fast as a sparrow's wing. Peering over the gunwale he saw the other two vessels locked together as their occupants fought out an unequal battle.

Common sense prevailed over family loyalty. There were at least fifteen men on board the Revenue boat, most of them armed.

Walter said, 'Ben, get back here to the tiller. I'll tell you what to do as we go along.'

Ben scrambled to the stern of the boat. He had only the vaguest idea about steering a boat, but it needed only a couple of experimental pressures on the tiller to give him the knowledge he would need. By this time the fishing-boat was cutting through the water, the sea slapping heavily against the bow.

Their desperate attempt to escape the attentions of the Revenue men was noisy. As they passed around the fringe of the light cast from the torches they were spotted. A cry went up from one of the King's men, and seconds later a musket-ball sped angrily above Ben's head. Fortunately for himself and his companions, the captured fishermen realised what was happening. They created such a disturbance that the Revenue men were hard pressed to hold them and quickly lost interest in Walter's boat.

Ben guided the boat through the wide gap in the harbour wall. Once inside, Walter shipped his oar and came back to take the tiller himself.

'Good work, Ben. I'll take her now. We'll need to get alongside and clear the boat before the Revenue men follow us in.'

'What will happen to the others?'

'It will be time to think about that when the Revenue men bring them in. We've men enough in Mevagissey to prevent them being taken off to gaol. If we fail . . .? We'll worry about that when the time comes. Here, take this rope and stand by to jump the moment we touch the steps.'

35

Although it was dark in the harbour, Walter brought the fishing-boat in skilfully and swiftly, guided by his knowledge of the lamp-lit windows of the houses around the harbour. Soon the boat scraped along the stone wall of the quay and Ben could make out the deeper shadow of the steps. Leaping ashore, he secured the rope to a huge iron ring.

He had hardly finished tying the knot when a number of men appeared from the shadows about him. At first he thought they must be Revenue men, but when one of them greeted Walter in a low voice Ben realised that smuggling in Mevagissey involved more men than were in the Dunn family.

In quick low monosyllables Walter explained what had happened out beyond the harbour. The Mevagissey men immediately set to clearing the boat of fish and contraband. Not ten minutes after entering the small harbour the boat had been emptied and pulled clear of the steps. Once it was moored amidst a jumble of other fishing-boats there was no way of connecting Walter with the events of the evening.

There was still work for the fishermen to do. With the boat safely tucked away they turned their thoughts to those who had been taken by the Revenue men. Surrounding Walter, they listened as he laid plans for an elaborate rescue attempt.

Ben was given no part in this promised action. Walter Dunn sent his nephew on his way with an order for him to go straight home. Ben was a boy – and this would be a night for men.

Ben made his way to his grandparents' house, not knowing whether he was disappointed or relieved to have no part in what was certain to be a desperate and dangerous exploit. Along the way many men passed him, all hurrying to the harbour. It seemed every fisherman in Mevagissey intended being on the quay to provide a reception committee for the Revenue men and their prisoners.

When he entered the Dunn house, Ben gave his news to the stunned occupants. Grandfather Dunn immediately reached for his coat and rushed from the house without a word. Grandma Dunn sank down on a chair, convinced that her two sons would be hanged. Not until much later did Ben learn that there was very good reason for her concern. It was

36

less than a year since a fisherman from a nearby village had been convicted of smuggling and publicly hanged for his misdeeds. The government of the land was determined to stamp out smuggling in Cornwall – and was prepared to adopt harsh measures to achieve its ends.

Ben's mother listened in white-faced consternation as Pearson Retallick questioned his son about the events leading up to the Revenue men's ambuscade.

When Ben told him the whole story, the sick miner rounded on his wife, who was now trying to comfort her mother.

'Do you realise how close Ben has been to getting himself arrested for smuggling?'

Martha Retallick looked up, startled. She was unaccustomed to angry outbursts from her even-tempered husband.

'They wouldn't have done anything to Ben. He didn't know what was going on. He just happened to be in the boat, that was all . . .'

Her argument died away, defeated by its own weakness.

'There's not a judge in the land who would have believed him – and you know it well. Is this your idea of a better life for our son?'

'I am sure nothing like this will ever happen again . . .'

'So am I.'

Pearson Retallick was overwhelmed by a violent spasm of coughing. When it subsided, he spoke more quietly. 'I may not be much use to you any more, Martha, but I can still think like a man. Ben is a miner and not a fisherman. He doesn't belong in this house. Neither do I.'

Turning, Pearson Retallick saw Ben watching him, wide-eyed.

'You have seen and heard enough for one day. Off to bed with you now.'

'I want to wait until Walter comes home.'

'What he is doing could keep him from the house all night – or for ever. Go to bed now, Ben. I need to talk with your mother.'

Reluctantly, Ben left the room and climbed the stairs to their bedroom. At the top of the stairs he opened the window and leaned far out, looking into the darkness towards the harbour. He could see nothing, and no sounds carried to him on the night air.

Ben slid between the rough blankets and began to think about the events of the last two days – especially of what had happened after the meeting between the two Dunn boats and the French barquentine. He now knew why the fishermen had expressed their misgivings about having a stranger go out with them. Smuggling was as much a part of their lives as fishing.

Ben had no objection to becoming involved in such activities, but he wished Walter had trusted him enough to tell him what was likely to happen. He wondered what the fishermen did with the contraband when it came ashore. He would prefer to help with this side of the operation. Ben knew he was no sailor and would never become one, no matter how hard he tried. Even thinking about boats and the movement of the sea made him feel ill.

From the room downstairs, the sound of voices came to Ben as a low monotonous drone. He could make out nothing of what was being said and eventually he dozed off.

He woke up with a start as the door was pushed open on ungreased hinges. Pearson Retallick entered the room and prepared for bed. There were many more people downstairs now; Ben could hear their voices raised in heated conversation.

'What's happening, Pa?' Ben whispered. 'Is Walter home yet?'

'Yes.'

Ben waited for his father to say more. When nothing was forthcoming, he said, 'What of the others – Mark and Billy?'

'Rumour has it they have been taken to Plymouth to be put on board one of the warships there. If it is true, they will be sailing for the Mediterranean before the week is out.'

Ben gasped. 'The Revenue men can't do that! Mark and Billy have families—'

'That should concern you no more than your future worried them. Think yourself lucky that you are safe in bed and not being pressed into the Navy, leaving your mother behind to weep for you.'

Ben lay quietly in the darkness for a long time before he asked his father quietly, 'Will Walter be going fishing in the morning?'

'He might – but you won't be going with him.'

'Why? What am I going to do?' Ben sat up on his mattress, a great surge of relief going through him.

'We will all need to leave this house, Ben. Someone will have to take in Mark and Billy's wives and children if they are not to be thrown on parish charity. Your grandma wasted no time in pointing that out to me. This is the obvious place for them to come. There will be no room for us.'

'Where will we go?' The news filled Ben with excitement. He hoped they might return to the mining district of Cornwall's far west where he could go back to work that was familiar to him. His hopes were dashed by Pearson Retallick's next words.

'The Vincent family up at Lamorrack House want a woman to work in their kitchens. Your ma and me are going up there to see them in the morning. I am hoping they might find a house for us if I do odd jobs in the grounds for them.'

'What about me?'

'I would like you to bide your time for a while, Ben. Likely I will need you to help me out for a while. Just until my strength returns, that's all.'

Ben understood. His father's pride was too great for him to admit that he was incapable of holding down a job of work without his son to help him. The knowledge brought a lump to Ben's throat, and he said no more of his own hopes.

Chapter Five

The following morning, Walter and the two men who fished with him put to sea about their normal business. By so doing they would stay clear of any questioning Revenue men who might search the village for the companions of the captured men. Ben saw Walter before he left the house and was shocked by his tired and haggard appearance. Walter was taking the blame upon himself for not having done more to rescue his two brothers. Nothing Ben said could convince him otherwise.

Pearson and Martha Retallick left the village to walk to Lamorrack House immediately after breakfast. They had not been gone many minutes before the families of Mark and Billy Dunn descended upon the small cottage. Soon it was filled with the noise of wailing women and the crying of bewildered children.

Ben beat a hasty retreat. For an hour or two he wandered the narrow streets of Mevagissey, unused to having so much time on his hands. He looked on without any great interest as a new boat was launched from the small boat-building yard in a corner of the harbour. Ten minutes later he was looking in through the door of the mill, watching huge granite grinding-stones rumbling one upon the other in powerful unison, driven by a creaking timber water-wheel revolving on an outside wall.

There was little else to interest Ben in Mevagissey. Eventually, he decided to set off to meet his mother and father. They should be on their way back from Lamorrack House by now.

Ben made his way along a rough track through the valley to the north-west of the village. Within minutes he was in a new world. Rounding a low hill, the track cut through a small wood and left all sight and sounds of Mevagissey behind. Only the bird-calls and the sound of a stream flowing swiftly over a shallow bed of stones disturbed the deep peace.

Ben was unused to such countryside. In St Just every tree had long since been cut down and burned as fuel for home and mine-engine boiler; the song-birds driven far away to undisturbed countryside where they could build their nests. The trees had been replaced by tall stone-built engine-house chimneys, bird-song by the clank and clatter of whim and stamp-hammer.

Ben stopped once to watch a crimson-crowned woodpecker scale a tree, tapping at a hundred crevices in search of insects. Next, he searched the skies for a bird that was sending out plaintive cries, like those of a lost kitten. It was a buzzard with blunt tip-tilted wings, circling high above a nearby field.

So intent was Ben on watching the hunting bird that he walked along totally oblivious to his surroundings, his head high, eyes following the progress of the buzzard.

The bird changed its flight-pattern, banking in a long gliding dive. Ben turned around, walking backwards as he followed the bird's flight.

Suddenly he bumped against something – something that moved and shoved him hard in the back, sending him sprawling full length on the path.

Ben looked up from the ground to see two boys of about his own age looking down at him. One was grinning, the other scowling. Ben was certain thay had not been ahead of him before he turned around. They must have been hiding among the trees.

'You want to watch where you're going,' said the scowling boy, the larger of the two. 'You nearly knocked us down.'

The second boy's grin widened, and Ben stood up slowly and carefully brushed himself off. Not until this was done to his satisfaction did he meet the larger boy's eyes.

'You're quite right. I *should* have been looking where I was walking. But I am not going to apologise. You could have stepped out of the way. There was no need to push me over.'

'Move out of the way for a fisherman?' The big boy's look was scornful. He nudged his companion with his elbow. 'Do you suppose all fishermen walk backwards? Perhaps it's because they row their boats that way. They get used to it, I

41

suppose. Makes you wonder how they get on when they go to bed with their women, don't it?'

Ben waited quietly until the two boys had finished laughing.

'You could wet yourself, laughing like that,' he said, addressing the larger of the two boys once more. 'I'm sorry to spoil your joke, but I'm not a fisherman. I'm a miner. Now, if you move aside, I'll be on my way.'

'Miners are no better than fishermen,' said the boy aggressively, the scowl once more on his face. 'And what is a miner doing along here, eh? We've got no mines in this valley. We don't want none, neither.'

'What I'm doing here is my own business.' Ben moved to step around the scowling boy. Quickly side-stepping, the boy blocked his path once more.

Ben's heart began to beat a little faster. He knew he was in for a fight. The thought did not trouble him unduly. He had been in many fights before. Among miners, fighting and wrestling were favourite pastimes. But Ben had two opponents here. He would need to land the first punch. He moved to one side as if to try to pass the boy in front of him again. Waiting until the other boy did the same, Ben quickly shifted his feet and put his shoulder behind a punch aimed at the larger boy's groin.

Ben had been working underground in a mine from the age of ten, and during the last year at the Money Box mine had been pushing heavy wooden wheelbarrows loaded with up to three hundredweight of ore. He had muscles that were the envy of grown men.

The scowling boy let out a cry of agony and slumped to his knees as Ben turned to meet the rush of the second boy.

He took him in a 'bear hug' and both boys crashed heavily to the ground, rolling over and over until they were brought up short by a tangle of briars.

Ben released one of his arms and aimed a blow at his adversary's face, but the other boy was quick and wiry. He got home with a couple of punches of his own before Ben's heavy fist landed.

42

By this time the first boy had recovered sufficiently to launch himself at Ben. For a while, Ben was hard put to hold his own against the two country boys. Then unexpected help arrived in the form of a shrill-voiced girl who pulled off one of the boys and held him by the collar of his shirt while she laid about him with a stick.

It was Jesse Henna, and she and her flailing stick proved too much for Ben's assailants. They fled along the path past a startled brown cow. Jesse's voice followed them until they were out of sight.

'You should be ashamed of yourself, Joe Teague. You too, Billy Rowe. Neither of you would dare start a fight on your own – nor stay when it's two against two . . . even though one's a girl. You're bullies and cowards, the pair of you.'

Turning back to Ben, Jesse's mood underwent a swift change.

'Are you all right? Have they hurt you? Here, let me look at your eye; there's a nasty graze just beneath it. Come over to the stream and let me bathe it for you.'

Ben allowed her to lead him to the stream. After washing his face, he brushed down his clothes as best he could while Jesse inspected his eye and 'tut-tutted' at him for not keeping still.

'It's all right,' he said at last. He felt she was making far too much of the graze. It only hurt when he blinked his left eye.

'It's not all right,' retorted Jesse. 'But it's better than it was before.'

Wiping a fragment of dirt away with a flourish of her pinafore, she asked, 'What started the fight?'

Ben shrugged, disconcerted by the closeness of this slim and dark-eyed girl whose whole being vibrated with life and energy. 'They just wanted a fight. But what are you doing here? I thought you lived up there.'

He waved a hand in the general direction of the head of the valley.

'I do, but our cow has been down at the valley farm – where Joe Teague lives. We use their bull. I'm taking her home now. Where are you going?'

Ben told Jesse about the interview his parents were having with Sir John Vincent and informed her he was on his way to meet them.

'Oh! I thought you might have been coming to Pengrugla.'

She sounded disappointed. Puzzled, Ben asked, 'Why should I be going there?'

Jesse coloured up and said quickly, 'It doesn't matter. Where will you live if your mother gets a job at the house? Perhaps Sir John will offer you Tregassick. It's empty at the moment. That would be nice. You would be close to our place there. But I thought you were going to become a fisherman. Why aren't you out with the boats today?'

'I doubt if I will go fishing again. There was some trouble last night . . .'

Jesse stared at him uncomprehendingly, but at that moment a horsedrawn farm-cart came into view along the track and Jesse had to shoo her cow out of its path. As they stood back to allow the cart to pass, Ben saw his parents seated in the back. They called for the wagoner to stop, and Ben's mother beckoned to him.

'What on earth have you been up to?'

Martha Retallick's hands went up to straighten Ben's hair and she peered closely at his grazed eye.

Jesse had driven her cow further along the track and now she returned to stand near the wagon. Feeling awkward and tongue-tied, Ben introduced Jesse to his parents, adding that she was the girl who had been knocked into the ditch by the wagon from St Just.

'Humph!' Martha Retallick began vigorously slapping the dust from Ben's jacket. 'It looks to me as though she has had her own back on you today.'

'It wasn't me who got him dirty,' explained Jesse cheerfully. 'He got in a fight with Joe Teague and Billy Rowe. That's how he hurt his eye. But you should see them. Ben gave them what for, even before I arrived to help him.'

'Did he, now? I'm sure I should be pleased to hear that, but I doubt whether Sir John Vincent will be interested to know how well Ben can use his fists. All he will see is a scruffy boy with a grazed face and dirt on his clothes. That's not the sort of lad he'll want working for him.'

'Work for Sir John Vincent? Doing what?' Ben looked apprehensive. 'Does that mean I'll have to work up at his house?'

'No, Ben,' Pearson Retallick answered his son. 'It seems Sir John owns the Happy Union mine down at Pentuan. It's tin-streaming – no underground work – but it's a mine. Sir John has given me a job, too. Counting the wagonloads of ore going on the ships down at the harbour. But you had better get up to the house. Sir John wants to see you, to learn what you are capable of doing.'

Martha Retallick sniffed. 'You needn't look so pleased, my son. It doesn't mean that I suddenly approve of mining. I don't. If this had been underground work, I wouldn't have let you take the job, even if it meant losing my own. Working above ground is different.'

Ben remembered that his mother had said much the same thing about fishing, but he did not want to remind her of the previous night. He felt happier than he had for a long time. He was going back to mining – and his father would be working, too. The future suddenly seemed much brighter for both of them.

'Did Sir John give you a place to live, Mrs Retallick?'

'Yes, he says there is a house and barn at Tregassick where we'll be comfortable enough. Why?'

Jesse gave Ben a brief triumphant glance. 'I thought it might be Tregassick. We'll be near-neighbours.'

'Not if we don't get a move on, you won't,' said the driver of the farm-cart. 'Stay here talking for much longer and my cart will take root. We'll never get your bits and pieces up to Tregassick at this rate.'

'Then what are you waiting for?' snapped Martha Retallick. 'Get your horse moving. I intend being in by nightfall.'

The driver shook his head in despair and cracked his whip above the flank of his startled horse. As they moved off, Martha Retallick called to Ben, 'You go straight up to Lamorrack House and see Sir John Vincent now – and brush

45

the dirt from your clothes before you get there.'

Waving his hand in acknowledgement, Ben turned his back on the trundling farm-cart. When they caught up with the cow Jessé gave it a sharp smack across the rump with her stick and the beast trotted along the track ahead of them, its udder swinging awkwardly from side to side. Jesse fell into step beside Ben, and when they cleared the trees and came out into a long meadow she pointed ahead of them. 'There's Lamorrack House.'

In the distance Ben saw a gigantic mansion set among tall trees. It was the largest house he had ever seen. It must have contained at least forty, or even fifty, rooms.

'What is Sir John Vincent like?'

Jesse shrugged her shoulders. 'He's rather nice really. A bit strict – but I expect that's because he's a magistrate. His son is a magistrate too – and a Member of Parliament – but I don't like Colman very much. Sir John owns all the land about here, and the fishing tithes at Mevagissey. He's always been very kind to me and my ma.'

She suddenly looked serious. 'You'd better not let him find out that Walter Dunn is your uncle. Sir John believes all reformers should be horse-whipped, then hung, drawn and quartered as traitors.'

'I know nothing of "reform", and before these last couple of days I hardly knew Walter.'

'All the same, make certain Sir John doesn't learn you are related. If he finds out, you won't be at Tregassick for very long.'

The track became steeper as they left the valley and began the climb up the hillside towards the house. At close quarters Lamorrack House looked even larger than before. The sheer size of it completely overawed Ben. Seeing this, Jesse decided to accompany him to the house. She gave the cow a sharp slap on its rump and it went swinging on its way along the track. It would find its own way to Pengrugla from here.

Ben was grateful for her offer. Ahead of them were at least three paths through the wooded gardens of Lamorrack House. He was terrified of ending up in the wrong place and incurring the wrath of the titled and all-powerful landowner.

Jesse led Ben along a track that kept to the trees. As they approached the house, hemmed in on either side by tall flowering rhododendrons, Ben saw a tall man of about thirty-five standing on the path ahead of them.

Jesse saw him, too. 'That's Reuben Holyoak, Sir John's gamekeeper.'

She greeted the gamekeeper as they drew closer, but Reuben Holyoak was scowling at Ben, and it was to him he spoke.

'What are you doing here? These are private woods.'

Ben was taken aback by the undisguised hostility of Reuben Holyoak to a complete stranger but he replied politely enough.

'I've come to see Sir John Vincent.'

'What for?'

Ben had no intention of telling his business to this man. 'You'd better ask Sir John Vincent. He wants to see me.'

'That's right,' agreed Jesse. 'Ben and his parents are moving in to Tregassick.'

Reuben Holyoak's scowl shifted to her. 'What has it to do with you? Why are you here with him?'

'Oh, Reuben! Ben is going to be a neighbour and he's new in these parts. He needs all the help we can give him.'

'Is that so?'

The surly gamekeeper gave Ben his attention once more.

'Then I'll give you some neighbourly advice. Keep out of Sir John Vincent's woods if you don't want to fall foul of me. I'll give you some, too, Jesse. Don't latch on to every stranger you meet. Walking with them in such out-of-the-way places can lead you into trouble.'

Jesse's mouth dropped open in astonishment. Then colour rushed to her face and surprise turned to anger.

'What I do is none of your business, Reuben Holyoak – and I don't "latch on" to every stranger who comes to Lamorrack. You'll do well to bridle your tongue – or I'll loose mine. It was no stranger who tried to get me into trouble in these very woods when I was thirteen years old. Sir John doesn't treat such matters lightly.'

Now Reuben Holyoak's face glowed a fiery red, and without another word he strode off along the path.

Jesse gave Ben an embarrassed grin. 'You mustn't take any of that too seriously, Ben. I don't think Reuben meant anything he said to you.'

'What about . . . the thing you reminded him of? When you were thirteen?'

Jesse laughed shakily. 'It was nothing. Reuben was feeling fatherly towards me and went too far. That's all.'

Jesse was being less than honest with Ben – and he was aware she was not telling the whole truth. Reuben Holyoak was old enough to be Jesse's father, but there was nothing paternal in the way he looked at her. He had been filled with jealousy when he spoke to Ben. Reuben Holyoak wanted Jesse. Ben did not doubt that he would do everything within his power to ensure she went to no one else.

The path they were on led to the servants' quarters, at the rear of the great house. Before reaching the back door, Jesse gave Ben a final brush down with her hand and inspected him in a manner that reminded him of his mother. Then she wished him luck and left him to knock on the door.

After passing through a huge kitchen, occupied by at least half a dozen servants, Ben was led along numerous dim passageways and then made to wait in a small stone-flagged hall.

It was almost an hour before the summons came from Sir John Vincent. During that time many servants passed to and fro through the hallway, but not one of them paused to speak to Ben. He became so nervous that he would have left the house had he thought he could find his way back to the kitchen door.

Then a stony-faced butler came to fetch him. Looking at Ben's heavy miner's boots, he sniffed loudly and told him to avoid walking on the carpets. Ben was taken to a large walnut-panelled study where the thick-piled carpet had him walking on tiptoe, wishing he owned a pair of shoes.

Sir John Vincent was seated at a desk in front of the study window, writing on a long sheet of paper. The quill pen scratched across the page with bold swift strokes and occasionally Sir John jabbed at the wide-rimmed ink-jar with unerring accuracy.

After a couple of minutes, he put down the quill and looked up at Ben. His eyes took him in from head to toe and lingered briefly on his face.

'How did you come by that graze?'

Ben fingered his eye quickly, 'I . . . I was watching a bird as I came through the woods . . . I walked into a tree.'

'Ha!' Ben could see that Sir John Vincent did not believe him. 'I want no troublemakers working for me, Retallick. No one is going to disrupt my mine by fighting. Do you understand me?'

'Yes, sir,' Ben gulped.

'You came towards the house a while ago with young Jesse Henna. How long have you known her?'

'Only a few days. She fell into a ditch. I helped her out and caught some of her ducks . . . sir.'

He added the 'sir' quickly because he sensed that Sir John was waiting to hear it.

The baronet frowned at Ben's disjointed explanation, but he did not pursue the matter.

'I see. Well, you will be neighbours, so it is as well that you get along. Now, tell me of your mining experience.' Sir John Vincent leaned back in his chair.

Happy to be talking of something he understood, Ben told the baronet of his five years spent working underground with his father, and of the things he had learned from him.

It was not long before Sir John held up his hand to silence Ben.

'All right, Retallick. It is clear you have not wasted your time so far. Keep up your interest in mining and you will one day become a much-sought-after miner. Get down to the Happy Union stream-workings in the morning. Tell Captain Ustick I have taken you on. He will put you to work. You will be on boy's wages until you have proved yourself. With shoulders like yours it should not take you too long.'

Sir John Vincent tugged at a bell-cord beside the desk, and a few moments later the butler arrived to show Ben out. He had reached the door when the baronet called to him.

'Retallick?'

Ben turned around.

'Don't fall into bad company at the Happy Union. I am
told some of the men have been heard talking about parliamentary reform. Any man reported to me for involving himself in such matters will be instantly dismissed. Remember
that.'

The baronet returned to his letter, and Ben was ushered
from the room. He was now the latest employee of Sir John
Vincent, eighth baronet. Champion of the 'rotten' boroughs
of Cornwall.

Chapter Six

Ben and his father set off for work together at dawn the following day. The diminutive harbour at Pentuan, where Pearson Retallick was to work, was less than a mile away. The Happy Union mine was half a mile further on.

The way was downhill. Even so, Pearson Retallick was forced to rest when they were no more than halfway to Pentuan. His impaired lungs were incapable of supporting him for any sustained effort – even walking.

'I think Ma likes the new house, don't you, Pa?'

Ben made conversation so the enforced delay would not seem any longer than it was.

'I'm sure she does . . . nothing to dislike about it. Roomy . . . no one overlooking us. It might be a bit lonely for a while . . . but that isn't a bad fault.' Pearson Retallick summoned up a faint smile when he was able to breathe more easily. 'Your young maid had no trouble finding us there.'

Jesse Henna had called at Tregassick within minutes of their arrival there. She brought with her milk, eggs and a pair of willing hands to help Martha Retallick scrub floors and tidy up the house. It had lain empty for many months, and there was much that needed doing.

'Jesse is nobody's maid,' Ben retorted with such indignation that Pearson Retallick's smile widened. 'She goes her own way. She felt like helping Ma, so she did. That was all.'

In spite of his own words, Ben knew there was the beginning of an understanding between Jesse and himself. After Martha Retallick had persuaded her that she had done enough work for one day, Ben had walked Jesse to her home. Not many words were spoken by either of them along the way, each content to be in the company of the other. The walk in the warm spring evening had passed all too quickly.

'We're not going to be much use to Sir John Vincent sitting up here talking of other things. We'll need to be on our way or the day will be half over before we get to work.'

Pearson Retallick had recovered sufficiently to go on. Pushing himself up from the grassy bank where he had been resting, he set off down the hill at a determined pace. Ben followed, wishing there was a way to tell his father to walk more slowly, without reminding him he was a sick man.

At the foot of the hill a small river met the sea on a beach of smooth sand. Here Ben parted company with his father, Pearson Retallick going to the loading-jetty, close to the beach, Ben making his way up-river to the tin-streamings.

The Happy Union 'mine' proved to be very different from those in which Ben had worked, farther west in Cornwall. The 'levels' were not tunnels deep in the ground, but trenches dug in the hillside to form an intricate interconnecting pattern. Water was pumped to the highest level and used to wash the ore-carrying gravel down to the lowest. Here it was picked out and crushed to extract the tin.

The captain in charge of the Happy Union mine was a huge bearded Cornishman who weighed at least three hundred and fifty pounds. His name was Loveday Ustick and he made Ben repeat the details of his mining experience.

Captain Ustick's shrewd eyes never left Ben's face during the whole time he was talking. When Ben finished, the big miner hooked his thumbs into the wide leather belt over which his stomach overflowed. His bushy eyebrows almost hid his eyes as he said, 'You think underground miners are God's chosen people, don't you, boy?'

Ben was surprised. 'Far from it, Cap'n Ustick. If they were, God would make life a whole lot easier for them. I know more about underground mining than I do about anything else. I have never stopped to wonder whether a miner was any different from a streamer.'

Captain Ustick's eyebrows returned to their normal position, and Ben saw that the tin-streaming captain had very blue eyes. 'Don't start thinking about it now, Retallick, and you'll get along fine at the Happy Union. I'm the best damn tin-miner you'll ever meet, but I've never found it necessary to try to squeeze this body of mine into any miserable little mole-run. Now, get to work in that bottom level over there and show me that you know what raw tin looks like.'

The task Ben had been given was children's work. He smarted at Captain Ustick's way of letting him know that his experience in deep mining counted for nothing here. But he said nothing and settled down to the fast rhythm of picking out the ore-bearing gravel from among the waste. He had been working steadily for a couple of hours when a shadow fell upon the trench. Looking up from his back-aching task, he saw the mine captain.

'All right, Retallick, you've had yourself an easy morning. Now we'll see how you manage a wheelbarrow. Someone is needed to take ore to the crusher farther along the level. Hurry up, now.'

That was the second of five different tasks given to Ben that day. At the end of it Captain Ustick declared himself satisfied with Ben's progress. He allocated him to a permanent team with the task of winning ore from the rich lower level of the valley. Ben had been accepted as a tin-streamer.

There was another boy of Ben's age working with the team and Ben looked up on more than one occasion on the second day to see the boy watching him, a frown on his face.

Not until they took their noonday break did the other boy approach Ben. He waited until Ben had moved away from the other tin-streamers to inspect the water-wheel that produced power for the stamps to crush the ore.

'You're Ben Retallick from the Money Box mine?'

'What if I am?'

There was such a natural belligerence about the other boy that Ben sensed trouble. Nevertheless, this boy's voice was familiar. Ben tried to remember where they had met before.

'I owe you my hand, Ben Retallick. I am Moses Trago. You pulled me up the ladder, the night the sea came into the Money Box mine.'

The hand that gripped Ben's was strong and firm. 'But for you I'd be down the mine now, along with all the others. I couldn't have held on in that torrent for long.'

Ben was delighted to meet someone who had also been an underground miner – and he was relieved he was not going to be called upon to fight this tough-looking dark-visaged boy.

'What happened to you when we reached the top of the

53

shaft? I looked around and you had gone. No one could tell me who you were.'

'I had my reasons for not staying.' Moses Trago looked embarrassed. He felt he owed Ben an explanation.

'I . . . I ran away from home, such as it was. I heard my father was trying to find me. To get me to go back. If word got around that I'd been saved from the Money Box mine, it might have led him to me. So I just upped and left. It's not bad here. Some of the streamers are a bit nosey, but loosen a tooth or two in their heads and they soon learn to mind their own business.'

Ben looked at the other boy's large hands and the wide spread of his shoulders. Moses Trago would have no problem holding his own against any man.

'Where are you living?' Ben asked.

Moses Trago waved his hand vaguely towards the valley, up-stream from where they were standing. 'Along there a way. A few of us have built places for ourselves in the woods. And you?'

Ben told Moses Trago about the house at Tregassick and of the work his mother and father were doing. He invited Moses to come and see them. The serious secretive boy said he would, but Ben was left with the feeling that social visits were foreign to Moses Trago's nature.

When the time came for them to resume working, Ben and Moses Trago took up their tools and worked side by side. They talked about mutual acquaintances in the mines of the far west, and Moses told Ben what the area around Pentuan had to offer. During their conversation, Ben learned a little more about the parliamentary reform movement. In spite of Sir John Vincent's opposition it seemed that the movement had a strong following among the tin-streamers of the Happy Union and the miners from the huge underground mines only a few miles away at the head of the valley.

There was an urgent need for reform. Votes were sold and bought like so many shares in a mine, yet the vast majority of the men in the country were unrepresented in the House of Commons.

The same cry for suffrage was going up from many of the

new industrial centres in the Midlands. It was a voice that was determined to be heard. Most miners, together with the men, women and children of the Midlands, lived and worked in appalling conditions – but nobody cared. Those who sat in Parliament were too busy keeping the country's ever-increasing wealth in the hands of the few powerful landowners who had made them Members of Parliament.

Ben learned from Moses that Walter Dunn was one of the most active local reformers, with a large personal following.

At the end of that day, Ben went home from work well satisfied with life. He was once again among miners – men who spoke the mining language, using mining words and sharing jokes that made no sense at all to anyone who was not a miner. Ben was almost back where he belonged.

During the next few weeks, Ben's happiness was marred only by the knowledge that his father's attempts to re-establish himself were not succeeding as well as his own. Pearson Retallick's problem lay in the distance they lived from the small harbour at Pentuan. The walk was too much for his dust-laden lungs. Once there, he was fine – the work was neither hard nor demanding – but he had to walk home up a steep hill at the end of the day.

At first, Pearson Retallick waited for Ben to finish work, and they would go home together. But, as the weeks went by he was obliged to rest more and more frequently along the way. Reluctant to allow Ben to witness his constant battle for breath, he began making excuses to walk home alone. Most nights he would remain at Pentuan, waiting until Ben had gone, before beginning his journey. Always he arrived home in a state of near-collapse.

It was a situation that could not last indefinitely. Pearson Retallick would soon have to give up working. Ben became desperately worried at the effect it would have on his father. He was not a man to spend his days happily at home, doing nothing but watch the seasonal changes in the fields and woods about the house.

One evening, when Martha Retallick was working late at Lamorrack House, Ben and his father were alone at Tregassick, and Ben tried to broach the subject.

He found his father excessively touchy.

'There's nothing wrong with me that I can't cope with. I can manage as well as the next man. You begin worrying about me when I ask for your help, not before.'

He spoke so sharply that Ben turned away, hurt. He went to leave the house, but before he reached the doorway his father called him back.

'I'm sorry, Ben. I shouldn't have spoken to you in that way. I know you mean well. I know you care. But this is something I must work out for myself. If I give up, or pass the problem on to you, I'm finished. I become a burden to everyone I love. I don't think I could live with myself if that were to happen, Ben.'

Ben wanted to argue with his father, to tell him that becoming a burden was not important. The only thing that mattered was for Pearson Retallick to stay alive and remain with his family for as many years as possible.

Ben could not bring himself to speak the words. His father had just said more to him about his illness than he ever would to anyone else. The subject was closed, and Ben left the house filled with unhappiness.

Then, in June of that year, an event occurred that, terrible though it was, gave Pearson Retallick a temporary respite.

For days a south-easterly gale had pounded Cornwall. It was particularly severe along the stretch of coast about Pentuan and Mevagissey. In Mevagissey the sea-wall was breached and heavy seas sank many of those boats that could not be quickly drawn up to the safety of the narrow water-washed streets.

At Pentuan things were even more serious, but the danger was not appreciated until it was too late.

The village was little more than a cluster of houses huddled in the lee of a hill, protected from the sea by a wide bar of sand that stretched across a gap between the cliffs. This sand also prevented the sea from running up the wide valley to where the Happy Union tin-streaming mine was situated.

During the days of the storm, this natural barrier took an unprecedented battering. Driven by winds of near-hurricane force, the waves from the bay roared up the beach, attacking the protective ridge. Each wave, as it made a grumbling retreat, took with it tons of irreplaceable sand. Not until the highest tide of the year was expected, and the storm showed no sign of abating, did the residents of Pentuan suddenly realise the very real danger they were in. By now, only a thin strip of sand stood between the village and the sea.

With every villager helping, the men from the Happy Union mine toiled all night to reinforce the inadequate barrier, using rocks and trees carried from the woods behind the valley. They were still working when the final dawn broke and the tide threw its great weight behind the raging storm.

News of the fight to keep back the sea had spread around the countryside. It was a Sunday, and the cliffs and slopes on both sides of the beach were soon crowded with sightseers. Some, more brave – or more foolhardy – than the others, lined the road behind the sand. They were mostly young men and girls. The former, outdoing each other in a bid to impress their companions, ventured ever closer to the inadequate breakwater. The girls, in their turn, gasped and screamed as waves hit against the reinforced sand-ridge and threw spray thirty feet in the air, drenching those young men daring enough to stand their ground.

'Damned young fools!' muttered Captain Ustick as he returned from ordering a group of the young men away from the makeshift breakwater. Wielding a broad pointed shovel, the captain of the Happy Union mine was working as hard as any of his miners – and perspiring more than any two of them. 'If they have so much energy to spare, they should come and help us, instead of showing off before the maids like stupid young fighting cocks.'

Although he had warned them off, Loveday Ustick never thought the young men were in any real danger, although the tide was already encroaching farther inland than anyone in the small coastal village could ever remember – and it still wanted half an hour before high tide.

The situation changed suddenly and dramatically at the very moment Sir John Vincent arrived on the scene to see for himself how the coastal barricade was withstanding the storm.

Driving a pony and trap, Sir John turned from the road on to the flat waste ground behind the barrier just as a series of huge waves broke against it. The waves had been building up across almost two hundred miles of English Channel. The first one roared up the beach, flinging hundreds of tons of sea-water against the hastily constructed barricade. As it subsided, it could be seen that a gap, fifty feet across, had been torn in the breakwater. Captain Ustick knew there would be no holding back the sea now. He bellowed for his men to run for their lives.

Even as they ran, a second wave, larger than the first, thundered in from the sea. It smashed through the gap, crumbling the sea-wall on either side as though it were a biscuit, and a ten-foot-high wall of water surged into the valley beyond.

The foolhardy young men and screaming girls were overwhelmed by the rushing water and carried away, struggling and shouting as sea-water poured into the valley. Driven by wind and tide, it swept away everything in its path.

The wave had rushed past Sir John Vincent, but his pony and trap were on low-lying ground. Within seconds, water was swirling about him, higher than the floor of the trap. The pony, chest-deep in water, was thrown into a panic. It reared and plunged in terror as Sir John fought to keep it under control.

Bowled off his feet by the sea-water, Ben regained his footing no more than two arms' length away from Sir John Vincent's terrified pony. Floundering towards the animal, Ben caught hold of the harness just as the baronet slipped and fell in the trap.

'Whoa! Whoa!' Ben's experience with horses had been limited to patting the rump of the old blindfolded beast plodding a never-ending circle on the whim of the Money Box mine, but he had no fear of them. Calming the animal quickly, he led pony and trap to the safety of higher ground.

Dishevelled and wet, Sir John Vincent regained his footing and began berating the animal. Ben turned away as screams rose from the throats of nearby spectators.

'Boy? Retallick?'

58

Ben turned as Sir John Vincent called to him.

'Thank you, boy. You kept your head and saved me from a thorough soaking – at the very least! Come and see me at Lamorrack. Do you hear me?'

Ben nodded; then, as the screams of the crowd of young girls and women rose in a crescendo, he turned to watch the drama being enacted across the flooded valley, where a river of water, now a hundred yards wide, poured in from the sea.

Some of the miners had formed a human chain in a vain attempt to reach three young girls in the centre of the torrent. Swept along by the force of the water, their dresses floating around them, they were as colourful as flowers in a stream – and equally as fragile.

When the men farthest from shore were out of their depth and floundering helplessly against the pull of the tide, a couple of them broke away and attempted to swim to the girls. Even as they did so, the girls disappeared, pulling each other down as they sank. For a brief second one of them rose to the surface, choking violently. She disappeared again and there was only the swirling water spreading ever wider across the valley.

Then Ben saw Jesse. Pale-faced, she stood at the edge of the flood, her hands up to her mouth, watching the spot where the three girls had disappeared.

As Ben reached her, she looked up at him, her eyes wide and frightened with the horror of the scene she had just witnessed.

'Did you see them?' she whispered hoarsely in disbelief. 'They just sank and disappeared . . . drowned!'

It was the first time Jesse had been a witness to such a tragedy. It came as a shock to Ben to learn that others had not witnessed violent deaths. He had lived all his young life in a mining community where death was commonplace and arrived in many guises. He knew that the three girls they had just been watching were not the only ones to lose their lives in this disaster. When the water subsided many more bodies would be recovered.

Reaching Jesse's side, he put a hand on her arm. 'You'd better go home now, Jesse.'

59

She stood as though she were in a trance, looking out across the flooded valley. 'I know one of those girls, Ben. Her name is Kathie. She sat next to me in church this morning . . .'

Jesse was in a state of shock and Ben put an arm about her shoulders. 'I'll take you home.'

As though in a dream, Jesse allowed Ben to turn her away from the water and lead her slowly up the hill towards Pengrugla. Not until they were well away from the sounds of the pounding sea and the cries of the crowd waiting ghoulishly for more excitement did Jesse emerge from her shocked state.

A sob came from her, racking her body from head to toe. She turned to Ben, and he held her while she cried as though she would never stop.

It was the first time Ben had ever held a girl in his arms. It made him feel older than his fifteen years, and more of a man than working a hard day underground among miners ever had.

He held her until she was able to control all but the occasional ragged sob. Then he pushed her gently away from him.

'Are you all right now?'

Her eyes and nose red from crying, Jesse bit her lip and nodded vigorously. 'I think so. Thank you, Ben.'

When they reached the junction in the path where they would go in different directions, Jesse stopped and caught Ben's arm.

'You've been very kind to me, Ben.'

Ben smiled at her. The memory of her warm body in his arms was still with him. It was a very pleasant feeling.

'You were upset, that was all. Anyone would have been . . . after what happened.'

'I'm glad you were there to look after me, Ben.'

Before he realised her intention, Jesse stood on tiptoe and kissed him on the lips. Then she turned away and ran off along the path to Pengrugla. Ben watched her go, his face as fiery as an autumn sunset and his chest puffed out with all the importance of his newly discovered manhood.

Chapter Seven

Moses Trago paid his first visit to Tregassick that afternoon. He came to tell Ben and his father that the flood had devastated the Happy Union workings. Choking the pumps, it had caused the engine to seize up. The giant water-wheel had been washed away and the main drain culvert from the mine was blocked for all its length. The deep levels of the stream-workings were under sixty feet of water.

There would be work for Ben, Moses and the other tin-streamers, helping to bring the mine back to production, but no ore would be mined for many weeks. It meant that Pearson Retallick would not have to make the daily return walk to Pentuan harbour for a while.

Moses Trago's makeshift home in the valley beyond the mine had also been swept away. Martha Retallick, pleased that her son had found himself a friend, tried to persuade Moses to stay at Tregassick for a few days. Moses declined the offer, accepting only the meal that she laid before him.

The truth was that Moses Trago did not feel comfortable inside a house. His makeshift home in the woods would have appalled Martha Retallick, but the home from which he had run away was little better. It was a rough cromlech, formed from huge slabs of rock set into a hillside, high on Bodmin Moor. It had once housed the bones and worldly possessions of a Bronze Age chieftain, but these had been removed long before Moses Trago's father and his young family took up residence.

Another visitor to Tregassick that evening was Walter Dunn. He was on his way to a reform meeting at the Crinnis mine, a couple of miles away. Learning of the disaster at Pentuan, he called in to check that his brother-in-law and Ben were safe.

'I hear that seven bodies have already been recovered in the valley, with as many more still missing,' he said. 'Half the houses in the village have been washed away. Mother says it's the Lord's way of wiping out sin, Pearson. First your mine in St Just, and now the Pentuan stream-works. She says nothing good ever came from burrowing so deep in the earth.'

'Is that so?' snorted Martha Retallick. 'I don't see that our Mark and Billy have much to thank fishing for! I don't like mining myself – but only because it kills far more than it will ever make rich. That doesn't mean that men who work beneath the ground are any less godly than those who earn their living on the sea. How many of those who died today were from the mine? Tell me that, if you can.'

'There's no call for you to get your dander up with me, our Martha. I am only repeating what Mother said.'

Walter Dunn stood up and grinned ruefully at Pearson Retallick. 'I came out of my own house to get away from women with tongues like fish-hooks. There are two of them down at Mevagissey who spend half their days weeping for their menfolk, and the other half blaming me for letting them go smuggling. I don't like to remind them that I'm the youngest brother. It was Mark and Billy who taught *me* about free-trading!'

'You were quick enough to learn,' retorted Martha Retallick. 'But what they are really blaming you for is not getting yourself caught along with Mark and Billy. It's as well for them that someone in the Dunn family was born lucky. They would be in a sore plight now without you at home to fish for them.'

'Thank you, sister. I'm glad someone is on my side. But I must leave now for Crinnis. We have an important meeting there today. With any luck we'll make some progress towards ridding ourselves of Members of Parliament elected to office by men like your Sir John Vincent.'

'I don't want to hear a word against Sir John Vincent in this house,' snapped Martha Retallick. 'He gave us work and a home when we needed both. Don't you forget that.'

'Moses and I will walk along with you a way,' said Ben hurriedly to Walter, hoping to avert an argument. 'I want to see how they are getting on with cleaning up at Pentuan.'

Pearson Retallick cast a glance out of the window and said,

'Well! Today is a great day for visitors. Here comes young Jesse Henna.'

Jesse was still looking pale after the events of the morning, but she produced a wan smile for Ben. It was the first time she and Moses Trago had met, and Ben was surprised at the surliness of Moses when Jesse said she would accompany them to Pentuan. It was apparent that Moses Trago had little time for girls, and his sullen silence had an effect upon them all as they walked down the hill to Pentuan.

It was as much to provoke conversation as anything else that Ben asked his uncle exactly what was meant by 'parliamentary reform'.

'It is just what it says,' replied the fisherman seriously. 'We are trying to reform a corrupt voting system – one that allows men like Sir John Vincent to buy votes and send his son to the House of Commons in London. He doesn't do it to help the people of Cornwall, but to protect his own selfish interests. Farmers, fishermen and miners have no say at all in the running of the country. Forty-four men are sent to Parliament from Cornwall, some of them with no more than ten votes behind them. Yet, up-country, there are whole towns with thousands of people and no Member of Parliament at all. That's why things in this country are so bad for the likes of us. Farmers' men are fed by the parish, and seven-year-old children work ten hours a day on the mines for threepence because their fathers can't find work. You've seen for yourself that good fishermen need to turn to smuggling to feed their families because their earnings are paid out on unfair taxes and tithes. When we speak up for ourselves we are branded as agitators by Sir John Vincent and his land-owning friends. The day will soon come when they'll need to change their tune. Many gentlemen elsewhere are beginning to think as we do and support our cause.'

Walter Dunn spoke with great feeling, and Ben realised how deeply he felt about the reform cause.

'You don't need to take my word for anything, young Ben. Come along to the meeting with me and hear what others have to say.'

Remembering Sir John Vincent's warning, Ben was about to decline the invitation, when Walter added, 'You'll enjoy seeing Crinnis. We are holding our meeting close by the new engine-house at the mine there – and what a mine it is, too! None of your tin-streaming. It's a deep copper mine, giving work to nigh on a thousand men.'

There was a hunger in Ben for the sight of an underground mine and, looking at Moses Trago, Ben saw his own eagerness reflected on the other boy's face.

'Sir John wouldn't like it if he knew you had been to a reform meeting, Ben,' Jesse warned.

Moses Trago rounded on her. 'What's it got to do with Sir John Vincent – or with anyone else? Come on, Ben. Let's go to Crinnis. We'll see again what a *real* mine looks like.'

'Will you come, too, Jesse?' asked Ben. 'You'll enjoy looking round a mine.'

Jesse shrugged. She knew she would not be able to prevent Ben from going now. 'I don't mind – but I'm coming with you to see the mine, not to listen to a lot of foolish talk.'

She looked at Walter Dunn defiantly as she spoke the words, but he only grinned at her.

Moses Trago lost much of his enthusiasm when Jesse agreed to accompany them, but he kept his thoughts to himself.

'How long will it take us to get there?' queried Ben.

'If we step out when we reach the top of Pentuan Hill, we'll be there inside an hour.'

Pentuan village was cleaning up in the wake of the great storm and flood. The water had subsided with the tide, and the villagers were hunting among the ruins of their collapsed houses for lost belongings.

As they passed through the village, Jesse fell silent, and Ben knew she was thinking of the girls she had seen drown. He would have liked to say something to make her feel better, but could think of no words that would not sound foolish in front of the others.

When they reached the top of the hill beyond the village, Walter Dunn pointed out the chimney and tall engine-house of the Crinnis mine. The mine was perched on the cliff-top just round the curve of the bay, and Ben imagined he could hear the clatter of stamp-hammers carried to them on the wind.

It was not long before they met up with others on their way to the meeting. Walter was known to most of them, and Ben fretted as their pace slowed to talk of reform and a preview of the evening meeting.

Eventually, Ben, Moses and Jesse hurried on ahead and left Walter to come on more slowly with his friends.

There was never any danger of losing their way. It seemed that all the men and boys, and a fair number of women, from the surrounding countryside were going to the reform meeting.

There were already at least five thousand people crowded into the flat piece of open ground between mine and cliff, but it was to the engine-house that the three made their way. As it was a Sunday, there were no men working underground on the mine, but the engineer kept the big engine at work pumping out water from the foot of the fifty-fathom-deep shaft. The huge cast-iron beam rocked easily on its greased pivot, with only the hiss of steam from the cylinder and the creak of chain and giant pump-rod to hint at its power.

This was a big mine, with far more equipment than they had possessed at the Money Box mine, but Ben and Moses moved from building to building, examining each piece of machinery minutely. Listening to their comments, Jesse thought a stranger could have been forgiven for thinking that the mine equipment had been made by the gods and not by Man.

The workings of the Crinnis mine extended far under the sea, and gradually the memories of the last minutes of the Money Box mine replaced the novelty of being on a deep-working mine. Ben and Moses allowed themselves to be drawn by the applause to the field where the reform meeting was being held.

The organisers had built a platform at one end of the field. On this stood the campaign officials and speakers. Ben saw that Walter Dunn was one of them. But, when they arrived, it was a thick-set grey-haired man who was drawing the crowd's applause. Ben and his companions pushed their way forward until they could hear his words more clearly.

'. . . all over the country, men – aye, and women, too – are rising in support of parliamentary reform and the cause of universal suffrage.'

'What does "universal suffrage" mean?' Jesse whispered loudly.

'Shh!' Ben understood it no more than Jesse, but there could be no misunderstanding the grey-haired man's next words.

'When are you people of Cornwall going to do something about the rotten boroughs within your own borders? When will you make your feelings known to those who spend a few guineas to buy votes for their own candidates, then sit back and grow fat on your labours? Not six months since, the people of London moved to seize the Tower of London! They would have succeeded had others come in from outside the capital to help them. Then, hardly a week ago, the workers of Derby fought against mounted soldiers for the right to be heard. Will you be left behind while other men fight for *your* rights? Will you do nothing here in Cornwall while the country continues to be ruled by a corrupt Parliament – and while a mad King sits upon the throne of England?'

The speaker's words stirred a feeling of excitement within Ben, but the roar of a concerted '*No!*' burst forth from five thousand throats startled him and Ben looked about him in alarm.

Inexperienced in the ways of mass meetings, and unaware of the transient nature of a crowd's enthusiasm, Ben believed he was in the midst of an imminent uprising against King and country.

Jesse felt the same way. Tugging at his sleeve, she whispered, 'Let's get away from here, Ben. I don't want to stay any longer.'

Ben would have liked to hear more of the speaker's words, but Jesse was already edging away.

'All right.' Ben looked about him for Moses Trago, but he

66

was lost in the crowd. It did not matter. Moses Trago was quite capable of looking after himself.

As the speaker continued to shout abuse and pile insults upon the names of the infirm King George III and his Ministers, Ben and Jesse pushed their way through the noisy and enthusiastic crowd.

They were almost clear of the noisy throng when Ben looked up – and saw Reuben Holyoak standing not twenty paces from them. The gamekeeper was looking in their direction, but Jesse was not yet clear of the crowd. If Reuben Holyoak did not see her, there was a good chance Ben would go unrecognised. Turning hurriedly, Ben bundled Jesse back towards the heart of the meeting, doing his best to silence her puzzled protests.

When they had been swallowed up by the crowd, Ben told her the reason for his actions.

'Are you certain, Ben? Reuben Holyoak would not get involved in parliamentary reform. You must have been mistaken. You've only seen him once . . .'

Ben shook his head vigorously. 'It was him.'

'Then he must have been sent here by Sir John to take the names of any Lamorrack workers at the meeting. Did he see you?'

Jesse's face was pale. Sir John Vincent had an unreasonable hatred of 'reformers'. He would dismiss any of his servants who showed an interest in their cause.

'I'm not certain – but we'll need to go a long way round if we're to be sure of missing him.'

They went through the Crinnis mine and over the nearby fields, circling around the noisy meeting before they were on the Pentuan road.

The roars of the crowd at the meeting pursued them halfway to Pentuan. If Reuben Holyoak was there to take names, he would be kept busy searching among the thousands of reformers for a familiar face.

Ben and Jesse hurried homewards as fast as they could go, but they lost their race with darkness when they were still in the Pentuan valley. With the lights of the battered village behind them, they could have been the only two people in the dark silent night. It was a warm and companionable feeling, and the problems of the morrow receded rapidly.

'How did you and Moses come to be friends ?'

The question from Jesse came suddenly, as though she had been thinking about it for some time.

'We both worked on the Money Box mine.'

After an initial hesitation, Ben told Jesse the story of the night the sea burst in upon the Money Box mine. It was the first time he had talked about it in detail since then. When he reached the point where he and Moses were clinging to the ladder while water poured down the shaft, trapping every miner in the mine, Ben's voice became hoarse and he found it impossible to continue.

In the darkness Jesse reached for Ben's hand and squeezed it sympathetically. 'I think you were very brave, Ben.'

'I was lucky, that's all.'

'Yet at the Crinnis mine you and Moses talked as though you looked upon a mine as being the most wonderful place in the whole world! Why, Ben ?'

Ben thought about it as they walked along the path together. Here in the clean air of the night, with a sky full of stars above them and not the slightest hint of danger in the surrounding countryside, the need of a born miner to wrest a living deep underground was not easy to put into words.

After thinking about it for a long while, he said, 'Mining is the only thing I know how to do well, Jesse. I feel at home on a mine. I was ten years of age when I first began working an underground shift with my pa. He was the same age when he went below grass – and so was his pa. The Retallicks have been miners for as far back as anyone can remember. My pa felt bad about making me go down there with him, but I can remember that I'd never felt so happy in all my life. Working underground is not easy to describe, Jesse, because it's like nothing else I know. When you begin digging out a new level, following a lode, you know you're going where no other man has ever been before. It's not just digging out earth and stones. Everything down there has its own meaning and its own colour – colours you don't see above ground . . .'

Ben faltered, unused to making such a long speech and laying his feelings bare in such a manner.

'I'm a miner, Jesse. One day I'll be as good as my pa. There's many a man would be proud to be able to say that.'

Jesse did not doubt him for one moment. She knew Ben had just shared a very important part of himself with her.

They walked in silence for a while, and Ben was very much aware of the fact that he was still holding Jesse's hand, but he made no move to do anything about it.

'I don't think I like Moses Trago,' Jesse said unexpectedly.

'You met him today for the first time. How can you say that?'

She shrugged. 'It's a feeling I have. There's something in his eyes when he looks at me. I find it frightening,' she shuddered. 'Let's talk of something else.'

Pushing aside all thoughts of Moses Trago, mines – and Sir John Vincent – they chatted about their houses, the livestock on the Henna 'farm' and the people who farmed the land in the area. Born and raised on the Lamorrack estate, Jesse knew everyone for miles around.

In no time at all they arrived at Jesse's house. Reluctantly, Ben released her hand. Somewhat gruffly, he announced that it was time he went home. But he made no immediate move to leave her.

'Thank you for taking me to see the Crinnis mine, Ben. I have often wondered what a mine was like – especially since you came here.'

Jesse, too, was reluctant to have Ben go, yet she was unable to think of words that might make him stay a while longer.

'It was good to see a proper working mine again.'

They stood in awkward silence, the familiarity of a few moments before gradually slipping away.

Suddenly, the door of the house, only a few yards away, opened wide and Jesse's mother was silhouetted in the doorway, the yellow light of a lamp behind her.

'Jesse? Jesse, are you out there?'

'I'm here, Ma.'

'Then you come in this minute. I've been worried sick about you.'

Maude Henna took a step outside the house and peered into the moonlit night. 'Who is that with you?'

'Ben Retallick.'

'Then it's time he was home where he belongs. You come straight indoors now, or I'll come out and fetch you.'

The door swung shut, and Jesse grinned at Ben. 'I think my ma wants me to go in.'

She leaned forward and kissed him quickly. Backing away from him, she said softly, 'I like you, Ben Retallick. I like you a lot.' Then she was gone.

Ben walked home with his hands in his pockets, whistling loudly. It was a song he had heard in the miners' inns around St Just – a man's song.

Chapter Eight

Ben felt less like a man the following day. After spending his working-hours fruitlessly searching for lost equipment at the flooded Happy Union mine, he arrived home to find his mother waiting for him in a state of some agitation.

'Hurry up and wash and get into your best clothes. They are upstairs laid out for you. Sir John wants to see you up at the big house.'

'Why does he want to see me?'

Although he asked the question, Ben was certain he knew the answer and his heart beat faster. All day long he had been thinking of the unfortunate meeting with Reuben Holyoak at the Crinnis mine, wondering if the gamekeeper had seen him. Now he knew, and it seemed Reuben Holyoak had wasted no time in informing his employer.

'How should I know what's in Sir John's mind? All I know is that the butler told me you were to come to Lamorrack House the minute you arrived home from work.'

'Sir John Vincent can wait until I've had something to eat. I've been working all day without a break to get his mine cleared up and I'm hungry.' Ben needed time to think.

'You can eat when you get back from seeing Sir John. So the faster you get up to the big house, the better for yourself. Hurry up, now. I have your father to tend to when you get off.'

Ben had looked for his father when he first entered the house. Not seeing him, he had assumed he was out somewhere.

'Tend to Pa . . .? What's wrong with him?'

'He's not feeling so good. He's gone upstairs to bed.'

In spite of Martha Retallick's repeated demand that Ben hurry off to Lamorrack House, Ben's immediate concern was for his father, and he went upstairs to the bedroom to speak to him.

Pearson Retallick was propped up in the sparsely furnished

main bedroom, looking wistfully out of the window at the sun-soaked fields and the blue sea in the distance.

Turning his head as Ben entered the room, Pearson Retallick gave him a tired smile, 'Hello, Ben. I wish we'd found this place a few years ago. Perhaps I should have listened to your mother after all. The three of us could have made a good life here together.'

'Doing what, Pa? You trundling a wheelbarrow in a stream-working and me sitting in a boat off Mevagissey, waiting for a French smuggler . . . or an English press-gang? No, it's nice enough out there but I would rather be following a lode along an underground level – so would you.'

Pearson Retallick coughed quietly, drawing shallow breaths of air into his dust-filled lungs. When he could speak again, he said, 'I've spent too many years following tin lodes, Ben. I carry a part of every one of them inside me now. I am thirty-seven – and I'm finished. I'll never work another pitch again. But what am I doing talking to you like this? Take no notice, Ben. I'm just feeling sorry for myself for being a-bed on a fine day. Didn't I hear your mother say that Sir John wants you up at Lamorrack House? You'd better get on your way. Likely as not he wants to make you captain of the Happy Union . . .'

Pearson Retallick's laugh brought on another bout of coughing, this one more serious than before.

It hurt Ben very deeply to see his father in this condition and he turned away. 'I'll go up to Lamorrack House now. You try and get some rest while I'm gone.'

'Ben . . .?' The word was forced out as Pearson Retallick fought hard for breath. Ben turned back to his father as he gasped out what he wanted to say. 'Whatever it is – whatever Sir John wants of you – go along with him, Ben. We depend on Sir John's goodwill . . . and your mother is happy here.'

Ben nodded unhappily. 'She'll not have to leave here because of me, I'll see to that.'

As Ben put on his best clothes, he wondered what he ought to say to the baronet. Then he put all the ideas from his mind. No doubt Sir John had already decided what he was going to do with Ben. If that was so, the only course of action left to him was to say he was leaving, going away somewhere. Then perhaps Sir John would allow Martha Retallick to remain at Tregassick.

When he went downstairs, Ben's mother fussed at his appearance. Brushing off the shoulders of his jacket, she tried to pull the too-short sleeves down over his exposed wrists.

'You be certain to call him "Sir John" when you speak. And listen to what he has to say to you. Don't say anything unless he asks you a direct question. Do you hear me, now?'

'I hear you, Ma,' Ben said irritably. 'I'll be polite to him, but Sir John is only a man, the same as any other.'

Martha Retallick stopped her fussing. Taking a step back from Ben, she wagged a finger only inches from his nose.

'That's just the kind of thinking to land you in trouble, my lad. Sir John Vincent is *not* just another man. The Almighty may rule the hereafter, but on this part of God's earth Sir John Vincent rules for Him. Upset him and you'll need to go a very long way to make a new start. I know; I work in his house. I see what goes on. You heed my words or we'll all suffer. Your father is ill upstairs, and it won't be long before you are the breadwinner for this family.'

'All right, Ma. I'll try not to upset Sir John.'

Secretly, Ben thought Sir John Vincent was probably already angry with him, but it would be no comfort to his mother if he told her the truth. She was worried enough already about his father's illness. A widow's lot was not an easy one in the unenlightened days of the early nineteenth century.

Ben set off from Tregassick displaying far more confidence than he felt, and it was fast seeping away by the time he reached the Hennas' small farm. There he saw Jesse turning out the Hennas' two milking-cows into a field.

She commented gaily on his smart appearance, but her mood changed abruptly when he told here where he was going.

'So Reuben did see us! He's wasted no time doing something about it. What will you say to Sir John?'

Ben shrugged. 'I'll think of something.'

'Wait a minute. I'll come to the house with you.' Jesse reached the decision suddenly.

'This has nothing to do with you,' said Ben in alarm. 'Keep out of it, Jesse. There's little sense in both of us finding trouble.'

'You needn't worry about me. I get on well with Sir John – you ask anyone. He won't do anything to me, and I may be able to help you.'

'Haven't you got work to do? What about the cows . . . ?'

'I've already milked them. The rest of my work can wait. This is far more important.'

The expression on Jesse's face allowed of no argument. Jesse Henna was a very determined young woman – as anyone who opposed her quickly discovered.

Ten minutes later they were walking through the trees surrounding Lamorrack House. Ben nursed a vain hope that Sir John might have forgotten he was coming and have gone out somewhere.

But there was to be no evading this issue. Sir John Vincent was at home. Furthermore, Ben was informed that the baronet was annoyed because Ben had not come to the house very much earlier.

The servant who took Ben to the library was not at all sure about allowing Jesse to accompany him. But Jesse thrust out her chin and told the servant that Sir John would wish to see her, too.

He did not. When she and Ben entered the room together, Sir John Vincent's grey eyebrows met in a heavy line across the bridge of his nose and he snapped at her, 'What the devil are you doing here? I did not send for *you*. Only for this whippersnapper.'

'If it's about yesterday, then you'll want to see me, too, because I was with Ben,' Jesse retorted, looking at the baronet defiantly.

Ben held his breath in dismay. It was just such an angry confrontation as this he had been so anxious to avoid.

'You were at this – this – meeting of rabblerousers?'

'We were both at Crinnis – but not at the meeting. Ben

took me there to see the mine. After we looked all over it we had to pass through a crowd who had gathered for some meeting. That was when Reuben Holyoak saw us – and I know it must have been him who told you he saw us there. Though I don't suppose he explained what he was doing there himself?'

'Reuben Holyoak was there on my instructions. But he made no mention of seeing you, only Retallick.'

'I don't suppose he mentioned the other boy who was with us, either. The one whose life Ben saved when they were both working on a mine, farther west?'

Sir John Vincent looked perplexed. He shifted his gaze from Jesse to Ben and back again . . . Then he threw back his head and laughed. 'By God, girl! You are snapping at me for all the world like a vixen defending one of her cubs. I swear you've got more guts than any man or woman on the whole of my estate. Now, the pair of you sit down and tell me what this is all about. No, you keep quiet for a few minutes, Jesse. You have said enough already. Let me hear what you have to say, Retallick.'

Taking his cue from Jesse's explanation, Ben told the baronet that, as it was a Sunday, he had decided to take Jesse to Crinnis and show her over the big mine there. When they left the mine they had found themselves caught up in the meeting of reformers.

Sir John Vincent asked Ben a number of technical questions about the lay-out of the Crinnis mine and the surface machinery they had there. He displayed a surprising knowledge of the cliff-top workings, but when Ben began answering his questions in detail Sir John Vincent threw up his hands to stop Ben's flow of words.

'Enough! You have no need to air your knowledge of mines in here. You said you went to Crinnis to look over the mine workings. Now I believe you. But what is all this about saving the life of some lad . . . ?'

Ben gave a very brief version of his first meeting with Moses Trago. As Sir John Vincent listened, he studied Ben's face.

'You seem to make a habit of rescuing people, Retallick. I

have not forgotten your assistance to me yesterday.'

He put a finger and thumb inside a pocket of his waistcoat and pulled out two dull golden guineas. Holding them out towards Ben, he said, 'Here, take these. I am told your father is not too well. I have no doubt you will find a use for them.'

Delighted with the sudden turn the interview had taken, Ben took the coins and thanked the baronet.

'I always reward those who do me favours, Retallick. I also deal harshly with those who do me ill. Remember that. As for this "reform" nonsense, I will have none of it on this estate. Neither will I tolerate such revolutionary ideas within my magisterial district.'

'What is revolutionary about a man wanting a say in his own future, Sir John?'

Jesse asked the question in apparent innocence, but Ben saw Sir John Vincent's expression harden and he was glad he had not asked the same question.

'Coming from anyone else that would be crass impudence, Jesse. I and the other landowners of this country have looked after our tenants and workers for centuries. I will continue to protect them – against themselves, if need be. The man in the field, or in the mine, knows only what food is short today, or what commodity costs more than it did yesterday. He knows nothing of the cause – or of the efforts being made on his behalf to set things to rights. There is no reason why he *should* know. Such things are better left to those who possess all the facts. Were he to be given power to act on his own behalf, or even to vote, England would go the same way as France. The mobs would take over and terror would stalk the countryside. Eventually, some blackguard like Bonaparte would come along, take over the country and lead it to total ruin.'

Sir John Vincent glared belligerently at Jesse for a few moments, then his face softened.

'Why am I telling you of such matters? They do not concern you, Jesse. Run along to the kitchen, now, and see if Cook can find you a cake, or something. I want to have a word with this young man. Oh! You need have no fear. It has nothing at all to do with your visit to Crinnis.'

In spite of Sir John's assurance, Jesse left the room with

76

obvious reluctance, but she knew better than to disobey a direct order from him.

When the door had closed behind her, the baronet eyed Ben in a speculative manner for so long that Ben began to feel uneasy. Suddenly, Sir John spoke to him.

'That girl is fond of you, Retallick.'

Ben did not know what he was expected to say, and so he said nothing.

'Well? Don't just sit there like a simpleton, boy. I said Jesse is fond of you. What are your feelings towards her, eh?'

'I am fond of her, too, Sir John.'

To Ben's great relief, the baronet beamed. 'Good! Good! But there is more to life than being fond of someone. What ambitions do you have for the future?'

Ben had no hesitation in answering this question. 'I want to work as a miner . . . in an underground mine. Perhaps one day become shift captain – or even a mine captain.'

'H'm! I can think of better ways of earning a living, but it so happens I will be opening a deep mine just outside Mevagissey before long. That should keep you in the area long enough for me to keep an eye on the pair of you. All right, young Retallick. You can go now.'

Ben left Sir John Vincent's library thoroughly bewildered, not at all sure of the reason for the last private session of questioning. He decided that Sir John Vincent must be taking a special interest in him because he had led his pony and trap from the flood waters of Pentuan. That was what he told Jesse when they were on their way home.

In Sir John Vincent's library the door swung open and a tall pale-faced man in his early forties entered the room.

'Good evening, Father. Did I see a couple of estate brats leaving the house just now? What had they been up to?'

'Estate brats, Colman?' The look Sir John Vincent gave to his only son was decidedly cold. 'The girl was Jesse . . . Jesse Henna.'

'Was it, now! I *have* been away from Lamorrack for a long time. She has reached an interesting age.'

Sir John Vincent looked at his son in disgust, 'Jesse is

77

almost fifteen, Colman – an age when many young girls are wedded off. As a matter of fact, that was partly why I had her and the lad in here. They make a good couple. I am thinking of settling the farmhouse at Pengrugla on them.'

Colman Vincent lost his air of indifference. 'Is that wise? Such a generous gesture is certain to set tongues wagging . . .'

'Damn the wagging tongues! It is a little late in the day for you to care what people say, or think, about the Vincent family.'

Colman Vincent shrugged. 'You must do what you think best, Father. But I trust you realise that marrying Jesse off to someone else is going to upset your faithful servant, Reuben Holyoak?'

'Holyoak? He is old enough to be Jesse's father!'

'Perhaps. But, of course, he is *not* her father. Reuben has told me more than once that he would like to wed Jesse.'

'You would not go along with such an indecent arrangement?'

'Why not? The girl would be gaining a respectable husband and a certain status in life. After all, Reuben Holyoak is a *head* gamekeeper. I don't suppose he would be too demanding, either. If the girl wanted an extra-marital romp in the hayfield with her young swain, I am sure the old stag would be only too happy to have someone blunt the edge of her appetite, so to speak.'

'I will thank you to keep your crude talk for your London friends, Colman. It is out of place in this house. Young Retallick will wed Jesse as soon as he is old enough to support her – and they will have Pengrugla. I will make my wishes known to her mother tomorrow. Now, you may leave me. I have work to do.'

Sir John Vincent turned his back on his son, leaving Colman Vincent to seek the amorous gamekeeper and inform him of the decision that had been made about Jesse's future.

Chapter Nine

Maude Henna called on the Retallick family late the following evening, bringing with her an unusually quiet Jesse. Pearson Retallick saw them coming along the path towards the house. He was feeling a little better today and occupied a wooden rocking-chair in the kitchen, looking out through the open doorway.

'Martha! We have company – and all dressed up in their Sunday frills, too. It must be something of importance.'

He looked across the room at Ben. 'Have you been up to anything I should know about?'

Ben's face turned a deep red, but he shook his head vigorously, hoping his guilty thoughts did not show. On the way home from Lamorrack House the previous evening, he and Jesse had followed the course of a stream through the woods surrounding the big house. They were still in the woods when dusk fell.

In the dark seclusion it had seemed perfectly natural for him to kiss Jesse. She had responded with inexperienced but enthusiastic ardour, and his hands had begun an exploratory journey of her body. Jesse stopped him before he was able to answer all the questions that had long plagued him, but not until he had made a number of discoveries to stir his own body physically and thrill him with their future promise.

Last night, their newly awakened passions had been an exciting experience for both of them, but if Jesse's mother had found out . . .

By the time Jesse and her mother entered the house, Ben's cheeks wore a fiery glow, fanned by his guilty and imaginative thoughts.

His sense of foreboding increased when Jesse entered the room without looking at him. Behind her, dressed in her church-going clothes, Maude Henna was tight-faced and serious. This was no informal neighbourly call. Martha Retallick responded to the mood of her visitors by bringing out the tea she kept for special occasions. Until it was made, they all sat or stood about the small room, making stilted comments about the weather and the ever-rising cost of foodstuffs.

Not until she had sampled her hostess's tea did Maude Henna broach the matter she had come to discuss.

'Sir John sent for me this morning. He wanted to speak to me about my Jesse . . . and young Ben.'

As Pearson Retallick flashed his son a 'What haven't you told me?' look, Martha Retallick threw up her head defensively.

'I don't believe my son has done anything to which Sir John can take exception.'

Maude Henna looked startled. 'Oh, no! Neither of them has done anything wrong. No, that's a long way from the truth of the matter. Sir John wants there to be an understanding between our two families. When Ben is old enough, Sir John wants him to wed Jesse. He said that on the day they are married he will settle our little farm at Pengrugla on the two of them.'

Jesse looked at Ben for the first time since she had entered the house. It was a look that contained both happiness and apprehension. Ben's answering smile contained a great deal of relief. But no one was paying any attention to them. While Pearson Retallick listened to Maude Henna's words in slack-jawed astonishment, Martha Retallick groped blindly behind her for a heavy wooden chair. Grasping it, she sat down quickly.

'Ben to wed Jesse . . . ? But they are both no more than children?'

Maude Henna snorted. 'Children? Jesse has been putting in a full day's work since she was big enough to hold a stick and drive a cow to pasture. From what I hear of your boy, he has led a similar life. They don't remain children for long these days, Mrs Retallick. There are maids a-plenty hereabouts who are wedded and bedded by the time they reach Jesse's age. Ben is a bit too young to take on the responsibility of a wife just yet, but he's a big boy. In a year or two he'll be able to call up a man's wage. Leastways, he would if he worked on the land, or on a fishing-boat.'

'But why should Sir John concern himself with who our Ben marries . . . and give him and Jesse land as a wedding gift?'

Pearson Retallick had heard none of the rumours concerning Jesse Henna's parentage.

'Sir John has always taken an interest in Jesse,' replied Maude Henna, meeting and holding Martha Retallick's eyes. 'My family have worked for the Vincents for as long as anyone can remember, and Sir John has always been a generous man. Mind you, I am not saying that I entirely approve of this arrangement and, if it were not Sir John's express wish, I might have more to say about it. I had hoped to see my Jesse married to a man with more of a future than a miner.'

Martha Retallick bristled. 'My family are fisherfolk with their own boats at Mevagissey, Mrs Henna. I had no thought of lowering my station in life when I married Pearson.'

'No, of course not. Besides, Ben won't be a miner when he has his own land.'

Martha Retallick did not share Maude Henna's confidence. She could not have wished for more for Ben . . . if he were able to settle to working on the land. She knew how much mining meant to Ben and was fully aware of the hold that mining took on a man. There was also her own future to consider. If Ben took over the farm at Pengrugla, he would have a wife and mother-in-law to support there. Little money would be left over to help his own mother and a sick father.

'Did you know anything about this, Ben?' Pearson Retallick questioned his son.

'No. Well . . . not exactly. Sir John asked me what my feelings were for Jesse, and I told him. That was all.'

'H'm! You must have left him in no doubt about them.' Pearson Retallick smiled happily. 'I am pleased for you, Ben. Pleased for you both.'

Martha Retallick said nothing. She was still thinking of what being related to the Henna family by marriage was going to mean. Jesse was a good girl, even if she did have a disconcerting habit of speaking her mind at times when most other girls would remain silent. She would be welcome in the family. But Maude Henna . . . ? She believed herself to be a sight too good for other working folk. Martha Retallick expected trouble with her.

Then Maude Henna began talking about the future wedding and, seizing their opportunity, Ben and Jesse slipped from the house.

As they walked through the wood behind Tregassick, Jesse took Ben's hand. 'So we are to be married, Ben? What did you really tell Sir John when he asked you about your feelings for me?'

'I can't remember now.'

'Oh, Ben! You can't have forgotten something of such importance so quickly.'

'All right, what would you have said to him had he asked you?'

Jesse was quiet for a few minutes. Then, softly, she said, 'I would have told him I love you very much.'

There was such sincerity in her voice that Ben knew she meant every word.

'Now tell me what *you* said.'

'I told him . . . I am very fond of you.'

'Honestly, Ben?' Jesse's face glowed with happiness. 'I'm glad, Ben. Very, very glad.' She hugged him excitedly in her happiness.

Ben grinned in embarrassment. 'Not so fast! I didn't tell Sir John I would marry you . . .'

'That doesn't matter. You will. You just wait and see.'

Ben held Jesse to him, but as the heat of the previous evening returned to both of them the voice of Maude Henna rang out, calling for her daughter to return home with her to Pengrugla.

The summer of 1818 passed faster than any season Ben could remember, and with it passed Jesse's fifteenth birthday.

Ben spent the hot summer days toiling, shirtless, in the re-opened Pentuan stream-workings, enjoying the unaccustomed luxury of sunshine on his skin, and he developed a healthy tan. Most evenings he went to Pengrugla to help Jesse with the chores. Afterwards, if they finished early enough, they would stroll through the woods to Mevagissey and there watch the return of the fishing-boats with their own daily harvest.

These were good days for Ben and Jesse, but there were many in Cornwall who shared little of their happiness. For the farmworkers and tenant farmers in particular, it was a difficult year. Prices, rents and taxes were cripplingly high – but wages remained low. Many more farmworkers were forced to rely upon parish relief to keep themselves alive. Others literally fought each other for work. Often it was no more than gathering seaweed to manure the fields, or weeding crops for the paltry sum of threepence a day. Given such a situation, it was not surprising that the reform meetings were increasingly well attended. At the meetings, desperate men with families close to starvation listened as speaker after speaker blamed all the ills of the country upon a government that did not represent the vast majority of the British people. It did nothing to help, but they gained comfort from the knowledge that *someone* was aware of their plight.

There was a great deal of truth in the arguments of the reform speakers. The country *was* run for the benefit of a privileged few. The distribution of parliamentary seats, in Cornwall in particular, was a disgrace. Cornwall held tenaciously to forty-four seats. The whole of Scotland could boast of only one more; Wales had only twenty-four; and the huge industrial cities of the Midlands – none!

But such facts were lost in the extravagant claims of those who spoke in favour of immediate parliamentary reform. They told their listeners whatever they wanted to hear. Reform would bring down the price of goods. Reform would give a living wage to the impoverished farmworkers, freeing them from the spectre of the dreaded workhouse. Reform would cure all ills.

Few men paused to ask how such a desirable state of affairs would be achieved – and no one attempted to tell them. Embracing parliamentary reform, universal suffrage, abolishment of tithes and taxes – and general freedom from want – the reform movement attracted anyone with a grievance against the established order in the land.

Ben met his uncle, Walter Dunn, frequently and the talk always turned to reform. In spite of his own reservations, Ben found his interest in the movement quickening and he asked many questions – for which Walter Dunn was always ready to provide answers.

But Ben was working hard at the Happy Union, determined to make the most of the opportunity Sir John Vincent had given him and Jesse. He would not allow himself to be drawn into the parliamentary reform movement. As it grew in strength throughout the country, it attracted to it the type of man about whom Sir John had warned Ben.

The new reformers used the general unrest to sow seeds of the revolution that had borne such bloody fruit in France. In the Midlands, workers wrecked the new machines that had taken the places of so many of their fellow-workers. In Manchester, troops were called to put down riots. Scores of protesters were arrested.

In a desperate attempt to quell the unrest the administration of Lord Liverpool hanged many of the ringleaders and sent others to the penal colonies of Australia. Yet still the people of the land clamoured for 'reform'.

Even the most innocent of meetings needed little provocation to make it erupt into violence, as Ben and Jesse learned for themselves, later in the year.

One of the Pengrugla sows had produced a fine litter of fourteen piglets and, as soon as they were weaned, Ben and Jesse took them to a Saturday market in Mevagissey.

By late afternoon the last of the piglets had changed hands for a very satisfactory price. Ben and Jesse were thinking of returning to Pengrugla when suddenly a sullen-faced Cornish farmworker entered the square where the market was being held, only yards away from them. At the end of a halter he led a drab and none-too-clean young woman.

'Hear me! Hear me!' the man called in a loud voice. As men gathered about him, he shouted, 'I've come to auction off my wife to the highest bidder. She's not too clever, and her looks aren't of the best, but she's a willing worker and has a still tongue in her head. What am I bid now? Do I have an offer of a shilling?'

'You do! I'll bid a shilling for her.'

The excited call came from a scrawny-bearded ancient who stood no higher than the woman's shoulder when he came forward eagerly to confirm his offer.

'Then I'll make it two . . .'

A broad-shoudered man wearing a military coat limped forward. Ben saw he had one leg cut off below the knee. In its place was a leather-topped wooden stump.

The old man glared at the newcomer, then he pulled out a worn purse. Opening it carefully, he slowly counted its contents with one bony finger.

Looking up again, he eyed the woman, then said to her husband, 'I'll give you two and fourpence – and that's my best offer.'

'Then you'll need to keep your trousers on in bed tonight if you want to stay warm,' cried the one-legged ex-soldier jubilantly. 'I have a bright half-crown here that says she'll be mine for certain.'

'Yours she is, then,' said the woman's lawful husband. Snatching the silver coin, he handed the end of the halter-rope to the ex-soldier before he changed his mind. 'You'll not regret your bargain – though she might need a good cuffing to drive her from bed on a cold winter morning.'

'I'll worry about pushing her out of bed after I've got her there,' said the one-legged man. Delivering a smart slap to the rump of his 'bargain', he gave the crowd about him a lewd wink.

Grinning at the ribald shouts of the onlookers, the ex-soldier led his purchase from the market. She, for her part, walked away behind him without so much as a backward glance at her husband. Indeed, throughout the whole tran-saction she had neither spoken nor shown a moment's interest in the proceedings.

Ben had been watching the auction with great amusement, but when he turned to Jesse he saw her hands were clenched to her side in a paroxysm of ill-controlled fury.

'Did you see that?' she hissed angrily. 'That . . . that man! He sold his wife as though she were a pig . . . or a cow for which he had no more use!'

'She didn't seem to mind,' replied Ben innocently. 'And I think she'll be happier with the one-legged man than with her husband.'

'What has that to do with anything?' Jesse rounded on him. 'She *chose* to marry her husband. That didn't give him the right to *sell* her in a market! If *that's* the way you think, Ben Retallick, you can forget about marrying me. I have no intention of ending up in Mevagissey market with a rope around my neck, being auctioned off for half a crown!'

Throwing up her chin, Jesse pushed her way through the amused bystanders and stalked away from Ben.

She allowed him to catch up with her at the edge of the harbour, where the crowd was thinner. He took her arm. 'Look . . . Does that please you?'

Ben pointed to an inn close to the water's edge. Seated on a bench outside the door were the one-legged man and the woman he had just purchased. As Ben and Jesse watched, a serving-girl came from the inn and put two large tankards on the table in front of the ex-soldier and his half-a-crown woman. Raising a tankard to his lips, the ex-soldier said something to the woman and nudged her in the ribs. She responded with a smile that transformed her dull features before they were hidden behind the second tankard.

'Well . . . she may be happier,' agreed Jesse, grudgingly. 'But no man has the right to sell his wife to anyone else.'

'That needn't trouble us. You said only a few minutes ago you'd decided not to marry me.'

'No, I did not!' Her good humour restored, Jesse linked her arm through Ben's. 'I said I wasn't going to be auctioned off at some market. Neither will I. You won't want to get rid of me, Ben Retallick. Not once I am yours.'

She was still smiling at Ben when a voice called, 'Hello, you two young sweethearts. Have you come to Mevagissey to attend our meeting?'

Walter Dunn fell into step beside Jesse and winked at her. To Ben he said, 'You had better hurry up and wed this young lady. She is prettier every time I see her. Wait too long and I'll take her to church and wed her myself.'

'You don't need to go to church to get yourself a wife,'

grinned Ben. 'They sell them at Mevagissey market.'

He told Walter of the incident he and Jesse had just witnessed and Jesse broke in to say, 'Can you really expect Parliament to give the vote to men who behave in such a manner?'

'They are little different in high places,' retorted Walter Dunn. 'There's not a landowner in the country who hasn't auctioned off sons and daughters to the highest bidder, in return for power or a title. The Prince Regent himself is only waiting until he is given the crown of England before he gets rid of his queen and puts another in her place. Come to the reform meeting if you want to learn more.'

Ben shook his head. 'I'll be staying clear of your reform meetings. Jesse and I have too much to lose. Besides, Sir John is opening an underground mine here in the spring. I intend working on it.'

'I doubt whether Sir John Vincent will appreciate your caution. He'll use you both in the same way he does everyone else. As and when it suits him. But I'll save my speeches for those who appreciate them. If you change your mind, you'll find us along the quay. Our main speaker today is one of the Spencean Philanthropists who marched on the Tower of London last year. Had they succeeded in taking it we would have parliamentary reform now – and everything else this country so desperately needs.'

Walter Dunn walked away, skirting the crowds attending the market.

As they watched him go, Jesse said to Ben, 'Walter will land himself in serious trouble one day if he goes around saying such things to people.'

'Trouble is as necessary to Walter as food. Without it he could not live. But it would break my grandma's heart if she lost the last of her sons. Let's forget about Walter and his reform movement. If we don't leave now, it will be dark before we get home.'

But Ben and Jesse had left it too late to avoid the trouble that suddenly flared up around them.

Mevagissey was only a few miles along the coast from the great naval port of Plymouth where three ships-of-the-line had been making ready to put to sea with a fleet setting out for the Mediterranean. The bulk of the fleet sailed along the English Channel from Portsmouth – only to learn that the Plymouth ships had been unable to find crewmen and were hopelessly undermanned.

The angry admiral ordered the three West Country vessels to break away from his fleet and make up their complements by sending press-gangs ashore along the southern coast of Cornwall. One of the Plymouth ships, the seventy-gun *Caesar*, sailed into St Austell Bay and sent two of her boats ashore at the tiny fishing-hamlet of Portmellon. When they landed, the found the village almost deserted. Most of the men were either at Walter Dunn's reform meeting, or had fled to the hills about Portmellon when they saw the boats coming inshore from the man-of-war. This coast had a long experience of press-gangs.

Aware of the admiral's anger, the young midshipman in charge of the press-gang was determined not to return to his ship empty-handed. Foolishly, he led his men over the hill to Mevagissey, a scant half-mile away. Along the road they scooped up a couple of unsuspecting fishermen who had been heading for the Portmellon boat-yard.

As they entered Mevagissey, the sailors found themselves in the midst of a thousand Cornishmen attending Walter Dunn's meeting. The two fishermen who had already been taken by the press-gang cried out for help, and the fishermen among the crowd were quick to respond.

With only twenty sailors under his command, the young midshipman had no chance of keeping the two impressed men and he let them go. His main concern was now to extricate his sailors before they were injured by the angry fishermen. There was no returning over the hill to Portmellon. He felt his only chance lay in fighting his way to the harbour in Mevagissey and commandeering a boat.

This the midshipman did with considerable skill until, when only yards from their goal, one of the sailors tripped and fell on the stone cobbles of the quay.

Had the midshipman merely stood his ground until the sailor regained his feet, all might have been well. The mob had secured a victory by rescuing the two fishermen, and they were content to drive the sailors back to their ship without any impressed fishermen. But the midshipman lacked experience. He saw only that one of his men was on the ground surrounded by angry fishermen. Drawing a pistol from his belt, he went to the aid of the downed sailor.

A young fisherman foolishly reached out and attempted to pull the pistol from the midshipman's hand. There was a noise like the crack of a packhorse driver's whip, and a puff of black smoke momentarily hid the fisherman and the young naval officer from view. When it cleared, the fisherman could be seen sitting on the ground. Clutching his stomach, he watched in disbelief as blood oozed between his widespread fingers.

A sudden shocked silence fell upon the crowd and it was far more terrible than the shouting that had gone before. Then a rumbling roar of anger broke from a thousand throats, and an avenging flood of men rushed forward. The sailors broke and ran.

The mob split twenty ways in pursuit, and it was one of these groups that engulfed Ben and Jesse. Unable to escape, they were forced to go along with the angry crowd or risk being trampled beneath the fishermen's boots.

They were still with the crowd when the sailor they were pursuing was cornered on the edge of the stone quay with no way to escape. He had a cutlass in his hand, but as the crowd advanced towards him he let it drop helplessly to the ground and opened his mouth to plead for mercy. His voice escaped as a terrified squeak, and Ben was distressed to see that the sailor was no more than a year older than himself.

Even as the boy sought for words with which to plead for his life, a cobblestone flew through the air and struck the young sailor in the face. He took an involuntary pace backwards – and stepped off the edge of the quay. As he dropped fifteen feet into the dirty water of the harbour, he struck his head against the stone wall. A cheer went up from the mob, but it died away in ragged discord as those in front moved forward and saw the motionless sailor floating face downwards amidst a stinking scum of fish offal.

89

'Ben! He mustn't be allowed to drown. Why doesn't someone get him out?'

There were others with similar thoughts. A big fisherman pushed his way to the edge of the quay and growled. 'Has the war with the French been over so long that we've forgotten what British sailors did for us? Has none of you got brothers or sons at sea who might be ordered to do no more than this lad did?'

Men shuffled their feet, discomfited, avoiding the fisherman's eyes.

'Someone get me an oar, or a hook. I'll pull him to the side.'

Ben ran to the harbour steps, where there were boats moored alongside the wall. A scream from Jesse stopped him.

'He's gone under!' she shouted.

When Ben looked from the fisherman to the harbour there was only the scum on the water to be seen, swirling with the falling tide.

Kicking off his heavy boots, the fisherman who had been addressing the crowd jumped into the foul water of the harbour. After some hesitation, two younger men jumped in after him. Others hurried past Ben to put out a boat.

The fishermen searched for fifteen minutes before a woman on the far side of the harbour called to them. She could see something floating beneath the surface, fifty yards away.

It was the missing sailor. He was quite dead. The fishermen in the boat brought him to the quayside where he was lifted ashore and gently laid out by some of the women.

'There will be hell to pay because of this,' muttered the big fisherman who stood wet and shivering, looking down at the body.

'It was an accident,' said one of the other men uneasily. 'No one is to blame. We did our best.'

'I hope to God the coroner believes you, but I wouldn't think it likely.'

A grim-faced Walter Dunn pushed his way through the crowd gathered about the body. 'He's not the only one. Two more sailors have died today – and they were not drowned. There will be murder warrants sworn out before this matter is settled.'

Chapter Ten

The investigation into the death of the three sailors was carried out by Sir John Vincent in his capacity as a magistrate. For a whole month Mevagissey had a full company of marines billeted in the village. Off-shore, a frigate patrolled the bay to prevent the escape of the unknown murderers and succeeded in totally disrupting all smuggling activities.

The sailors who manned the frigate were in a vengeful mood, and more than one Mevagissey fishing-boat lost its nets, run down by the naval vessel. The fishermen could make no complaint – there was no one to whom they dared report the incidents. The occupants of the fishing-boats had to accept that they were lucky to have escaped with their lives.

Sir John Vincent learned nothing from the tightly knit little fishing community. Angrily, he banned all future meetings of the reformers, and as a punishment to the village declared they would have a Revenue prevention-boat stationed permanently at Mevagissey.

The fishermen grumbled among themselves, but they realised they could have been dealt with in a much more severe manner. Had the killers of the sailors been discovered, there would have been more than one fisherman's body hanging outside the grim grey walls of Bodmin's gaol.

The reformers still met, but only in small groups now, each man known to the others. The meetings were held in houses, where no outsider could hear what was being said.

Such secrecy soon became essential throughout the whole land. Alarmed by the gathering momentum of the reform movement, the government of Lord Liverpool increased its efforts to repress the reformers. Troops were used to disperse even the most orderly of meetings. Lord Liverpool's own agitators were sent out to stir other meetings up to such a pitch that magistrates had to be sent for to break up the meetings and order the arrest of the speakers. Many leaders of the reform movement were thrown into gaols in towns and cities all over England. Those who came to trial were quickly transported to places where survival and not reform became every man's goal.

Survival of a different kind was going on in the Retallicks' house at Tregassick. During their first long winter there, Pearson Retallick fought for life with every painful breath he took. To his family he made no complaint, assuring them he would be all right when the warmer weather arrived.

In February of 1819 work began on the long-awaited underground tin mine just outside Mevagissey, and Ben and Moses Trago both moved there from Pentuan. Ben was grateful for the opportunity it offered to earn more money. With Pearson Retallick's continued ill-health, money had become a matter of some importance to himself and his mother.

The first task facing the miners was to dig a vertical shaft through ground that was mainly clay and shale. It needed boarding up for every foot of the way. Eventually, a depth of twenty fathoms was reached. Here Moses Trago and Ben left the shaft-digging gang and teamed up with a hymn-singing miner five years Ben's senior. Together they would drive a horizontal tunnel from the shaft, in search of the tin believed to be there. Wrightwick Roberts, at twenty-one years of age, was as thick-bearded and broad-shouldered as any man working the Mevagissey mine – and he was twice as industrious. He thrived on hard work. As he swung a pick, or hammered a drill into a rock-face, he sang from the sheer joy of mining – and from his unshakeable love of God.

Once Ben asked him why he sang hymns the whole time he worked. Wrightwick Roberts wiped perspiration from his eyes and looked at Ben with great seriousness.

' 'Tis necessary, Ben. Up at grass there's the Lord's good air and the trees and birds to remind us of His great works. Down here in the darkness of the earth the Devil is always on the look-out for new disciples. There's nothing like a good hymn to remind him that we belong to the Lord. Shout "Allelujah!", Ben. You'll feel better for it, and the Devil will have to work his mischief elsewhere.'

Moses Trago grumbled that they had so much waste rock and shale to shift that he would welcome the Devil himself if he brought his own shovel and paid for his own candles.

Wrightwick Roberts hastily made the sign of the Cross and warned Moses Trago against calling on the Devil, even in jest.

'He has keen hearing and a mind for mischief, Moses. If you need more help than you have already, then call upon the good Lord. Pray to Him, and He'll give you the strength of ten men.'

Behind Wrightwick Roberts's back, Moses Trago signalled to Ben that he thought the religious miner was soft in the head. But no one could dispute the strength of Wrightwick Roberts's arms. He was one of the strongest men Ben had ever known. When, after a week, they came upon a wide seam of rich tin ore, his redoubled efforts kept Ben and Moses Trago toiling harder than either of them had ever worked in their lives.

The trio were soon bringing more ore to the surface than any other team in the mine. One day, as they were cleaning up in the boiler-room of the mine, Ben asked Wrightwick Roberts what he intended to do with his share of the money they were making.

Wrightwick Roberts's face glowed with the fervour of his thoughts. 'I intend using it to become a preacher, Ben. To follow in the footsteps of the great John Wesley. I want a circuit of my own and a chance to carry the Word to those less fortunate than myself.'

Ben had learned something of Wrightwick Roberts's upbringing during the time they had been working together. Now he looked at him in amazement.

'To those *less* fortunate than yourself, Wrightwick? You were an orphan, brought up by the parish and sent out to work as soon as you could tell ore from rock. You look upon yourself as being *fortunate*?'

'Above all men, Ben. The good Lord chose me, and from the day I accepted Him I have known true happiness. Yes, I am a *most* fortunate man.'

Such simple faith made a deep impression on Ben, but Moses Trago was more convinced than ever that the big black-bearded miner was a simpleton.

93

Since they had been working at the Mevagissey mine, Ben and Moses had become close friends. Ben had managed to overcome Moses and Jesse's mutual dislike for each other to such an extent that Moses now lodged at Pengrugla. He slept in their barn, but ate his food with the Henna family. His contribution to the family's income would be a great help during the winter months when the farm was producing little that could be sold.

Once the rich seam of ore had been found, Ben saw little of Jesse. He and his partners needed to mine as much ore as possible before settling-day and they worked as many hours as was physically possible. Because of this, Moses Trago saw things that escaped Ben's notice.

Late one evening, as they walked home from the mine in the darkness, Moses said to Ben, 'You haven't been to Pengrugla for a few days.'

'No,' agreed Ben. 'It's been a busy time for us all. When I last went to Pengrugla, Jesse spent all her time fussing over a cow that's due to calf at any time.'

'The cow had twin calves two nights ago, Ben.'

Moses Trago's words made Ben feel guilty, although he knew Jesse understood how hard he was working. In two days' time it would be Sunday. He would spend the whole day with Jesse then.

They walked in silence for a while, then Moses said, 'Look, Ben, I don't want to cause any trouble, but . . . do you know Sir John Vincent's head gamekeeper?'

'Reuben Holyoak? Only too well. Why?'

'It's probably nothing . . .' Moses Trago already wished he had kept quiet. 'But he's been hanging around Pengrugla a lot lately. Last night when Jesse went out late to shut up the pigs I heard her arguing with someone. I thought it must be you at first, until I heard a man's voice. It was an older man. I got up to go and find out what it was all about, but before I'd got my boots on I heard Jesse run into the house and bang the door.'

Ben went cold at the thought of Reuben Holyoak molesting Jesse again.

'I'll come up to the house with you and see Jesse tonight.'

'Good . . .'

Suddenly Ben put a restraining hand on Moses Trago's arm and brought him to a halt.

'What is it, Ben ?'

'Shh! I saw a light across the far side of the pigs' field – there!'

It was the small dancing light of a flame being put to a pipe.

'That must be Holyoak waiting for Jesse now. He'll meet up with me instead.'

Ben was slow to anger – but he was angry now. His aching limbs forgotten, he was grateful for the hours of hard physical labour he had performed in recent weeks. It had given him rock-hard muscles and a strength that went far beyond his years.

'If you intend tackling a gamekeeper at night, I'd better come with you,' declared Moses Trago. 'Otherwise he'll go to Sir John Vincent and swear you and he fought because he caught you poaching.'

Ben knew Moses Trago was right. Men who protected game were powerful enemies. The distant colonies were peopled with a great many young men whose only crime had been to fall foul of a vindictive gamekeeper. The game laws were among the harshest on the statute-books. But Ben did not want Moses involved in what he had to do.

'I don't intend fighting Reuben Holyoak unless I have to. I'll wait until Jesse comes and see if I can learn what this is about. You go home – and take the long way. Don't disturb Holyoak.'

Moses Trago hesitated, but before he could argue Ben had gone, slipping away into the shadows of the high earth-covered wall surrounding the Hennas' pig-field.

Ben knew where the wall was at its lowest. Climbing over carefully, he dropped to the ground in the field and stealthily made his way to the side of the building that housed the pigs. Inside, the pigs snored, twitched and squeaked in sheer bad temper as they huddled together in restless sleep.

Ben was no more than fifteen yards away from the gate here, and the aromatic smell of tobacco smoke was carried to him on the night air.

For almost half an hour Ben waited in the darkness. He began to think that Jesse might already have completed her chores. The same thought must have come to Reuben Holyoak.

Ben heard the gate creak open as Reuben Holyoak came into the field to check that the pigs were not already locked away.

Ben held his breath and pushed back into the shadows as Reuben Holyoak passed only a few feet from him. The game-keeper reached the door of the pig-sty just as one of the pigs squealed and began to snort and snuffle noisily.

Reuben Holyoak drew a small fire-pistol from his pocket and struck sparks from it. A feeble flame flickered in the doorway, and he leaned in to look at the restless pigs.

It was an opportunity too good to be missed. A few hurried steps took Ben to the doorway and, before Reuben Holyoak could turn, Ben's shoulder hit him in the back. The game-keeper was knocked to his knees inside the pig-sty, the extinguished fire-pistol flying from his grasp.

As Ben slid the heavy wooden bolt into place on the outside of the door, the pigs complained vociferously from within as Reuben Holyoak stumbled clumsily amongst them.

Ben stood back and grinned wickedly. The door had been made to withstand the combined weight of ten hefty pigs. It would not budge beneath Reuben Holyoak's fists.

'Let me out! Do you hear me? Let me out! I'll have you for this, whoever you are. Let me out!'

Ben walked away from the pigs' house to the gate of the field. Passing out on to the path, he closed the gate behind him and met Jesse hurrying towards the field.

'Ben! What are you doing here? And what's that noise from the pigs' house? What's going on?'

Ben took Jesse's arm. Turning her around, he began to walk her away from the gate. 'Everything is all right. The pigs are locked away for the night – but they have company. Ask Moses to come down and let them out tomorrow morning.'

Jesse pulled against Ben and stopped.

'Is Reuben Holyoak in there with them?'

'Yes.'

'But Napoleon is in there, Ben! He's the most evil-tempered pig in Cornwall. He'll have Reuben's leg off.'

'Not if Reuben climbs up on one of the beams and sits there all night.' Ben smiled at Jesse, and she saw his teeth gleam in the darkness. 'Reuben won't get any sleep, but he'll be safe enough.'

He chuckled, and a moment later Jesse was giggling with him.

'Reuben won't forgive you for this, Ben.'

'He can never be certain it was me – and, if all I've heard is true, he is too vain to complain to anyone. He would become a laughing-stock.'

'How did you know Reuben has been bothering me, Ben?'

'Moses told me. Did Reuben try anything with you, Jesse?'

'No.' Jesse shook her head, but much of the lightheartedness had gone from her. 'He only wanted to talk.'

'About what?'

As they walked, they had swung away from Pengrugla, taking a path that led to a grassy bank above a stream. It was one of their favourite spots.

Jesse said nothing until she and Ben were seated on the grassy bank and he had his arm about her.

'Reuben asked me to marry him, Ben.'

Her answer took Ben by surprise. He knew the gamekeeper wanted Jesse. He had seen the way he looked at her. But Ben had not expected Holyoak to declare himself now. He must know how things were between Ben and Jesse – that their understanding had Sir John Vincent's blessing. He expressed his thoughts to Jesse.

'I think that's why he is so persistent now, Ben. He knows about Pengrugla and is trying to make me change my mind before it's too late. Reuben has big plans for his own future and he told me I could be a part of them.'

'What sort of plans. He's a gamekeeper. He'll never be anything more.'

'Don't be too sure of that, Ben. Reuben is well thought of by Colman Vincent – and Lamorrack will be his one day. But

97

Colman prefers to live on his Devon estate, and Reuben hinted that *he* will be given the job of running Lamorrack when that day comes.'

Ben had to admit that Reuben Holyoak had made an offer that would impress many girls – and most mothers. If Reuben had been speaking the truth, he and his wife would live like the lord and lady of the manor during Colman Vincent's long absences.

'What did you tell him, Jesse?'

She looked up into his face quickly. 'Do you *really* need to ask me that question, Ben? I told Reuben that I love you and would marry you in preference to him if you were a beggar.'

Ben kissed her and Jesse snuggled against him.

'But, if you made it so clear to Reuben Holyoak that you want nothing to do with him, why is he still bothering you?'

'Reuben just can't accept that I won't one day change my mind. Perhaps I am partly to blame for that, Ben. When my pa was killed I leaned on Reuben a lot. He was kind to me; but then he wanted to be more than just "kind", and I stopped seeing so much of him.'

After a brief pause, Jesse said unhappily, 'Reuben would think twice about bothering me if my pa were still here.'

She sounded so miserable that Ben's arm tightened about her.

'What was he like, Jesse . . . your pa?'

'He was fun. He never let anything or anyone trouble him. He had a temper, though. No one would take any liberties with him. He was brave, too. Sir John had a letter from one of the officers who was at Waterloo with him. It said that my pa was one of the bravest soldiers in the regiment . . .'

She was silent for a long time; then she whispered, 'Sometimes I wish he hadn't been so brave. He might still have been here with me and Ma . . .'

Ben kissed her again. This time he tasted the tears on her cheek and held her to him until she wriggled in his arms.

'I'm all right now, Ben.' Her voice was muffled and she rubbed her face against his shirt. Then she looked up at him in the darkness. 'I wish Pa could have met you, Ben. He would like you.'

'Would he?' As Jesse disentangled herself from him to tie her hair behind her neck, Ben lay back on the soft turf with his hands beneath his head. 'Perhaps he would prefer you to marry someone with Reuben's prospects.'

He half rolled over, towards Jesse. 'I sometimes worry about myself, Jesse. I listen to Walter talking about his reform movement and wonder what it is inside him that drives him on all the time. He believes wholeheartedly in what he is doing. There is no doubting voice inside him to tell him that perhaps he might be wrong. That reform might not achieve all he claims it will. I wish I had such unquestioning faith in something – anything!'

'I'm glad you haven't, Ben. Walter has no time for anything but "reform". I suspect that's why he has never married. No girl is going to take second place to parliamentary reform.'

'All right, then, take Wrightwick Roberts – he's the miner who works with Moses and me. He believes so strongly in religion that he is determined to become a preacher. He works like two men because he's after something special – an ambition. Even Reuben Holyoak has that – but I don't, Jesse! I dig in the ground. I'm excited when we find good ore and I enjoy digging it out. If we haven't found the ore, I'm just as happy to be underground looking for it. I don't want any more. I'm happy with my work – and I'm happy with you. But when I look around me I feel I should be after something more in life.'

'Ben Retallick, just so long as you're happy with me, I don't care if you never have an ambitious thought in your head. One day you'll be the best miner in the country, and everyone will want you to work for them. Don't feel ashamed of enjoying your work. There are many people so busy trying to get somewhere that they never have time to enjoy what they have. I'm *glad* you're not like that, Ben. I love you just as you are. I wouldn't want you to be like Reuben Holyoak – or even Walter Dunn.'

Ben reached out for her, and she went to him. Jesse had

realised, as had Martha Retallick before her, that Ben might one day own Pengrugla, but it would never make him a farmer. Ben was a miner – and a miner he would remain.

Much later that night, Jesse let herself quietly into the darkened house and slipped into her bed with a sigh of relief. Her mother had not heard her come in. Jesse lay awake for a long time, remembering. Occasionally she ran her hands down the body that had been brought to life tonight and given a whole new meaning.

Jesse had given Ben peace of mind about his love of mining to the exclusion of all ambition. She had also come to an understanding with her own tangled emotions.

She had realised tonight that she belonged to Ben Retallick – and he to her. She determined that she would hold nothing back from him – ever. Mining was a dangerous occupation, and Ben might be taken from her at any time. She dreaded the thought of such an end to her happiness, but, if it happened, she knew she would regret nothing they had done together – only the things they had *not* done.

Now she would never have the greatest regret of all.

In the darkness of the night, with only the stars to bear witness, Ben and Jesse had consummated their love, and Jesse had crossed the threshold of womanhood.

Chapter Eleven

During that year of 1819, Jesse and Ben's relationship became one of deep love and understanding. It was a time of constant discovery for them both. They laid their plans for the future, for themselves and for the family they would have and raise at Pengrugla.

They agreed that Ben should continue to work at the Mevagissey mine. The money he earned would be used to build up the stock on the small farm. When Jesse and Ben had a son he would have a choice – to follow in Ben's footsteps, or to become his own master. A yeoman farmer, working his own land.

They decided the wedding would take place late in 1820, when both of them were seventeen. By then, with the aid of the industrious Wrightwick Roberts, Ben hoped to have saved enough to ensure the success of both Pengrugla and his marriage.

During these happy summer months, Mark and Billy Dunn returned from their enforced voyage to the Mediterranean. England's problems there had been temporarily solved and half the huge fleet ordered back to their home ports.

The two men returned to Mevagissey as heroes, and accepted the new status as their due. But Mark, at least, had served his country with something less than distinction. Ben learned of this when he went to Mevagissey one day and unexpectedly walked into the backyard of the Dunn home when Mark was stripped to the waist, washing.

The whole of the fisherman's back was crisscrossed with scars, grim evidence of a brutal lashing.

Mark Dunn slipped his shirt over his head hastily and scowled at Ben. 'No other man in Mevagissey will see me without my shirt on, boy. You hold your tongue about what you've seen today. Do you understand me?'

'I carry no tales of things that are none of my business,' retorted Ben. 'I have other things to think about.'

'I wish I could forget as easily.'

Mark Dunn fastened his shirt and tucked it inside his trousers. 'I'll carry the memory of two hundred lashes with me to the grave.'

Ben winced, it was a beating to sear the mind of the strongest man, 'Why . . . ?' he began; then stopped. As he had declared earlier, it was none of his business.

However, as his secret was now shared with Ben, Mark Dunn seemed not to mind telling him the details.

'You were going to ask why I was tied to the mast and humiliated before the whole ship's company, right? Well, I'll tell you, Ben. It was because I know more about sailing than some of the fools they put in charge of King George's ships – and because I wasn't above telling them so.'

Mark Dunn's eyes glittered angrily at the memory. 'We were off the coast of Greece when we were caught in as fierce a storm as any I've seen anywhere. The fool captain ordered more sail shaken out in a bid to outsail it. I said we stood in danger of foundering if we did as he told us. Some of the other men agreed with me, and the captain had us secured in irons. The ship lost a mast and five good seamen – but I was still in the wrong for having spoken my mind. I took two hundred lashes and the others a hundred apiece. That's your fine navy for you, Ben boy.'

Ben murmured sympathetically about the wrong that had been done to Mark.

'Aye, it were wrong, boy. But as every one of those lashes bit down on my back I swore it would be another nail in the coffins of the Revenue men who put me on that ship.'

Ben looked at his uncle in alarm. 'You know there's a Revenue boat stationed here now?'

'I know. I also know it's manned by some of the men who took Billy and me. I'll have 'em, Ben boy. I promise you that. It may not be this week, or even this year, but I'm a patient man. I'll have 'em.'

Ben was to remember Mark Dunn's words. Before the year was out, three of the Mevagissey Revenue men had died from unexplained 'accidents'. Two were found drowned in the harbour, having apparently fallen in when intoxicated. The third was keeping a night watch from the cliffs to the north of the village and it was believed he missed his footing and tumbled down the cliff to the rocks below. Each of the three had been a member of the crew of the boat which had taken Mark and Billy Dunn prisoner.

With the return of the two brothers, local smuggling activities immediately increased, despite the presence of the Revenue men. Contraband was landed in various coves around Mevagissey and packed on ponies for carriage up the hill past Tregassick. Pearson Retallick, kept awake by the pain in his chest and his difficulty in breathing, heard the muffled hoofs of the ponies passing by almost nightly.

So regular were the illegal night journeys, Pearson learned to tell how many ponies were being used and even how heavily laden they were. He felt a great deal of sympathy for their lead pony. Its breathing was almost as noisy as his own.

One night, earlier than usual, Pearson Retallick heard a new sound in the quiet night. It was the furtive movement of men, betrayed by a whispered order, a stifled cough, and the careless rattle of a powder-horn against a musket lock.

Fighting against his own coughing, Pearson Retallick struggled from the bed and made his painful way to Ben's bedroom.

'Ben! Ben, wake up!'

Disturbed from a deep sleep, Ben was momentarily confused. 'What is it? What's happened?'

'Shh! Keep your voice down. Get dressed and go to Mevagissey. Find Walter, or one of the others. Tell them the Revenue men are out and about. It sounds as though they are setting a trap up by the wood. Go quickly – and take care, Ben.'

Ben asked no more questions. Swinging his feet to the floor, he dressed swiftly.

'Remember, go with caution, Ben.'

His father's hoarse whisper reached him as Ben let himself quietly from the house.

There was a full, smugglers' moon hanging bloated above the tallest trees of the wood, and Ben took a detour around the deep shadows. Once clear of the wood he made good time until he reached a place where the path divided, going in three different directions. Ben paused uncertainly before choosing the middle path. It led directly to Mevagissey and was the most unlikely path for the smugglers to use, but it was the quickest way to the Dunn cottage. Grandfather Dunn would know where his three sons were carrying out their nocturnal trading.

Ben was only a hundred yards along the track when he heard the blowing of a pony somewhere to his right. It had to be the smugglers, already well on their way along one of the other paths. The moon chose that moment to slide behind a large silver-fringed cloud. Cursing beneath his breath, Ben stumbled blindly back the way he had come.

Reaching the junction, he collided bodily with the unseen man leading the first of the smugglers' ponies.

'Who's there? Speak up or be shot!'

The demand came as a hoarse whisper, but Ben recognised the voice of Ned Hunkin, one of the two men who fished with Walter.

'Keep your voice down and speak no names, or we'll all be shot. There are Revenue men up ahead. They're hiding close to the wood, waiting for you.'

'Are they, be damned!' This was Walter's voice. 'Do you know how many there are?'

'No.' Ben repeated everything his father had told him.

'Good boy! Get along home now and leave us to attend to this.'

'What will you do?'

'Ask no questions. The less you know, the better it will be for you. Hurry now.'

Ben did as he was told, smarting at his curt dismissal. However, when he reached home and repeated what had been said, his father agreed with Walter.

'Walter is no fool, Ben. He'll have made plans for just such an occurrence as this. It's best that there's no one else around to see what happens.'

Martha Retallick had been woken by the comings and goings in her home and she said, 'I hope Walter has planned well. The family have just got Mark and Billy home. It will be the end of your grandpa and grandma if they are taken again, Ben.'

Martha Retallick need not have worried. This was a night for smugglers.

Led by only a few men, the laden ponies headed inland along a lesser-known path. Walter took the remainder of the smugglers in a wide circle around the Revenue men's ambush. He waited for the moon to show him the position of every one of the Revenue men, then he mounted a swift but brief attack.

Coming as it did from such an unexpected direction, the assault took the Revenue men completely by surprise. In the ensuing confusion they shot two of their own number and were still fighting each other long after the Mevagissey men had faded into the night.

It was a notable victory in the age-old battle between smugglers and the authorities. For weeks the Revenue men had to endure the jokes of small boys, warning them to 'Look out! There may be another Revenue man creeping up on 'ee.'

At Tregassick, they woke on the morning after the fight to find a keg of best French brandy on the doorstep. For many nights afterwards it served to dull the constant pain of Pearson Retallick's clogged lungs and he slept in a welcome drunken stupor.

But Pearson Retallick's relief from pain lasted only as long as the brandy. Afterwards, the deterioration in his health caused Ben more concern than ever. Now the sick man was able to leave the house only to sit for hours in a chair set outside the door. This was pleasant enough during the long fine summer days, but when the deep mists of November rolled in from the sea the door had to be kept tight shut, and Pearson Retallick was forced to spend long hours alone in the house.

Ben knew the pain in his father's chest increased with the cold weather. More and more often, when Ben looked at him, there was an expression of resigned weariness on Pearson Retallick's face. Gradually, the sick man became increasingly withdrawn and morose. Ben worried about him every time he left for work. One morning, when his mother had already left to go to Lamorrack House, Ben went to his parents' bedroom and, to his consternation, found his father seated on the edge of the bed, dressing with painful difficulty.

'What do you think you're doing, Pa?'

Pearson Retallick turned his face towards his son and gave him a weary grin that reminded Ben of better days, when such a look regularly passed between them.

The memory struck deep – and it hurt.

'I'm getting out of bed and going downstairs, Ben. If I don't, I'll lie up here and rot away. That's no life for a man, or for his wife and son, is it, now?'

'You'd be better staying in bed until the days warm up a bit. There's a frost outside this morning. If you insist on getting up, I'll light a fire for you before I leave. In an hour it will have warmed the house. Stay in bed until then.'

'Cold mornings don't trouble me, Ben. Do you remember some of the winter mornings when we were at the Money Box mine? We'd go outside the house together and break the ice on the barrel to get water to wash with. You were no more than seven or eight when we began doing that together, Ben. At times it tore the very guts out of me to see your poor little body shivering in the cold, knowing you had to go off and spend a full day breaking ore in the cold wind without enough warm clothing on your back.'

Pearson Retallick screwed up his face, fighting the tears that threatened to expose his extreme weakness. He eventually managed a laugh which was quickly chased away by a bout of coughing.

'It's funny how life turns about, Ben. Now it's your turn to stand over me like some young giant, looking at my poor thin body and feeling pity for *me*.'

Pearson Retallick looked up at his son, and the muscles in his face twitched with the emotion he was feeling.

'You're a good boy, Ben. We've had some grand times together, you and me. We've never been overburdened with goods and chattels, but there has always been more than enough love in the house for all of us.'

'There still is, Pa – and there are many more good times yet to come. It's not pity I feel for you, it's pride. Pride that you've always worked so hard for Ma and me. Pride that you kept going long after most other men would have given up.'

Pearson Retallick was unable to control his tears now. They ran unchecked down his cheeks, and his voice came out as a whisper. 'Thank you, Ben. But I've always been an honest man – to myself and to you. I know how much of a burden I am. No, Ben, don't try to hide behind kind words. You know it's the truth, just as I do.'

Fiercely, Pearson Retallick cuffed his eyes with the back of his hand. 'Now, go down and light that fire, then get yourself off to work. Don't let a good pitch of tin lie idle because you're back here, humouring your foolish old pa.'

Ben had never seen his father in such a melancholy mood. He set off for work more worried about him than he had ever been before.

All that morning, as Ben swung a heavy hammer, driving a borer into a narrowing tin lode, he kept seeing the tortured face of his father, fighting for control of himself.

By mid-afternoon, the unsettling nagging at his mind was so strong that he could bear it no longer. Telling his two workmates that he was worried about his father, he announced that he was returning home early.

Moses Trago grumbled that he would never be able to keep up with Wrightwick Roberts on his own, but the religious miner sympathised with Ben.

'It's written that you should "Honour thy father and thy mother, that thy days may be long in the land which the Lord has given". Go and obey the Lord, Ben. I only wish I had known a father about whom I might concern myself.'

Leaving the mine behind him, Ben felt suddenly foolish about going home so unexpectedly. What would he tell his father? That he could not work for thinking about him? Pearson Retallick would give his son a gentle smile and send him back to the mine. Perhaps Ben should say they had lost the lode and stopped work early.

Then, as he drew close to the house at Tregassick, Ben's earlier anxiety returned a hundredfold. There was no smoke coming from the fire he had lit that morning, although the day was still very cold. He had left a pile of logs, ready cut, beside the fireplace. His father needed only to place them upon the fire. Ben's first thought was that his father had been taken ill before he finished dressing and had not made it downstairs. He broke into a trot.

When he reached the house a quick glance in the kitchen confirmed that the logs had not been touched. The fire had died an early death. Running up the stairs, Ben called to his father and flung open the bedroom door. The room was empty. Ben checked his own bedroom; then every room in the house.

Pearson Retallick was not there.

By now Ben was thoroughly alarmed. His father had not left the house for weeks. He was far too weak to go off on his own.

He went outside and looked about him wondering where to begin his search. Then he saw the door of the old barn standing half-open. It had been closed when Ben set off for work. There was no reason why Pearson Retallick – or any one else – should have gone inside. The barn held only a broken-down farm-cart and a miscellany of rubbish that needed sorting and throwing out.

The door protested noisily as Ben pulled it wide open.

'Pa? Are you in here?'

For a moment Ben saw nothing. Then, in the light from the evening sun shining through a broken window, he saw an exaggerated distorted shadow cast on the wall beside him. His eyes widened in horror. Shielding his eyes against the sun's rays, Ben took two unsteady paces into the barn.

His agonised cry sent a cluster of roosting birds fluttering in panic from a crevice high up in the wall.

Ben had found his father.

Pearson Retallick was dangling at the end of an old length of rope, secured to a wooden beam. His head was laid sideways on his shoulder, the toes of his heavy mining-boots swinging only inches above the dusty barn-floor.

Weary of life after years of constant ill-health and bouts of excruciating pain, Pearson Retallick had relieved his family of the burden of nursing him during his last years of total incapacity. It was the final act of a caring and courageous man.

*

Pearson Retallick was buried on a wet and stormy night, at a spot where the path from Tregiskey to St Ewe crossed the track from Mevagissey to St Austell.

By taking his own life he had put himself beyond the absolution of the Church. In spite of the pleas of Ben and his mother, the vicar of Mevagissey was adamant. Pearson Retallick could not be laid to rest in consecrated ground. He had committed a sin that carried its stigma to the grave – and beyond.

The funeral took place, as tradition decreed it should, at an hour as dark as the deed itself. Pearson Retallick's mortal remains were laid to rest where two paths met – and passed on. This was the only cross he would ever have to mark his grave, a diluted balm to soothe the unhallowed soul that was doomed to haunt this place until men's memories grew dim and unreliable.

All ordinated clergy were forbidden to officiate at such an internment, but after helping Ben and Moses Trago to dig the grave to a respectable depth Wrightwick Roberts pleaded Pearson Retallick's case to the Lord with a powerful prayer. He reminded Him of the pain the miner had been given to bear during his lifetime and begged pardon for the deed that had hastened God's own mercy.

The mumbled 'Amen' went up from only a few throats. Ben, Martha Retallick, Moses Trago, Jesse and Walter Dunn were the only mourners to brave the cold night and risk the displeasure of the Church.

Afterwards, Ben and his two miner companions used their long-handled shovels to fill in the grave and cover up their work as well as they could. Body-snatchers were active, even in this remote part of the country.

It was as well that none of those who trudged homeward from the unmarked grave could see into the future. Pearson Retallick's suicide was only the first incident in a winter that was destined to change the life of each one of them.

Chapter Twelve

Standing at the cold damp graveside and sharing in a small way the grief of Ben and his mother, Moses Trago had inexplicably felt himself to be a part of a family again. It was an uncomfortable disturbing feeling – but one that would not be shaken off.

For the first time since running away from home, Moses began to think about those he had left behind at Sharptor, high on Bodmin's moor. Most of all he remembered his mother. A colourless beaten women, she had given birth to five sons and seen three of them laid in the ground before they were old enough to know her. The two who survived were brought up in abject poverty in the cave home on the moor.

Matthew Trago, Moses' father, spent much of his time and all of his money in moorland gin-houses. He found his amusement in beating his wife and whichever of the two sons was not quick enough to run from the house when he staggered home roaring drunk.

John was the younger of the two brothers. Moses remembered him as a quiet, almost simple boy who rarely spoke his own thoughts. John had a stoicism that stood him in good stead when he fell foul of his father's fists. Because he neither showed pain nor defended himself, his beatings became brief perfunctory affairs.

With Moses, it had always been different. He had fought back from the very beginning, his rage increasing with every blow his father rained upon him.

It was Moses Trago's memories of his father that he had tried hardest to forget. His earliest recollections were of the terror he brought with him into the makeshift house. The first sounds Moses could recollect were his mother's screams as his father pummelled her from corner to corner of the home. Moses grew up hating his father and the cromlech home on the tor.

His very few happy memories began when, at the age of six, he was old enough to accompany his mother to the mine and help her to sort the ore. There, for the first time in his life, he heard voices raised in conversation or laughter, and not in anger or terror.

As he grew older, it became evident to everyone who knew him that Moses had inherited his father's dark temper. It flared up repeatedly at Matthew Trago, bringing Moses some severe beatings. The worst of them on the occasions when he tried to protect his mother.

Eventually, life at home became unbearable for Moses. One night he stole away and headed for the deep tin mines of St Just.

Now, after four years, the sharp edge of his hatred had dulled. When he stood looking down at Pearson Retallick's lonely grave, Moses Trago remembered a few long-forgotten things: the feel of his mother's hand holding his as they set out for work before dawn on a winter morning; the sympathy in his brother's eyes as he looked at Moses' face, bruised and battered by yet another beating.

There was still nothing but hatred for his father in Moses Trago's heart, but now Matthew Trago was no more than a dark shadow. He loomed large behind the others, but no longer carried the menace he had once possessed.

Moses realised he wanted to see his family again – alive. He did not wish to return to Sharptor to stand at a meaningless graveside and think of them as they had once been.

Moses Trago grappled with his new and unwanted sentiments for many days before giving Ben and Wrightwick Roberts the surprising news that he was leaving the Mevagissey mine and returning home to Sharptor. Wrightwick Roberts accepted the news in silence. After mulling it over for many minutes, he said generously, 'You could not have chosen a better time to leave, Moses. We have lost the lode and it might be many weeks before we find it again. Go now, and you will have money in your pocket to take with you. Stay, and you will spend it before there is more to take its place. Set off now, before you change your mind.'

Ben received the news with mixed feelings. He was sorry to

be losing his friend, and he said so, but he understood why Moses had to go.

Moses was relieved that his two colleagues had accepted his decisions so readily. He smiled at Ben's words.

'Given a week or two you will need to stop and think if my name is mentioned, Ben. Besides, you will have other things to think about soon. A wedding to arrange. But if ever you feel the need to work in a big mine again, one going deep enough for copper as well as tin, come to Sharptor. You will be able to choose from a dozen mines, many of them already down to the two-hundred-fathom level.'

'I would like to see them, Moses. But I intend staying here. I might even become a farmer one day, when Jesse and I are married.'

Moses Trago shook his head. 'You are a miner, Ben. A good miner. Mining is in your blood. You'll never settle down to milking cows and feeding pigs and chickens. That's women's work.'

That evening, Moses Trago treated Ben and Wrightwick Roberts to a couple of ales in a Mevagissey inn. The next morning he set off for Sharptor, and home.

It was little more than twenty miles distant. Moses Trago knew he would make the journey fairly comfortably in one day. On the way he passed the great Crinnis mine. The size of the working made him more eager than ever to return to an area where mining was a serious business. Sir John Vincent had opened the Mevagissey mine to satisfy a whim. He would not make a fortune, and the mine would never amount to much. The ore was not there in sufficient quantities.

At Lostwithiel, Moses Trago paused to view the great round castle of Restormel and marvel at the ancient workmanship of the Norman fortress. From here, the road began to rise steadily, and he caught occasional glimpses of Caradon Hill rising above the edge of Bodmin Moor. It was no more than a stone's throw from Sharptor. Then he saw Sharptor itself, its granite heights perched on the slope above Henwood village.

As Moses drew closer and felt the springy turf of the moor beneath his feet once more, the first doubts about the wisdom of returning stirred within him. He had been away a long time and had left without a word to anyone. He had never thought what his going would mean to his mother or brother John.

Moses slowed, reluctant to cover the final mile. By the time he arrived at the heights above the strange dwelling it was dark. He moved forward ever more slowly until he could have pitched a stone in through one of the high window-openings.

There was a flickering orange glow inside the home, and Moses knew it came from a cooking-fire in the centre of the cromlech.

Moses Trago squared his shoulders and strode to the door. Pushing it open, the foul smell from inside rushed out, threatening to overwhelm him. He stopped inside the entrance, shocked at the chaos he saw there. It looked as though no attempt had been made to tidy the place for many months.

Before the open fire, a boy of about fourteen years of age squatted, stirring a pot that was perched at a crazy angle on sagging iron bars above the flames. There was no sign of his mother.

Moses stood inside the door waiting for the boy to turn and look at him. When nothing happened, Moses said quietly, 'Hello, John.'

For a few long seconds, the figure crouched at the fireside with the ladle poised in his hand. Then John Trago rose to his feet and slowly turned to face his brother, an expression of sheer joy spreading across his face.

'Moses! Moses . . . it really is you?'

Suddenly the two brothers were clasping each other, both laughing stupidly. Finally, holding his brother away from him at arm's length, Moses said shakily, 'Well, it's nice to know someone is pleased to see me – but where's our ma?'

The happiness slipped away from John Trago's face, and the shoulders beneath Moses' hands rose and fell in a shrug.

'I don't know.'

'You don't know? What do you mean?'

John Trago shrugged again. 'She left us, about a year after you went – and took the baby with her. Yes, that's right, she had another child. A boy again. I came home from the mine one day and they were both gone. I searched for weeks, but no one had seen them go. She must have gone off over the moor . . . somewhere.'

John Trago made a helpless gesture in the direction of the moors that extended for ten empty miles to the north-west.

Moses gnawed at his lower lip as he looked at the boy standing before him. Almost as broad-shouldered as himself, brother John yet looked very vulnerable and helpless dressed in clothes that had obviously been handed down from their father. They were neither clean nor in good repair. Where they hung too far from his body they were tied in with string.

'How have you managed without her?'

Another shrug. 'We get by. Sometimes Pa brings a woman home with him. She stays until he beats her too hard. The rest of the time I do whatever needs to be done.'

Pity welled in Moses for his younger brother. 'And Pa? How is he?'

'He doesn't change, Moses. He works, he drinks and he fights. Sometimes he does more of one than of the others, that's all.'

Moses Trago's spirits sank within him. He had secretly hoped a miracle might have occurred to change his father's ways. He should have known better. Miracles happened only in the pages of the book Wrightwick Roberts carried about with him – and already Mevagissey could have been a million miles away.

Moses accepted some of the weak and foul-smelling stew cooking in the pot on the fire, then he sorted out some of his own clothes for his brother. They were old working-clothes, but John Trago's delight was such that Moses might have presented him with a suit of velvet.

The two brothers talked together well into the night. They were still talking when they heard the noise made by someone staggering along the path towards the house. Moses rose to his feet slowly, his heart pounding at the thought of the encounter to come. Moments later the door crashed open and Matthew Trago stumbled drunkenly into the stone house.

Moses was shocked at his father's appearance. John had

declared that their father had not changed. He was wrong. Years of dissipated living had taken a heavy toll on Matthew Trago. There was less weight on his bones, and his face was bloated and stained. He had the look of a wild animal about him, and an expression approaching madness in his eyes.

Matthew Trago opened his mouth to release his habitual roar of anger at John, then realised he was looking at his eldest son. For a brief moment something akin to pleasure showed on his face, but it went before Moses could be certain.

'Oh, it's you! Decided to come home again, have you?'

Moses nodded.

Matthew Trago belched noisily. 'If you've eaten my supper, I'll knock you back outside again. D'you hear me?'

'I hear you.'

Something in the quiet way Moses spoke the words caused Matthew Trago to look at him again. This time it was not the look of a drunken man, but the shrewd assessment of a fighter. He saw the wide shoulders and hard muscles that filled out the shirt his son wore.

'You think you've grown big enough to take your father now, do you?'

'I *know* I have.'

Moses whispered the words and tensed himself for what was to come.

Father and son stared at each other for what seemed an age to the anxiously watching John. Then Matthew Trago grunted.

'H'm! Happen you could be right.'

Turning to his other son, he roared, 'What are you standing there like an idiot for? Give me my supper.'

Moses Trago had returned to Sharptor – and he was now a man.

Chapter Thirteen

As the spring of 1820 neared, Ben found himself working longer hours than ever before. Wrightwick Roberts had once more found the tin lode. It was wide enough now for two men to work at it standing side by side. They brought in two boys to help, but at the end of each shift they all had to lend a hand to clear the ore that had been mined in the rich working.

Nevertheless, when he left the mine each evening, Ben went to Pengrugla to help Jesse complete her day's chores. Jesse's mother had fallen ill. A doctor had been called in and, after muttering vaguely of 'palpitations' and 'heart flutters', he ordered her straight to bed. At first, Maude Henna scorned his instructions, but when she fainted whilst carrying food to the pigs Jesse insisted that she go to bed immediately and remain there for a while.

Contrary to Moses Trago's gloomy predictions, Ben enjoyed working at Pengrugla. Without the constant presence of Maude Henna, it was almost as though he and Jesse were already married.

Then the second blow of the winter fell.

Ben arrived home from Pengrugla one night to find Tregassick in darkness. There was no sign of his mother, and for one panic-stricken moment Ben thought it was a tragic repeat of the day he had returned home and discovered his father's body hanging in the barn.

The barn was empty and, sagging with relief, Ben realised that his mother must still be at Lamorrack House. She had said nothing about there being any social function for which she would need to work late, so Ben set off to the big house seeking her. He had gone no more than a hundred yards when he heard someone hurrying towards him in the darkness.

'Is that you, Ma?'

'Ben! Thank goodness! I thought I would never get home. It's been a terrible day.'

Reaching Ben, his mother clung to him, breathing heavily.

'What's happened ? Why are you so late ?'

'Sir John was thrown from his horse this evening,' Martha Retallick began to cry. 'At his age he should have known better than to go riding alone.'

'Is he badly hurt ?' Ben felt genuine concern for the aged baronet.

'Hurt ? He's dead, Ben. He died not an hour since, with only his sister at his bedside, poor man.'

When Martha Retallick had brought her tears under control, she said, 'There'll be changes at Lamorrack House now, Ben. Colman is not the man his father was. I'll never get used to calling him "Sir" Colman. They can make him a duke, he'll still have all his father's faults and none of his virtues. Sir John's servants are shedding tears tonight – but as much for themselves as for poor Sir John.'

Sir John Vincent's funeral was held a week later. Every servant and all his employees were given time off to attend. The Mevagissey mine was closed for the day, as was the Happy Union stream-working. All the miners attended the service. Wearing their Sunday clothes, they stood awkwardly at the back of the church. In the main they were chapel-goers, followers of John Wesley. Unused to the pomp and medieval symbolism of the Church.

Sir John Vincent had been a well-known and respected county figure, and most of the pews in the church were filled by Cornwall's gentry. The Carews, Boscawens, Edgcumbes and St Aubyns were all there. Outside the church their carriages filled the narrow lane for a hundred yards, the foot-men in unfamiliar livery subjected to many sidelong glances from the young servant girls from Lamorrack House.

Once the funeral was over, the tenants and workers on the late Sir John Vincent's estate waited for their new landlord to declare his intentions. No one had any doubt that he would bring about changes. They were inevitable. Sir John's life had been filled with a great many interests, but they all revolved around his estate at Lamorrack. It had been the hub of his whole life.

Not so Sir Colman Vincent. He had been born at Lamorrack House and was the Member of Parliament for nearby Pengony, but he had spent very little time in the county. His time was divided between the estates he owned in Devon, and his London business commitments. His visits to Lamorrack House had been infrequent when his father lived. There was little reason to believe they would increase now.

Over the next week, things gradually returned to normal as the tenants of Lamorrack went about their familiar daily tasks. They began to relax. Perhaps things would not change after all.

Then came the day when Ben's whole world collapsed about him.

He came up to grass after the day's shift to find Jesse waiting for him. This itself was unusual enough. She should have been busy at Pengrugla. But one look at her face told Ben that something was very seriously wrong.

'Jesse . . . what is it ? Your mother . . . ?'

'No, Mother is the same. Let's get away from here, Ben. I must talk to you.'

Ben's immediate thought was that Jesse had learned she was expecting a child. It was a matter that was bound to concern her, but to Ben it mattered very little. It meant only that they would need to marry earlier than they had intended. More than half the marriages in Cornwall were advanced for the same reason. The tongues of the village gossips would wag only until the next couple came in for their attentions.

Ben said as much to Jesse – but she was not with child. This problem would not be solved in such a simple manner.

They had climbed the hill from the mine now, and Jesse was unable to keep the news to herself any longer. Turning to Ben, she blurted out, 'Ben, Sir Colman Vincent is taking Pengrugla away from us!'

Ben looked at her in disbelief. 'He can't do that. It was promised to us by Sir John.'

'*We* know that, but Sir John must have forgotten to put it in writing. Sir Colman claims he knows nothing about any such promise. What's worse – he's given Pengrugla to Reuben Holyoak!'

Ben was stunned. This must be a bad dream.

'I don't believe it. Why should he do this to us?'

'I don't know. It was Reuben Holyoak who came to the house to tell me. Sir Colman has made him his agent, as we knew he would. He's leaving Reuben to run the whole estate. But I never dreamed he would take Pengrugla from us . . .'

Jesse choked on the words. Desperate with worry, she had been turning the same questions over and over in her mind since Reuben Holyoak had come to the house. Unable to say anything to her sick mother, she had brought the insurmountable problem to Ben. Now she broke down. 'I don't know what to do, Ben. We can't leave Pengrugla. Ma is so ill the move would kill her.'

'We'll marry right away, Jesse. Then as soon as your ma is well enough we'll take her to Tregassick with us.'

Ben was mentally groping for a solution – any solution.

'It wouldn't work, Ben. Tregassick is part of the Lamorrack estate. Reuben Holyoak would have us out in no time. Besides, things are not that simple.'

Ben was angry and confused. Turning all the possible alternatives over in his mind, he was not listening to what Jesse was saying.

'We can go to the far west of Cornwall, back to St Just. Yes, that's the answer. I'll find work tributing on one of the deep mines. I can earn enough to keep us all. You, me and your ma. I expect my ma will want to stay at Mevagissey – or even Tregassick. Reuben Holyoak will have no cause to turn her out with us gone—'

'Ben, stop! Listen to me, please! You don't understand. When we first moved to Pengrugla, Pa borrowed a lot of money from Sir John. It was never repaid; Sir John never asked for it, but the debt is still there. When Reuben came to the house today he told me that, if we try to go away anywhere, Sir Colman will demand full settlement of the debt. He'll commit Ma to a debtor's prison, if necessary. Oh, Ben! What can we do?'

Ben suddenly realised the full extent of Reuben Holyoak's scheming.

'Reuben Holyoak is moving into Pengrugla – but he wants you to stay there with him?'

119

'Yes. He says that, if I marry him, Sir Colman won't press for the money Ma owes him.'

A sob prevented Jesse from saying more. Ben held her to him until she stopped trembling and had regained control of herself. He knew now what he had to do.

'Reuben Holyoak may be lying. I'll go and see Sir Colman first thing in the morning, Jesse. He probably knows nothing of what's happening – or of Sir John's promise to us.'

Ben was wrong. Sir Colman Vincent knew very well what was going on.

It was almost noon before Ben was shown into the room where Sir John Vincent had first questioned him about his feelings for Jesse. In spite of the late hour, Sir Colman had the appearance of a man who had not been out of bed long enough for good humour to have caught up with him.

For Ben, the matter he had come to discuss was of the utmost importance. The whole future of Jesse and himself hinged upon its outcome. Slowly and carefully he began to explain the purpose of his visit, determined not to leave out anything that might be important.

He had scarcely begun when the new baronet cut short his well-thought-out appeal.

'Yes, yes! I know very well why you are here, Retallick. Before you say any more you should know that I took all this into consideration before reaching my decision. Nothing you have to say will persuade me to change my mind, I assure you. Reuben Holyoak is to manage the Lamorrack estate and he wishes to move into Pengrugla at the earliest opportunity.'

'Sir John promised Pengrugla would come to Jesse and me when we married—'

'I have only *your* word for that. Even if it *were* true, I would not consider myself bound by such an extravagant promise. My father was a generous man – far too generous. I am surprised there are any Lamorrack lands left.'

'But . . . Mrs Henna and Jesse? What will they do?'

'I understand Reuben intends asking Jesse – Miss Henna – to marry him. It is a good match. I support it wholeheartedly.

So there would seem to be no problem. Was there anything else, Retallick ?'

Ben was able to contain his anger and frustration no longer. 'You are going back on Sir John's word – and forcing Jesse into a marriage with a man she detests. It's wrong—'

'Hold your tongue, Retallick! To give you Pengrugla would make me the laughing-stock of the county, whatever my father's intentions. As for the Hennas, I am forcing them to do nothing. Jesse is free to make up her own mind. She can marry Reuben Holyoak and stay – or she can wed you and move out. I will not influence either decision.'

'What of the debt Mrs Henna owed your father ? Are you willing to forgo that ?'

'No, I am not. But it does not concern you – unless, of course, you intend paying it off ?'

Sir Colman Vincent gave Ben an amused smile, then signalled his dismissal as though he were a dog.

'Get out, Retallick. Oh! . . . One thing more. Tell your mother I intend pulling down Tregassick and rebuilding a house for my aunt there. You will both need to move out as soon as possible. Shall we say . . . by the end of the month ?'

It was now the twenty-first day of March. Ben and his mother had ten days in which to find somewhere else to live.

Ben held his hands tightly to his sides, resisting the almost overwhelming urge to step forward and knock Sir Colman Vincent to the floor.

Instead, he said, 'There's a strong move in this country for parliamentary reform, Sir Colman. I've never fully understood it before. Now I do. It's to rid ourselves of men like you.'

'Damn your insolence, Retallick! Come back here . . .'

Ben stormed out of the house, forcing startled servants from his path. leaving Sir Colman Vincent mouthing threats to an empty room. Ben knew he had just thrown away his job at the Mevagissey mine, along with everything else. It did not matter now. Nothing mattered. He had lost Pengrugla for himself and Jesse – Jesse herself was no longer his. For her mother's sake she would be forced to bow to Sir Colman's pressure and marry Reuben Holyoak. Ben did not know how he was going to tell her . . .

It would have been wiser for Reuben Holyoak to have stayed well away from Ben that day. He had seen Ben go to Lamorrack House – and it was not hard to guess the reason for his visit. Reuben Holyoak knew Sir Colman would give Ben short shrift. He waited at the edge of the wood for Ben to make his way home, prepared to gloat over his downfall.

Reuben Holyoak stepped into Ben's path confidently, a long-barrelled flintlock fowling-piece cradled in the crook of his arm.

'Has Sir Colman told you you'll need to move from Tregassick by the end of the month ?'

'Out of my way, Reuben.'

Ben's cold anger fooled the older man. He believed Ben was returning from Lamorrack House a thoroughly defeated young man.

'Keep away from Pengrugla between now and then. I'll be moving my things into the house and I don't want you hanging around Jesse—'

Ben swung his fist with all the force of the pent-up anger that was in him behind it. The blow knocked Reuben Holyoak backwards, the long flintlock flying from his grasp. Ben stooped to pick it up, and as Reuben Holyoak struggled to one knee Ben swung the gun, clubbing him to the ground again.

Suddenly, all Ben's anger and desperation broke free. The man lying on the ground shielding his head with an arm was responsible for the disaster that had fallen upon the Henna and Retallick families. Without Reuben Holyoak, he and Jesse would still have had a future with each other. Ben raised the gun again and again, each time bringing it crashing down on the other man's head and face.

Ben did not come to his senses until he realised he was holding only the long chiselled barrel in his hand. The stock was lying broken and splintered upon the ground.

There was blood everywhere. It was on Reuben Holyoak's face and head – and even on Ben's trembling hands.

Ben looked down at them in horror. He had no doubt that he had killed the gamekeeper. He had *meant* to kill him. Sir Colman Vincent would know immediately who was responsible for the death of his new estate manager. He would issue a warrant for Ben's arrest – and Ben would surely hang for what he had done today.

Ben let out an agonised cry and began running. He did not stop until he reached the house at Tregassick and stumbled in through the door.

He called out, but there was no answer. His mother was not at home. Panting hard, Ben ran up the stairs and sat down heavily on the edge of the bed in his room, his head in his hands.

He had gone to Lamorrack House to try to persuade Sir Colman to honour the promise made by his father, to make everything all right again for Jesse and himself. His efforts had gone disastrously wrong. Nothing would ever be the same again now. Ben was a fugitive. A hue-and-cry would be raised for him. Someone might already have discovered Reuben Holyoak's body and be hurrying to Lamorrack House to tell Sir Colman at this very moment . . .

Ben sprang to his feet and began bundling a few items of clothing together. He had to get well away from Mevagissey. He desperately wanted to go to Pengrugla, to explain to Jesse what had happened – but he knew he dared not. If Ben were taken at the Henna house, Jesse might become implicated in Reuben Holyoak's death. No, Jesse would understand. She would know why he had been forced to leave so hurriedly.

At least there was no question of Jesse being forced to marry Reuben Holyoak now. He had resolved that problem, at least.

As he left the house, Ben's anguish increased as he thought about his mother – but she would make out. Mark and Billy Dunn had taken their families from Grandpa Dunn's house. There would be room for her there.

The sudden combination of unforeseen circumstances had shattered the thin shell of manhood Ben had built up around himself. He had been doing a man's work, and his relationship and future marriage with Jesse had given him the status of a man. Now all that was gone.

Ben left Tregassick close to tears, desperately aware of his scant experience of life. Confused and afraid, he could think only of getting as far from Tregassick as was possible.

Chapter Fourteen

Fleeing from Mevagissey and the expected wrath of the law, Ben headed eastward. He was deeply unhappy and totally bewildered by the sudden change in his fortunes, aware that he had failed Jesse when she most needed him. He tried to think where he had gone wrong. What other approach he might have made to Sir Colman Vincent for things to have turned out differently. If only Sir Colman had been prepared to give him a hearing . . .

It had been the sheer frustration and hopelessness of the situation that had caused Ben's anger to explode into such violence when confronted by Reuben Holyoak. Now he was a fugitive and acutely aware of the dangers he faced. More than once on the road eastwards he heard the sound of a horse and rider coming along the road behind him and he hid in a ditch or hedgerow until they had passed by. As soon as he was able, Ben left the road and struck out through woodland, away from the eyes of man. But always he headed towards the east.

Not until he reached the busy mines along the wide valley of the River Tamar did Ben begin to breathe more easily. Here he was once more in a mining community. The call 'One and All' meant something to these people. When a miner was in trouble the others closed ranks to protect him. Ben was as safe here as he would be anywhere.

He found work in the mines, but was unable to settle down to enjoy mining. As a precaution against being traced, he changed his place of employment again and again. Before long Ben had vanished in the tide of miners who ebbed and flowed from mine to mine along the length of the Tamar valley.

The parliamentary reform movement was strong here but, although his sympathies were with them, Ben avoided their meetings. There was always the chance that someone in the huge crowds might have been a magistrate's agent.

Gradually, though, Ben's nervousness decreased. He was

able to walk the roads without the urge to hide whenever a horseman rode by. One day, Ben met up with an old miner who was on his way to the stream-works at Pentuan. He was sick with lung disease. To him Ben entrusted a guarded verbal message for Jesse. Afterwards, Ben worried for a month lest it be overheard by someone who would pass news of his whereabouts to Sir Colman Vincent. But no constables arrived to arrest Ben, and there was no reply from Jesse.

Ben moved from mine to mine in the Tamar valley for a full year and then felt the need for some permanence in his life. He had cut all ties with his earlier existence and could never return to take them up again, but neither was he able to settle here.

His eyes turned to the dark hills of Bodmin Moor, not very many miles to the westward. Moses Trago lived there. He was a link with the life Ben had once known. It was as close as Ben would ever come to finding it again – yet far enough removed to be safe.

When Ben arrived in the shadow of Sharptor's rocky crags and made enquiries, he learned that Moses was working at Stowe's Hill mine, with his father and brother John. On a fine summer evening, Ben waited at grass for Moses Trago to come up from his shift. Moses now sported a fine curly black beard, and Ben would have allowed him to pass unrecognised had his friend not seen him and let out a loud howl of greeting.

Excitedly, Moses introduced Ben to his brother as the man who had saved his life in the Money Box mine disaster before insisting that Ben accompany them to the ale-house in Henwood village.

It was apparent as soon as they walked through the door of the dingy miners' inn that Moses was well known here. He was hailed by the landlord and many of the miners already inside, but Ben wondered whether it was his imagination, or whether there was a lack of warmth in the greetings. They were given in a manner suggesting that the inn's customers were fearful of offending the broad-shouldered miner, rather than pleased to see him.

Moses Trago was more garrulous than Ben could ever remember. He spoke expansively of all the mines in the district, of the rich ore they were bringing to grass, and their bright hopes for the future. Not until the third mug of gin was on the table in front of him did he think of asking Ben what he was doing in the village.

Ben took a hasty look about him before replying, but nobody else in the ale-house was paying him any attention. He told Moses only that Sir Colman Vincent had forced him from his home, that he had taken back Pengrugla – and that Jesse had been unable to leave. He added that Reuben Holyoak had been at the root of all their troubles.

Moses slammed his mug down on the rough wood of the table in front of him and let out a bellow that turned every head towards him.

'I knew it, Ben! After I let him out of that stinking pigs' house I said you should have made sure he was unconscious before you put him in. There would have been nothing left of him in twenty-four hours. He would simply have disappeared and nobody would have been any wiser. You are too soft by half, Ben Retallick.'

Every man in the room was staring at him, and Moses glared back at those who were not quick enough to avoid his eyes. 'But I'm not – and I know what to do to anyone in this cheap ale-house who doesn't mind his own business.'

Suddenly everyone found something to occupy him. The young black-bearded miner was a powerful man, his shoulders wide enough to seat a man on each of them. It was a feat he had performed more than once in this very room. He was also a man with an uncertain temper. That, too, was equally well known.

'But to hell with Reuben . . . whatever his name is. To hell with Sir Colman Vincent, too. Let either of them come here, if they dare. We are all miners in this place, Ben. We bend to no man. "One and All" is the cry, and one and all it is. If someone from outside takes on one, he takes on every man of us.'

Moses Trago clapped a hand heavily on Ben's shoulder,

'You'll be all right with us, Ben. You stay here and learn how we look after our own.'

Ben's senses gradually faded away in a sea of cheap gin. He remembered Moses saying he must come with him to his home on Sharptor, but later in the night he had a hazy recollection of stumbling through tangled fern and needle-sharp gorse. Then Ben remembered no more until he felt drops of water splashing on his face.

At first he thought it must be raining. But when he opened his eyes he looked into a sky so bright and blue it was painful to behold. With a groan of self-pity, Ben screwed his eyes tight-shut once more.

This time a deluge of water hit him in the face, and a young female voice said, 'If you think I've nothing better than to stand here trying to bring you out of a drunken stupor, then you'd best be thinking again, mister. I've got work to go to.'

The sky was still excruciatingly bright when Ben opened his eyes again. Not until he turned his head sideways did the clanging in his skull settle down to a brain-crushing pounding.

Ben found himself looking at a pair of none-too-clean feet, peeping from beneath a long and equally grubby dress. He raised his eyes slowly and carefully. No more than five feet above him was a sharp-featured young face, looking down at him with an expression of intense scorn.

Ben struggled to sit up, and the whole nauseous world swung about him. He groaned again, putting finger-tips to his painful forehead.

'Jesus! You must have had yourself a time last night. What were you celebrating?'

Ben had never before heard an Irish accent. It sounded strange to his ears.

'I wasn't celebrating anything.'

His tongue felt three times its normal thickness.

'Are you telling me you got into this state for no reason at all? Holy Mother! I've found myself a looney. Here, looney. Get this down you.'

She had a jug in her hands. Stirring its contents vigorously with a wooden spoon, she handed the jug to Ben. He put it to his mouth, only to recoil violently when he got a whiff of the mixture.

'Ugh! It smells terrible. What is it?'

'Herbs to clear your head. The smell doesn't matter. You're meant to drink it, not sniff at it.'

Ben threw back his head and downed the drink as quickly as hc could. For a long timc hc sat on the ground gagging and spluttering. The mixture was spicy and attacked his throat every inch of the way down.

'My, but you're a baby! What's your name?'

'Ben . . . Ben Retallick. Who are you?'

'Aileen Brenahan – but what am I doing standing here talking to you? I'll need to be getting to work or they'll find someone else to take my place. Are you working?'

'Not yet. I arrived here only yesterday.'

'Then you'll not have a place to stay, either. Speak to my father. That's him over there by the stream. I'll be away now.'

Ben discovered he could now turn his head without fear of it falling off. As Aileen Brenahan hurried away, he looked to where she had pointed. He saw a wizened dark-skinned little man squatting at the edge of a fast-running stream. He was soaking grasses in the water and weaving them into the framework of a basket with incredible speed.

Climbing carefully to his feet, Ben staggered to the stream.

'Good morning to you!'

The little man had the same accent as Aileen Brenahan and spoke without looking up from his work.

Ben mumbled an inaudible reply before dipping his head in the water of the stream. It was icy cold and he came up gasping for breath. He plunged his head under the water again and held it there until his ears sang. Shaking much of the water from his hair, Ben unwrapped the kerchief from his throat and wiped his face. When he stood up he had a magnificent view over the wide Tamar valley to the high hills of Dartmoor, more than fifteen miles away.

Bringing his attention back to his immediate surroundings Ben saw that Aileen Brenahan and her father were not the only ones living on this moorland slope. Clustered about the ruins of an early and long-abandoned Newcomen engine-house were a number of makeshift dwellings. Built from turf and tree-branches, they were supported here and there by a dry stone wall. There were many babies in evidence. They crawled loose-legged across the space between the shanties and squatted in full-bellied satisfaction, enjoying the early-morning sun. Not one of them wore a stitch of clothing.

Ben had stumbled upon an encampment of the Irish peasants who came to England seasonally to work on the land. For the last couple of seasons they had learned that employment here was as scarce as in their own country, but still they returned, taking work wherever it was to be found. Under-cutting the already-low wages of the English workers, they earned for themselves the bitter resentment of miner and farmworker alike.

'You'll be a mining man, I'm thinking? Leastways, you drink like one. If my Aileen hadn't found you last night, you'd most likely be at the bottom of a shaft by now. There are two of them not fifty paces from where you're standing at this very moment. Ah, but she's one for helping helpless creatures, is my girl. Back home in dear old Ireland we always have a house full of poor injured creatures of the wild. Al-though I say it, who shouldn't, there's not another girl in the whole world with more kindness in her heart than Aileen Brenahan. She takes after her dear departed mother – may the blessings of our Holy Mother be upon her soul. She has the same beauty of looks, too. Yes, you'd go far to find another girl like my Aileen.'

Dowal Brenahan looked up at Ben with dark bright little eyes that made Ben think of a weasel he had once snared.

'Would you be from around these parts, young sir?'

'No, but I'll be staying . . . if I can find work.'

'Is it work you're after? Well, now, you're talking to the right person.'

The Irishman put down the half-completed basket. Rising to his feet, he advanced upon Ben with outstretched hand. 'My name is Dowal. I'm happy to make your acquaintance.

If you are looking for work, then you'll do no better than to hurry down to the Wheal Slade.'

Dowal Brenahan pointed to the floor of the valley, where an untidy jumble of mine-buildings and heaped ore-waste was dominated by a round-chimneyed engine-house throwing out dark coal-smoke. 'Aileen works there as a bal-maiden. She was telling me only last night that a ladder slipped and three men were killed yesterday – may God rest their souls.' Dowal Brenahan crossed himself piously. 'They'll be looking for strong young Cornishmen like yourself. Get on down there now, before they find someone else.'

Ben hesitated. 'I'll need somewhere to leave this.' He picked up the bundle of belongings he had somehow managed to keep with him throughout the previous night's drinking.

'You needn't fret yourself about that. Give it to me. It will be here when you finish work tonight. I'll do more. As my Aileen has taken you under her wing, I'll have a couple of the women put up a shanty for you. Nothing grand, you understand? No more than a place to sleep and keep your things dry. Away with you, now.'

Ben hurriedly changed into his underground working-clothes and set off down the hill to the Wheal Slade.

When he reached the mine, Ben saw it was even more of a mess than it had seemed from the hillside. Wires supporting the shaft-head lifting gear were loose, roads were half-buried in mine-waste, and there was a general air of slackness and apathy about the place.

Ben had seen such mines before, but he had never before worked on one. It was typical of a mine that was being run by a lazy and inefficient mine captain. When Ben entered the mine office, he understood why. It was early in the morning, but there was a strong smell of gin hanging on the breath of the mine captain.

'Bad news travels fast in these parts,' grunted the captain, when Ben told him why he was there. 'Yes, I *am* in need of men. If you have the experience, you'll do. One of the men who died was a tributer, the others tut-workers. Which would you prefer to be?'

Ben said promptly that he preferred to work as a tributer. He did not fancy the idea of working for this man on a fixed wage.

'Please yourself,' shrugged the captain. 'Most of the tut-workers are Irish anyway – and there is no shortage of them. The tribute team needing a man is on the forty-fathom level. Tell Tom Shovell I sent you.'

As Ben closed the door behind him, he heard the clink of a bottle against a pewter mug. The mine captain was fortifying himself against the problems of the coming day.

Ben had reached the top of the shaft when a young girl left the nearby dressing-floor and ran to speak to him. It was Aileen Brenahan.

'Are you coming to work here?'

'Yes, down at the forty-fathom level.'

'I'm glad you were able to find work so quickly.'

Aileen Brenahan smiled, and Ben noticed the way the dark skin crinkled at the corner of her pale-green eyes. 'Where will you be staying?' she asked.

'Your father said some of your women will build a place for me up on the hill.'

'I thought he might do that. I'm glad, Ben.'

For some sudden inexplicable reason, as Ben looked at Aileen Brenahan standing loose-limbed and happy before him he thought of Jesse. It was as though he had been dealt a severe body-blow. Although he had tried not to think about her since leaving Tregassick, there had been many times like this, when memories flooded back and he knew he was not succeeding.

Abruptly, he swung on to the ladder in the shaft.

'Wait a moment.'

Aileen Brenahan drew a cloth from a large pocket beneath her apron and unfolded it to reveal a huge pastie. Breaking it in two, she handed one piece to Ben.

'Take this. You'll have had nothing to eat for a while, I'm thinking. It will keep you going.'

She was right. Ben had eaten nothing since noon the previous day.

Taking the food from her, he pushed it inside his shirt. He intended eating it on his way down the ladders, but he found such a feat quite impossible. The ladders were flimsier than any he had ever trodden. It needed no feat of imagination to realise why three men had fallen to their deaths on these ladders. Most mines had a man, or a team of men, constantly checking and repairing all ladders. It seemed that the captain of the Wheal Slade gave the safety of his miners scant attention.

At the forty-fathom level, Ben realised he had no candles with him. Taking a lighted one from a niche in the tunnel wall, he made his way along the level. Suddenly there was a rush of feet from somewhere ahead, and a collision of bodies. Ben's candle was knocked from his hand and he was grabbed and dragged to the ground behind a pile of granite rock. Moments later there was a roar in the level that hurt Ben's ears and momentarily deafened him. The explosion was followed along the tunnel by a dense rolling cloud of dust and fumes that caught at Ben's throat and set him coughing, along with the unseen men about him.

It was some minutes before the air cleared enough for one of the men to scrape a light for a candle. It spat and spluttered indecisively, but in its dim yellow light Ben saw the faces of two men, dirt-caked and red-eyed from the dust that still hung in the air.

One of the miners looked at him angrily. 'What are you doing on this level? You could have got yourself killed – and us along with you!'

'The captain sent me down here. He said you were short of a man.'

'The Wheal Slade might well have been short of three more. Didn't Captain Clymo tell you we were using explosives?'

'He told me only that I would find you at the forty-fathom level.'

The two miners exchanged glances.

'If Captain Clymo didn't live on the mine, he would forget where he had to go to work each day,' said the younger of the two miners. 'I'm Tom Shovell. This is Ezra Hooper. He's on night shift but stayed on to help me out.'

'You have only two men working at a time? No boy to carry the ore, or shift the waste?'

Ezra Hooper snorted. 'This is the Wheal Slade, not one of your big St Just mines. Captain Clymo keeps the rate of tribute screwed so low that after paying for powder and candles we're lucky to break even on settling-day. We're working for a shilling in the pound, and all we have to show for our efforts so far are heaps of waste rock. Unless we find tin soon we'll end the month owing money to the mine!'

'Then perhaps we should be looking for tin now and not sitting here talking about it.'

Tom Shovell and Ezra Hooper looked at each other; then both men grinned at Ben's words.

'He's right,' agreed Ezra Hooper. 'I think he'll keep you working, Tom. I'll go home to my bed and see you both tonight.'

He clapped Ben on the shoulder and walked away with the weary step of a man who had spent too many years working below ground for a living.

Tom Shovell was perhaps five years older than Ben, and tall and lean. Wiping some of the dust from his face, he said, 'Since you're so eager to be working we'll make a beginning. You can use Ned Rodda's tools. He was killed on the ladder yesterday. If we make any money, you can pay his widow for them. She'll have need of every penny she can get with three young maids to bring up.'

Ben said nothing as he followed Tom Shovell along the level. He would pay Ned Rodda's widow for the tools – but he would buy new tools at the earliest opportunity. Ben was as superstitious as any other miner. He would not be happy working with a dead man's equipment.

Ezra Hooper had not been wrong about the amount of tin to be found in the forty-fathom level. The tributers were following a seam no more than inches wide. It was hardly worth the effort they were putting into the work.

During the morning, Ben helped Tom Shovell to drill holes for more gunpowder. He also stacked the waste rock and carted away what little ore they had won. During his journeys to and fro along the tunnel he stopped many times to examine the walls. By the time they stopped for a midday break he was so thoughtful that Tom Shovell commented upon his silence.

'I've been looking along the level. I think you're following the wrong lode.'

Ben expressed his opinion with a certain amount of hesitation. He had been working underground at the Wheal Slade for no more than a few hours. He knew nothing of the ground they were working. Yet here he was implying that the men he had joined did not know their jobs.

He saw by Tom Shovell's expression that the same thoughts were going through the mind of the other man. He hastened to explain his audacious remark. 'I think the main lode was thrown off course about thirty yards back. Am I right?'

Tom Shovell nodded. He was not unduly impressed. Such an observation proved nothing. A young lad in his first year below ground could usually see where a lode had suddenly ended and a search made to find it again.

'We lost it right enough, but Ezra found it again.'

Ben shook his head. He was committing himself fully now. 'No. He found what he *thought* was the lode. It was a "whisker" – a breakaway lode. I remember my pa showing me a similar mistake in the Money Box mine. Nobody believed him then, but he persuaded his partners to go out a few feet, and the main lode was there. He could tell by looking at the rock. Come with me; I'll show you.'

Tom Shovell was sceptical, but he followed Ben along the tunnel. Ben led him unerringly to the place where the original lode had been lost.

'Here you can see where the old lode was. Now look at the ground on this side of it – where the new "whisker" was found. It's different.'

Tom Shovell took the candle from his hard hat and held it up to the rough-hewn wall of the level. It would have taken a very keen eye indeed to discern any difference in the composition of the ground, and yet . . .

Ben moved to the far wall of the tunnel. 'Now look here.'

135

Once again it would have taken a keen and expert eye to notice a difference, but on close examination it could be seen that the grain of the rock here was similar to that which had been worked along the level as far as this spot.

'If we went out from here, we would find the main lode again. I'm certain of it.'

Tom Shovell rubbed the stubble about his chin and wondered just how experienced Ben was in tin mining. He knew nothing about this young man. For all he knew, he might have been thrown out of mine after mine for making similar rash assertions. Ezra Hooper was a miner with years of experience behind him. It had been his decision to follow the present lode. On the other hand, Tom Shovell knew that after so many years of underground work a man became tired, liable to make simple, yet costly, mistakes.

'How far off the lode do you think we might be?'

Ben shook his head. 'I don't know. I doubt if it will be more than six feet.'

Tom Shovell frowned. 'We will need to use powder. A charge here will block the tunnel. If you're wrong we'll have lost half a shift's work.'

Tom Shovell looked at Ben again and made up his mind.

'If you are right, we'll take home a sight more money than we can look forward to at the moment. All right, Ben. I'll go up and get some more gunpowder from Captain Clymo. You begin boring the holes to take it – and, Ben, I hope you're right.'

Ben tried not to think about the possibility of being wrong. He hammered at the long spade-tipped drill as though his life depended upon the hole he was making in the tunnel wall.

When Tom Shovell returned they both worked hard. For a long time the only sound in the confines of the tunnel was the clang of steel upon steel. Neither man felt like talking.

When the holes were deep enough, the gunpowder was carefully tamped home and the fuse, made from gunpowder-filled straws, carefully inserted in the holes. Finally, when all was ready, a candle was set at the end of the fuse and both men ran to safety.

After the fumes from the explosion had cleared, Tom Shovell and Ben returned to the spot and examined the newly exposed rock face eagerly. They found nothing but more rock.

Ben tried not to look at Tom Shovell's face as he said, 'I think we should drill and set the powder again.'

'Of course,' Tom Shovell realised how Ben was feeling and he tried to sound cheerful. 'We've hardly put a dent in this rock yet.'

Picking up his drill and hammer, he began to chisel out another hole in the wall of the level. Ben followed his example.

They had been hammering without rest for twenty minutes when Tom Shovell let out a whoop and pounced upon the waste he had just scooped for the hole he was drilling. He picked up a piece no larger than a pea and held it out to Ben. It was cassiterite – tin ore!

'You were right, Ben. It *is* here.'

Ben tried unsuccessfully to hide his relief. 'We'd better wait until I've brought down the rock and seen how much ore is there before we get too excited.'

After the second explosion they could not wait until the smoke and dust had cleared completely. Coughing and choking, they made their way back to the scene of the explosion.

Starved of oxygen, their candles were slow to light and burned unevenly. But the feeble light was sufficient to show them they had uncovered an unmistakable lode of tin ore. With a pick, Ben worked at the lode to test its richness. Tom Shovell joined in, and by the time they had cleared a fair-sized area neither man could hide his delight. The lode was at least three feet wide, and it was rich ore.

'You were right, Ben. You were absolutely right.'

Tom Shovell was known as a quiet undemonstrative man, but now he wrung Ben's hand enthusiastically and both men grinned at each other like two foolish boys.

When they had recovered from their initial enthusiasm they began breaking out the ore. By the time the two men of the night shift came down to relieve them they had an impressive heap of ore ready to be hauled to the surface.

Ezra Hooper was quick to admit his error, and he praised Ben's mining skill ungrudgingly. When Ben tried to shrug it off as mere luck, the older miner said, 'No, Ben. There is little luck to this. You've a keen eye and a feel for mining. Looking at you now I am not so tired, I can see why. You're Pearson Retallick's boy, aren't you?'

Ben looked at Ezra Hooper in pleased surprise. 'Yes. You knew him?'

'Aye, I knew him.' Ezra Hooper had not missed Ben's use of the past tense. 'We were tributing together in the far west, for a while. I've never worked with a finer partner. If you turn out to be half the man he was, there won't be a better miner on the Wheal Slade – and you've made a good start. Away you go, now, the pair of you. The longer you wait about down here, the quicker the morning will arrive.'

Chapter Fifteen

When Ben and Tom Shovell climbed wearily from the shaft, the sun had already gone down below the ridge of the moor and long shadows lay across the valley. With the satisfaction of a good day's work behind him, Ben felt happier than he had for many months, but his throat felt as though he had swallowed a spadeful of dry ore. As he and Tom Shovell washed in the boiler-house, Ben announced he was going to the ale-house in the village and invited Tom Shovell to join him.

Tom Shovell shook his head. 'Richard Hampton is preaching in the chapel at St Cleer tonight. I shall be there to hear him. You'll be more than welcome if you care to come, Ben.'

Ben shook his head. He should have realised from his companion's quiet and serious manner that he was a staunch follower of John Wesley. There were a great many of them in the mines of Cornwall!.

'No, thank you, Tom. I've heard your Richard Hampton preaching on the mines of St Just. Folk there call him "Foolish Dick", but there's little foolishness in Richard Hampton. He'll have you stamping your feet for the Lord and emptying your pockets to pay for a new chapel before the night is over. I haven't the throat for shouting "Hallelujah!" I'll see you in the morning.'

After parting from his companion, Ben was no more than a dozen paces along the path to Henwood when a slim figure rose from the tall fern of the moor and fell in beside him.

'Hello, Ben Retallick. Are you on your way up the hill now?'

'No, I'm going to Henwood village to wash some of the tin dust from my throat.'

'Oh!' Aileen Brenahan sounded disappointed. 'I suppose that means you'll not be back up the hill until late.'

'And if it does?'

Aileen Brenahan shrugged unhappily. 'Nothing. You can

139

do as you please . . . but father caught a rabbit in one of his snares today. It made a fine stew. I saved some for you.'

Ben felt ashamed of his churlishness. Aileen Brenahan and her father had been very kind to him.

'I couldn't eat a bite of food until a couple of pints of ale have washed away this dust. When that's done I'll come up there for some of your stew.'

'Is that a promise?'

Aileen Brenahan sounded happy again, and Ben was reminded that she was still a very young girl.

'It's a promise. What's more, I'll bring a jug of gin with me for your father.'

In spite of his good intentions, Ben was at the ale-house for much longer than he had intended. Moses Trago was there when Ben arrived. He declared that Ben's success in finding work was a good excuse for a celebration.

It was almost three hours later when Ben made his way up the hill to the moor in the darkness. He went carefully, lifting his feet high to clear imagined obstacles as he nursed a flagon of gin to him.

When he reached the Irish encampment the fires were burning low. At first he thought everyone was a-bed, and he was relieved. Then a voice from the shadows beside one of the fires said softly, 'Is this how you keep your promises, Ben Retallick?'

'Ah! There you are, Aileen. I met a friend, Moses Trago, in the ale-house. He insisted I have a drink with him.' Ben's tongue felt lazy, and he heard the distortion of his words, 'But I've brought the gin for your father.'

'He's sleeping – and so is everyone else who has any sense. I've kept this stew on the fire for you. Will you eat it now?'

'I've thought of nothing else all evening,' Ben lied.

'Ha! You have the blarney of an Irishman. I know that Moses Trago. If you've been with him, you'll have thought of little else but drinking and finding trouble. I'm surprised you haven't got a few bruises for me to tend to. Here, take your food and pass that gin over.'

As Ben began eating, Aileen Brenahan pushed two mugs

forward into the dim firelight. Filling them both from the flagon of gin, she pushed one towards Ben. When he protested he had drunk enough already, she interrupted him curtly.

'I've been sitting around here waiting for you since sunset. Now you've finally arrived you can sit awhile and talk to me while I catch up with some of your drinking. Like most men, I've no doubt you talk better with a drink in front of you.'

Ben watched in disbelief as Aileen Brenahan lifted one of the mugs to her lips and drank the contents as though it were spring water.

The moorland gin sold to miners was reputed to be capable of dissolving a guinea of the realm within five minutes, and it brought hot tears to Aileen Brenahan's eyes. When she trusted herself to speak, she croaked, 'Well . . .? What's happened to all the talking you've been doing down at the ale-house? Have you nothing left to say to me now?'

'Yes. I suggest you go easy on that gin. I've known a grown man fall flat on his face from less than you've drunk already.'

'I was weaned on the stuff,' replied Aileen Brenahan defiantly as she splashed more into her mug. 'Tell me something about yourself, Ben Retallick. Have you got a girl somewhere?'

'No.'

It came out so quickly that Aileen Brenahan knew it was a lie. But it mattered little. Whoever the girl was, she was not here. Aileen Brenahan was. She watched Ben take a swig of his gin and sipped her own more circumspectly now. The world was beginning to sway uncomfortably. She had no intention of allowing it to fall flat on its face.

'Where were you before you came to Sharptor?'

Ben told her about his life in the mines of St Just and of the last year spent moving from mine to mine in the Tamar valley. He made no mention of Mevagissey.

If Aileen Brenahan was aware that there was an unexplained gap in his life story, she made no mention of it. She kept Ben's mug topped up until, with his stomach full of food and a sense of well-being brought about by gin and the nearness of the fire, Ben announced that he was going to get some sleep.

Aileen Brenahan was immediately full of concern.

'I'm sorry, Ben. Here I've been keeping you talking and you haven't even seen the place that Father had built for you. Come along, I'll show you now.'

She thrust a dry twig in the embers of the dying fire. When it was well alight she drew it out and shielded it with her hand as she led the way through the gorse.

The lean-to built by Dowal Brenahan for Ben was no more substantial than any of the others occupied by the Irish families. A loose stone wall stood four feet high at one end. Leaning against it, a wooden-framed turf roof sloped away to the ground, and the open ends had been filled in with stacked turf.

Aileen Brenahan stooped to enter the lean-to through the low doorway and put the lighted twig to a candle stub.

Ben followed Aileen inside, going down on his knees to inspect his new 'home'. His belongings had been taken out of their bundle, the clothes folded neatly and placed upon a large dry flat stone. A wooden bucket filled with water stood in a corner, and a bed of sweet-smelling ferns filled half of the limited floor-space. On the bed was a blanket, apparently donated by the Brenahans.

'Do you like it, Ben?'

It was cramped inside the sod lean-to, and as Aileen Brenahan kneeled beside him her animal smell increased his awareness of her. He gave her a sidelong glance and saw she waited for his answer.

'It's grand.'

This was an exaggeration. The makeshift home would keep out the rain and much of the wind. No more.

'I knew you'd be pleased.' Aileen turned in the cramped space and brushed against the candle which stood on a piece of stone protruding from the wall.

Ben saw it falling and reached across her to catch it. He was too late. The candle fell wick downwards to the floor and the lean-to was plunged into darkness.

'Damn!' As Ben drew back, Aileen's hair brushed against

his face and the smell of her was in his nostrils again.

In the darkness he reached for her. As his mouth sought hers, her two hands found his shoulders. She swayed against him as his arms went about her. He mouthed her hungrily and his body leaped into urgent life against hers.

'Wait a minute, Ben.'

Her voice was a hoarse whisper as she wriggled free of his hands. When she came back to him once more he felt her nakedness. Then they were lying body to body on the bed of fern, straining to each other.

Her hands coaxed him as she gasped for him to love her, and Ben was swallowed up by the eager ferocity of her body as he took her.

He had no recollection of falling into a deep exhausted sleep. When he awoke the sunlight was streaming in through the door-space. Ben sat up, his first thought that he must be late for work. Then memories of the previous night flooded back to him . . .

Ben sank back on the bed with a groan. It had been a long time since he had left Mevagissey, but he felt the betrayal of Jesse very deeply. He tried to tell himself such a feeling was absurd. He had been away for more than a year. During that time much must have happened.

For a long time now Ben had begun to doubt whether Reuben Holyoak was dead when he left him. Had he died, Ben was sure there would have been a determined hue-and-cry for him and he would have heard something of it by now – and, if Reuben Holyoak lived, he would be married to Jesse. Ben did not wish to dwell upon that thought. One day he would return to Mevagissey and face the truth. Now was still too soon. Ben had always known that one day another girl would come into his life, but he had never imagined it would be someone like Aileen Brenahan. He wondered what would happen when Dowal Brenahan learned of their relationship – and there was no doubt that he *would* soon find out. It surprised Ben that he had ever been accepted by these people in the first place. They were a strange, tightly knit community who seldom welcomed outsiders.

Ben groaned. He foresaw nothing but trouble as a result of

his involvement with this Irish gipsy girl.

He wondered when she had left him. Last night, when he had fallen asleep? Or had she lain beside him all night, until the sun had woken her – and everyone else on this Irish-occupied hillside?

Ben sat up quickly. What was he doing lying here thinking about his romantic involvements? There was work to be done at Wheal Slade.

When Ben emerged from the hut he saw it was not as late as he had thought. The lean-to hut was so positioned that the first rays of the rising sun shone in through the doorway from across the wide valley.

Aileen Brenahan was crouched before a fire on which a pot bubbled and stewed. She had her skirt drawn above her knees to keep it clear of the earth. There was a raw primitiveness about her that made him remember the abandoned way she had come to him the previous night. As though his thoughts had reached out to her she slowly turned and smiled at him.

'Hello, Ben. I'm cooking some eggs, and we have bread. It's not fresh, but it's eatable. Would you like some tea, too? We don't usually have tea in the morning, but I made it specially for you.'

Ben looked about him. His lean-to was a little distance from the others. Surrounded as it was by yellow-flowering gorse, it might have been the only dwelling on the whole hillside.

'Where is your father?'

Aileen shrugged. 'He's probably just thinking of rising. He doesn't believe in fighting the sun to be first up.'

Hesitantly, Ben asked her the question that was troubling him. 'Does he know you were with me last night?'

'What does that matter? Will you leave Sharptor and move to another place because a tinker knows you shared a bed with his daughter? Is that why you left the last place, Ben? Because you slept with someone's daughter?'

Ben looked at her sharply, then turned away.

'I'm sorry, Ben. Really I am. What you've done in the past is none of my business. Please don't go.'

Aileen clung to his arm. 'Ben, I wanted you last night. I

need you this morning . . . now!'

She saw his expression change and knew he would not be going away from her today. Perhaps not any day.

'Ben! Ben Retallick, I'm hot for you now.' She took his hand and held it to her body. 'Come with me, Ben. Come . . .'

He allowed himself to be led back to the lean-to shack. No sooner were they inside the entrance than she drew him down to the bed, breathing like a bitch that had just coursed a hare.

The sun had climbed clear of the distant hills when they emerged from the lean-to. Dowal Brenahan was squatting beside their fire.

'I took the eggs off. The water was almost boiled away. It seemed a pity to let a good pot burn through.'

He looked from one to the other of them with an expressionless face and Ben was embarrassed. No one who looked at either of them could be in any doubt about what they had been doing this morning. Aileen Brenahan's eyes had the mauve thumbprint of lovemaking beneath them, and Ben knew his own were the same.

'I . . . I'd best be getting to the mine,' he said awkwardly.

'Then take these eggs and this bread with you.'

Aileen tied them quickly and expertly inside a cloth and handed them to Ben, her hand lingering on his as he took the food from her.

'I'll walk down the hill with you a way.' Dowal Brenahan stood up, and Ben's hopes of making a quick escape were dashed.

The two men walked together in silence until they were well down the hillside.

'Is the shanty to your liking?'

'Yes, it's fine. Thank you for putting it up for me.'

'It's no more than a place to sleep, but there are many in Ireland with less. Aileen's mother and me had no more when we were first married.'

Ben made no comment. He felt sure the Irish tinker had more to say. He was right.

'Ah! but she was a good woman. Since she died it's been just Aileen and me, but we've got along well enough. You'll not be a Catholic, Ben?'

Ben shook his head.

'No, I wouldn't expect you to be. I'm not a religious man myself, but Aileen takes after her dear mother. Every Sunday she walks all the way to Liskeard to renew her faith. She goes to church twice every Sunday when we're home in Ireland. She's a good girl, Ben. Wilful, yes, but she'll make a good wife for a man.'

Still Ben remained silent. They were almost at the foot of the slope when Dowal Brenahan announced that he would come no farther.

Turning to Ben, he said, 'We are simple folk, Ben. We live by few rules. What a man takes or a woman gives is of no concern to anyone else. Mind you, if anything should happen to bring shame upon the girl's family, then the man is ex-pected to do the right thing by her. You understand me, Ben ?'

Ben nodded, his face flaming red. He knew exactly what Dowal Brenahan was telling him. The bastardy laws of the kingdom were harsh in the extreme. An unmarried girl who had a baby was likely to languish in prison for many years unless she could bring a man to court and prove beyond doubt that he was the father of her bastard child.

'Good! I knew you for a man of honour the first time I clapped eyes on you. I'll be away about my own business now with a greatly relieved mind. I have a feeling there'll be a pheasant in the pot when you reach home tonight, Ben. I should try not to be late for it, if I were you.'

With a broad wink the little man swaggered away, and Ben realised Dowal Brenahan had just given his blessing to the irregular relationship between his daughter and Ben. He had given it without rancour and with a total lack of emotion. He could have been giving Ben an unwanted cooking-pot. Somehow, it made Ben feel more ashamed of himself than he had been before.

Chapter Sixteen

That summer saw a brief upsurge in the parliamentary reform movements. It was, perhaps, inevitable. The country was being governed by some of the most hated Ministers of all time, supported by an unpopular king. King George IV had earned the contempt of his subjects by his dissolute life and the hypocritical way in which he had treated Caroline, his foolish but likeable Queen.

When Queen Caroline died in August 1821, the discontented elements in the land took to the streets in a noisy demonstration of their sympathy for her. Raising the banner of parliamentary reform, they used the occasion to reiterate their ever-growing grievances.

They resurrected all their old demands – among them the removal of Members from the 'rotten' boroughs. The demonstrators wanted these seats to be reallocated to the new industrial towns of the Midlands. The call for universal suffrage, too, was now much louder. Events in Europe had called the attention of the world to the real power held in the hands of the peasants, the artisans and all those who, until now, had been considered beneath the notice of their 'betters'. Now the ordinary people of England were clamouring for recognition. At the moment they were *asking*. But, by taking to the streets and market-squares in ever-increasing numbers, they were demonstrating their willingness to wrest power from the landowners if they had to.

These were disturbing and perplexing times for the country's gentry. They had been brought up to believe they were superior in every way to those they employed, and accepted without question their right to make decisions for the untaught masses.

Now they were being called upon to change their way of life, to reassess their traditional values and dismantle the barriers separating them from those who laboured without responsibility.

Some landowners paused to consider the new order of things. The more astute among them were prepared to give way to a number of the popular demands. They realised it was possible to harness the new mood and gain maximum advantage from minimum change.

Others vowed they would yield nothing. Among their ranks was Robert Jenkinson, 2nd Earl of Liverpool, Prime Minister of Great Britain. Backed by his Cabinet, the full weight of the law was thrown against radical reform. By introducing harsh new laws, Lord Liverpool tried not only to clear the rabble from the streets, but also to gag the writers and speakers who protested so vehemently against the Government's actions. For the first time since Cromwell's Commonwealth, the country was ruled by naked oppression.

In that hot and sultry August of 1821, the people of England let it be known they *would* be heard. They left their houses and gathered in their tens of thousands. In such numbers they could not all be arrested, and the army of the land was hard put to contain them.

In the face of such overwhelming civil disobedience, and aware of his personal unpopularity, the Home Secretary resigned. With him went many of the repressions brought in during his term of office. The reformers hailed it as a great victory for their movement and howled for the most outrageous new concessions. Workers met in the big cities of the Midlands and burned effigies of Lord Liverpool – and even of the King himself.

In Cornwall, too, the reform movement thought the end of their long campaign was at hand. The residents of the county needed good news. It had been a bad year for the deep tin mines in the west. A drop in the world price of tin had caused a number of the smaller mines to close, putting hundreds of men out of work. The miners drifted eastwards, tramping from mine to mine, seeking work.

They swelled the numbers at local reform meetings. With nowhere else to go, the miners welcomed such meetings. They offered an opportunity to air grievances and express the anger they felt at not being able to find work. But there were some who needed more than shouted words to express their dissatisfaction.

Late one pay-out evening, a meeting organised by a local reform speaker was held in the valley below Sharptor. Halfway through an unusually dull meeting, the inevitable question was raised, 'When are things going to improve in the tin industry in Cornwall?'

'I'll tell you when they'll improve,' replied the speaker, emphasising his words with a clenched fist. 'They'll improve when shareholders stop demanding an excessive return for their money.' He was giving the stock answer to a regular question. 'When tin prices drop the mine captain has to cut his costs, too. If he didn't, he would be looking for work himself. If the men who represent Cornwall in Parliament were put there by us and not by the landowners, we would have the system changed. No man would be thrown out of work just to put an extra few pence on the dividend of a man who might never have seen a mine. This is the reason we demand a change in the way Members are elected to the House of Commons.'

'If we have to wait for that to happen, we'll none of us have any families left alive to support,' shouted a miner from the back of the crowd. 'We need work to live – and we need it *now*.'

There was a loud roar of approval from the crowd. The man who had shouted the remark, a big red-bearded miner, pushed his way through the crowd and jumped upon the heap of granite waste to stand beside the meeting's speaker.

His voice boomed out above the swelling applause. 'There *is* something we can do about our jobs right away. It has nothing to do with reform, and nothing to do with landowners or shareholders.'

The applause of the miners died away and a puzzled murmur took its place.

'What happened to our jobs in the west of Cornwall I can't tell you, but I *do* know why there is no work for us here. Every man in this crowd with eyes to see must know the reason, too. We can lay the blame on the Irish. They come here in their thousands and take work that's rightly ours.'

The meeting organiser tried to regain control. 'We're not here to discuss Irish workers. They, too, have wives and children to support—'

'Then let them stay in Ireland and support them there.'

The red-bearded miner was dangerously belligerent. He had been drinking with more fortunate colleagues who had drawn wages that day.

'The Irish are no friends of the Cornish miner. They come here and take our work for half-pay. *That's* why we can't get work. *That's* why our families are starving.'

His words brought a mighty roar of agreement from the crowd. There were farmworkers present who had seen the same thing happening on the farms. An Irishman would take on any task for a wage that put himself and his family barely above starvation level. It had been a source of anger among Englishmen for many years.

'So what are we going to do about it?'

The red-bearded miner glared at those about him.

'Will you wait for God knows how many years to be given the vote and elect someone to Parliament who *might* send the Irish back to the country where they belong?'

There were a few shouts of 'No! No!' but most of his listeners waited to hear what he had to say next.

'The Irish are living here among us right now. They're up there on the moor, living in hovels fit only for pigs. Will you let them stay and take over all your jobs? Or will you come up there with me and throw them out? Tell them to clear off and go back to their own country?'

There was a tremendous roar of approval from the crowd. The red-bearded miner had given them a target for their anger and frustration: something positive to achieve *now*. They knew they could throw the Irish out of their temporary homes with no fear of retribution. The Irish were as unpopular with the authorities as they were with the people of the country as a whole. With their own language and ritualistic Papal religion, they formed an alien community wherever they went. They were bitterly resented by the conservative Cornish.

The meeting organiser tried desperately to recapture the attention of his fast-disappearing audience. His voice was lost in the uproar as the miners and farmworkers turned their backs on him and surged away up the slope to the moor.

Ben was seated across the fire from Dowal Brenahan and Aileen when he heard the first great roar from the crowd in the valley below.

'It sounds as though they are having a good meeting down there,' Ben said cheerfully. 'The reformers haven't stopped applauding themselves since the Home Secretary resigned.'

'You call *that* a good meeting?' said Dowal Brenahan, scornfully. 'How many men would you say were there – five hundred? Why, I've been to some of Daniel O'Connell's meetings where his stewards got cramp in their fingers and had to stop counting when they reached twenty thousand! Ha! A meeting, you call it? In Dublin that would be no more than a small family gathering.'

'Well, whatever it is, there are many things I would rather be doing on a fine evening such as this.'

Ben smiled at Aileen, but she looked hot and tired and did not respond to his smile. She had been in an ill-humour for some days now.

Ben lapsed into a gloomy silence; then the noise from the valley attracted his attention once more. 'Dowal, that may not be much of a crowd, but it sounds to me as though it's moving this way.'

'I would not be calling you a liar, Ben. It *is* coming closer.'

Dowal Brenahan rose to his feet and walked clear of the gorse-bushes around the camp. Ben followed.

The slope up to the high moor was steep, and the men from the meeting were strung out on the hillside. They were quieter now. Hurling threats and insults came easier when a man stood still.

'What would you think they are after, Ben?' Dowal Brenahan spoke uneasily. 'There's nothing for them up here.'

Ahead of the mob, two young Irish boys scrambled up the hillside as though their lives depended upon reaching the camp before the Cornishmen.

When the first of the two boys stumbled into the untidy Irish encampment, he gasped, 'We've got to get out . . . They are after killing every one of us.'

This dramatic information was given in Gaelic, but there was no mistaking the meaning, even before Dowal Brenahan translated the boy's message for Ben's benefit.

Ben wanted to ask the boy what had happened to make the miners turn upon the Irish, but this was no time for explanations. He did not doubt the boy's statement. There was no other reason for the men from the reform meeting to be swarming up the hill towards them.

'Get the women and children together and keep them well out of the way,' Ben ordered Dowal Brenahan. 'If they panic and run across the moor in this light, you'll lose half of them down old mine shafts.'

The warning was a necessary one. The moor had been mined for tin for centuries and was pock-marked with pits and shafts, many of them hidden by gorse and fern.

Dowal Brenahan passed on Ben's instruction and the Irish women ran from their pathetic homes. Dragging bewildered and frightened children, they took with them whatever belongings they were able to snatch on the way.

As the women and children fled to the tangled safety of the moor, the Irishmen came to join Ben and Dowal Brenahan. Each of them carried either a pick-handle, or a long pointed shovel. Without a word, they formed a long line on either side of Ben. There were not more than two dozen of them, but they were prepared to fight hard for what little they had up here on the moor. Famine and poverty had defeated them on many occasions – but famine and poverty were intangibles. The enemies advancing up the hillside were men. Men had brittle bones. Men would bleed. None of the Irishmen questioned Ben's right to be with them as they nursed their weapons and waited for the first of the Cornish miners to reach them.

Toiling up the hillside, the men from the meeting saw the line of silent Irishmen above them. Those in front slowed, waiting for more of their companions to catch up with them.

When they felt they were in sufficient strength, they began to advance again, more cautiously.

'That's far enough,' Ben shouted his message when the advancing men were fifty yards away. 'What's your business up here?'

'You're a Cornishman. This doesn't concern you.'

The red-bearded miner was still the spokesman for the men from the meeting.

'I'm making it my business. You . . . Moses. What are you doing here?'

Ben had spotted his friend in the front ranks of the advancing crowd.

'We're here to drive out the Irish, Ben. There's no place for them in Cornwall. They are forcing good men out of jobs by accepting lower rates for doing the same work. Taking food from the mouths of our wives and children.'

'You have neither wife nor child,' retorted Ben. 'And how many local men have been put out of work by Irishmen? The men here work for as much as they can get – the same as any one of us. You all know the truth of that. You also know it's not the Irish who hang around a mine waiting for an accident to happen, then fight each other to take work from an injured man. Cornishmen do that without help from anyone.'

Ben was reminding Moses and the other miners of a recent incident in the Wheal Slade when a miner blew off two fingers in an underground blasting accident. By the time he was carried to grass, news of the accident had reached a group of men newly arrived from west Cornwall. The injured miner had to fight his way through a huge crowd of men outside the mine office, each of them shouting to be given his job.

'That still doesn't make this any of your business . . .'

'Neither is it yours, John Carne.' Ben had recognised the red-bearded miner. 'You've never lost a single day's work because of an Irishman – but many a man has lost his job because of your troublemaking. How many mines in the west sent you packing? I can name three for you: Wheal Stennack, Boswedden and the Balleswidden. There's not a mine left in west Cornwall where you would be employed. Is that why you've come here, Carne? If it is, I suggest you keep moving. You are not wanted.'

John Carne's face was the colour of his beard.

'I don't know who you are, lad, but if you don't move out of the way you'll go down with your Irish friends. We came up here to burn them out, and that's what we are going to do.'

The cheer of support that greeted his words came from no more than a dozen throats. Ben was quick to take advantage of the sudden lack of support for John Carne.

'There are women and children up here who have done no harm to anyone. If you are spoiling for a fight, you can have one – but it will be you and me, Carne. No one else.'

John Carne stood a head taller than Ben and he had been involved in many ale-house brawls. Eagerly stripping off his coat, he handed it to a nearby miner and began to roll up his sleeves as he stepped forward, 'I'll deal with you first – whoever you are. Then we'll come up there and clean those Irish rabbits out of their burrows.'

His words brought a great shout from the miners. They surged forward again, this time to form a large open square about Ben and John Carne. Above them, on the ridge, the Irishmen, who enjoyed a fight as much as any other men, leaned on their spades and pick-handles and looked down upon the sloping arena.

Ben and John Carne circled warily, each waiting for the other to make the first move. All round them the men forming the square shouted impatient encouragement.

John Carne was the first to take the initiative. He rushed forward open-armed in an attempt to carry Ben to the ground in a rib-crushing embrace. Instead, Ben ducked low to his left and brought his right fist up into the bearded face. Carne stumbled to his knees at the edge of the jeering crowd. When he stood up and turned to face Ben again, there was blood spreading across his beard from his nose.

Three times more the bearded miner repeated his initial mistake. Each time Ben evaded his grasp and staggered the bigger man with a well-aimed punch.

Then Carne changed his tactics. He rushed in, as before,

154

but at the last moment launched himself feet first at his adversary. Ben dodged aside quickly, but not soon enough to prevent a flailing boot from catching him on the shin. Then the other man's legs tangled with his own and brought Ben crashing to the ground.

John Carne was a wrestling man and now he fell upon Ben, wrapping his strong arms about him. Locked together, the two men rolled through a low gorse-bush and Ben felt the needle-sharp foliage scrape against the side of his face.

When they crashed to a halt, the bigger man was uppermost. Ben grimaced in pain and struggled to free himself as John Carne's grip tightened and his face came down within inches of his own. Ben smelled the gin-laden breath as Carne panted, 'I'm going to break your back now . . . and you can do nothing about it. Feel that ?'

Carne jerked his shoulders back to increase the pressure, forcing out what little breath Ben had left in his lungs.

Ben was not defeated yet. Allowing his head to drop back as far as it would go, he suddenly brought it forward with all the strength he could muster. His forehead cracked against the bridge of Carne's nose, and the big man's grip slackened for a second. Flinging his shoulders wide, Ben broke the killing grip and threw Carne from him.

Ben stumbled to his feet in time to see the red-bearded miner's fist close around a broken piece of granite. He jumped forward, his heavy boots landing on the other man's wrist.

John Carne shouted with pain and jumped to his feet, nursing his wrist. It was the end for him. Two heavy punches sent him reeling backwards on legs as unsteady as a new-born foal's. Two more punches knocked him towards the excited crowd, and it parted to allow him to fall to the ground. He remained there, unmoving.

Ben pushed his way through the men who had followed John Carne up the slope from the meeting. With shoulders heaving, he turned to face them.

'You all know why I fought with John Carne. I'll fight any other man with the same ideas.'

He glared about him, hoping there would be no takers. His heart sank when there was a movement in the crowd and

Moses Trago stepped forward.

But Moses Trago walked to his side and turned to face the crowd. 'You'll need to fight me, too. I stand with Ben Retallick.'

A silent figure moved to join them. It was John Trago. More men stepped out from the crowd, and Ben recognised each of them as a miner from Wheal Slade.

The danger to the Irish families on Sharptor was over. It was not only Ben's decisive victory over John Carne that had dissuaded the miners from pursuing their aims. Attacking the Irish had seemed right when they were at the reform meeting. Now they had seen frightened Irish women with children clinging to their skirts the enthusiasm had gone.

Looking sheepish, the men began drifting away down the hill, two of them dragging the semi-conscious John Carne between them.

'I'm obliged to you for your support,' Ben thanked the men who still stood about him as he nursed a knuckle swollen to twice its normal size.

'You needed little support from us,' grinned Moses Trago. 'You'd have taken that crowd on, one by one, and beaten every man of them. You pack a mighty punch, Ben. A fist like yours is wasted wrapped about a shovel-handle. You should be earning your living as a prizefighter.'

'I'll stick to mining – and there are many others hereabouts who would be wise to do the same. There will be jobs a-plenty if the militia are called in to break up meetings such as the one you held this evening. Lord Liverpool has transported men for less.'

'There will be no repeat of tonight's happenings. We'll not be stirred up by the likes of John Carne again. We'll be on our way now. Your friends are coming to see you aren't hurt. You'll not need us . . .'

Moses Trago turned abruptly and strode off down the hill. Looking up towards the Irish encampment, Ben saw Aileen Brenahan running down the slope towards him.

She arrived in such a hurry that she stumbled and fell at his feet. As he helped her up, she cried, 'Ben . . . Are you all right? Oh, your poor face!'

Ben put a hand to his cheek and it came away wet with blood.

'Come up to the fire and let me tend to that.'

Aileen took him by the hand and led him up the slope. When they reached their own fire, she sat him down and bathed his face, picking out gorse-needles and making sympathetic noises the whole time.

'My poor Ben. It's fortunate the gorse missed your eye. You might have been blinded.'

' "Poor Ben", indeed! Did you see the other fellow? They had to carry him away. He'll be lucky if he has enough teeth left in his head to hold a pipe!' Dowal Brenahan poured gin into a mug until it flowed over the brim. Handing it across the fire to Ben, he said, 'I'm proud of you, me boy. You fight well enough to be an Irishman.'

'Is that all you can think of – fighting? Away with you, Father – and the rest of you standing here gawping. When I've cleared up my man he'll be wanting something to eat. Go on with you. Ben and I have things to talk about.'

Aileen spoke the last sentence in Gaelic. It was a special message for her father. He and the other men backed away from the firelight grinning, leaving Ben and Aileen together.

'What was all that about? You didn't need to be rude to them. They meant no harm.'

'I don't care about them, Ben. I wanted us to be left alone. There's something I need to say to you.'

'Keep it until the morning. All I want to do now is go to bed.'

'That's all you've wanted to do since we first met, Ben Retallick. Now it's time for us to have a talk. If we don't have it very soon, you'll find others doing the talking for me. I won't be able to hide it for very much longer.'

'Hide . . .? What are you talking about, Aileen?' Ben looked at her in alarm.

'Ah! I knew you wouldn't have to think about it for too long. Yes, Ben, I'm having a baby. You are going to have to marry me.'

Chapter Seventeen

For the next two months Ben lived out a nightmare. He had agreed to marry Aileen Brenahan, for the sake of the baby, but he did his best to delay the date of the wedding for as long as possible.

His reluctance to stand beside her in church did not please Aileen Brenahan. She accused Ben of having used her and now wanting to cast her aside. She stopped cooking for him and made a narrow bed for herself against the far wall of their tiny lean-to hut. Finally, in October, when cold night winds began to blow across the wide valley of the Tamar and heavy moorland mists closed in upon the tors of Bodmin Moor, Aileen refused to get up from her bed and go to work. She said that the other bal-maidens were beginning to talk about her. It was certainly true that she had put on a great deal of weight about her waist, and it would not have been missed by the sharp-eyed Cornishwomen who worked with her.

When Ben remonstrated with her, saying they would need all the money they could both earn, she bluntly announced that he would have to provide for her when they were married and he might as well get used to doing it right away.

Each night Ben dreaded the thought of going home to the miserable lean-to on the moor and the sharp-tongued Irish girl. He took to meeting Moses Trago at the Henwood alehouse once more. There, he and Moses would drink until the landlord closed his establishment and pushed them out through the door.

Occasionally the two young men went farther afield to do their drinking. There were a number of small ramshackle gin-houses dotted about the moor, selling alcohol of doubtful origins. It was strongly rumoured among the miners that drinking such spirits would send a man blind, or mad, but the gin-houses were never empty. Their custom came from sick and ageing miners, with legs too feeble to carry them to authorised drinking-houses, from beggars and tinkers – and young men out to gain new drinking experiences. They were also frequented by old hags, eager to take advantage of any man too drunk to be fussy. All but the hags and aged miners were transient drinkers. Few retraced their drunken footsteps.

One memorable Saturday night, Ben and Moses made their way to Liskeard, a fair-sized market-town only a few miles distant. Their visit coincided with the autumn fair and the settling-day for almost every tin mine in the district. The town was crowded beyond capacity. There was such a crush of bodies in every tavern and ale-house that a serving girl risked all but her dubious honour attempting to satisfy the prodigious thirst of the mining men.

Ben and Moses made for one such establishment. After pitching two drunken townsmen from a seat beside a window, they settled down to an evening of heavy drinking. The drinking was accompanied by the singing of bawdy songs, familiar to every tinner.

By midnight, with the thirst of the hard-drinking miners still unquenched, the landlord announced he was closing his tavern. Amid loud protests, he called for the miners to leave.

Not a miner moved from the premises. As their tankards were emptied they began to beat upon the tables in a steady and increasing rhythm, shouting 'Drink! Drink! Drink!' in a continuous chorus.

One giant of a miner, bolder and thirstier than his fellows, carried his tankard personally to the landlord, who stood guarding the huge ale-barrel in a corner of the room.

'I'll have this filled again, if you please, Landlord.'

'Not here, you won't. I am closed. If you want serving, you'll need to go elsewhere.'

The miner leaned closer and looked into the landlord's eyes from a distance of no more than four inches. 'You've taken my money and served me ale all evening to suit yourself. Now you'll serve some more to please me.'

Taking the landlord's hand, the miner opened his clenched fist as though it were a child's and dropped a couple of pence into his palm.

'There. Now, be good enough to serve me with a pint of ale, Landlord.'

The landlord allowed the coins to drop to the floor. 'You'll pick up your money and get out of here – now.'

'Will I, indeed?' said the displeased miner. 'I have a feeling that when I leave your tavern you'll be outside to greet me, Landlord.'

With that, the big miner cuffed the landlord on the side of his head, the blow spinning the unfortunate man around. With one hand grasping the landlord's collar and the other gripping the belt of his trousers, the miner propelled him through the cheering customers until he reached the table at which Ben and Moses were seated. With a mighty heave, the miner threw the landlord bodily over the table and through the window. The unfortunate man landed heavily on the pavement outside, surrounded by broken glass and splintered woodwork.

'Since the landlord isn't here to serve us it seems we'll need to help ourselves,' shouted the big miner. 'The first pint from the barrel is mine.'

For fifteen minutes the uproar in the tavern continued unabated. Then the landlord reappeared at the door, accompanied by half a dozen constables, taken on by the mayor for fair-day.

The landlord pointed out the big miner who had tossed him so unceremoniously from the tavern. Laying about them with heavy wooden staves, the constables forced their way to the offender. After a brief exchange of blows, they beat him to the ground and dragged him outside. Two miners who pressed the constables too closely were dealt with in a similar manner. The mêlée spilled out into the street, and immediately the age-old rallying cry of the Cornish miner echoed through the streets of the market-town.

'One and all!' 'One and all!'

The constables were surrounded on three sides by drunken miners in a fighting mood. Their lives were in very real danger. Hammering at the door of the dwelling-house at their backs, they forced their way in past the startled occupant, taking their prisoners with them.

They had hoped to make their escape through the back door of the house, but the miners had foreseen the move. Scores of men ran to the lane behind the house, shouting angrily when the constables showed their faces at the back door.

The constables ducked back into the house, and the miners began howling for the release of their colleagues. When there was no reply to their demands, stones were prised from the roadway and thrown at the windows. As breaking glass showered inside the rooms, the unfortunate tenant pleaded with the constables to release their prisoners.

Not until the miners began using a heavy stool from the inn as a battering-ram did the constables concede that they had no hope of reaching the lock-up with their prisoners. Shouting for the angry crowd to stand back from the battered door, the constables threw it open and pushed the captured miners out into the street. A great cheer went up from the besiegers, and the three rescued miners were carried away on the shoulders of their colleagues. The miners had won the night.

As they made their unsteady way homewards in the early hours of Sunday morning, Ben and Moses Trago agreed it had been one of the finest night's drinking they had enjoyed.

That Sunday was the day the new circuit preacher came to the Methodist chapel in Henwood village for the first time.

The occasion was of no interest to Ben. It had been many years since he last attended a service in church or chapel, but it drew a larger congregation than had been seen in the tiny village for a very long time.

They were all leaving the small chapel as Ben made his bleary-eyed way towards the ale-house that evening.

'Ben! Ben Retallick, surely it is you? Allelujah, boy, but it's good to see you.'

Not until the preacher stood toe to toe with him did Ben recognise the face beneath the wide-brimmed hat. It was Wrightwick Roberts, the Bible-reading miner from the Mevagissey mine.

Looking at Wrightwick's heavy black serge suit and spotless white shirt, Ben was acutely aware of his own disreputable appearance. He was wearing the same clothes he had worn to Liskeard the previous evening. He had not taken them off when he fell upon his bed of fern in the moorland lean-to. Involuntarily, Ben's hand went to his face and scraped against the stubble that had not been challenged by a razor for a full week.

'Wrightwick . . . What are you doing here? You were a miner when last I saw you.'

'The call finally came, Ben.' Wrightwick Roberts's face was flushed with joy. 'After wrestling with my soul for far too long, I bowed to the Lord's will. In His infinite wisdom He sent me to preach His word here, on the edge of the moor where John Wesley himself spent many waking-hours. But you . . . ? Why did you leave Mevagissey so suddenly? One day you were at the mine working, the next you were gone. No one was able to tell me the why, or wherefore.'

Ben looked at Wrightwick Roberts sharply. So there had *not* been a hue-and-cry. Had the magistrates' men searched for him they would have been certain to question Wrightwick Roberts. Ben shook his head wearily: this was not a day for thinking.

Wrightwick Roberts looked to where a group of neatly dressed villagers were patiently waiting for their new preacher to finish his conversation with this disreputable young miner.

'Where are you living, Ben? I will come visiting.'

'No!' It came out more sharply than Ben had intended. 'I . . . I'm living up there at the moment.'

Ben waved a hand vaguely in the direction of the great rock mass of Sharptor, poised above the village. 'I'm only there for a while . . . I'll be moving soon. I'll come to see you.'

Wrightwick Roberts smiled. 'That will be even more difficult. I have nowhere of my own. I stay with whoever is kind enough to offer me lodgings for the night.'

The well-dressed chapel-goers were showing signs of impatience. Wrightwick Roberts did not want to begin his new ministry by offending them. Grasping Ben's hand warmly between both of his own, he said, 'When I'm back around this way I'll look for you and we'll have a long chat about old times and old friends. God bless you and keep you well.'

When Wrightwick Roberts left him, Ben stood staring after the preacher until he passed from view behind a row of cottages. Once, Wrightwick Roberts's companions looked back at Ben, and he knew the ex-miner was telling them about him. It made Ben uneasy. He did not like to be noticed. He did not wish to think about the implications of Wrightwick Roberts's news. If he was not a wanted man . . . ! But it did not matter now – it could not matter. He would marry Aileen Brenahan and move on somewhere – anywhere.

This latest thought did nothing to cheer him. For the next few hours Moses Trago had a very morose drinking companion: one who had to be helped home to his rough bed at the end of the evening.

Wrightwick Roberts was a very observant man. He had not missed Ben's reluctance to have the preacher pay him a call. Neither had Ben's unkempt appearance passed unnoticed. When Ben was working at the Mevagissey mine he had always been exceptionally clean and tidy for a mining man. Now he had joined the ranks of those miners who neither washed nor changed when they came to grass at the end of a shift. Wrightwick Roberts wanted to know why there had been such a dramatic change in Ben, and he wasted no time in finding out.

Ben was on night shift that next week. One morning he made his way up the hill to the lean-to and found Wrightwick Roberts seated beside the fire waiting for him. The preacher explained his presence by telling Ben he was staying at a house only a mile away. He had thought this would be a worthwhile dawn stroll.

When he first saw Wrightwick Roberts, Ben tried to think of a story to excuse the circumstances in which the preacher found him – and for the presence of Aileen. Then he shrugged off any idea of lying. The whole situation was quite clear. Wrightwick Roberts was no fool.

Aileen was no less surly than she had been of late, but at Ben's insistence she reluctantly produced some moderately fresh bread and scalding-hot tea.

For weeks Aileen Brenahan had been telling Ben he must go with her to see the Catholic priest in Liskeard and make arrangements for their marriage. She thought Wrightwick Roberts's presence here now had something to do with the wedding and she was deeply disturbed. She was determined

163

to marry Ben, but she would have nothing to do with a Reformed Church ceremony, whether the reformer was Henry VIII or John Wesley.

As soon as she could get away, Aileen went in search of her father. Wrightwick Roberts watched her disappear into the moorland mist as he sipped hot tea.

'You are blessed with few of life's comforts up here, Ben.'

Ben grunted. It had been a hard night shift, helped along by a pitcher of gin he had taken with him in lieu of food. 'It's a place to sleep.'

'I always took you to be a man who expected more from life, Ben. What went wrong? What has happened to you since you left Mevagissey? And the girl you were going to marry there – Jesse, I think her name was – where is she?'

Ben was as reluctant as ever to talk, but he was tired and unhappy. Gradually, coaxed by Wrightwick Roberts, the story of all that had happened to him came out. Ben told of Sir John Vincent's promise, his son's subsequent refusal to honour that promise, and of the fight with Reuben Holyoak. Of Jesse he said little. Here, in this place, he did not wish to think of her.

After telling Wrightwick Roberts of the things he had done since leaving Mevagissey, Ben explained to his friend about Aileen Brenahan and of the way she and her father had befriended him. The result of that 'friendship' Wrightwick Roberts could see for himself.

'Do you love this Irish girl, Ben?' Wrightwick Roberts asked the question after a lengthy silence.

'I don't think I ever have, Wrightwick. Oh, I fooled myself for a while. I enjoyed playing at being married. But that doesn't matter now. Aileen is having my child. I'm *obliged* to marry her.'

'That's just what I thought,' said Wrightwick Roberts. 'As a preacher, I am bound to say that you are reaping the harvest of your sinful ways. As a friend, I will ask whether you are quite certain the child is yours?'

Ben looked at the preacher in surprise. 'Of course it's mine. We've been living together since I first came to Sharptor.'

'When was that?'

'At the end of June. What are you suggesting?'

'I am suggesting nothing, Ben. I don't doubt that the lump in Aileen Brenahan's belly will one day be a noisy smelly brat. However, I am curious to know how soon that day will be. If the baby is yours, it should not arrive in God's world until next March, at the earliest. I am not experienced in such matters, but I will be very surprised if Aileen Brenahan is not suckling a child before the new year is a week or two old.'

'No. You're wrong, Wrightwick. You must be wrong. Aileen knew about the child only two months ago. It is mine. It *must* be.'

As the initial shock of Wrightwick Roberts's suggestion wore off, Ben remembered the eagerness with which Aileen had come to him that first night in the lean-to. She had displayed an experience that outweighed his own. He remembered, too, her father's unexpected acceptance of their relationship when Aileen moved into the lean-to Dowal Brenahan himself had built for him. Ben had asked no questions of Aileen's way of life before he came upon the scene. He had accepted her as a warm-hearted young girl who made exciting demands on him during the darkness of the night. Even after she had soured towards him he had thought it no more than a temporary state of mind brought about by her condition and their difficult situation.

Ben had been a gullible fool, but it was too late now to do anything to right the situation. He had been living openly with Aileen since his arrival at Sharptor. No court in the land would declare for him in a bastardy hearing. But Ben knew it would never come to court. He could not spend the whole of his life running away from difficult situations.

He would marry Aileen Brenahan.

Chapter Eighteen

When Ben told Moses Trago for the first time about the baby, Moses treated the matter as a huge joke – until Ben said he intended to marry Aileen Brenahan.

'You're not serious, Ben?' Moses Trago looked at him aghast.

'Of course I am. What else can I do?'

Moses saw the determined set of Ben's jaw and he expressed his bewilderment. 'But you must know about Aileen? How she was before you came to Sharptor?'

'I know nothing of Aileen Brenahan before the morning I woke up to find her throwing water over me.'

Moses Trago gulped unhappily. 'Ben . . . Aileen would take any man up on the moor for a shilling. I know. I took her there myself, more than once. I thought you knew all about that.'

Ben shook his head angrily. He had been a stupid young idiot. He had been led into a carefully arranged trap by Aileen Brenahan and her father. Or had he? Ben would never be certain.

'She's not been doing the same thing while we have been living together?'

'No, she gave all that up when you came along. But you won't be marrying her now you know the truth about her, Ben?'

'I don't know the truth, Moses. Can't you see that? Aileen has told me she's expecting *my* child. It may well be a lie, but I have no way of proving it beyond all doubt. If I don't marry her, I'll be haunted all my life by the thought that somewhere in the world a child that may be mine is growing up without its father. Taunted by other children because he, or she, is a bastard. I'll not have that on my conscience, Moses. I'll go through with this wedding, even if she does insist on some Papist priest doing the marrying.'

Moses Trago tried hard to argue Ben out of his decision.

166

Ben, for his part, did his best to drink himself into forgetfulness. But he had made his decision and it was not going to go away.

That night, Ben arrived on time for the night shift at Wheal Slade, in spite of the amount he had drunk. Soon he was working hard, doing his best to keep his semi-drunken state from Tom Shovell. If the older miner realised that Ben had been drinking heavily, he said nothing, and by the time the shift was half over Ben had succeeded in sweating most of the alcohol out of his system.

There was little more than an hour of the shift left to work when, from somewhere deep in the heart of the mine, Ben heard a dull thump and the ground began to tremble beneath his feet.

'It's a bit late in the shift to be using explosives,' he said to Tom Shovell.

'Shh! Listen . . .'

Ben was hammering a drill into the rock-face. He stopped and lowered the heavy hammer to the floor of the level. He could hear a distant rumbling that continued for many seconds before a rush of displaced air swept through the level, extinguishing their candles.

'It's a run!' cried Ben. This was an occurrence feared by every underground miner. It sometimes happened when an explosive charge was badly sited, or made up of too much gunpowder. The roof of a level would come down in a run that could outpace the fastest man.

Tom Shovell scraped a light to his candle, and both men hurried along the level to the main shaft. As they drew near they ran into clouds of choking dust billowing upwards from the lower levels of the mine. Not until it began to clear were they able to clamber down the ladders.

Twenty fathoms below their own workings, they found a number of men huddled together at the entrance to the level from which the dust was still pouring out. The men were choking and gasping for breath.

'How long is the run?' Tom Shovell shouted at one of the crouching miners.

'We don't know yet.' The miner who coughed out the

167

reply had only his eyes and mouth showing through a mask of dust that clung to his face. 'The roof is still falling in parts.'

'That's no more than loose stones,' said Tom Shovell contemptuously. 'Come on, Ben. We'll need to go in and find out for ourselves.'

Ben groped his way after Tom Shovell through the billowing dust. An occasional trickle of earth fell, and once half a dozen pieces of rock, each the size of a man's head, crashed to the floor beside him. But Tom Shovell was right: the run had ended. They came upon it not fifty paces further along the tunnel. They could go no further.

A couple of miners had followed them, and Tom Shovell asked, 'How much farther does this level go?'

'About a hundred feet. I haven't been along here for a week or two, but it wouldn't be much farther. All the same, I doubt whether any one will come out alive, not by the time we could reach them.'

'The miners in there wouldn't have been at the far end of the level,' retorted Tom Shovell. 'They were blasting and would have come back a fair distance. There could be a man only a few feet from us – and he might still be alive. Do you know how many men were working this level?

'Yes, seven.'

The miner saw Ben's surprise and explained, 'This level is being worked by two families, one working nights, the other days. The Kelynacks have the night shift this week. I saw them coming down the ladder last night. There was Bob Kelynack, his five sons, and Ken Pardoe, his son-in-law.'

'Good God!' Ben uttered the words in a hoarse whisper. An explosion killing all the men in a particular level was nothing new in any mine. But the thought of seven men from a single family buried beneath the rubble ahead of them appalled Ben.

'We've wasted enough time talking,' said Tom Shovell to the two unknown miners. 'Go off and fetch tools and more men. As many men as you can find. While you're away we'll pull out some of this rock.'

Within an hour there were as many helpers in the level as it would hold. They all worked furiously to dig out the earth

168

and rock that filled the narrow tunnel. It was noon before they found the body of the first of the Kelynack family. A boy of no more than twelve years of age, he must have been runing along the tunnel towards the safety of the shaft when the roof-fall overtook him. He was lying face downwards beneath ten tons of loose rock. Behind him, in a line, were the bodies of all but one of the others. Last of all was Bob Kelynack, the father of the family. He lay over the body of the youngest of his sons, a boy of no more than eight years of age. It looked as though the father had fallen on him in a last desperate attempt to shield his small body from the stone and earth that pursued them relentlessly along the level.

Ben and Tom Shovell continued digging for another couple of hours, but the missing member of the family, Ken Pardoe, was still not found. Wearied beyond belief, the two men allowed others to relieve them and made their way up the shaft to grass.

When they emerged the sun was already sinking beyond the moor at the end of another day. A large crowd, mostly women and children, were squatting about the mine, waiting in silence for the last body to be discovered. They were not related to the missing men, but it was not mere curiosity that kept them here. This was the traditional way of paying respect to those who had died, and expressing sympathy to their families. Many of those who waited had been paid similar simple tributes.

Ben could not remember ever being wearier than he was that evening, as he trudged up the steep slope to the moor. He hoped Aileen would not be in one of her more difficult moods.

He would have gone to the ale-house in Henwood, but it would be full of men wanting to know what was happening underground at the Wheal Slade. Ben was not in the mood for talking. All he wanted was to lie down and sleep until the weariness drained from him.

He arrived at his lean-to to find the cooking-fire no more than a small heap of cold grey ashes, and his spirits sank. Aileen had stopped cooking for him long ago, but there had always been a fire upon which he could cook for himself, or make some tea.

It did not matter; he would not argue about it now. He wanted sleep. He made his way to the lean-to hut. Just as he was about to duck inside the low entrance, he stopped. Straightening up, he looked about him.

Something had been nagging at him ever since he arrived at the camp on the moor, but he had been too tired to appreciate its significance. Now it had come to him what was different. There was an unnatural silence up here. Usually, at this time of the day, the camp was noisy with the shouting of children and the cries of the babies, all vying with the unnecessarily loud voices of the women, raised in Gaelic conversation. Today there was nothing. Not even a whisper.

At first, Ben thought they must have gone to the valley, to the Wheal Slade. He immediately dismissed the notion. He would have seen some of them there. Tired though he had been, Ben was ready to swear there was not a single Irish woman among the crowd about the head of the Wheal Slade shaft.

Uneasily, Ben made his way from his own makeshift hut to the main camp of the others. He walked on the hard-packed earth about their huts and saw that the cooking-fires were as cold as his own. Finally, he looked inside one of the huts. It was empty. Not a pot, an item of clothing, or a scrap of food was to be seen anywhere. The Irish had gone.

A thought struck Ben, and he hurried back to his own lean-to. A look inside was enough to show him it had been stripped clean. The blanket from his fern bed was gone; so, too, were all his clothes.

His tiredness forgotten, Ben ran across the moor, ignoring the gorse that snatched at him, scratching his torn and dusty arms. He ran on until he reached the rocky outcrop of Sharptor itself. Scrambling upwards, he did not stop until he reached the summit. Here he sank to the ground, his chest heaving with his efforts, perspiration running down his face and neck.

From this peak a man had an unsurpassed view for miles around. Ben scanned the four points of the compass: the trackless moor, the farmland of the valley, and the network of paths and tracks that joined the two. He saw men and horses plodding slowly across the shadowed land, homeward bound from the ploughed fields that lay behind them. Nearer at hand, long lines of panniered ponies headed for the mines along narrow paths. There were a couple of creaking wagons, a sprinkling of pigs, cows and sheep – but no Irish tinkers.

The moor itself was an emptiness patrolled by a pair of late-hunting buzzards. Nothing moved beneath them for as far as the eye could see. It was as though a hundred Irish men, women and children had been snatched from the face of the earth.

Ben made his way back to the lean-to hut because he had nowhere else to go. As he drew near he could hear someone moving in the space about the fire.

'Aileen? Is that you?'

He hurried towards the clearing. It was not Aileen Brenahan but Wrightwick Roberts.

The preacher took in Ben's state, the weariness on his face, and his bewilderment.

'You look all in, Ben. Sit down here for a while. You've had a bad time at the Wheal Slade . . .'

'What's happened *here*, Wrightwick? Everyone has gone. Aileen, her father . . . everyone!'

Wrightwick Roberts nodded his head.

'You knew? Have you had something to do with this?'

'Yes, Ben, this is my doing. Sit down and I'll tell you about it.'

Ben looked at the preacher, trying to read something from his expression. Then he sat down heavily, shaking his head.

Squatting in front of Ben, Wrightwick Roberts leaned towards him. 'When I was last here I asked you whether you really wanted to marry Aileen Brenahan. You answered me honestly, Ben. It was a marriage you did not want but felt honour-bound to see through . . .'

'But the baby . . . ?'

Wrightwick Roberts silenced Ben with a wave of his hand. 'I'm coming to that. I told you at the time I thought Aileen Brenahan was more than five months pregnant. I was right. She confessed her state to a priest weeks before you arrived here at Sharptor.'

'The priest told you this?' asked Ben in disbelief.

'Yes – albeit reluctantly. You see, I told the priest you believed the child was yours and intended bringing it up as a follower of John Wesley. The good father wrestled with his conscience for a while, then told me you were not the father. The child was conceived almost three months before your arrival here. The rest was easy, Ben. I came up here last night and told Aileen Brenahan and her father what I knew. I said you would not be marrying the girl and I suggested they would be well advised to pack up and leave as quickly as they could.'

'And they left . . . with no argument?'

'I did not say that, Ben. I was reluctantly forced to knock down Aileen's father – and a couple of his friends – but they put up no strong argument. They knew very well that once the story got out they would receive rough treatment at the hands of the miners about here.'

Ben remained silent for a long time, then he asked, 'What will happen to Aileen now?'

'Don't you fret about that young woman, Ben. From what I have learned about her, she is more than capable of taking care of herself. She'll return to Ireland with a child in her arms and wearing a black shawl. As a poor young widow she'll get all the sympathy she needs – and likely a husband as well.'

Ben hardly knew what to say. For months he had been living with the knowledge that he would one day have to marry a girl he did not love; one who wanted him only as the father of her child, to escape the stringent penalties of the law. Now he was free again.

He began to thank Wrightwick Roberts, but the big preacher brushed his thanks aside. 'I did what needed to be done and I was the only one able to approach the priest. But I haven't finished with you yet. I'll not rest until you are more like the young man with whom I worked at the Mevagissey mine. In order to bring that about we both need to know what happened in Mevagissey after you left there in such haste. I think we can take it for granted you did *not* kill Reuben Holyoak, but that still leaves a great many unanswered questions. I'll find the answers for you, Ben, but it will take time. I am a busy man these days. When your life is back to normal you can thank me by coming to chapel and falling on your knees to thank the Lord.'

Wrightwick Roberts stood up. 'I'll leave you now, Ben. I must return to a poor woman in Henwood village to whom I can give only spiritual comfort. During last night the Wheal Slade took every male member of her family. They were her past, her present . . . and her future. What have you suffered to compare with that, Ben?'

On settling-day, when other miners contributed a shilling or two to the fund for the woman so tragically widowed in the Wheal Slade roof-fall, Ben gave half his pay to Wrightwick Roberts. He asked his friend to take the money to the bereaved woman and tell her he had collected it from the parishioners on his circuit. Ben felt guilty because on the day his own immediate troubles came to an end the Kelynack family had been dealt such a terrible blow.

'I would have given the lot,' apologised Ben, 'but I need to buy a few things for myself. Aileen and her folks took everything I owned.'

'This is a generous gesture, Ben. With Christmas so near, they will have need of the money. I am on my way to visit them now. Come with me and meet the family for yourself.'

Ben would have preferred to decline Wrightwick Roberts's invitation. The Kelynack family had known much grief. In common with so many young men, Ben found other people's grief an embarrassment. Wrightwick Roberts persisted, and eventually Ben agreed to go with him. There was little else to do on this Saturday evening. Moses Trago had already left for Launceston Town with another of his friends. They had invited Ben, but he knew the jaunt would prove too expensive for him this month.

The Kelynacks had one of the larger cottages in Henwood village. Fortunately for them it was not a mine cottage, but one rented from a local landowner. At least they would not be thrown out with nowhere to go – until they were unable to pay the rent.

Mary Kelynack was a thin pale woman with prematurely

grey hair and a body worn out by years of hardship and constant child-bearing. She was not yet thirty-seven, but during nineteen years of marriage had borne eleven children. Of these eight had survived – until the tragic night of the roof-fall at the Wheal Slade. Now she was left with a widowed daughter of seventeen years of age, and two younger girls, aged ten and twelve.

Dressed in brand-new trousers, shirt and jacket, bought on credit from the mine store, Ben was introduced to Mary Kelynack. As he murmured his condolences, she looked at him with dark eyes that still retained a hint of the attractive young girl she had once been.

'I have wanted to meet you, Ben Retallick. I owe you my thanks for your efforts in trying to rescue my husband and the boys. Many miners have told me that no men worked harder than you and Tom Shovell.'

'They would have done no less for us,' replied Ben gruffly. He had grown unused to such compliments.

Eager to escape, he said, 'I saw an axe and some uncut wood outside. You'll be needing some logs for that fire.'

Ben nodded towards the kitchen fire on which burned some crumbling dead wood.

He made his way outside again and hung his jacket in the shed. Rolling up his shirt-sleeves, he began chopping and stacking logs. He worked hard, finding pleasure in the physical energy expended in his voluntary task.

After a while, the axe blade began to lose its keen edge, and he was searching in the small stone-built woodshed for a whetstone when a shadow fell across the floor in front of him. Looking up, Ben saw Kate Pardoe, the widowed Kelynack daughter, standing in the doorway.

'I'm looking for a whetstone . . .' Ben began.

Without answering, the girl reached up and took down a worn whetstone from a recess between roof and wall. Ben carried the stone outside, splashed water on it from a bucket beside the door and carefully honed the axe. When he was satisfied with the edge on the axe, Kate Pardoe took the whetstone from him and replaced it in the shed, still without uttering a word.

174

Ben began chopping wood furiously, disconcerted by the girl's presence and irritated by her silence. As he worked, Kate Pardoe watched him. She stood leaning against the wall of the house, her hands behind her, occasionally bumping her body back against the stone wall. She was a tall, gaunt, ungainly girl, with big capable hands, but she had her mother's dark unfathomable eyes.

'Where do you live, Ben?'

She finally spoke to him as he took a brief rest.

Ben looked up at her quickly. 'Up there.' He waved in the direction of the moor and resumed his task of splitting logs.

'But Aileen Brenahan has left now.'

Ben looked at her with such a surprised expression that Kate Pardoe laughed. 'Oh, Ben! Don't tell me you believed you were living up on the moor with her in secret? I work on the Wheal Slade, too. Everyone there knew. Aileen made quite sure of that. She wanted a father for the child she was having and intended tangling you up so tightly in her little web that you would never be able to escape. How *did* you get rid of her? What made all the Irish leave Sharptor so suddenly?'

Ben shrugged his shoulders. Swinging the axe, he struck a log with such force that the two halves flew high across the small yard and the blade of the axe bit deep into the hard wood of the chopping block.

As Ben struggled to wrench it out, Kate Pardoe walked round him. Gathering an armful of chopped logs, she carried them inside the shed. Returning for more, she asked, 'Don't you get lonely up there on the moor?'

'No.'

It was a lie. Since Aileen and the others had left, Ben was desperately lonely in the moorland lean-to. It gave him far too much time for thinking.

'I'm quite happy keeping my own company.'

'I wish I was. Since I lost Ken, Dad and the others, the house seems so quiet I sometimes want to scream.'

'I'm sorry. It must be very hard for you.'

Kate Pardoe nodded, and the capable hands tangled in her apron. 'We had been married for only six months, Ken and me.'

With sudden understanding, Ben realised that this tall, outwardly unemotional girl wanted desperately to talk to someone. He leaned on the axe and prepared to listen.

'They never found Ken.'

'I know.'

It was believed on the Wheal Slade that a charge had failed to explode on the level where the Kelynack family were working. Ken Pardoe, Kate's husband, must have gone back along the tunnel to re-ignite the fuse and somehow caused the explosion. There would have been little of him to collect for burial. The level had been sealed off and would remain that way until a new generation of miners came along.

'He wouldn't have felt anything, you know.'

This was why Ben had not wanted to come to the Kelynack house with Wrightwick Roberts. He was expected to find words of comfort to say to members of a bereaved family and Ben had long ago learned that all such words are totally inadequate.

'It isn't that, so much . . .'

Kate Pardoe screwed the apron into a tight ball. 'We had an argument, Ken and me. Before he went to work that night. The last words I said to him were that I didn't care if I never saw him again. I didn't mean it . . . It was just a silly quarrel.'

'I expect he knew that.'

'I wish I could be certain. What if he believed I was serious? That I *didn't* want to see him again? What if . . . ?'

The apron-strings tore away as Kate's plain face distorted and she fought the anguish inside her. Quickly, Ben took her arm and led her into the shed just as she lost all control. Great shuddering sobs racked her gaunt body, and he held her to him, stroking her hair and speaking to her as though she were a small child.

Eventually the sobs became less frequent, but Kate still leaned heavily against Ben. Not until they both heard the door of the house open did she move away from him.

'Kate? Kate, where are you, girl?'

Kate Pardoe knuckled her eyes and lifted her broken apron to her face just as Mary Kelynack put her head around the

176

door of the shed. She looked from Kate to Ben, and a suspicious frown formed on her face.

'What have you two been getting up to in here?'

Ben opened his mouth to speak, but Kate put a hand on his arm quickly.

'It's all right, Ma. Ben and me got to talking about Ken. I . . . I'm afraid I wept all over Ben's shirt-front. It will need to be dried before he goes off anywhere.'

Another sob broke from her, and Kate Pardoe fled from the shed, pushing her mother aside. She ran in through the open door of the house, and Ben heard her wooden-soled shoes clattering on uncarpeted stairs.

'Thank God for that!' Mary Kelynack said to Ben, 'You have done more today than I have been able to achieve these last few weeks, Ben Retallick. I knew the tears were there, but she wouldn't let them come out. I have been worried sick about her. Bless you, boy. You've earned your dinner. Come indoors and eat it now, before that hungry preacher has it all.'

Kate did not come downstairs to take her place at the table until the meal was half over. There was an ugly puffiness about her eyes, but she had regained control of herself and managed a weak smile for Ben's benefit.

As they ate, Mary Kelynack directed most of her conversation at Ben in an effort to learn more of his background. He was determinedly reticent, and it was Wrightwick Roberts who provided her with much of the information she sought.

Then Kate volunteered, 'Ben is living by himself in an old hut up on the moor. Can't we persuade him to move in here, with us? We have the room – and he's very good at chopping wood.'

'Now, that's a splendid idea,' boomed Wrightwick Roberts, before Mary Kelynack could reply. 'A woman's influence would do Ben the world of good, and he could make a useful contribution towards the rent.'

Mary Kelynack was slow to answer. When she finally made her reply, she looked squarely at Ben. 'Well, Ben Retallick? You have heard what Kate and Wrightwick think. All I have to add is that I would be delighted to have you here. It's a strange house without a man or my boys about the place. I can offer you only plain food and fare, but with four women in the house I doubt if you'll ever have a loose button or unwashed shirt. You'll be as spoiled as any man in these parts. What do you say?'

In the ensuing silence, Ben's spoon scraped noisily across an almost empty plate as he thought about the offer. It would curtail his drinking habits, but Ben was honest enough to admit to himself that he did not enjoy long evenings in the false bonhomie of the ale-house. Living here would also encroach upon his independence, but there had been many nights in his Irish lean-to when independence was no more than another word for loneliness. Life had held little meaning for him since he left Mevagissey. Living here would give him the opportunity to pull himself together again; to think things out and plan a future.

Pushing away his empty plate, Ben said, 'Your cooking puts forward its own argument, Mrs Kelynack. I would love to move in here – if you really don't mind.'

Later that night, when Ben left the house with Wrightwick Roberts to collect his few belongings, the preacher said seriously, 'You'll be well looked after in the Kelynack house, Ben. You have also taken on a great responsibility. Until the family gets over the shock of the accident you will need to be brother, father and uncle to them all.'

'It's high time I took on some responsibility, Wrightwick. Since leaving Mevagissey I have drifted from one job to another with little thought for anyone but myself.'

Ben grimaced at his companion, 'Hark at me! Before you've done you will have me riding a circuit as a Methodist preacher.'

'You could do worse, Ben – and the Lord has need of good servants.'

Chapter Nineteen

Ben soon settled into the routine of the Kelynack household. It was more comfortable than anything he had known since leaving Tregassick. He had his own clean and bright bedroom, but, except when he slept, it was no more private than any other part of the house. There was always one or more of the Kelynacks in his room with him. The two younger girls seemed afraid to allow Ben out of sight in case he, too, went away from them.

Ben knew they would miss their father and brothers most of all at Christmas and he set out to make it a specially good day for them all. For Holly, the youngest Kelynack girl, he had a large peg-doll carved by the engine-man in the Wheal Slade. The engine-man's wife sewed clothes for the doll, while one of the long-suffering whim-ponies donated four inches of mane to give the doll a head of coarse black hair. Jenny Kelynack was twelve and a tall girl for her age. Consequently her clothes had always been Kate's home-made cast-offs. For her Ben bought a blue calico dress from a shop in Liskeard. It was the first shop-bought dress she had ever owned. For Mrs Kelynack, Ben bought a family present. A big plump goose from Liskeard market for the Christmas dinner.

Ben found choosing a present for Kate Pardoe the most difficult task of all. She was a good-natured, infinitely patient girl, and Ben had become very fond of her. She was all he would have wished for in a sister. But Ben realised she regarded him as something more than a brother. Because of this, he had to buy her a present of a fairly impersonal nature. He finally chose a sewing-bag, divided into many compartments, and had her name embroidered upon it by the obliging wife of the Wheal Slade engine-man.

It proved to be a much happier Christmas Day than Ben, or any member of the Kelynack family, had dared hope for.

Not until the time came for them to sit around the table for their midday Christmas dinner was the loss of the male Kelynacks brought home to them all with some impact.

The kitchen table was a huge affair, large enough to seat a dozen comfortably. Today, half the places were empty. The empty seats might have meant the collapse of the carefully nurtured spirit of Christmas, had Wrightwick Roberts not called at the house.

The preacher was paying brief visits to as many of his Methodist flock as was possible between his Christmas Day chapel services. His bluff good humour and joyful acclamation of this holy day put an abrupt halt to the family's slide into painful memory. Declining a seat at the table, Wrightwick Roberts left the house after promising to return later that evening, on completion of his last evening service.

After the midday meal, Ben sat beside the fire chatting to the others until the combined effects of heat and a surfeit of food made him feel drowsy. He announced he would go to bed to rest for a while. His decision brought a chorus of protest from the two youngest Kelynack girls, but their mother quickly silenced them. She knew Ben had worked until almost midnight the previous evening – and then he had gone on to have a few drinks with his friends in the Henwood ale-house.

When Ben awoke, his bedroom was in darkness. He sat up with a start. Something had brought him out of his sleep. There was a knocking at the door of his room and a voice called, 'Ben, are you awake?'

'Yes, I'm awake. Come in.'

The door was pushed open, and weak light from a candle standing on a shelf in the passageway outside advanced half-way across the room.

'I've brought you some tea.'

Kate whispered the words, as though afraid to waken the remainder of the household. Still stupid from sleep, Ben said, 'It's dark. How long have I slept? Is everyone else a-bed?'

'No. They've gone to chapel for Wrightwick's evening service. I said I would stay at home . . . in case you woke.'

'Oh! That's a relief,' Ben leaned back against his pillow.

'For a moment I thought I must have slept Christmas Day out.'

Kate put Ben's tea on the chair at the side of his bed. After a moment's hesitation, she sat on the bed beside him.

'I thought I heard you stir. The tea was ready so I brought you a cup. I didn't mean to wake you.'

Ben stretched himself lazily. He felt warm, rested and content. 'It's as well you did, or I would have slept until morning. I wouldn't want to waste Christmas in such a way.'

'Our Christmas hasn't been wasted, Ben – thanks to you. Had you not been in the house we would all have spent the whole day weeping. I'm glad you came to stay with us.'

'So am I,' said Ben truthfully. Had he not come to live here with the Kelynacks he would have spent Christmas Day in a corner of the ale-house, until he collapsed on the floor and was pitched out into the village street. The landlord's duty towards his customers ended when they became incapable of reaching inside a pocket for coins with which to buy more drinks.

'It seems strange to see you lying here, in this bed. This was our room . . . mine and Ken's.'

In the faint light from the passageway, Ben could make out a thin line of perspiration on Kate's upper lip.

'I miss him, Ben.'

'Of course you do. He was your husband . . .'

Kate continued to speak as though she had not heard Ben; as though she were repeating something she had carefully rehearsed.

'I miss him in ways that shame me, Ben. Before we were married there were some things I thought I would never be able to do. Things that the other women on the mine joked about to us younger girls. Now . . . now I lie awake some nights and my body screams out with wanting. You know what I mean, Ben. You know what I'm saying. Please, Ben . . .'

Tears had joined the perspiration on Kate's face now, and Ben sat up in alarm as she swayed towards him.

Her hair brushed against his face . . . Then there came a hammering on the kitchen door.

Wide-eyed, Kate sprang to her feet. 'Who can that be? You'll have to answer the door, Ben. I can't.' With that she fled from the room.

Ben swung himself from the bed and hastily pulled on trousers and shirt.

In the kitchen he paused momentarily to smooth his tousled black hair, and the banging on the door was resumed with renewed vigour.

'All right! All right! Leave the door on its hinges. I'm coming.'

Ben swung the door open, and Moses Trago stumbled into the room. He wore a wide grin on his face and in his hand waved a large earthenware flagon.

'You took such an age to open the door I thought you must have gone to bed. I've brought you a present. A merry Christmas, Ben! This is none of your cheap Holland gin, either. It's good brandy, carried from France within the month – and not a farthing wasted on Excise revenue. Taste it, Ben. It's as smooth as a virgin's bosom.'

Moses Trago sat down heavily upon a chair. Ben took the proffered flagon from him and lifted it to his own lips, sceptical of Moses Trago's claim. He was pleasantly surprised. It *was* good brandy. Ben had tasted nothing to match it since leaving Mevagissey.

'This is a *real* drink. How did it come into your hands?'

Moses Trago gave Ben an exaggerated wink. 'I won it, Ben. I was sitting on the old track across the moor behind our place, when I saw a stranger riding towards me on a donkey hung with flagons and the like. He didn't seem any too pleased to see me, but that matters little. By his accent I knew him to be a Polperro man, and they are well known to be a mite surly. Anyway, he had the nerve to order me from the path, telling me it wasn't wide enough for him to pass me with his donkey. I bet him a flagon of his brandy that it was.'

Ben smiled at Moses Trago's audacity. 'And you won the bet?'

'No, I lost. But any man who uses a donkey to push another from the path deserves to lose a flagon of brandy.'

At that moment Kate came into the room, carefully avoid-

ing looking at Ben. Moses Trago's eyes went from her to Ben
. . . and back again. He stood up abruptly, upsetting his chair.
'I'm sorry, Ben. You won't want my company. I didn't know
Kate was here with you.'

'Sit down, Moses.' Ben righted the chair. 'We are waiting
for the others to return from the chapel.'

Ben looked quickly at Kate. She had regained her composure now, but Ben wondered what would have happened
had Moses not paid them his Christmas visit. 'Fetch some
cups, Kate. We'll all have a drink.'

Kate brought three cups and set them upon the table.
Moses filled them clumsily from the flagon, then he called for
a toast in honour of Christmas. Kate and Ben raised their
cups in reply. When they drank, Ben was alarmed to see Kate's
cup empty as quickly as his own.

By the time Mary Kelynack returned with her other two
daughters and Wrightwick Roberts, Kate's cheeks were
flushed and her laugh rang out more loudly than Ben had
heard it since coming to live in the Kelynack house.

Mary Kelynack frowned at Moses Trago and his flagon of
brandy, but Wrightwick Roberts came to his rescue. He
declared that brandy was just what was needed to drive away
the chills of the evening and the draughts of the chapel. He
insisted that Mary Kelynack sample the unexcised liquor,
commenting that it was better drunk in the confines of the
home than in an ale-house where a man was surrounded by
temptation.

The unexpected Christmas party broke up when Kate
began to sway in her seat and lost the ability to focus her
eyes. She tried to stand, and Ben moved around the table just
in time to catch her as she fell.

He carried her upstairs, hoping that the hand stroking his
hair and neck could not be seen by Kate's mother. Setting
her down very gently on her bed, he broke the grip of her
arms as she tried to pull him down with her. He left Mary
Kelynack to undress her and mutter angrily about the evils of
drink.

Wrightwick Roberts was much more philosophical about
the outcome of Kate's drinking.

'It will do her no harm,' he said. 'And the drum that will be beating in her head tomorrow will give her no peace to think about her other problems. I wish I knew of some way to bring lasting happiness to her, but I fear it is beyond me. For reasons best known to Himself, the Lord makes the sun to shine on some, while others see only the clouds. I fear poor Kate was born with her back to the sun.'

Outside the house, Moses Trago stayed close to Ben until they had waved Wrightwick Roberts on his way. Then he spoke of what had been on his mind all that evening.

'Kate Kelynack – or Pardoe as she is now. She's a fine girl, Ben.'

'Yes, I am very fond of her.'

'What do you mean by that? Is there something between you?'

'Nothing at all, Moses.'

It was the truth, but Ben did not want to speculate on how long such an innocent relationship could last. 'I look on her as a sister, why?'

'No special reason.' Moses Trago's reply came too quickly. 'Like I said, she's a fine girl . . . Do you think she would mind if I came calling?'

Ben's answering smile carried relief as well as pleasure. 'I am quite sure she'll welcome you, Moses. But I suggest you delay your next visit until she has had time to forgive you for the headache she'll have tomorrow.'

Moses Trago became a frequent visitor to the house. At first Kate's mother did little to make him welcome. Because of his wild ways, Moses Trago had earned an unenviable reputation for himself. Few mothers would have been pleased to have him call on their daughters. Not until Kate's mother learned a great deal more about his family background did her manner towards him soften a little.

It was more difficult to learn Kate Pardoe's feelings. She did nothing either to encourage or to discourage Moses Trago. She still leaned heavily on Ben and looked to him for advice and assistance.

For months, Moses Trago fluctuated between hope and

184

despair until, in the spring of 1822, an event occurred to drive away all thoughts of romance.

Matthew Trago had done nothing to curb his drinking since his son's return to Sharptor. Indeed, it was doubtful if he was capable of giving up drinking now, had he wanted to. Alcohol had as firm a grip on Matthew Trago's life as religion on Wrightwick Roberts's. But it brought him none of the preacher's love of life.

Matthew Trago had always been a man of dark moods and long brooding silences, but his capacity for work was such that mine captains were eager to have him work for them and they overlooked his many faults.

At least, that had been true when the big miner was a younger man. More recently, drink had taken a heavy toll on Matthew Trago's faculties, both mental and physical. It now needed half a bottle of gin to get him off to the mine at all on a cold morning. Once there he sought frequent support from a gin-bottle.

While Matthew Trago was working with his sons it was possible for them to cover up his mistakes, some of which would have been disastrous in a deep mine. Then, in one of his angry drunken moods, Matthew Trago fought the captain of the Stowe's Hill mine and was dismissed on the spot.

John Trago would have left the mine to follow his father, but Moses persuaded him to stay on. Their father had taken the first inevitable downward step on the path that many miners had trodden before him. For his two sons to throw away their livelihoods and follow suit would be foolish. It was far better for them to continue to earn good money. When the day came when Matthew Trago could no longer find work, they could at least supply him with enough drink to keep him reasonably happy.

Moses Trago had made the right decision. Matthew Trago moved from mine to mine in quick succession, each period of employment briefer than the one before. He was not only a nuisance; he was also a dangerous man to have working below ground. One man, trusting enough to hold a steel drill while Matthew Trago wielded a four-pound hammer, was carried screaming from the shaft with all the bones in his

185

right hand smashed. Eventually, the head of the Trago family was reduced to the status of a piece-work labourer – a 'tut-man' – on the worst-paying mine in the district, the Wheal Slade.

After the Wheal Slade there was nowhere for Matthew Trago to go. At first he seemed to realise this. For a few days he worked hard to keep up with his fellow tut-men. If he smelled of gin and staggered a little more after the midday meal break, nobody appeared to notice. Certainly not Captain Charles Clymo. The Wheal Slade captain was never seen outside his office after midday. His affair with the gin-bottle was well known to every miner in the district.

But Matthew Trago's attempt at self-control did not last. One morning he and another tut-man, a young simpleton, had an argument about which of them was entitled to work with a brand-new wheelbarrow. The simpleton repeated many of the phrases he had heard his fellow-workers use to describe Matthew Trago. He called the older miner a useless old drunkard, a sot, and a scrounger who drank so much he could not keep a wife.

Without further ado, Matthew Trago swung his long-handled shovel. The flat of the blade hit the simpleton full in the face, bowling him over. The young man rose to his feet holding a bloody nose. Howling like an injured puppy, he ran to the mine captain's office. By the time Captain Clymo had coaxed a coherent story from the blubbering young man, Matthew Trago was seated on a heap of ore at the top of the shaft, downing the gin he usually reserved for the midday break.

'What's all this about, Trago?' demanded the mine captain. 'What's been happening?'

Moses Trago shrugged nonchalantly and jerked a dirty thumb at the bloody-faced young man. 'Ask him. He's the one who is doing all the squealing.'

'I've already heard his story. Now I'm asking for yours.'

Matthew Trago downed the last of the gin in apparent unconcern and stared up at the sky, saying nothing.

Captain Charles Clymo looked at him disdainfully. 'I should have known better than to take you on, Trago. You are trouble. A drunken troublemaker whose mining days are behind him.'

'Are you telling me you're a better man, Cap'n? What do you see when you stare at yourself in a looking-glass? The only difference 'twixt you and me is that I sit here on a heap of tin drinking from a bottle for other men to see me. You hide behind a locked door and take yours from a glass.'

Matthew Trago tossed the empty bottle down the gaping shaft in front of him. 'That's my second this morning, Cap'n Clymo. What's your count?'

Every man and woman working above grass at the Wheal Slade had moved closer to hear the exchange between the two men. At Matthew Trago's words one of the women sniggered. The sound was hurriedly stifled, but Captain Clymo heard and he was angry.

'Damn you, Trago! I'll have none of your insults. Get off my mine – now.'

'I'll go, Cap'n, in my own good time. You owe me money. I'll take payment in drink from your office.'

Before the captain of the Wheal Slade could stop him, Matthew Trago leaped from the pile of tin ore and made for the mine office. With a bellow of rage, Captain Clymo ran after him.

The watching mine workers erupted in cheers of encouragement. It was not every day they were treated to the sight of their lazy and much disliked mine captain moving so swiftly.

Matthew Trago gained the mine office well ahead of Charles Clymo and must have located the store of liquor almost immediately. When the mine captain flung open the door, the delighted onlookers heard him shout for Matthew Trago to 'Put them down!' Then the door swung shut behind him.

The surface workers and bal-maidens crowded around the office, and from within there came the unmistakable sounds of a furious fight. Unable to see through the curtained windows, the outcome of the altercation was the matter of excited speculation.

Suddenly, all went quiet inside. Seconds later the office door was flung open. Those closest to the door pushed back against those behind as Matthew Trago staggered out. His left hand clutched the slim necks of two full bottles of gin. In his right hand he held a short-handled cobbing-hammer, raised in a threatening attitude. The head of the hammer glistened with blood, and the women about the door gasped out their horror.

As Matthew Trago advanced through the crowd of on-lookers, they fell silently back before him. Once clear of the mine he began running up the hill towards Sharptor. Those nearest to the office pushed their way inside and screams escaped from the throats of the women among them.

Charles Clymo lay sprawled on his back on the stone floor in a spreading puddle of blood. His head was battered and broken, his wide-open eyes staring into eternity.

Ben was working underground when the news of Captain Clymo's violent death was brought to him. The bearer was a surface worker sent down to find him by Kate Pardoe.

Ben immediately set off for the Stowe's Hill mine, armed with the knowledge that a man was already on his way to Liskeard to inform the magistrate of Captain Clymo's violent death. Ben wanted Moses Trago to have the opportunity to find his father before the constables arrived.

By the time Moses and John Trago scrambled to grass at Stowe's Hill, a hue-and-cry had been raised. Crowds of eager miners armed with shovels, crowbars and picks were being formed into hunting parties to scour the moor.

Moses began running up the hill to the high moor with John Trago. Ben ran with them.

'Do you have any idea where he'll go?' he asked as the three men toiled up a steep section of the slope.

'Of course. He'll go home. He has always gone home, no matter what happened to him and however drunk he might be. There's nowhere else for him to go now.'

They arrived at the cave home on the moor and Moses Trago put a hand on Ben's arm. 'Stay outside until John and I have had a chance to talk with him, Ben.'

Moses Trago and his brother went inside the moorland home and there was the murmur of voices from inside as the first of the miners came into view up the narrow track.

'Is he in there, Ben?'

Flushed from their exertions and the excitement of the chase, the miners reminded Ben of a pack of baying hounds.

'I don't know – but Moses and his brother are. You'll do well to wait here until they come outside.'

The miners held a hurried consultation among themselves. There was not one of them with enough courage to go through the door of the unusual home and risk the wrath of the uncertain-tempered Trago brothers, so they waited.

It was a long time before Moses came out. He looked taut and strained.

'What do you want?' he demanded of the waiting miners.

'We've come for your father, Moses,' said a miner from the safety of the rear of the crowd. 'He killed Captain Clymo. He'll have to answer to the magistrate.'

'He'll answer to a magistrate. When he wakes he'll be taken to Liskeard by brother John and myself. Not by a mob of vengeful miners.'

There was some angry muttering in the crowd at his words, and the same miner shouted, 'He's a murderer. You won't be able to hide him.'

Moses Trago's anger flared. He took a pace towards the crowd and they fell silent. 'I said John and I will take him to the magistrate when he wakes. Does anyone here want to call me a liar?'

His challenging stare passed slowly over them. There was not a man in the crowd willing to meet his challenge. Moses Trago spat contemptuously on the ground. 'That's what I thought. You can all go home and leave us up here in peace. When we go to Liskeard we'll not need any help from you.'

The door behind Moses opened and his silent brother came out and stood beside him.

Slowly and reluctantly the crowd began to move away. Once the movement had begun it quickly gathered momentum. Many of the miners looked back at the Trago brothers as they went, but they kept moving.

'He's in there, then?' Ben asked.

'Yes, Ben, he's in there.' Moses Trago had a strained look once more. 'Something has happened to him. It's not just the drink this time. He has no recollection of doing anything wrong. John and I could get no sense from him at all. We might have been talking to a babe.'

'What are you going to do?'

'What can we do? We can't hide him up here, and he's incapable of making an escape. When he awakes, John and I will deliver him to the magistrate in Liskeard. We'll see he is properly cared for until he's brought before the court.'

Moses Trago ran a hand through his tangled hair. 'You'd better go back to the Wheal Slade now, Ben. I am obliged to you for getting word to me so quickly.'

Two constables rode to Sharptor that evening. By the time they arrived, the two Trago brothers and their father were well on the way to Liskeard, having taken the direct route across the moor.

One look at Matthew Trago's wild expression convinced the magistrate that it was in everyone's interest to have him placed in a cell away from the other prisoners. He readily acceded to Moses Trago's request that his father be given special consideration.

The next day, at a hastily convened hearing, the magistrate committed Matthew Trago for trial at the next Assizes on a charge of murdering Charles Clymo. Pending the trial he would be held in Bodmin Gaol.

Before the Assize Judge arrived, a raving Matthew Trago had been transferred to the Lunatic Asylum in Bodmin Town, palpably unfit to plead his innocence or guilt.

Moses Trago gained much sympathy among the miners for the manner in which he had handled the situation, together with his determination that his father should be properly cared for, in spite of the harsh manner in which Matthew had always treated his family.

Mary Kelynack insisted that Moses and his brother John should come to the house and get a good meal inside their bellies at least twice a week.

Yet Kate's attitude towards Moses showed no sign of changing. She still had eyes only for Ben. Life in the Kelynack house became something of a game, Kate doing her best to get

190

Ben alone, he in his turn ensuring there was another member of the family in the house when he was with her.

In April of that year, Wrightwick Roberts went away for more than a month to introduce a new preacher to another Methodist circuit, farther west. He returned to Sharptor on a warm May evening. Although tired after a long day on his aged sway-backed nag, he rode straight to the Kelynack house.

Ben was carefully shaping a new leg for one of the family's ageing chairs when the preacher arrived. Mary Kelynack bustled about, preparing a meal, but Wrightwick Roberts was so full of news that he stomped about the room on stiff legs, unable to sit still for even a few minutes.

'I spent last night in Mevagissey,' he blurted out when he found it impossible to remain silent for a moment longer.

Looking up at the preacher, Ben slowly lowered the half-completed chair-leg to the floor.

'Yes, Ben. I have news for you.'

'My mother ,. . . ?'

'She is well, Ben. I spoke to her only last evening. We were seated in the house of your grandparents. Stalwarts of the Wesleyan movement, both of them . . .'

Ben made an impatient gesture and Wrightwick Roberts returned to his narrative.

'Your mother is living in Mevagissey now, Ben. She works in the family salting-cellar. She told me to tell you she is well, but she would like you to return home, if only to pay her a brief visit. She misses you, Ben.'

'What of Reuben Holyoak?'

'Ah, yes! Reuben Holyoak. He runs Sir Colman Vincent's Lamorrack estate and distributes malevolence and injustice to those who fall foul of him. That means most of the men on the estate. He is a much hated man, Ben.'

'So he didn't die?'

Ben whispered the words to himself. He did not know whether he was relieved or angered at the news. There was a huge emptiness within him. Had he known Reuben Holyoak would live, Ben's own life would have taken a very different course.

191

'He lived, Ben. What is more, it seems no complaint was ever laid before a magistrate. Your disappearance came as a complete mystery to your mother at first.'

'Jesse would have told her why I left,' said Ben brokenly. 'She must have made Reuben Holyoak promise not to make a complaint against me. No doubt it was part of the marriage agreement between them.'

Wrightwick Roberts frowned thoughtfully. 'I am not sure there ever was a marriage, Ben. Leastwise, your mother mentioned that Reuben Holyoak was living alone at Pengrugla and, as a result, the farm has been allowed to run down very badly.'

'What of Jesse's mother? She was too ill to be moved from Pengrugla. That was the main reason why Jesse had to marry Reuben Holyoak – that and the money they owed to Sir Colman.' Ben was bewildered.

Wrightwick Roberts shrugged his wide shoulders. 'I'm sorry, Ben. It seems there are many questions of importance I should have asked. Unfortunately, your grandmother was in the room the whole time I was there. She insisted on telling me of the arrest and transportation of your Uncle Walter.'

'Walter transported . . . ? For what? Smuggling?'

'No, I fancy it was as a result of his involvement with the parliamentary reform movement. Whatever the reason, it seems Sir Colman Vincent and Reuben Holyoak were involved, and Jesse did her best to have Walter released.'

'Jesse and Walter . . . ?' Ben shook his head. 'There is much here beyond my understanding, Wrightwick.'

'All you need to understand is that you are not a wanted man, Ben. The rest you can learn for yourself.'

'What's all this nonsense about Ben being a wanted man?' Mary Kelynack had understood little of their conversation. 'Wanted for what?'

The Kelynack family listened in amazement as Ben gave a brief account of the events that had caused him to leave Tregassick in such a hurry.

When he ended his story, it was Kate Pardoe who put the question that was in all their minds.

'What will you do now, Ben?'

Ben had no need to think about his reply, 'I must go home. I need to know what has been happening there.'

'And to see Jesse?'

Kate spoke quietly, but from her manner Ben knew that his answer would mean a great deal to her. Nevertheless, anything less than the truth would be unfair.

'Yes, most of all to see Jesse.'

There were a few moments during which no one in the room said anything. Then Kate got to her feet abruptly and ran from the room. Her mother went after her, calling her daughter's name.

Chapter Twenty

When Reuben Holyoak was left lying battered and unconscious at the edge of the wood on that spring day in 1820, Jesse waited at Pengrugla for Ben to return from Lamorrack House. She waited to be told that Reuben Holyoak had not been telling the truth. She wanted to hear Ben say that everything was all right once more. That they would marry, continue to live at Pengrugla, and allow life to fulfil its promise to them.

But Ben did not return. By noon, Jesse knew that nothing would ever be the same again. Ben must have failed in his attempt to persuade Sir Colman Vincent to allow them to keep Pengrugla.

Bitterly, Jesse told herself she had been foolish to keep her hopes alive. Sir Colman was no different from any other landowner in the country. Those who worked the land were no more important to him than domestic animals. That one's tenants occasionally tried to plan their own lives was a tedious burden imposed upon the rich, and no more than that. It was certainly not necessary to consider their views.

By mid-afternoon, Jesse could remain in the house no longer. She walked to Lamorrack and asked after Ben. She was told he had left the house more than three hours before . . . in a furious mood. Now Jesse knew for certain that things had gone badly for him – for both of them.

She hurried from the big house, following the same path to Tregassick taken by Ben earlier in the day.

At the edge of the wood she found Reuben Holyoak.

The gamekeeper had taken a beating which few men would have survived. Both his eyes were swollen and tightly closed. Unable to see, he was crawling about among the undergrowth, his hands scratched and torn by brambles. As he crawled, he whined and pleaded for someone to help him.

There was no need for Jesse to ask Reuben Holyoak who had given him his injuries. She knew it must have been Ben.

Jesse was in a dilemma. She wanted desperately to find Ben, to learn the outcome of his talk with Sir Colman. Yet she could not leave Reuben Holyoak here in his present state. If he was found by someone from Lamorrack House, Sir Colman would have Ben arrested.

She would have to take Reuben Holyoak to Pengrugla. Supporting him as best she could, Jesse went home by a roundabout route, being careful to keep out of sight of the big house.

At Pengrugla she half carried the injured man inside and laid him on a settle. On his stumbling way across the room, Reuben Holyoak knocked against the furniture, and a determined rapping on the bedroom floor with a stick informed Jesse that the noise had disturbed her mother.

Hurrying up to the bedroom, Jesse had first to listen to her mother's complaint that she had been knocking on the floor for almost an hour. Then Maude Henna demanded to know what was going on downstairs.

Jesse had not told her mother of the decisions reached by Sir Colman Vincent and his newly appointed estate manager, and she did not tell her now. Jesse said only that Reuben Holyoak had met with an accident and she had brought him to the house.

As soon as she had made her mother comfortable, Jesse set off for Megavissey to fetch a doctor. Reuben Holyoak's face was such a mess that only a qualified doctor could say with certainty how much damage had been done.

On her way back from the fishing-village, Jesse struck off across the fields to Tregassick, hoping to find Ben there. The house was empty, but in the kitchen she found evidence that food had been hurriedly removed from the food-cupboard. Jesse ran upstairs, calling Ben's name.

The door of Ben's room stood open, and one quick look was enough for her to see that all but his oldest working-clothes had been taken away. Then Jesse realised the truth. Ben had gone away.

She knew why. Reuben Holyoak had taken a severe beating. In his emotive and imaginative state of mind, Ben would have been convinced he had left Sir Colman's new estate manager

195

lying dead. There, in Ben's bedroom, Jesse sat down and wept for Ben, and for the life together they had planned.

When Jesse returned to Pengrugla, she found her mother standing pale and dark-eyed beside the settle in the living-room, prodding Reuben Holyoak with the stick she kept in her bedroom.

Full of remorse and concern, Jesse said to her mother, 'What are you doing out of bed? Come, I will take you back upstairs.'

'You will do no such thing! I want to know what is going on in my own house. I lie up in bed while doctors come and go. Then this idiot . . .' She prodded Reuben Holyoak viciously in the ribs with her stick, bringing a shout of pain from him. 'This idiot falls from the settle and screams for someone to come to his aid, shouting that he is blind. What else can I do but rise from my bed and find out what is happening? Then, after I have done my best to help him, he tells me some cock-and-bull story about Pengrugla belonging to him now. He says he is taking you for his wife! What has been happening while I have been lying a-bed, girl? What *is* going on?'

'Reuben has told you the truth, Ma. Sir Colman says he has no knowledge of Sir John's promise to give Pengrugla to me and Ben. He has made Reuben his estate manager and given him this house to live in.'

'He has done what?' Maude Henna gasped painfully. Reaching for a high-backed chair, she sat down quickly. 'He . . . has . . .!' Maude Henna began panting so heavily she was unable to continue speaking.

'You must get back to bed right away.' Jesse was alarmed. The news had affected her mother exactly as she had known it would. It was for this reason she had said nothing to her.

'Bed can wait,' gasped her mother. 'There are things that need to be dealt with first. What has all this to do with the absurd notion that you must marry this . . . this . . . *thing*?' Maude Henna waved her stick dangerously close to Reuben Holyoak's face. 'You are promised to Ben Retallick.'

'How can I marry Ben now?' Jesse cried bitterly. 'You have lived at Pengrugla for most of your life and now you are ill. If we have to move, it will . . . it will make you worse. Besides, there's the debt owed to Sir John. If we try to leave without settling it, Sir Colman will have you put in prison. I won't allow that to happen.'

'Sir Colman will have me sent to prison? He told you this himself?'

'No, but Reuben did.'

'And I spoke the truth . . . Oh! Ah!'

Reuben Holyoak struggled to sit up as Maude Henna's stick whistled through the air and cracked down hard across his shoulders.

'Your idea of the truth has never been the same as other folks, Reuben Holyoak. Save your breath.'

Angrily, Reuben Holyoak squinted painfully in a vain attempt to see something through his tightly closed and swollen eyelids.

'I'll tell you something you had better believe!' he shouted. 'Jesse won't be marrying Ben Retallick. When I tell Sir Colman what that hooligan miner did to me he'll have him thrown into gaol. He'll be sent to Van Dieman's Land for the rest of his life. Ben Retallick tried to kill me – and he came damned near to succeeding.'

'It's a pity he didn't work at it a little harder,' snapped Maude Henna. 'It would have saved everyone a great deal of trouble. Now I'll tell *you* something, Reuben Holyoak. Whoever my Jesse marries it will *not* be you. I've seen the way you look at her. At times I've felt like taking a billhook to you myself.'

As Reuben Holyoak lay back on the settle muttering vague threats, Maude Henna said to Jesse, 'Help me back to my bed. Then you go to the village and find someone to take Reuben Holyoak back to his own home before nightfall. This is not his house yet – whatever Sir Colman might say. I'll not sleep with him under my roof.'

Once upstairs, Maude Henna eased herself back into bed with a deep sigh of relief. When she closed her eyes, Jesse made to leave the room. Before she reached the door, her mother called her back.

'Jesse! I appreciate what you tried to do, child. But you

shouldn't have kept things from me. You might have made a terrible mistake – one you would have regretted all your life. Now, listen to me carefully. Before you go to the village I want you to go to Lamorrack House. Ask to be taken to Miss Eulaliah Vincent, old Sir John's sister. Refuse to speak to anyone else. When you see her, tell her you are the daughter of Maude Henna – who was Maude Carvinicke. She will remember me. Tell her I must see Sir Colman urgently. He is to come here. I have some papers I want him to see . . . No, Jesse, ask no questions. Just do as I say . . . please.'

Jesse left Pengrugla with her mind in a confused whirl. She wondered whether her mother had taken leave of her senses. *Ordering* Sir Colman Vincent to come to Pengrugla to see her!

There was a moment as she approached the big house when Jesse's courage almost left her and she thought of ignoring her mother's instructions. Then Jesse remembered all that had happened and she cast her doubts aside. There was nothing to be lost now. With Ben gone nothing really mattered.

Jesse found things changed at Lamorrack House. The servants appeared fearful of doing anything that might cost them their jobs. The maid who opened the door to Jesse was reluctant to allow her inside the house. Eventually, Jesse managed to convince her of the importance of her errand. After a brief wait in the servants' hall, Jesse was shown upstairs to a magnificent room with a huge window, giving a spectacular view down the valley to Mevagissey and the sea beyond.

Jesse had not seen Eulaliah Vincent for many years and she marvelled at the white-haired frailty of the late Sir John Vincent's elder sister. But, for all her years, the old lady had a keen eye and a sharp mind. Jesse had no need to explain who she was. When she entered the room, Eulaliah Vincent put down the small circular tapestry on which she was working and beckoned for Jesse to approach her.

'Closer still, girl. Ah! I thought as much.' Eulaliah Vincent reached out and took Jesse's hand, 'I would know those looks anywhere. You are Maude Carvinicke's child. I think your mother's married name is Henna?'

Jesse nodded, fascinated by the bright bird-like eyes of the old woman. 'Yes, I am Jesse Henna.'

Eulaliah Vincent snorted in gentle derision. 'Jesse, indeed! What sort of a name is that? I would hardly have expected your mother to call you Eulaliah, but I suggested many other names to her. Nice names. Alice, Harriet, Grace . . .'

'I was baptised Jesse Harriet.'

A pleased smile crossed Eulaliah Vincent's face. 'Harriet was my mother's name. Maude would have known that. She was brought up in this house and knew this room well. Did you know your mother was my personal maid from the time she could reach high enough to hang up a dress? But of course you know. Ah! Maude was more than just a maid to me. She could almost have been the child I was never fortunate enough to have myself. I— But you have not come here to hear the reminiscences of an old lady. Your mother must have sent you to me. Is she ill, child? Are you in need of help?'

Jesse passed on her mother's message and, in answer to Eulaliah Vincent's persistent questioning, she filled in many of the background details that had led to the request.

By the time Jesse ended her story, the old lady was trembling with anger.

'Colman did this? How *dare* he! That *he* of all people should make Maude suffer . . . No matter. I will attend to this immediately.'

Eulaliah Vincent tugged at a bell-pull beside her chair. When a maid answered the call, she snapped, 'Where is Sir Colman at this moment?'

The startled maid was unused to finding her mistress in such an angry mood. 'He's downstairs, entertaining friends, ma'am.'

'Is he, indeed! Go down and tell him I want to see him in my room – this instant! And on your way down you can show this child out.'

Eulaliah Vincent patted Jesse's hands. 'You can stop worrying, child. Go off and find this young man of yours. Tell him there has been a dreadful mistake. Arrange your wedding – and don't forget to send me an invitation. Go now.'

Jesse left Lamorrack House bemused by the course events

were now taking. How could her mother possibly influence Sir Colman's decision on Pengrugla? And why was Eulaliah Vincent so angry with her nephew because of his actions? But there remained one problem about which Eulaliah Vincent had been able to do nothing. Ben had gone. Unless Martha Retallick knew his whereabouts there was no way of letting him know that all would be well.

Jesse did not need to go all the way to Mevagissey to fetch help for Reuben Holyoak. She had not long left Lamorrack House when she met a party of men who knew him. They promised to go to Pengrugla and see him safely home while Jesse went on to Tregassick.

Martha Retallick was home, but she was as distraught as Jesse had been earlier. She knew no more about Ben's hurried departure than Jesse herself.

Jesse stayed for a while comforting Martha Retallick before anxiety for her own mother drove her home to Pengrugla.

Reuben Holyoak had gone, but a saddled horse stood outside the door and the sound of raised voices came from the bedroom. Jesse called up the stairs to ask her mother if all was well, then had to retreat hurriedly as Sir Colman Vincent came down. He was in such a hurry that he slipped down the last two stairs. Steadying himself, he stood tall in the narrow hall and glared down at Jesse, his face contorting in rage.

'Damn you and your mother! If you want to marry a nobody, then so be it. I have done my best to arrange a satisfactory marriage for you. I will do no more. Tell your mother you can remain at Pengrugla as non-paying tenants, but stay away from Lamorrack House. I do not want to see either of you there, ever again.'

With this final remark, Sir Colman Vincent pushed past Jesse and stormed out of the house. He slammed the door so hard behind him that a heavy piece of mortar fell from around the door-frame.

Concerned at what his anger might have done to her mother, Jesse ran upstairs and into the bedroom.

Maude Henna lay back against her straw-filled pillow, looking utterly exhausted. When she opened her eyes, Jesse was distressed to see tears trembling there.

'It's all right, Ma. Everything is all right now. We can stay at Pengrugla. I'll work hard and we'll manage.'

'Have you found Ben?'

'Not yet, but he'll be back, you'll see.'

'When he returns he'll not have to fear what Reuben Holyoak might do; I have seen to that. But I don't want to stay at Pengrugla, Jesse. I want to give it back to Sir Colman.'

'But he said . . .'

'He said many things, Jesse. Most of them hurtful. There is no debt to be paid off on Pengrugla now. We can leave and let Sir Colman have it for his new manager – but Reuben Holyoak will occupy it alone. You and I will sell off the stock and rent a small cottage in Mevagissey. You'll need to work, but there will be money set aside for bad days, and enough to pay for your wedding when Ben returns.'

'*If* he returns,' said Jesse despondently. 'Ben thinks he has killed Reuben Holyoak. He'll put as many miles between himself and Pengrugla as he can.'

'He'll be back one day, but waiting for him may call for a deal of patience. Go away and let me sleep now, Jesse. This has been a long, long day. I am tired . . . so very tired.'

Chapter Twenty-One

Maude Henna died in her sleep during the night. Distressed as she was, Jesse knew her mother had died as she would have wished – at Pengrugla.

The knowledge gave her little comfort. In the course of a single day, Jesse had lost everything she loved: Ben, her mother, and Pengrugla.

Had she wished, she might have kept Pengrugla. Eulaliah Vincent told her so on the day of Maude Henna's funeral. She came to the house to collect some letters that had been in Maude Henna's keeping. Eulaliah Vincent told Jesse she had written them to Maude Henna – or Maude Carvinicke, as she had then been – to be kept by her should she ever find herself in trouble. Now the need had passed.

Jesse found the letters in a tin by her mother's bed and handed them over without question. Unable to read, she had little interest in them, only a great curiosity about their contents. She did not doubt that the letters had been responsible for making Sir Colman change his mind about Pengrugla. But Pengrugla held nothing but bad memories for Jesse now. She wanted no more to do with it. She would go.

A widowed mother and daughter setting up home together was one thing. A lone sixteen-year-old girl doing the same thing was very different. It was now that Ben's mother came to the rescue. Ordered to quit Tregassick, Martha Retallick returned to the home of her parents and took Jesse with her.

For a few days, Jesse found her new surroundings bewildering. She had lived all her life at Pengrugla, enjoying the freedom of an isolated farmhouse. Now she was living in a house in a village, crowded on every side by similar houses. There were people wherever she went, wherever she looked.

Walter Dunn recognised how miserable she was and one morning took Jesse with him on a fishing trip. The unique experience made her forget her misery for a few hours, and from that day she began to gather the threads of her life about her once more.

Walter wanted her to go fishing with him again, but Jesse had seen the frowns and the scarcely concealed disapproval of the other fishermen and their womenfolk. She did not want to antagonise them unnecessarily. Instead, she asked Martha Retallick to take her with her to the Dunn's fish-cellar to learn how to salt fish. She needed to earn a living until Ben returned to Mevagissey – and she was determined never to lose her faith that he *would* return.

The work in the cellar was hard on her uncalloused hands, unused to the effect of constant immersion in heavily salted water. They soon became raw and painful. She managed to hide her discomfort from the others, but Walter was more observant than the rest of the family. One evening, when they were all seated for a meal, Walter reached across the table and took one of Jesse's hands in his own. Turning it over, he looked at the raw and inflamed fingers.

'Good God! Why haven't you said something about this before now, Jesse?'

Jesse pulled her hand away. 'It's nothing. It will be all right once I am used to the work.'

'Of course it will,' declared Grandma Dunn. 'Every other girl in Mevagissey manages well enough.'

'Every other girl in Mevagissey is handling salt and fish by the time she can walk. Jesse has had to keep smooth hands for milking cows and nursing young livestock. No, salting is not for her. She can come down to the quay and gut fish, but she'll do nothing at all until her hands are better. Tomorrow I am going to Gorran Haven. Jesse can come with me.'

Grandma Dunn was not pleased, but her displeasure was not aimed solely at Jesse.

'Why do you have to go to Gorran Haven? Haven't they got enough fishermen there?'

'They have, and they'll have more tomorrow,' the St Mawes men are coming. That is why I need to be there. Their tithes have been doubled. Mevagissey could be the next. I am going to see what needs to be done to prevent it happening here.'

'You'll be leaving Mark and Billy to do your share of the work, no doubt? It's a good job all the fishermen hereabouts don't just walk away from their boats and go off seeking trouble at every opportunity. If they did, the tithes would never get paid – however low they might be.'

'I did my share of Mark and Billy's work when they were off on the King's business. If someone doesn't do something to stop the tithes increasing very soon, we might as well give the landowners our boats and work for *them*. As it is, we risk our lives every day to line the pockets of men who don't know one end of a boat from the other. Sir Colman Vincent is one who wouldn't recognise a seine-net if he fell over one. But it is no use talking about it in this house.'

Walter spoke to Jesse again. 'I'll be leaving early in the morning. Be sure you are ready, young lady.'

Uncertain whether she should accept his invitation, Jesse looked to Martha Retallick.

After a moment's hesitation, the older woman nodded. 'Yes, you can go, Jesse. It will be a day or two before those hands are fit for work. Why didn't you tell me of the state they were getting into? Come along with me, now. I'll put something on them. I have some salve in my room.'

Later, as Martha Retallick smeared Jesse's lacerated hands with a thick, green, greasy ointment, she gave her some words of advice.

'Walter is my favourite brother and he has a warm and generous nature, but he also has a certain reputation where young girls are concerned. Don't let him take any liberties with you. If he becomes too persistent, tell me. I'll soon put a stop to his nonsense.'

Jesse smiled. 'It's all right, Mrs Retallick. I'll have no trouble with Walter. I know of his reputation, and I don't think he'll put it at risk with me. I'm Ben's girl, and will be until Ben himself tells me he no longer wants me.'

'I wish to heaven we knew where he was, Jesse. If only he had waited to discuss things with one of us . . .'

'He did what he thought was best. He didn't want to get us involved. He'll be back as soon as he learns the truth. I hope that will be soon. I miss him.'

Jesse repeated the same words to Walter the next morning when they had climbed the steep hill out of Mevagissey and

204

were walking along the quiet and narrow track to Gorran Haven.

'Word has gone about that Reuben Holyoak took a severe beating at Ben's hands,' said Walter.

'Yes. Bad enough for Ben to believe he had left him for dead. That's why he went, I'm certain of it.'

Walter looked down at the slim dark girl walking beside him. 'The sooner he learns different the better. You can't be expected to wait for him for ever. Not when there are handsome fishermen like myself waiting to marry a pretty young thing like yourself.'

Jesse grinned at him. 'If marriage was mentioned to you, Walter Dunn, you'd run so fast your boots would catch fire.'

'You shouldn't take notice of village gossip,' Walter smiled back at her. 'All the same, Ben will be foolish to stay away too long.'

At the small fishing-village of Gorran Haven, they had to wait for the St Mawes men to arrive. Walter took the opportunity to discover the extent of the local fishermen's tithe problem.

It was new only in the amount now being demanded. For years the fishermen of Cornwall had been fighting to maintain the pilchard industry against great odds. During the recent Napoleonic wars many of their traditional markets had been closed to them. Coupled with an incredible duty of sixpence a pound on the salt essential for curing the fish, this had reduced many of the fishermen to starvation level. When the war ended, the fishermen tried to overcome the continuing salt duty and regain their old markets. But in recent years the pilchards had not been running in their former numbers. Many thought it was due to the large deep-sea drift-trawlers from the Devon ports, fishing farther offshore. Whatever the reason, times were hard – and the tithe-holders chose this year to increase their tithes.

The custom of paying tithes had begun somewhere in the mists of ancient history, both the lord of the manor and the local priest demanding a share of the catch of fish as their 'tithe'. Grudgingly given at first, it had become an accepted practice over the centuries. More recently, it had been found more practicable for the boat-owners to pay a small sum of money per boat in lieu of tithes. Others paid so much per hogshead of fish caught.

This arrangement had worked well until a needy landowner hit upon the ingenious idea of selling his tithe rights to a speculator. The enterprising purchaser immediately raised the tithes to a level that could be met by only the largest and most efficient fishing-boats. Not to be left behind, many landowners promptly raised their tithes, too.

This was the problem that had first hit the Gorran Haven fishermen and, more recently, the men of St Mawes. The Mevagissey tithes were owned by Sir Colman Vincent, and Walter knew it was only a matter of time before the baronet followed the others in demanding higher dues.

The Gorran Haven fishermen told Walter they had refused to pay the new rates, but they were a very small community and could not hope to succeed on their own. Only if every fishing-village faced with the same problem followed their example could they hope to break with an ancient custom that had got out of hand. This was why they had invited Walter and the St Mawes fishermen to meet them.

The St Mawes men did not arrive until almost noon. They were in an aggressive and angry mood. Their new tithe-owner had heard of the proposed meeting and, in an attempt to prevent them from attending, had reported them to the local magistrate. He argued that the meeting was treasonable, and would most likely result in a serious breach of public order.

The magistrate, backed by members of the militia, currently stationed at St Mawes Castle, had stopped them on the road outside their village. Fortunately for all concerned, the magistrate was a sensible local man. After questioning the fishermen closely on the purpose of their visit to Gorran Haven, he had allowed them to proceed on their way. The incident served only to anger the St Mawes fishermen and harden their determination to fight the tithe increases.

It was in dealing with such men that Walter Dunn was at his very best. Jesse listened in admiration as he shaped and moulded the men's belligerent mood to suit his own ideas. He finally persuaded them to delay taking any further action until Sir Colman Vincent had shown his hand – as Walter told the men he would, very soon now.

By the time that happened, Walter promised he would have persuaded every fisherman along Cornwall's south coast to withhold his tithes. He insisted that, in the meantime, the fishermen must keep away from the tithe-owners and their agents. He suggested they use their womenfolk to carry out any 'negotiations' that might prove necessary. The fisher-women had a vocabulary every bit as colourful as their men-folk's. What was more, they were quite capable of standing up to any man the tithe-owners cared to send against them, and it was doubtful whether a magistrate would commit the militia to deal with women.

The longer the men from St Mawes talked about Walter's idea, the more enthusiastic they became. There was not a man at the meeting who did not know at least one fisherwoman who was the physical equal of any one of them; but, as a woman, the chances were that her physical prowess would never have to be put to the test.

The St Mawes fishermen left Gorran Haven amused with the thought of setting their women against the tithe-owner's men. They knew that Walter would keep his word to bring every south-coast fisherman into the fight when the time came.

On the way back to Mevagissey, Jesse asked Walter, 'Do you really think Sir Colman will raise the tithe dues?'

'He's already brought in a solicitor to draw up the papers,' declared Walter. 'I have friends at Lamorrack House who keep me in touch with what is going on.'

'Then why did you lie to the men at the meeting? Why keep the news from them?'

'Had I told them the truth there would have been no way of preventing the St Mawes fishermen stirring up more trouble than they can handle on their own. They are in a dangerous mood. There are too few of them to defy the law by themselves – and win. Troops would be brought in from Pendennis Castle to deal the reform movement a blow from which it would never recover. As it is, I can persuade a dozen villages to take action when the time is right. That will increase tenfold the number of men refusing to pay tithes. With the womenfolk dealing with tithe-collectors there will be no men for the troops to arrest and no one to punish as an example. By doing things my way we stand a reasonable chance of succeeding. Success is what this is all about, Jesse. If we win the first battle, the next will be easier. Eventually we'll be able to demand our full rights. The rights of free and equal men . . . The right to have our own man represent us in Parliament.'

Jesse looked at Walter Dunn with something akin to awe. 'Walter Dunn, if I hadn't found Ben first, I might have fallen in love with your clever mind.'

Walter Dunn rubbed his chin ruefully. 'Do you know, you are the first girl who hasn't been charmed by my good looks and splendid body. Ben really *had* better return quickly. You're quite unlike any other girl I've ever known.'

Walter Dunn's affection for Jesse was quite genuine, as Jesse herself quickly realised. By the time she had spent a month in the Dunn house she knew she could not remain there for very much longer. Walter was spending far too much time in her company. He invited her to accompany him to all the villages he visited in connection with the parliamentary reform party and more recently had taken to coming to her room and talking to her for hours.

At first Jesse was grateful to him. She missed Ben dreadfully, especially when she was alone. She had also begun to feel responsible for her mother's death. If she had not allowed her mother to assume the problems of Pengrugla . . . She talked her thoughts out with Walter, and his reassurance helped her a great deal.

But, as time went by, Walter's attentions drew comment from other members of the family, and Jesse knew she had to leave.

Deciding to go was one thing. Implementing the decision without offending the Dunn family – and Walter in particular – was another.

The solution came when Jesse paid a visit to the Happy Union mine. She went there seeking news of Ben and was immediately referred to Captain Loveday Ustick; but this was not the rough belligerent mine captain Ben had known. A huge man he still was, but at the age of fifty Loveday Ustick had been tamed and converted to Wesleyism – by a woman.

Not that Fanny Furse was any ordinary woman. Mevagissey-born, she had been taken at the age of five to hear the aged John Wesley preach. At the end of a characteristically fiery sermon, the great man had picked Fanny out of the crowd and sat her on his knee. Before returning Fanny to her parents, Wesley had urged her to give her future to the Lord.

Neither Fanny nor her parents ever forgot his words. Teaching herself to read, Fanny learned every sermon and scrap of teaching attributed to John Wesley and his brother Charles. Nowhere did she find anything to say that a woman should not emulate the great evangelists. While other young girls walked in pairs around Mevagissey harbour, giggling together and giving boastful young men sly glances from beneath their bonnets, Fanny Furse tramped miles, attending any Wesleyan gathering willing to let her stand up and offer a prayer for their souls.

It was not long before realisation came to Fanny Furse, as it had to Wesley before her, that those most in need of the word of the Lord were the miners of Cornwall. Fanny began a personal crusade in the tough mining communities. The slim five-foot-nothing woman preacher soon became a familiar figure in the shadow of the smoking chimneys of Cornwall's tin mines. She preached her message to hundreds of miners on the cliff-edge mines, pointing to the pounding surf of the Atlantic Ocean as a physical manifestation of the power of *their* Lord. Sometimes she prayed in miners' hovels, bringing comfort to the newly widowed women who wept beside her.

On a rare visit to her home village, Fanny Furse was asked to preach to the miners at the Happy Union mine, up-river from Pentuan. There she met Captain Loveday Ustick. It was a day when the Lord smiled and handed back some of the love He had carefully stored for Fanny Furse during the years she had served Him.

When they married, Loveday Ustick was in his fiftieth

year and Fanny Furse was forty – but there was not a happier couple in the whole of Cornwall.

Fanny still preached to the miners, but now she rarely went further than the Crinnis and Polgooth mines, both within walking distance of her new home at Pentuan. She and Loveday set to work to convert a house in the village into a chapel. Here she shared the pulpit on Sundays with itinerant Wesleyan preachers who were always sure of a warm welcome at the house of the Happy Union stream-works' captain and his wife.

Miners too old for underground work were frequent visitors to the Ustick house. They came to the Happy Union seeking to restore their flagging self-respect with employment close enough to mining for self-delusion. Most of these men were beyond any type of work, but in the Ustick house they received a good meal and a powerful prayer. More often than not, a night or two's much needed lodging were thrown in for good measure.

Jesse paid a visit to the Happy Union mine in search of news of Ben in the summer of 1820. Loveday Ustick remembered Ben well, but had not seen him since Ben left to work at the Mevagissey mine, more than a year before. He wished he could have helped, he said. He had liked Ben, but neither Captain Ustick nor any of the men working the stream-works knew his present whereabouts.

At the end of the day's work, Loveday Ustick took Jesse along to his house to meet Fanny. The experienced older woman immediately recognised the unhappiness in Jesse. Before the three of them sat down together for an evening meal, Fanny had learned a great deal about their guest. After a hurried whispered conversation in the kitchen with her husband, she asked Jesse to come and live with them at Pentuan. Loveday Ustick also offered Jesse work, sorting ore at the Happy Union.

Jesse eagerly seized the double opportunity to leave the Dunn house and take work where she was more likely to hear news of Ben. Mining men came to the Ustick house from all over the county. Surely one of them would have word of Ben?

Jesse announced her decision to leave Mevagissey the next evening, when she and the Dunn family were gathered together for their evening meal. The news was received with consternation by Ben's mother.

'Why, Jesse? I thought you were happy here.'

Instinctively, Martha Retallick turned a frown upon Walter, and Jesse hurried to explain.

'I'm going to work at the Happy Union stream-works. I know Ben is working on a mine somewhere, and many miners come to the Happy Union. I'm more likely to hear news of him there than here.'

Much to Jesse's relief, Martha Retallick's suspicions immediately fell away. Her words made sense, and Ben's mother was as eager as Jesse for Ben's return. But Martha Retallick asked Jesse why she could not work at the Happy Union and still live at Mevagissey.

'When Ben and I are married we'll be living among miners,' explained Jesse. 'I would prefer to get used to it now.'

Martha Retallick guiltily approved her decision. She had never really tried to fit in with those about her when Pearson Retallick had taken her to live on the Money Box mine. She admired Jesse's forethought.

Walter took the news very quietly, but later when Jesse walked with him to a reform meeting on Mevagissey quay, he said, 'You're leaving the house because of me, aren't you, Jesse?'

Jesse strenuously denied his accusation, but Walter Dunn knew the truth. 'If you stay, I promise not to bother you. I won't even speak to you, if that's what you wish. But, please . . . don't go.'

'I must, Walter. Finding Ben is the most important thing in my life.'

Walter was reluctant to accept her decision, but he could not persuade her to change her mind. Eventually, he said, 'If you can't find him, or if you change your mind, will you tell me?'

'I promise, Walter.'

'Then I must be satisfied with that – for now. When the right time comes I will have more to say to you. Until then it's better left unsaid.'

'Thank you, Walter. I'll always be grateful to you for the way you've helped me. No one has been kinder.'

Putting a hand gently on his arm, she stood on tiptoe and kissed his cheek.

Rubbing the place where her lips had rested, Walter said, 'Young Ben may think himself a fugitive, but I would willingly change places with him to have what he has.'

Jesse looked to where a noisy crowd milled about the quay. 'If that crowd gets out of hand you may well become a fugitive, Walter. You tread a dangerous path.'

'One day it will prove worth while. Stay and hear what I have to say, Jesse. Much of it concerns Sir Colman Vincent. You'll find it of interest.'

'No doubt, but I have to pack.'

'When are you leaving?'

'Tomorrow.'

'So soon? Surely another week or two will make no difference, Jesse?'

'It could make *all* the difference, Walter, as well you know. Go to your meeting, now. They are calling for you.'

Jesse turned and walked away. Before she went from sight along one of the narrow alleyways leading from the quay, she looked back. As the dejected figure of Walter Dunn approached the crowd who were calling for him, the sagging shoulders straightened, his stride lengthened and he gave them a cheery wave.

Jesse smiled ruefully. Walter had the ability to immerse all his problems in his reform activities and wash them away. Had he been born of a less humble family he would have made a splendid Member of Parliament. As it was, he would probably end his days in the colonies, sent there as an agitator, an exciter of the people. Jesse wondered whether she, or any other woman, could change him. She doubted if it were possible. Walter Dunn had a destiny to fulfil. He would see it through to the end.

On the day Jesse began work at the Happy Union mine, a notice was posted on the quay at Mevagissey. It informed the fishermen that Sir Colman Vincent had raised their tithes from eight shillings to two guineas per boat.

It was the action for which Walter had been waiting. Word went out to all the fishing communities along the south Cornwall coast. The 'tithe revolt' had begun. It quickly spread. One by one, the fishing towns and villages throughout the whole of Cornwall announced their refusal to pay the new tithes imposed upon them. Some made it an outright refusal, others clouded the issue by declaring they were now 'driftnet' fishermen. Traditionally, tithes could only be claimed from those who used a seine-net.

Whatever the alleged reasons behind the refusals, the titheholders of Cornwall became thoroughly alarmed. They saw their unearned and totally undeserved incomes slipping away from them.

Only in the port of Falmouth were the refusals accompanied by violence. Then, when the garrison of nearby Pendennis Castle was called out to restore order and arrest the leading troublemakers, it was discovered the so-called 'fishermen' were in fact the crews of the packet boats, using the occasion to air a few grievances of their own.

Elsewhere in Cornwall, many of the tithe-holders hurriedly reverted to the old tithe rates, but Sir Colman Vincent was determined he would not be so easily cowed. He sent Reuben Holyoak to 'talk things over sensibly' with the men of his home village.

When Reuben Holyoak arrived in Mevagissey's village square and called upon the fishermen to gather round and listen to what he had to say, there were few men to be seen. However, there *was* an unusually high number of women. Reuben Holyoak saw nothing sinister in their presence. He spoke to them, urging them to persuade their men to come and hear what he had to say.

'Why don't we do as he says?' shrieked a girl who had worked in the Dunn salting-cellar alongside Jesse. 'Send for Ben Retallick, someone.'

Reuben Holyoak looked angrily at the girl. 'My business is with fishermen. I have nothing to say to Ben Retallick . . . or to you.'

'Oh! Then 'tis a pity you didn't give up talking to women before you drove poor Maude Henna to her death.'

Only when the shouted accusation brought a noisy response from the other women did Reuben Holyoak realise he was surrounded by a very hostile crowd. He tried to push his way through them, but he was already too late. Hands grabbed at his clothing and held him back. The more he struggled, the greater was the determination of the women to hold him. Finally, Reuben Holyoak struck out in a last desperate attempt to break free.

It was the worst thing he could have done. The clutching hands became fists. Pummelled unmercifully Reuben Holyoak was propelled towards the filthy waters of the harbour – and thrown in.

The Mevagissey women cheered loudly as he rose to the surface, coughing and spluttering. 'That's where the money for tithes is earned, and that's where you'll collect it,' shouted one of them. 'You can tell Sir Colman Vincent he'll end up in the same place if he comes down here.'

For an hour Reuben Holyoak alternately trod water and clung to the stones of the harbour wall, pleading through chattering teeth for the fisherwomen of Mevagissey to allow him out of the cold waters of the harbour. Not until the tide had dropped sufficiently for him to stand up in the muddy harbour did they go on their way, laughing uproariously at the success of their day's work.

Sir Colman Vincent made one final attempt to convince the fishermen of his right to increase tithes. This time he sent a solicitor to talk to the fishermen on his behalf. When the unfortunate lawyer eventually made his escape from Mevagissey, he wore only his long woollen stockings and the tattered remnants of his breeches. His dignity and much of his exposed body had been badly bruised by the coarse fisherwomen and their derisive laughter pursued him along the road to Lamorrack House.

A few days later, after the Sheriff of Cornwall had called upon all the tithe-holders in the county to meet him, notices went up in every village. The fishermen were informed that, with immediate effect, all tithe dues would be charged at the rate applicable twelve months before.

Walter Dunn and his fishermen had won their first battle.

Chapter Twenty-Two

Jesse found working on the mine harder than working in the Dunns' fish-cellar, but there was no salt to aggravate the cuts she sustained on her hands. She also gained a great deal of satisfaction from going home at the end of a day's work thoroughly tired. After performing her share of the household chores, she wanted only to go to bed and sleep until morning, too exhausted for thoughts or dreams.

Occasionally, Fanny Ustick would arrange a prayer meeting for miners and their families at the house. As she spent every spare penny of her money on tea and cakes for her guests, Fanny Ustick's meetings were always well attended.

Jesse helped out at these prayer meetings. It was not for any religious reason, but because it gave her an opportunity to ask newcomers to the mine if they had met with Ben Retallick.

Unfortunately, the Cornish miners were entertained so lavishly with food that they did not wish to disappoint Jesse by saying 'No'. As a result, she received vague reports of young miners answering Ben's description being seen at places as far apart as St Just, Camborne and Kit Hill.

All that first summer Jesse believed someone would soon come to the Happy Union with definite news of Ben's whereabouts, but her hopes were in vain. By the time the fogs and rains of winter spread over the land, Jesse was as miserable as the weather.

Walter Dunn often came to Pentuan to see her. One day, as she walked with him to visit Martha Retallick, he asked her to marry him.

At first, Jesse thought he was joking. But one look at his face was enough to tell her that Walter Dunn was desperately serious.

'I've been patient, Jesse. I respected your feelings towards young Ben. But it's now November. Ben has been gone for eight months without sending word to you. For all you know, he might be dead. How long are you going to keep yourself for him ?'

For just a moment Jesse weakened. It would be so easy to say 'Yes' to Walter. He would take care of her and provide her with a home of her own. The Usticks were very kind, but living with them was not the same as having a place where she really belonged.

Then Jesse thought of Ben. She remembered what they had been to each other. Had it not been for her he would have done nothing to run from. He, too, would be enjoying the comfort of his own home. Suddenly her whole being ached for Ben. She knew she would find no real and lasting happiness without him.

'I'll wait for Ben for as long as is necessary, Walter. That means until he returns home.'

Walter shook his head helplessly. 'That's what I thought you would say. Oh, well! I'll ask you the same question next year . . . and the year after. One day you'll weaken. But I warn you, you are missing my best years!'

It was good to be with someone who made her smile. Jesse had grown increasingly fond of both Loveday and Fanny Ustick, but they took themselves and their religion very seriously.

Walter continued his half-teasing banter until they were almost at the Dunn house. Then he said something to prove there was more than romance on his mind.

'I heard an interesting piece of gossip this week. If it's true it will mean the end of Sir Colman Vincent's parliamentary career. It will also provide a powerful argument for reform. It seems Sir Colman purchased the votes in his constituency – a grand total of seven, for fifty pounds apiece!'

'Don't tell me that surprises you, Walter. Every thinking man in Cornwall knows such a practice is commonplace.'

'No, Jesse. It's common practice for a prospective Member of Parliament to "persuade" the voters to elect him and to put up a reasonable amount of expenses towards that end. Handing the mayor of a borough a sum of money to purchase votes is something very different. Even the government we have today dare not ignore this. If I can prove the rumour is true, Sir Colman Vincent will be out and the whole country will scream for parliamentary reform.'

'First you have to provide proof.'

'That shouldn't be too difficult – thanks to Reuben Holyoak. Ah! I thought the mention of his name would interest you. As a reward for his part in the election, Sir Colman granted the mayor of Pengony a parcel of land at a very low rent. Unfortunately for him, the mayor "forgot" to pay any rent at all. He didn't think Sir Colman would chase him for arrears. However, Reuben Holyoak knew nothing of the service rendered by the good gentleman of Pengony. Without reference to Sir Colman, he repossessed the land and rented it to someone else. He also sold the mayor's livestock and kept the money in lieu of unpaid rent! Can you imagine that? The mayor of Pengony is so furious that he tells the story of Sir Colman Vincent's ingratitude to anyone with the price of a pint of ale and the time to listen.'

'Would he tell the same story in court after Sir Colman has been given the opportunity to speak to him?'

'He wouldn't dare lie, Jesse. I can produce twenty men who have heard what the mayor has said.'

Jesse was not convinced. Anxiously, she said, 'Be very careful, Walter. Sir Colman has much to lose – so much that he'll go to any lengths to silence you.'

'Anything he did would merely confirm his own guilt.'

'Don't be a fool, Walter. Sir Colman won't come after you himself. He gets others to do his work. Remember, with you out of the way there's not another man in Cornwall who would dare try to bring him down.'

Jesse's fears were well founded, but her warning came too late. Walter had already told too many people of the information he had.

Two days after his conversation with Jesse, Walter brought his boat into Mevagissey harbour to find two constables from the nearby town of St Austell awaiting him. They had with them a warrant for his arrest. The charge was preaching sedition.

It was useless for Walter to argue that the whole thing was

a ridiculous mistake. The charges were far too serious to be taken lightly. Earlier that same year a group of extremist reformers had plotted to murder the hated Lord Liverpool's entire cabinet. Only a last-minute betrayal by one of their number prevented the desperate plan from being carried out. Government and judiciary were in a state of jittery vigilance, informers reaping a rich reward for their dubious activities. The merest hint of an organised protest was enough to provoke hasty overreaction.

Walter Dunn was swiftly arraigned before the magistrate at St Austell. Only then did he begin to appreciate the dangerous predicament he was in. Sir Colman Vincent was the examining magistrate. Walter had been arrested on the baronet's warrant.

The proceedings in the magistrate's court were brief. Two hesitant and unsatisfactory witnesses only were called. One was the constable who had arrested him. The other was Reuben Holyoak.

Sir Colman Vincent's estate manager told the court of two speeches he had heard Walter Dunn make at meetings. He failed to add that both had been made more than a year before. On this flimsy 'evidence', Walter was sent to Bodmin Gaol to await an escort to London. There he would face trial on the charges laid against him.

Walter protested loudly, but he was hustled from the court to a waiting covered van which immediately set off for Bodmin at a teeth-rattling gallop. By the time Walter arrived at the prison, his wrists and ankles had been skinned by the heavy irons securing them, and all the protest shaken out of him.

There had been good reason for such indecent haste in removing Walter Dunn from St Austell. So incensed were the fishermen of Mevagissey by his arrest that, after a hastily convened meeting, they were marching on the magistrate's court, determined to secure Walter's release.

Along the way the fishermen were joined by adherents to the reformers' cause from the mines of Polgooth and Crinnis. By the time they arrived at the outskirts of St Austell they were six hundred strong, shouting bold defiance against the magistrate who had ordered the arrest of Walter Dunn.

218

The marchers never entered the town. Before they reached the first of its houses their way was barred by a troop of blue-uniformed dragoons. Mounted on tall horses, the soldiers waited with swords drawn.

The commander of the troop had selected his position well. The lane at this point crossed a wide common. The soldiers were drawn up in a double line across the full width of the common. There was ample room here for them to ride through the marching column again and again, if need be.

The fishermen and miners were unarmed, and the officer in charge of the dragoons rode to the head of their column, calling on them to disperse quietly and return to their homes.

When the marching men shouted for the release of Walter Dunn, the officer was able to tell them in all honesty that Walter had already been taken to Bodmin Gaol.

This unexpected news threw the would-be rescuers into confusion. A few were for marching on to the county town, but the listening dragoons' officer strongly advised them against such a course of action. He told them that the foot soldiers currently garrisoned in Bodmin had, until recently, been stationed in the Midlands. Many of their number had been injured by rioters there. They would not have the same patience as his own dragoons.

His words had the desired effect. The Mevagissey men had walked six miles from their village on a cold November day. The thought of marching another twelve miles only to be turned back by a company of angry soldiers held out little appeal for them. The brave little army that had set out with such enthusiasm broke up in confusion under the scornful eyes of the dragoons.

Walter Dunn was not kept in Bodmin Gaol for long, but it turned out to be a harrowing experience for him. The charges against Walter were so serious that his gaolers took no risk of an escape attempt. He was placed in the most secure cell in the prison, sharing it with a prisoner who was to be executed the following day at the end of a hangman's noose. The man was not ready to die and refused to believe that the sentence of the court would be carried out. All night long he wept and pleaded for Walter to give him some glimmer of hope.

An out-of-work miner, Michael Stephens's crime had been to kill a sheep grazing on the moorland. The meat from the stolen animal had been used to keep his starving children alive. Such extenuating circumstances meant little to the Assize Judge, himself a livestock-owner. The law was quite clear. The unlawful killing of a sheep was a capital offence. Michael Stephens was guilty. He must hang. Because he had moved from his own home area in a bid to find work, Michael Stephens had no friends or employer to plead his cause, to urge that the sentence be commuted.

The young miner's abject pleading went on until noon on the day of the execution. Then, struggling and protesting to the end, Michael Stephens was carried to the scaffold by two soldiers and supported whilst the rope was placed about his neck. His terror came to an end when the hangman flung the lever controlling the drop and the sheep-stealing miner was flung into the arms of his Maker.

In the silence that followed the hurried execution, Walter heard a blackbird singing in a nearby tree. Then the voice of the crowd, gathered to witness the death of a felon, swelled to an excited roar. It had been an execution to remember. The reluctance of young Michael Stephens to die would be talked about for a long time.

Through the barred window of his cell, only a short distance from the gatehouse upon which the gallows stood, Walter Dunn winced at the crash of the trapdoor, his manacled hands clenched tightly before him.

Walter Dunn was not a religious man, but when the crowd roared its approval of the spectacle it had just witnessed he fell to his knees and prayed for the soul of the unfortunate young man.

The hours of horror spent in the company of the condemned miner inflicted a deep wound on Walter Dunn's mind. From that time, little that happened had any reality. It was as though he was looking at his own life from a distance, seeing but not feeling the things that happened to him. When he was transferred to a London gaol guarded by a large escort of soldiers, it meant nothing, the journey passing as though it were an unreal dream.

Walter Dunn's family learned of his transfer from Jesse. She walked to Bodmin expecting to see him, the weekend after his arrest.

Her frustration and anger at having undertaken such a long and wasted journey were tempered with concern for Walter. London was a whole world away from Cornwall. Ordinary men and women had no control over the things that happened there. As she made the long return walk to Mevagissey, Jesse tried to think how best she could help the one real friend she had.

It was Sunday evening and the whole Dunn family was gathered in the little house close to the harbour, after attending the evening service in the chapel. Jesse arrived, footsore and tired, and told the family what she had learned. She waited for their anger, but it did not come. Old Mrs Dunn began crying quietly to herself while the grandchildren looked on in consternation. The remainder of the Dunn family received the news in silence. Not one of them muttered a single word of sympathy for Walter.

'Well, what are we going to do to help Walter?'

Mark Dunn shrugged his shoulders. 'What can be done? He was told often enough that a fisherman should tend to his nets and leave changing Parliament to them as understands about such things.'

'What you mean is you'll do nothing.'

Jesse gave Mark Dunn a scornful look, then turned her back on him to speak to his brother.

'How about you, Billy? What do *you* think we should do?'

Billy Dunn looked uncertainly from his scowling brother to Jesse. Before he could reply, his wife answered for him.

'Billy is not going to do anything. He's got me and his children to think about. Mark is right; there's nothing to be done. Besides, what did Walter do for Mark and my Billy when the Revenue men picked them up and carried them off to the Fleet?'

Jesse looked at Billy Dunn's wife in disgust. 'Walter made certain that you and your children – yes, and Mark's family, too – had a roof over your heads and were never short of food. He worked hard so that his brothers had fishing-boats to come home to. *That's* what he did – though why he bothered, I don't know! You are none of you worth an hour of Walter's time.'

Angrily she slammed out of the house.

Tight-lipped, Billy Dunn's wife said, 'It's as well your Ben never married that girl, Martha. We can do without her in this family.'

'Can we?' Martha Retallick picked up her shawl and flung it across her shoulders. 'It's a pity your man hasn't got half the spirit of Jesse Henna. As for marrying Ben . . . if she had, he'd be here now and *he* wouldn't need to be pushed into doing something to help Walter.'

Martha Retallick ran from the house and caught up with a tear-blinded Jesse as she wandered aimlessly at the edge of the harbour.

'I'm sorry if I lost my temper back there,' Jesse said as she clung to Martha Retallick's hand, 'but someone *must* help Walter.'

'You said what needed saying,' declared Martha Retallick. She squeezed Jesse's arm comfortingly and added, 'I wish our Ben was here with us.'

'So do I, Mrs Retallick. So do I.'

Jesse closed her eyes, and for a moment she appeared to be in physical pain. Taking a deep breath, she regained control of herself.

'I'm certain Sir Colman is behind Walter's arrest. Walter knows more than he should of something that could harm Sir Colman. If I am right, no one in Mevagissey can do anything for him. I've thought about it all the way from Bodmin. I know of only one person who might be able to help. Sir Colman's aunt.'

'Help Walter? Against her own nephew?' Martha Retallick was sceptical. 'Why should she want to get Sir Colman into trouble?'

'I don't intend asking her to do anything against Sir Colman; only to see if she can persuade him to have Walter released. Perhaps if he promises to say nothing of what he knows . . .'

Jesse's voice faltered. She saw the weakness of her own argument before Martha Retallick pointed it out to her.

'Walter's a stubborn man. If he believes the information he has will further the aims of his reform movement, he'll use it and damn the consequences. Anyway, the whole thing is out of Sir Colman's hands now Walter is in London.'

'You may be right, Mrs Retallick, but I can't just give up and do nothing. If there is any possible way to help Walter, I'll find it, be sure of that.'

'What if you succeed, Jesse? What will you do then – you and Walter?'

'You know he asked me to marry him?'

'Yes, he thought I should know. Walter is not a guileful man, Jesse.'

'If he were, he wouldn't be in trouble now. Walter has been very kind to me, but I can't marry him. I still love Ben.'

'Ben left here believing he'd killed Reuben Holyoak. There's little reason for him to return to Mevagissey. Ben is my own son, Jesse, but don't waste your life waiting for him.'

They were standing at the harbour steps now, and Jesse remembered how Ben had looked on the day he returned from his very first fishing trip, his face as green as the waters of the English Channel today.

'I'll wait a while yet, Mrs Retallick. I think Ben has a right to expect that from me.'

Eulaliah Vincent had moved into the new house that had been built at Tregassick, the one in which Ben and his mother had lived having been pulled down to make way for the extensive gardens. Although not on the same grand scale as Lamorrack, it was a fine house.

When Jesse arrived, the silver-haired Eulaliah Vincent was in the garden supervising the planting of rose-bushes around a newly seeded lawn. She was delighted to see Jesse.

'Why, child, what a pleasure this is! Have you come to see how I am settling in at the new Tregassick?'

Jesse began to explain the purpose of her visit, but Eulaliah Vincent quickly stopped her.

'This sounds like a story best told behind closed doors. These are Sir Colman's men working here. Tale-bearers find much favour with my nephew.'

Inside the new house, Eulaliah Vincent ordered a maid to make tea, fussing over Jesse as though she were an invited guest and not a girl whose mother had once been her maid.

Not until tea had been served in front of a roaring fire in the lounge did the old lady settle back to hear what Jesse had to say.

Jesse told her of Walter's long association with the reform movement and of the story he had passed on, concerning Sir Colman's election to the House of Commons.

If Jesse expected Eulaliah Vincent to be shocked she was disappointed.

The landowner's aunt snorted. 'If every man who paid for his votes was thrown out of the House of Commons, Lord Liverpool would not have enough men left to govern – but please go on, child.'

Jesse continued with the story of Walter's arrest and hurried transfer to London.

'You *walked* to Bodmin and back to Mevagissey again just to speak to this Walter Dunn? That is more than thirty miles. What is he to you?'

'He is Ben's uncle. He has helped me a great deal since my mother died.'

'I see. But what of your Ben? You were supposed to be marrying him. Has he changed his mind now you no longer have Pengrugla?'

Jesse told Eulaliah Vincent of Ben's disappearance and the reason why he had left the area so hurriedly. By the time she ended her story the old lady was trembling with rage.

'My nephew has much to answer for – he and that damned upstart estate manager of his!'

Controlling herself with some difficulty, she put a hand on Jesse's arm and said, 'Try not to hate Sir Colman, Jesse. If you did, it would distress me greatly – though God knows, you have reason enough. One day he will bring about his own downfall by his stupidity. Most of the Members of the House of Commons may have paid for the votes that put them there, but that does not make it legal. If a specific case was brought to his attention, Lord Liverpool would be forced to take action. He is already thoroughly alarmed that this agitation for parliamentary reform is getting out of hand. Oh, you need not look so surprised, child. Do you think your friend Walter Dunn has been carrying on a lone campaign? No, reform fever has the country in as firm a grip as the black plague once had. For this reason I must hold out very little hope of securing Walter Dunn's release. Lord Liverpool is determined to stamp out reform agitation once and for all. He sees it as a greater threat to England than Napoleon ever was. That does not mean you need despair. I will think carefully about what might be done. Sir Colman is in London at present. The first thing I will do is go there and speak to him.'

Jesse protested that such a journey was unnecessary. Surely a letter would suffice? Her concern now was for Eulaliah Vincent. She was a frail old lady, and the journey to London by road would take at least ten days.

Eulaliah Vincent waved Jesse's protests aside.

'Nonsense, child. I have made the journey many times. Besides, it has been far too long since I was last in London. I will make arrangements immediately. I have many friends there, and a personal appeal is worth a hundred letters. Now, where may I find you when I return?'

Jesse left Tregassick wondering yet again why Eulaliah Vincent was prepared to go to such lengths to help her – possibly at the expense of her own nephew. Eulaliah Vincent must have been very fond indeed of her one-time maid.

Jesse did not see Eulaliah Vincent watching her departure from one of the large windows of the house. As Jesse went from sight around a curve of the path, Eulaliah Vincent turned back into the room. Shaking her head, she whispered fiercely, 'The past is coming back to haunt you, Colman Vincent – and this girl will not be as easily bought off as was her mother.'

Chapter Twenty-Three

As the weeks stretched into months, Jesse waited in vain for news of Walter and began to wonder whether Martha Retallick's scepticism about Eulaliah Vincent might not have been well founded.

Then Jesse began to worry that the journey to London had proved too much for the oldest member of the Vincent family. When the snows of winter were decorating the leafless trees and hedgerows, and lying thin and crisp underfoot, Jesse walked from Pentuan to Tregassick. There she enquired after Eulaliah Vincent.

The servants were quickly able to put Jesse's mind at ease. A letter from the mistress of the house had been received only two days before. Eulaliah Vincent was well and enjoying the almost forgotten social pleasures of London. She had written that she did not expect to be returning to Cornwall until a change of weather had brought about an improvement in the condition of the roads. There was no mention in the letter of either Sir Colman Vincent or Walter Dunn.

On the return journey to Pentuan, Jesse did not take the usual path. Instead, she made a slight diversion along an overgrown path that was more sheltered from the cold northerly wind. Along the path she met a young girl hurrying in the opposite direction. It was Judy Lean, the simple-minded daughter of one of the late Sir John Vincent's kitchen maids. Jesse and Judy were of a similar age and had often played together in the woods about Lamorrack House. A straightforward game of hide-and-seek, which might have given a normally restless child half an hour's pleasure, had kept Judy Lean happy and laughing for as long as Jesse had the patience to play with her.

But this was no carefree little girl playing hide-and-seek in the woods today. The simple girl was dressed in a summer frock that was totally inadequate to keep out the cold winds of winter, and the chilblains upon her feet owed much to the broken and ill-fitting shoes she wore. In addition, Judy Lean was dirty – and noticeably pregnant.

Jesse greeted the other girl warmly, but Judy was reluctant to stop and talk. Jesse had to take her by the arm to prevent her from hurrying on her way.

'Judy, it's me . . . Jesse. Surely you remember me? We used to play together, up at the big house.'

For a fleeting moment a shaft of light pierced the tangled darkness of Judy Lean's mind and she smiled. The moment quickly passed, and she became agitated and eager to move on her way.

'Mr Holyoak said I was to hurry back from St Austell and not gossip to anyone. He says local folk are just out to make mischief for me.'

'Reuben Holyoak sent you to St Austell in that condition?' Jesse's anger was fanned by the mention of the estate manager's name. 'What right has he to tell you where you must go and to whom you may speak along the way? Where is your husband . . . ?'

'I'm not married.' Judy Lean looked down at the ground beside her broken shoe. 'I work for Mr Holyoak now. I look after his house at Pengrugla. He relies on me . . . he told me so.'

Pity welled up inside Jesse as she stared at the ill-dressed girl standing shivering before her. 'I'm sure he does, Judy. Your mother must be very proud of you now . . .'

The simple girl's expression changed, and Jesse said quickly, 'Your mother . . . she's well, Judy?'

'I don't know.' Judy Lean's bottom lip began to tremble. 'When I went to work for Mr Holyoak she went off with a sailor who worked into Pentuan. They went to Plymouth to get married. She's living there somewhere. Mr Holyoak says she don't care nothing about me now.'

Judy Lean's mother was a widow and had been forced to work very hard to bring up her simple daughter.

'I'm quite sure she *does* care, Judy. She probably thinks about you a great deal – just as I shall now. Look, I am living in Pentuan village, at the house of the captain of the Happy Union mine. I want you to come and visit me there. Will you promise to do that?'

The agitation returned to Judy once more. 'I . . . I can't. Mr Holyoak doesn't let me go visiting. He says I'm better off at home, where he can keep an eye on me.'

'You must meet other people sometimes, Judy. You'll need the help of other women soon' – she looked pointedly towards Judy Lean's distended stomach – 'when the baby comes.'

'Baby? What baby? Mr Holyoak won't have a baby at Pengrugla. He told me so.'

Judy's bewilderment was quite genuine. Jesse realised that this simple girl was not aware that she was pregnant!

When Jesse tried to pursue the matter, Judy Lean became very upset and finally turned and fled along the path, ignoring Jesse's pleas to return.

All the way to Pentuan, Jesse worried about the simple-minded girl, but there was little she could do immediately. She would mention Judy Lean to Eulaliah Vincent – when she returned.

Before then, Jesse had sudden and unexpected news of Ben that drove all thoughts of the unfortunate Judy Lean from her mind.

It came at one of Fanny Ustick's Sunday prayer-meeting teas, attended by a number of men new to the Happy Union mine. One of them, a man in his early forties, was well on the downward path trodden by older miners. Too old to cope with the ladders on the deeper and more prosperous mines, he was now drifting round the county, seeking smaller mines and stream-works. Before long he would be forced to swallow his pride and join the army of odd-job men, willing to undertake any job in order to stay on a mine.

'Ben Retallick?' He frowned in reply to Jesse's routine question, 'Why, yes. I worked with him about four or five months since, on the Luscombe mine, down on Tamarside. I remember him well. A good strong lad. I wouldn't mind working with him again.'

Jesse could hardly believe her luck. 'You actually worked with Ben? Where exactly is the Luscombe mine? Is Ben still there?'

The miner shook his head, and some of the hope died within Jesse.

'No, missie. He left there before I did. He's one of those miners who don't care to stay in one place for long. A month is plenty long enough for the likes of him, I reckon. He'll have worked in another half dozen mines by now.'

Jesse continued to question the miner, gleaning every scrap of information about Ben, until Fanny Ustick called for her assistance in the kitchen.

By the time Jesse came back to the room, the miner had gone. It was the last opportunity she had to talk to him. He, too, was a soldier of the army of drifters. The rumour of an easy surface-job on a deep mine was all he needed to put him on the road to another mine, another district. Jesse never saw him again.

Nevertheless, it was the first positive news of Ben that Jesse had received in almost a year. It now seemed certain that Ben had not left the country, and was probably still in Cornwall.

For the whole of one evening, the patient Fanny Ustick wrote and rewrote a letter to the captain of the Luscombe mine, at Jesse's dictation.

This was a most important letter, and Fanny realised it could not be hurried. Jesse spent so much time trying to make up her mind *exactly* what should be written that Fanny Ustick wrote a brief note of her own to accompany the letter. She begged the mine captain to give them *any* news of Ben.

For weeks, Jesse faced each new morning with the thought that this might be the day when she would have news of Ben. Perhaps Ben himself would arrive, informed by the captain of the Luscombe mine that there was now nothing to keep him away.

Jesse waited in vain. No reply to the letter was ever received.

In the spring of 1821, two young boys were walking along the little-used path where Jesse had met with Judy Lean, when they saw a brightly coloured bundle tucked beneath the leafless hedgerow. Thinking they had discovered some exciting booty, abandoned by the Mevagissey smugglers who used the path, they pounced upon the bundle and unwrapped it with excited anticipation. As the last wrapping was turned back, the boys dropped the bundle quickly, recoiling in horror.

They had found the body of a newly born child, wrapped inside a bloody apron.

News of the grisly find was given to Loveday Ustick by the constable from St Austell when he called at the Happy Union stream-works to water his horse. The constable had been despatched by a St Austell magistrate to view the tiny body and try to establish the cause of its death – and also to seek the dead baby's mother.

Loveday Ustick mentioned the matter quite casually that evening, when he was sitting down to supper with his wife and Jesse. Before he had finished talking, Jesse jumped up from the table, leaving her meal, and announced that she was going out.

'Out? Where are you going at this hour? It will be dark soon.'

'I know, but I must go. I'll tell you all about it when I return.'

Before the Usticks could ask any more questions, Jesse was out of the house. She had no doubt that Judy Lean was the mother of the dead baby. She was equally certain the constable would reach the same conclusion before very long. She wanted to find Judy Lean before he did.

Turning in at the gate of Pengrugla, Jesse had a moment of indecision. She had not seen Reuben Holyoak since she had left this house after her mother's death. She was not happy at the thought of meeting him again now, but it could not be avoided.

The light was failing fast, but it was sufficient for her to see that Sir Colman Vincent's estate manager did not concern himself with the appearance of his own house. Winter gales, heavy with salt from the bay beyond the hill, had scoured much of the paint from doors and window-frames. The house had a sadly neglected air.

There was a light in the kitchen, but when Jesse knocked on the door no sound came from within. She was about to move to the kitchen window to look inside, when a voice spoke from close behind her. Reuben Holyoak had lost none of his gamekeeper's silent ways. Jesse had heard nothing of his approach.

'Well, this is an unexpected pleasure.' Reuben Holyoak looked at her in feigned surprise. He had seen her coming towards the house when she was a quarter of a mile away. 'Welcome back to Pengrugla, Jesse. It's been a great disappointment to me that you should have stayed away for so long. Come into the house.'

Reuben Holyoak went in first and held the door open. Jesse took a single step inside. It was far enough for her to see that the neglect outside had its beginning here. It both saddened and angered her. But she reminded herself that she was not here to take issue with Reuben Holyoak over the condition of the house that had been her home for so long.

'I've come to see Judy Lean. Where is she?'

'Judy?' Jesse had caught Reuben Holyoak off guard, but he recovered quickly. 'I don't know. What's more, I don't care. I sent the slattern packing.'

Jesse was certain he was lying. She said, 'Was that before or after the baby was born?'

'I know nothing of any baby,' Reuben Holyoak blustered. 'What baby? If I learn who has been spreading such rumours, I'll take them before the magistrate.'

'The chances are that you'll have an opportunity to speak to a magistrate sooner than you expect. People around here are not fools. Some of them will have seen Judy. She was with child – and now a dead baby has been found not a stone's throw from here. The constable from St Austell is most likely on his way to this house at this very moment. Now, take me to Judy.'

Jesse sounded far more confident than she felt. She was close enough to Reuben Holyoak to smell the alcohol on his breath, and she knew him well enough to fear him.

'Judy Lean and her baby have nothing to do with me. What that girl does is her own business.'

'Then I've been wasting my time – and yours. I came here to help Judy. I haven't found her and I'm worried. I'll seek out the constable and tell him everything I know.'

231

Jesse turned to walk from the house.

'Wait!' Reuben Holyoak was not certain how much Jesse really knew, but he did not want her talking to the constable. 'I . . . I'm not sure . . . She may be down at the pigs' house.'

'Why should she be there?' Jesse looked at Reuben Holyoak suspiciously.

'She's been living there for a month or two.' Reuben Holyoak's eyes would not meet hers.

'You mean since you learned she was expecting a child.'

Jesse made no attempt to hide the contempt she felt for Reuben Holyoak. Now she knew for certain he was the father of Judy Lean's dead child. Had he not been, he would have sent her away from Pengrugla the moment he knew she was pregnant.

'Bring a lantern. We'll have need of it if we are to find her.'

Jesse set off down the path in the darkness. Halfway to the pig-sty Reuben Holyoak caught up with her. In his hand he carried a fish-oil lantern that cast a flickering yellow light about them.

'I knew nothing about the baby's death, Jesse. You must believe me.'

Jesse said nothing.

'I swear to you I've done everything in my power to help Judy. I will do so now, but we must keep the constable from learning her whereabouts.'

They arrived at the low windowless building that had once housed the pigs owned by Jesse and her mother. Jesse remembered that Reuben Holyoak had once spent a night here, but the thought raised no smile tonight. The sty was in darkness, but as Jesse pushed the door open on creaking hinges she heard a startled rustle of straw. It was too loud to have been caused by a rat.

'Hold the light up,' Jesse called to Reuben Holyoak.

In the weak yellow light cast by the lamp, she saw that the sty had not been cleaned out since her pigs had been sold.

At first, Jesse could see little in the dark interior of the sty, but as she advanced further inside, with Reuben Holyoak behind her, she made out the shape of someone lying on a heap of last year's straw.

It was Judy Lean.

She lay covered with only the tattered remnants of an old blanket. Her head moved on the straw as she followed the progress of the shadowy figures across the sty towards her. Her face was taut and haggard, but it was her eyes that alarmed Jesse. They were wide and feverish, full of the pain she had borne alone.

Jesse dropped to her knees on the straw and sought to reassure the girl. 'You are going to be all right now, Judy. I've come to help you.'

Judy Lean looked apprehensively towards the lantern held high behind Jesse.

'Don't worry, Judy. That's Mr Holyoak.'

Instead of relaxing, Judy Lean drew an arm from beneath the blanket and gripped Jesse's arm painfully. 'I didn't do nothing wrong, Jesse. I didn't want to make no trouble for Mr Holyoak. Don't let anyone take me away.'

'Hush, now! No one is going to take you anywhere.'

It was doubtful whether Judy Lean heard her words, so caught up was she in her own tangled fears.

'I'm hurting so, Jesse. It happened along the path . . . I didn't know . . . The baby just came.'

Judy Lean's fingernails dug into Jesse's arm, and Jesse winced with pain.

'I spoke to it, Jesse, but it didn't do nothing. I cuddled it, too, but I don't think it loved me very much. It wouldn't make a sound for me. Then I heard some boys coming along the path. I wrapped the baby in my apron and put it in the hedge. I knew they'd see it . . . I thought it might love them more than it loved me . . .'

Tears were streaming down Judy Lean's face and, before Jesse could prevent her, she struggled to a sitting position. 'I wouldn't have brought the baby to Pengrugla, Mr Holyoak. I remembered what you said to me. If the baby had loved me, I'd have found somewhere else to keep it. I would . . .'

The tattered blanket had slipped from Judy Lean in her agitation, and, as Jesse held the girl close in a bid to calm her, she saw that Judy had lost a great deal of blood.

Over her shoulder, Jesse spoke to Reuben Holyoak. 'Judy

needs a doctor. I doubt if he'll want to work in a pig's house. You must help me to take her to Pengrugla.'

'What about the constable? If he finds here there, I'll be in trouble with Sir Colman.'

Jesse snorted angrily. 'Your neck will be safe enough, Reuben Holyoak. So will Judy's if we get a doctor to her quickly. You heard what she just said. The baby must have been dead when it was born. There will be gossip, but that's never bothered you before. Help me lift her up, now – and be careful with her.'

'All right. Hold this lantern.'

Handing the lamp to Jesse, Reuben Holyoak bent down to Judy Lean. With a muffled grunt he lifted her from the straw, avoiding meeting her frightened gaze.

When they reached the house, Reuben Holyoak carried his burden up the narrow stairs to the small bedroom that had once been Jesse's own. It now contained nothing but a hard straw mattress.

Laying Judy Lean on the mattress, he said gruffly, 'I'll find a blanket for her.'

'When you've done that you can go to the village and fetch the doctor. She's still bleeding badly.'

For a moment it looked as though Reuben Holyoak might argue, and Jesse said quickly, 'You'll not want it said you have reason to wish this girl dead, Reuben? Go, now. I have things to do here that you won't want to see.'

Without another word, Reuben Holyoak left the room. A few moments later, much to Jesse's relief, she heard the front door slam shut behind him.

Jesse quickly set to and stripped and bathed Judy Lean ignoring the girl's weak protests. She frowned at the extensive bruising she found on Judy's pale body, but by then Judy Lean was so drowsy she made no reply to Jesse's questions.

Jesse had just completed her task when she heard footsteps on the stairs outside. Thinking it was the doctor, she went out to meet him and have a brief discussion with him before he examined the ill and exhausted Judy Lean.

It was not the doctor but the constable from St Austell.

Looking at Jesse, he said, 'I was told I would find Reuben Holyoak here. Would you be Judy Lean?'

'No, Judy is in there.' Jesse jerked her head at the door behind her.

As the constable made to move past her, Jesse blocked his path, 'Judy Lean is not going to run away, Constable. She's a very sick girl. Reuben Holyoak has gone to Mevagissey to fetch a doctor for her.'

The constable put his head to one side and looked quizzically at Jesse. 'I don't doubt your word, young lady, but I have some questions to put to her.'

'You'll receive no answers from her tonight. Judy is ill and very, very tired. I think I can tell you all you want to know. Yes, the child that was found is hers – but it was dead when it was born.'

'I wouldn't dream of arguing with you, miss. However, the rights of that will be decided at a Coroner's inquest. Have you known Judy Lean for long?'

Jesse nodded. 'We grew up together, but I hadn't seen her for some years until we met again a couple of months ago. It was obvious to anyone that she was expecting a child, yet when I asked her about it she became terribly confused. I'm quite sure she never realised what was happening to her.'

The constable nodded sympathetically. 'That is more or less what others have told me – but someone must have known. The child's father, for instance. Would you have any idea who he is?'

'Thoughts, I might have; but the gossips will already have given you theirs.'

'Perhaps Reuben Holyoak can tell me more.'

'I don't doubt it. Whether he *will* is another matter altogether. But you'll have an opportunity to talk to him soon; I think I hear him.'

When Reuben Holyoak entered the house the doctor from Mevagissey was with him, complaining bitterly at being called out to roam the countryside in the dark of a moonless night.

Reuben Holyoak came up the stairs behind the doctor.

When he saw the constable, he stopped, the blood draining from his face.

The doctor ignored the constable, but to Jesse he said, 'You had better come in the room with me. I may have need of your help.'

The Mevagissey doctor's examination was so crude it came close to brutality. He handled Judy Lean with a roughness that brought screams of pain from her. When he had completed his cursory examination he left her whimpering softly.

As Jesse looked at him in silent disapproval, the doctor wiped his hands on a bloody cloth. 'The bleeding must be stopped if she is to recover. Find some woundwort – there should be plenty growing about here. Make a strong tea from it and give it to her as often as you can force it down.'

'Is that all you can do for her?'

'Go to church and pray if you want a miracle – but I saw a constable outside the door. He will have been sent here by the Reverend Hawkins. Hawkins is a magistrate who pays scant heed to the Bible's dictum of tempering justice with mercy. He has more control over this girl's future than I.'

Jesse said sharply, 'Judy's committed no crime. Her baby was dead when it was born.'

'The Coroner's jury may agree with you, I doubt if their verdict will convince Hawkins. Judy Lean has sinned against the Church by bringing a fatherless child into the world – dead or alive. If he had his way, the Reverend Hawkins would make all such sins capital offences.'

His ablutions completed, the doctor strode from the room and called to Reuben Holyoak as he went down the stairs.

Jesse remained in the bedroom and did her best to comfort Judy Lean. She did not leave the room until the girl had fallen into a sleep punctuated by long quivering sobs.

When Jesse went downstairs the doctor had left the house. The constable had gone with him.

'Judy will need a woman to look in and help her each day,' she said to Reuben Holyoak.

'Will you come and do whatever needs to be done, Jesse?'

'I have my own work at the Happy Union. You can get a

woman from Lamorrack House, but I would like to visit Judy occasionally.'

'You are always welcome, Jesse. You know that.'

Jesse saw the brandy-bottle on the table alongside a half-empty glass. She knew it was time she left.

'I've missed seeing you about, Jesse. It was always my hope that this would remain your home. I've not changed. I still want you here as my wife.'

Jesse looked around her at the neglected and unloved house that held so many memories for her. On her way to the door she paused to throw her words back at Sir Colman Vincent's estate manager.'

'This is no longer the house I grew up in, Reuben. You've succeeded in destroying my past; but you'll have no part of my future, I promise you that.'

Chapter Twenty-Four

The Reverend Hawkins sent his constables to Pengrugla to arrest Judy Lean two days after the dead baby had been found. He ordered that she be kept in custody pending the verdict of the coroner's court.

One of the constables was the man who had been to Pengrugla to investigate the death of the baby. He called at the Happy Union mine to give the news to Jesse.

'I wouldn't like you to believe this is any of my doing, miss. To my way of thinking the girl might just as well remain at Pengrugla, but I have to carry out my orders. I'll make sure she is well looked after, don't you worry about that. I've brought along a wagon to carry her to St Austell, and my wife will tend her while she's there. We'll have a doctor look in on her, too, if he's needed.'

Despite the constable's reassuring words, Jesse worried about Judy Lean. She was thinking about the matter on her way home from the stream-works that evening when a passing horseman hailed her. It was Reuben Holyoak, dressed in clothes that would not have disgraced a country gentleman. He told Jesse of Judy Lean's arrest.

Jesse thanked him politely but coolly and continued on her way. Undaunted, Reuben Holyoak swung himself down from the saddle. Leading the horse by the reins, he fell in beside her.

'I've helped Judy as much as I dare, Jesse. Now she has been arrested I can do no more. I have my position to think of. All this is none of my business . . .'

Jesse snorted loudly and walked faster. 'Tell that to those who might believe you, Reuben Holyoak.'

Striding out to keep pace with her, Reuben Holyoak said, 'I was hoping for an opportunity to talk seriously to you, Jesse. As Sir Colman's estate manager I occupy a good position. I have much to offer you. Marry me and you'll be the envy of every girl for miles around. I can give you back

Pengrugla. You would have a good life there with me, Jesse.'

Jesse stopped and turned scornfully upon Reuben Holyoak. 'Is that what you told Judy Lean when you bedded her, Reuben? That she would have a good life with you? She's simple enough to have believed you – I am not! Pengrugla means nothing to me without Ben Retallick. You have nothing I want, Reuben Holyoak. Set your fine clothes back in the saddle and find another simpleton to impress.'

'You are angry and upset now, Jesse. We'll talk again another time.'

Reuben Holyoak pulled hard on the rein of his horse as it backed away from him. 'In the meantime I suggest you forget Judy Lean. Allow justice to take its course.'

'Judy Lean needs more than justice right now. She needs friends. I count myself as one of them and I'll do all I can to help her.'

Some of the bal-maidens from the Happy Union streamworks came around a bend in the lane, laughing and joking. Jesse, who was usually content with her own company, waited for them. They had not gone far before Reuben Holyoak rode by, looking neither to left nor right, ignoring the whistles of some of the younger girls.

The inquest on Judy Lean's baby was held in a Mevagissey inn, much to the chagrin of the Reverend Hawkins. He felt the proceedings were robbed of dignity by such surroundings.

No one at the inquest knew why the ecclesiastical magistrate had chosen to attend. Possibly he was expecting to be called upon to give evidence of having arrested Judy Lean.

Jesse was there. So, too, was Reuben Holyoak. He looked ill at ease when called to the witness-box. The estate manager denied knowing that Judy was pregnant. In truth, he solemnly declared, it was not often that he saw the girl. He worked long hours and ate most of his meals at Lamorrack House. Judy Lean had been employed by him to keep Pengrugla clean and cultivate a small vegetable garden there.

According to Reuben Holyoak she was rarely at home when he returned in the evening and he had no idea how she spent her time. He added that Judy's mother had run off with a

239

sailor and he doubted whether Judy's morals were any better . . .

At this point Jesse jumped to her feet and accused Reuben Holyoak of deliberately attempting to blacken the character of Judy Lean.

The coroner was not in the least perturbed by Jesse's interruption. He calmly asked her whether she had something to say to the court. When Jesse said she most certainly had, the coroner asked Reuben Holyoak, 'Have you anything further to say that might help to throw light upon the death of this child, Mr Holyoak?'

Reuben Holyoak shook his head.

'Very well, you may step down and we will hear what this young lady has to tell the court.' The coroner waved Jesse forward.

Jesse's manner was in sharp contrast to Reuben Holyoak's. Firmly and clearly she said she had known Judy Lean since childhood, and she told the coroner of Judy's simple ways. Then she spoke of meeting Judy Lean on the path where the dead baby was found and of her belief that Judy had not realised she was pregnant. Finally, Jesse told of finding Judy Lean in the pig-sty at Pengrugla. Her voice faltered for the first time as she repeated what Judy Lean had said to her about the failure of the baby to move or make a sound.

When Jesse ended, it was apparent to everyone in the improvised court-room that she had made a great impression upon the seven-man jury. But the coroner seized upon another aspect of her story.

'Miss Henna, will you clear up one small point for me? Was Mr Holyoak present when Judy Lean told you about the birth of her baby?'

'He was.'

'I see. Thank you.'

The coroner fixed Reuben Holyoak with a look that made the estate manager squirm. 'No doubt Mr Holyoak has his own reasons for not telling this court such an important piece of evidence.'

Two more witnesses were called by the coroner. One was the constable who had investigated the baby's death; the other was the surgeon who had conducted a post-mortem on the child. Neither man had found any marks of violence on the tiny body.

When the last witness had sat down the jury had a brief discussion then returned a verdict that it had not been proven the baby was alive when born. The coroner recorded their verdict accordingly.

A coroner's jury would rarely bring in a verdict that might lead to criminal proceedings being taken against the mother of a baby found dead under circumstances such as these. If the bastardy laws of England were harsh, the criminal law was pitiless. More than one young girl climbed the steps to a prison gallows, guilty only of earning the disapproval of a jury of her peers, backed up by a stern judge's lack of compassion.

One man in the crowded court-room disagreed with the verdict. The Reverend Hawkins had come to Mevagissey to hear a verdict of 'wilful murder' recorded against Judy Lean. Jumping to his feet, he shouted that Judy Lean had sinned against the Church and that the verdict reached by the jury would offend God himself.

The onlookers responded with a barrage of jeers. When the coroner had succeeded in restoring a degree of order, he addressed the angry magistrate.

'Sir, had it been your wish to address this court I would have been most happy to afford you the opportunity. As it is, the jury has arrived at a verdict with which I am in complete agreement. This hearing is now over.'

The coroner smiled fleetingly at the angry magistrate. 'I am aware that the verdict has placed you in a difficult situation, Reverend Hawkins. You should have waited the finding of my court before making an arrest. I suggest you release the young lady at the earliest opportunity.'

'Damn you, Varcoe. I will do no such thing,' retorted the fiery magistrate in a most unclerical display of bad temper. 'Wickedness must not go unpunished. Indeed, it *will* not! Judy Lean has no employment and no place to live now that Mr Holyoak has dismissed her from his service. I'll not release her to a life of sinful vagrancy, to tempt other men.'

Before the Reverend Hawkins had ended his tirade, Jesse was on her feet again. She shouted, 'Judy Lean is no vagrant, and neither you nor Reuben Holyoak will make her one. She can share my room. There will be work for her, too, when she is well enough.'

When the jury had reached its verdict, the innkeeper had immediately flung open his establishment, anxious not to lose so many prospective customers. Now, with glasses and tankards in their hands, jurors and spectators alike raised a cheer for Jesse, drowning the Reverend Hawkins's angry reply.

Unable to make himself heard above the din, the red-faced magistrate stormed from the inn, calling down the wrath of heaven upon the heads of all those who condoned sinfulness.

Later, the constable released Judy Lean, and she went home with Jesse to the Ustick house. Fanny Ustick had heard all about the unfortunate girl from Jesse and she displayed a great deal more Christian charity than had the Reverend Hawkins. For the first time in many years Judy Lean slept in a house where she was welcome.

It was a full month before Judy Lean was well enough to commence working at the Happy Union mine. She was a hard-working girl, lacking all deceit, and she was well received by the other girls and women with whom she worked.

When Judy Lean had been at the mine a week, she and the other bal-maidens were sorting ore and chattering together when a carriage turned off the road and swayed down the steep pitted track to the workings.

The bal-maidens watched with great interest as Captain Loveday Ustick hurried from his office to meet the carriage and they saw him say something through the open window. Then he turned, shielding his eyes against the light of the sun, and pointed to where the bal-maidens were working.

Jesse knew immediately that the occupant of the carriage must be Eulaliah Vincent. Without waiting to be called, Jesse hurried to where Loveday Ustick was holding the carriage door open.

'Hello, child.' Dressed in clothes that were the height of London fashion, Eulaliah Vincent took Jesse's arm, heedless of the dust that clung to Jesse's coarse dress and apron. 'Walk with me to the far side of the river. I fancy there is less mud underfoot there.'

'You have some news of Walter?' Jesse asked eagerly.

'I have, but I fear it is not the news for which you have been hoping. Walter Dunn has been sentenced to fourteen years' transportation.'

Jesse reeled as though she had been struck, and Eulaliah Vincent's grip tightened on her arm.

'Fourteen years! For what? For speaking the truth?'

'No, child. He was found guilty of sedition. Of advocating violent changes in the order of our society. It is probably the most serious charge that could be levelled against a man in these uncertain times – but there, do not upset yourself so, child. Things might have been much worse for Walter Dunn.'

'But he did nothing . . .' Jesse's voice trailed away in an agony of despair.

'That was not what the evidence implied. Indeed, during the course of the trial it was rumoured that Walter Dunn would suffer the same fate as the Cato Street conspirators.'

Jesse gasped. Even in this remote corner of England news had reached them of Arthur Thistlewood and his misguided fellow-reformers. They were the men who had plotted to murder the whole Cabinet of Lord Liverpool. They had reached an advanced state of preparation when one of their number had betrayed his fellow-conspirators.

Captured and convicted by the due processes of English law, Arthur Thistlewood and four of his lieutenants were hanged by the neck until they were semi-conscious – then removed from the gallows and beheaded by an axeman.

'Fourteen years is a lifetime,' whispered Jesse.

Eulaliah Vincent smiled sadly. 'It is only a lifetime when you reach my age, child. For you it is no more than a passing chapter in the book of life. When Walter Dunn returns to Mevagissey you will still be a beautiful woman – but you must expect very little from him, or I fear you will be terribly upset.'

They had crossed the bridge, and now Eulaliah Vincent turned to Jesse and said gently, 'I went to see Walter Dunn

243

in Newgate prison. I wanted to know if there was anything he needed. Sadly, I fear that imprisonment has proved too much for Walter Dunn to bear. His mind has escaped to the sea and the clean air he loves so much. I am sorry to be the bearer of such sad news, but I felt you should know.'

Jesse was stunned. She had come to believe that Walter was able to cope with anything. Jesse thought of the time she had told him she was leaving the Dunn house. When he walked away from her to the reform meeting, she had admired the way he shrugged off his problems and put them behind him. For such a man to be broken was unthinkable.

Jesse wept openly, and Eulaliah Vincent did her best to comfort her.

When Jesse regained her composure, she walked slowly back to the stream-workings with Eulaliah Vincent. Along the way she thanked her for all she had tried to do. Jesse was convinced Eulaliah Vincent had used her influence to save Walter from the gallows.

When she expressed this opinion to the Dunn family that same evening, only Martha Retallick agreed with her. Billy Dunn said bluntly that, had Jesse not interfered, things might even have gone better for Walter. He told Jesse she had been foolish to expect one Vincent to act against the interests of another.

There was a similar reaction from men who had attended Walter's meetings. When Jesse told them her news and urged them to make some form of protest against his sentence, they did no more than mutter among themselves, carefully avoiding committing themselves to any particular course of action.

Bitterly, Jesse was forced to the conclusion that Sir Colman Vincent's victory was absolute. With Walter Dunn gone from the scene, the reform movement in Cornwall was dead.

Chapter Twenty-Five

To Walter Dunn, his conviction and sentence meant nothing. They were no more real than the surroundings in which he now found himself. He blotted out the words of the Judge, witnesses and court officials as effectively as he did the noises of his rowdy companions in the communal cell of Newgate prison.

It was ironic that Walter Dunn, champion of the rights of others, should be incarcerated in such a place as this. All his life he had bitterly attacked the power of landowners to control the lives of their tenants from birth to the grave. He fervently believed a man had a right to choose his own home, his work, and the wife he took. Now Walter was locked away in a prison, his mode of life dictated by the whim of justice and the mood of his gaolers.

It was the continuous din and the total absence of privacy that Walter found most difficult to bear in Newgate. The noise of crowds was not new to him, but at home he had been able to turn his back upon a reform meeting and walk for an hour or two along a Cornish cliff, with only the wind and the surf as companions.

In his imagination, Walter Dunn spent much of his time there now, looking out to a far horizon across the silver-grey sea he loved so much.

It was a scene he knew well. He had been able to tell the time of day to within minutes, merely by the way the light was reflected from the water beyond Mevagissey.

The sea had provided Walter Dunn with his living. It had also been his barometer, calendar and clock. *That* was Walter Dunn's real world and the place in which his mind sought refuge. Newgate prison was an unreal nightmare.

Walter spent much of his day clinging to the bars of a small window. Three feet away, a dirty grey wall rose higher than he could see, but he knew the sky was up there and he clung to his vantage-point tenaciously, the blows and curses of his fellow-prisoners failing to move him.

During the long months he was in Newgate, Walter Dunn slept little. There was no physical exertion to tire his body, and whenever he closed his eyes he was haunted by the sobs and pleadings of Michael Stephens, as the soldiers dragged him to the gallows from the cell they had shared. Walter would wake to find himself beating the straw-strewn floor with his manacled hands, screaming for them to spare his late companion.

Each week more and more convicted felons were placed in the heavily overcrowded cell. The days passed in constant squabbling and fighting. The area closest to the small barred window, with its relatively fresh air, became the most fought-over site in the cell.

Eventually, Walter Dunn was ousted by some of the more violent newcomers. Pushed to one of the darkest corners, he sat huddled against the wall, his chin sunk upon his chest. He fought only when he was crowded too much, or when food was brought to the cell. There was no comradeship here. Each man had to fight to stay alive.

When it seemed the cell could not possibly accommodate one more prisoner, the transportation agent and his men arrived. They were to convey the convicted men to a prison hulk moored on the River Thames at Woolwich. Here they would await transportation to the penal colonies of Australia.

The enclosed prison-vans were brought into the yard and backed up to the rear of the gaol. The convicts, shuffling clumsily in their irons, were herded into the vans, each man linked to his neighbour, front and rear.

Packed so tightly that they were unable to sit or lie, the convicts complained long and bitterly – yet to Walter it was the most wonderful day he had known for many months. He was jammed against the side of the van, and high above his head was a tiny opening through which he could see the sky.

He stared up at this tiny grey square of freedom for every inch of the bone-shaking journey through the streets of London Town and along narrow lanes beside the River Thames, until the vans drew to a halt by the side of the stink-

246

ing mudflats of Woolwich Reach.

It was raining hard now. As they were pulled from the vans the convicts slipped and fell about in the black mud, hampered by their heavy chains and cursing their escorts.

The tempers of guards and convicts were not improved by Walter Dunn. He dropped to his knees in the ooze, his mouth wide open to receive the rain that fell upon his upturned face. Holding his shackled hands high in supplication to the dark and stormy sky, Walter wept salt tears that mingled with the rain streaming down his sunken cheeks.

The initial reaction of the guards was to laugh and jeer at Walter, but as the rain continued to beat down on them their merriment turned to anger. When Walter ignored their orders to get to his feet and make his way to the waiting boat with the others, they kicked and pummelled him, then began to beat him with their long wooden staves.

Impervious to their blows, Walter was finally hoisted to his feet and dragged to the waiting boat by his fellow-prisoners.

The prison hulk to which they were taken had once been a proud seventy-four-gun ship-of-the-line, with an honourable record of service. At the Bay of Aboukir she had followed close in the wake of Nelson's *Vanguard*. Later, at the battle of the Nile, she had taken part in the destruction of Napoleon's fleet. Finally, at the battle of Trafalgar, scarred and dismasted, she had been towed clear of the carnage, her guns still spitting anger and defiance at the enemy.

There was little honour in the old warship's present role. With the broken remains of her masts sawn away and stout iron bars securing her gun-ports, she lay in Woolwich Reach, just clear of the foul mud that glistened black at low tide. The quarterdeck, once trodden by the heroes of England, now housed a blood-stained whipping frame where lesser men screamed their pain.

Below decks, the prison-holds were as dark as a Newgate cell – and equally as crowded. It was also indescribably filthy, the guards not daring to go below decks to supervise any cleaning activities.

This would be Walter Dunn's home for the first twelve months of his fourteen-year sentence.

While Walter Dunn was settling into the routine of his new surroundings, Jesse became increasingly depressed because she had received no reply to the letter sent to the captain of the Luscombe mine.

There had been no further news of Ben, and she knew the difficulties he would experience in trying to let her know where he was and what he was doing. Unable to read or write, Ben would have to entrust a message to anyone he met with who was coming to Mevagissey. Believing himself to be a wanted man, Ben could not afford to trust a complete stranger. Nevertheless, Jesse could not help feeling that Ben would have found *some* means of informing her of his whereabouts – had he wanted to.

Jesse was not aware of Ben's belief that, had Reuben Holy-oak lived, she would now be married to the estate manager. Reluctantly, she came to the conclusion that Ben no longer loved her.

There were many who were ready to persuade Jesse that this was so. The bal-maidens with whom she worked told her she was foolish to wait for Ben for so long. Jesse was now a very attractive girl of eighteen years. It was an age when most respectable young women were married and had begun a family.

She would have had no shortage of suitors. A new deep-water dock was under construction at Pentuan. It was planned to use it for the export of china-clay from the rapidly expanding clay industry about St Austell. Young men were flocking to the area from all parts of Cornwall.

For a few Cornishmen it was a prosperous time. Fishing had taken a sudden, albeit brief, upsurge. For years the numbers of the pilchards taken around the Cornish coast had been steadily declining, but this year they returned in huge shoals that ruffled the waters of every bay from Sennen to Rame. The fishermen were kept busy from dawn to dusk.

Mevagissey reeked with the tang of fish, the cobbles of its steep and narrow streets glistening with spilled pilchard oil.

If the Dunn brothers ever thought of Walter, it was only to grumble that he was not there to help them with the increased work.

The parliamentary reform movement missed him more. Meetings were still called when an important member from another part of the country visited Cornwall, but they attracted only a fraction of their previous support.

Many reasons could be found for the failing interest. Chief among them was the arrest of Walter Dunn. Shocked and angry at first, men fell silent when the news of his sentence became known, fearful lest the same fate befall them. There were few Cornishmen willing to risk arrest and transportation for a cause they hardly understood. Most believed Sir Colman Vincent had proved his invincibility beyond any doubt. They had no wish to have his wrath turned upon themselves.

At first, Jesse attended the reform meetings in a vain attempt to stir up support for Walter. A few men listened to her, but whenever she tried to address a full meeting she was quickly shouted down. The fishermen of Cornwall were not prepared to listen to a woman who upbraided them for not saving one of their own.

The lack of direction at the few meetings held in the district depressed and saddened Jesse. Eventually she stopped attending them.

Her failure to influence the men at the meetings was not due entirely to the fact that she was a woman. Many a disappointed man had also learned that it needed something more than words to move Cornishmen.

By the end of that year, disillusioned and unhappy, Jesse made up her mind to leave Pentuan and the Happy Union mine. She had gone there because she believed she might hear news of Ben. Now she was ready to admit that he had probably gone for ever. She decided to return to the work she knew and had enjoyed in the past. She would move inland and seek work on a farm. In these difficult days, many farmers preferred to employ women. Taxes were high, profits low, and farmers could not match the wages paid by the mines and clay works about them.

But when Jesse told Fanny Ustick of her decision, the

Happy Union captain's wife had a surprise of her own for Jesse.

God had smiled at the Usticks and their settled way of life. At the age of forty-two, Fanny Ustick had become pregnant. She and her huge good-natured husband were absolutely delighted. They accepted it as one of the Lord's miracles and spent much time on their knees, thanking Him for laying His hands upon them.

Now, to Jesse, Fanny Ustick confessed that she was desperately afraid of giving birth to a child. She begged Jesse to remain with her, at least until after the baby was born.

'Loveday and I want this baby so much, Jesse, but I am not a strong young girl to whom child-bearing comes as the most natural thing in the world. I am a staid old woman who should be past this sort of thing – and I am terrified of something going wrong.'

Then Fanny Ustick told Jesse of the reason for her fears.

'My mother died in childbirth when I was ten years old. I can remember lying in my bed crying while my mother screamed and fought for two days and nights to give birth to a child that wouldn't come. I don't believe the Lord will allow me to suffer in the same way, Jesse, but should things be difficult I would like you to be with me.'

Fanny and Loveday Ustick had been very kind to Jesse. After such a plea she could not possibly leave Pentuan until the baby was born.

The child was expected during the first days of June 1822, and Fanny Ustick struggled with an uncomfortable pregnancy through one of the worst winters in living memory. Wild storms raged from end to end of the county, lifting roofs and felling trees that had stood for centuries. For weeks snow blocked the narrow Cornish lanes, cutting off isolated farms and villages, and April arrived ushered in by yet another violent snowstorm. It seemed to the unhappy inhabitants of the county that they had lost the sun for ever.

The snow persisted for most of that month. Dark grey clouds hung low over the countryside from coast to coast and only the most determined of spring flowers showed themselves in the shelter of the hedge-bottoms.

One morning, Jesse and Judy Lean made their way to the stream-works through four inches of snow and all morning sorted ore with fingers stiff from the cold. Loveday Ustick had gone to the St Austell foundry to order some new equipment, and when the midday break came around Jesse decided to return to the Ustick house at Pentuan. She thought Fanny Ustick might need help to clear the snow from about the house. Judy Lean remained behind at the stream-works, her dependence upon Jesse much less now she knew the women with whom she worked.

When Jesse arrived at the house, she received no reply to her first call. She called again. This time she thought she heard a sound in the kitchen. Hurrying there, Jesse found Fanny Ustick seated in an old rocking-chair, clutching her distended stomach, her face the colour of the sky outside.

Shocked by Fanny Ustick's appearance, Jesse crouched down beside her, deeply concerned. 'What's happened, Fanny? What have you done?'

Fanny Ustick was about to reply when a fierce spasm of pain attacked her body. With her face contorted in agony, she fought against the pain for about half a minute. Then she expelled her breath noisily and sank back in the chair.

Slack-mouthed now, Fanny Ustick looked up at Jesse and gasped helplessly. 'I slipped in the snow this morning. I have hurt myself somehow. I think the baby is on its way. Help me, Jesse.'

Jesse had a brief moment of panic, but it passed quickly. She had never before been present at the birth of a child, but she had brought a great many calves and lambs into the world. A baby could not be so very different. Even one that was arriving six weeks before its time.

'We must get you upstairs to your bed. I'll make you comfortable then fetch the mine doctor—'

'You'll do no such thing!' Fanny Ustick spoke through gritted teeth as she struggled to her feet with Jesse's help. 'I'll not have that drunken atheist in my house. I'll go to bed now you are here, but stay with me, Jesse. Please . . .!'

Halfway up the steep and narrow staircase, another spasm caught Fanny Ustick. She was forced to rest on a stair, gasping with pain and clutching her stomach. Jesse realised the baby was well on its way. Coming so much before its time, she wished she were able to call on someone to help her. But there were no other houses within hailing distance, and little likelihood of help until Loveday Ustick or Judy returned to the house. The bal-maidens at the stream-works would miss her, of course, but Judy would tell them she had returned to the house. They would merely assume she had taken the afternoon off work. By the time anyone came to the house it might already be too late . . .

Seated on the dark staircase, Jesse shook off her morbid thoughts. Helping Fanny Ustick to her feet, she half carried her into the bedroom. There she helped Fanny to undress and got her into bed.

The birth of the baby was much closer than Jesse would have wished. Fanny Ustick's muscles were already contracting involuntarily in a powerful bid to expel the child from her body. Fanny Ustick's fear had been that she would suffer a painful labour for days. There was no likelihood of that happening now. Whether the baby would be born alive was another matter.

For the next two hours, Jesse's main problem was preventing Fanny Ustick from throwing herself out of bed as she threshed about wildly, driven on by the ever-increasing labour pains. Jesse had hoped to make hasty preparations for the baby's arrival, but, in constant pain, the older woman would not allow her to leave the bedside.

The child was born as the dark clouds outside lowered over the surrounding hills, hastening the night. The actual birth was over so quickly that Jesse had no time to worry about doing the right things.

At one moment, all that could be seen was the dark damp hair on the crown of the baby's head. The next, it was lying full length in her hands – and very much alive.

With its eyes screwed tight shut, the baby's tiny fists and feet jerkily attacked the stormy world into which it had been so precipitously flung. As Jesse used a finger to clear the baby's mouth, it fought her. Then, sobbing breath into tiny untried lungs, it uttered its first, uncertain cry.

The effect of the sound upon Fanny Ustick was remarkable. The pain of her ordeal immediately forgotten, she struggled to sit up.

Jesse tried to hold her back. 'Lie still, Fanny. There are things to be done yet. The baby is fine.'

'What is it, Jesse? Have I given Loveday a son or a daughter?'

'You have a son, Fanny. A healthy noisy little boy.'

Fanny Ustick sank back on her pillow. Bringing her hands together, she whispered hoarsely, 'Praise be to God! The gift of a son. That is what I will call him, Jesse. Nathaniel . . . the gift of God.'

Jesse felt a great elation. She had successfully brought Fanny Ustick's baby into the world. Cutting the umbilical cord, she tied it off and bound the baby's stomach. Then, with the afterbirth chores completed, Jesse wrapped the tiny wrinkle faced Nathaniel Ustick in his swaddling-clothes and placed him in the eager arms of his mother.

She was tidying the bedroom when she heard the front door open, and the voices of Loveday Ustick and Judy Lean came to her. Alarmed by the absence of lights downstairs in the house, Loveday Ustick's deep voice boomed through the house as he called to ask where everyone was hiding.

'We're up here, Loveday,' Jesse called. 'Come on up.'

'Is everything all right, Jesse? Judy told me you didn't return to the mine after the midday break.'

The boards creaked noisily as the heavyweight mine captain stumbled clumsily up the stairs in the darkness.

Jesse swung open the bedroom door. Blinking in the light of the lamp, Loveday Ustick saw Fanny lying in the bed. Such was his immediate concern for his pale and exhausted wife that he saw nothing else. Suddenly, hidden by the bed-clothes, the baby stirred and uttered a thin complaining cry of protest.

Loveday Ustick's mouth dropped open in disbelief and he took a quick step to the bedside. Fanny pushed back the blankets and exposed the blotchy red face of their hour-old infant.

Looking down upon his son for the first time, Loveday

Ustick's face crumpled. Falling to his knees, he took his wife's hand without once shifting his gaze from the baby. There was such wonder and love in his expression that a great lump rose in Jesse's throat.

Judy Lean had come to the top of the stairs to look silently into the room. Turning her about, Jesse led her down the stairs, leaving the happy couple to enjoy these first shared moments with their newborn son.

Chapter Twenty-Six

Jesse remained at the Ustick house for two weeks after the birth of Fanny's son. The mine captain and his wife urged her to stay longer but, with their family now so blissfully complete, Jesse felt herself more of an interloper in their home than ever.

After a period of uncertainty, Judy Lean decided to accompany Jesse. It was a difficult decision for her to make. She adored Fanny's baby and glowed with happiness whenever she was allowed to help with him. Nevertheless, she felt a fierce loyalty towards Jesse and would not allow her to go from Pentuan alone.

Jesse knew her decision to leave was the right one. Apart from the lack of meaning in her present way of life, Jesse could foresee additional problems coming her way by remaining at the Happy Union stream-workings. Reuben Holyoak had paid two surprise visits to the mine in recent weeks. On both occasions he had carried messages from Sir Colman Vincent to Loveday Ustick. The information contained in them was unimportant; it might have been sent with one of the servants from Lamorrack House.

The messages were merely excuses for Reuben Holyoak to come to the mine, and on both occasions he sought out Jesse. She did not wish to speak to him, and his presence reduced Judy Lean to a quivering wreck, unable either to work or speak. It was apparent to Jesse that Reuben Holyoak had been drinking before both his visits. It was rumoured that just lately Sir Colman Vincent's estate manager was drunk for more hours than he was sober. Jesse had no wish to fall foul of the amorous drunkard.

All the same, Jesse could not dismiss the feeling that by quitting the area she was breaking faith with Ben. She told herself many times that he had been away for two years without sending her a single message. She could not waste her whole life cherishing a dream that Ben Retallick had long abandoned. But still the feeling remained.

Jesse had no fixed plans. She intended striking inland and seeking work on a farm, that was all. Her one big regret was in leaving the sea behind. It was something she would miss. The sea had been no more than a glance away for as long as she could remember.

It was for this reason that on the day before she left Jesse took a long walk along the cliff-top. She went beyond Mevagissey, to a spot where she had spent many hours as a child. On the narrow fern-covered promontory known as Chapel Point she sat down to think.

Jesse stayed there for a long time. When she stood up to return to Pentuan, she saw a large ship under full sail heading westward, about a mile from the shore. As she watched, it suddenly heeled over and turned about in a wide arc, to lie wallowing in the swell of the English Channel, its sails flapping in a most unseamanlike display. There was much unusual activity on the white, holy stoned deck, but minutes later the vessel got slowly under way once more and returned to its original course.

Jesse watched until the ship had passed from view beyond the next headland. Then she turned her back upon the sea and slowly made her way homewards.

On board the prison-hulk moored off Woolwich, each day began at five-thirty in the morning. At this hour the convicts were awakened and their dead carried on deck, to be buried in shallow graves in the foul mud of the Thames, as the tide permitted.

At five forty-five, the convicts had their breakfast. Afterwards, it was usual for them to be taken ashore to work on the new docks being built at Woolwich. Unfortunately, no cut stone had been available for many weeks and the convicts remained locked in the holds of the hulk all day.

Life on board the rotting hulk was cruel, degrading, and primitive in the extreme. Many of the convicts were the dregs of human society. With nothing to do to occupy their time, they plotted ridiculously impractical escapes, quarrelled among themselves and bullied those too weak to retaliate. The younger criminals, many of them no more than children, cried themselves to sleep every night and longed for the new land and the promise it held out to them of a better life.

Walter Dunn suffered much at the hands of his fellow-convicts because he was mentally less alert than the others. But after the first few harsh weeks their cruelty became sporadic. There was little pleasure to be gained from tormenting a man to whom all indignities meant nothing.

Walter did all that was necessary to stay alive, but life meant little now. Outwardly he lived. Inside he was already dead. Hate, fear, love, anger – they were all feelings that no longer existed for him. Walter Dunn the man had died when they cut him off from sea and sky. Only Walter Dunn the convict remained.

For a while, hopes were raised on the hulk when rumours began to circulate that a transport was now available to convey the long-term prisoners to Van Diemen's Land, in Australia. It mattered little to the convicts that few of them would ever return. The thought of leaving the stinking overcrowded hulk for the comparative freedom of colonial life filled every man with excitement. Many of them, like Walter Dunn, had already spent a year on board the hulk.

For days, one unsubstantiated rumour followed close on the heels of another. Hopes fluctuated first high and then low in the convict-filled holds. Arguments and fist-fights broke out as men's tempers became frayed with the strain of uncertainty.

The days of eager waiting became weeks, and gradually hope died. Then came the morning when the hatches were not opened at the usual time. Breakfast-time, too, came and went without any movement from above decks. Beating upon the stout wooden planks of their holds, the convicts protested in vain. For an hour it was bedlam below decks. Then, with a crash of complaining timbers, a ship came alongside the hulk, the force of the impact sending convicts sprawling into the dark corners of the prison-holds.

The transport-ship had arrived.

The howls of complaint turned to cheers and hysterical relief. The convicts congratulated each other on surviving the harsh rigours of imprisonment on a convict-hulk. Many had been less fortunate. One in three of the convicts sentenced to terms of transportation were dead before the transports arrived to carry them to the colonies.

A few of the younger men who were leaving families behind them in England wept for the children they would never see again. But they, too, were grateful that their lease on life had been renewed.

They had to wait until after noon before the hatch-covers were removed; then they were herded, two by two, into the harsh light of day.

Under the watchful eyes of heavily armed guards, names were checked and double-checked. Lists were signed and countersigned, and finally passed from the superintendent of the hulk to the mate of the transport *Perseus*. Finally, fetters and chains were carefully inspected and the convicts taken to the Australia-bound ship.

Once on board *Perseus*, half a dozen convicts were segregated from their fellows. Taken to one side, they had the heavy iron chains struck from wrists and ankles. Walter Dunn was one of them.

A boatswain, as gruff and ruffianly in appearance as any convict, explained why they had been singled out for such unexpected treatment.

'The *Perseus* is short of seamen. Good sailors don't want to take a cargo of stinking convicts halfway around the world. They can get better berths, these days. We have to make do with second-best. Even so, we're hard put to make up a full crew. This trip has started worst than most. Half the crew deserted the moment we returned from our last voyage and we've been delayed in London for a week trying to make up a crew. We are still short-handed, so you are going to be put to work. Every one of you has been chosen because he is a seaman, and because your records show you haven't been convicted of violent crimes. Behave yourself on board *Perseus* and you'll enjoy a more comfortable voyage than any one of you has a right to expect. Put a foot wrong and you'll be thrown back into the hold to rot with the others. Do you all understand me ?'

The boatswain glared fiercely from man to man. Each newly unfettered convict – with the exception of Walter Dunn – nodded emphatically, eager to please. Walter, rubbing his chafed and emaciated wrists, was gazing up at the sun as though it were the most beautiful object he had ever seen.

The boatswain of *Perseus* took an angry pace forward and jabbed Walter Dunn in the ribs with a calloused finger. 'You! Did you hear what I said ?'

Reluctantly, Walter Dunn pulled his gaze away from the bright sun and gave the boatswain a bewildered look.

'He's a bit simple, sir,' explained one of the convicts to the glowering boatswain. 'But he's a good worker and I've never seen him lose his temper. Not even when he's set upon by the others . . .'

For a long fear-filled moment the convict wished he had remained silent as the boatswain switched his scowl to him. 'For your sake, you'd better be right. Keep him working or I'll have you *both* back in the hold.'

The boatswain rubbed his dark stubbled chin and came close to a smile.

'He's not so very different from the rest of the crew on this flat-bottomed scow; they're most of 'em idiots. I must be one myself, or I'd be off earning good wages on a sweet-smelling slaver instead of putting up with the stench of this pig-boat.'

After delivering this parting comment, the boatswain turned his back on the six seamen convicts. They were led away by an armed guard and locked in a cabin until the ship slipped away from the prison-hulk on the late-evening tide.

The next couple of days were happy ones for Walter Dunn. He clambered among the rigging, scrubbed decks and cheerfully carried out every chore he was given, rejoicing in the feel of rain and sunshine on his skin.

On the third day, the ship was sailing close to the coast. Her captain wanted to make a call at the busy Cornish port of

259

Falmouth. Here the ship would take on a final supply of fresh provisions and load mail for the penal colonies of Australia.

The holds, packed with their human cargo, were not yet throwing out the stench that caused strong-stomached sailors to sail well to windward of ships on the transportation run. The captain of *Perseus* set his seamen to scrubbing decks and generally smartening up the ship. Falmouth was his home port and he had no intention of spending the remainder of his career in command of a convict transport. He meant to prove to the ship-owners that he could keep *Perseus* clean and tidy. Any man who could do that with a transport-ship deserved a chance to command one of the fast new packets operating out of the port.

Below decks, Walter Dunn and the other convict seamen were splicing ropes and stitching spare sails. Suddenly, the boatswain's bellowed order sent them clambering to the rigging to furl sail for the run-in to Falmouth harbour.

Walter Dunn obeyed the order eagerly. High in the rigging, with the sea and sky all about him, he felt quite alone in the world. He hurried up the ladder to the deck, smiling as the sunshine touched his face. Breathing in the salt air, he shinned up the rigging of the mainmast and edged his way skilfully out along a yardarm.

Not until then did he take a look about him.

The scene that met his eyes gave him such a tremendous shock that it drove the self-protecting mists from his mind. In an instant it was as though the long months of imprisonment had never happened.

Walter Dunn was looking across a mile of water to where the village of Mevagissey nestled in a fold of the hills, just beyond Chapel Point. It was a scene he had looked upon so many times before. It had been there whenever he raised his head from his nets, or rested on an oar and glanced over his shoulder. It was home.

As he looked spellbound at the unexpected miracle in front of him, the boatswain bellowed to another member of the crew on the bows of the ship – and the spell was broken.

Walter Dunn remembered he was no longer a free fisherman. He was in the rigging of a convict ship heading for a rigorous exile twelve thousand miles away.

The coxswain, at the wheel of *Perseus*, saw Walter Dunn's curving dive into the sea from the rigging. Shouting a warning to the other seamen up aloft, he spun the wheel and put the cumbersome craft into a wide slow turn.

By the time *Perseus* came about and stopped with all sails flapping, there was half a mile of choppy water between the rolling ship and the spot where Walter Dunn had plunged into the sea, and none of the seamen crowding the side of the ship could see him.

As the ship wallowed uncomfortably in the Channel swell, the captain hurried on deck from his cabin. When he was told what had happened, the captain angrily berated the mate who had chosen Walter Dunn to help out with the duties of a seaman. Then, with the Gwineas rocks only a few hundred yards distant, the captain ordered the coxswain to turn the ship to catch the wind and resume course for Falmouth.

'But what about the convict? We can't allow him to escape. Shouldn't we put away a boat and search for him?'

'Escape, you say?' The captain looked at his mate scornfully. 'Look again at that sea, mister. It's a full mile to the shore. The tide is on the ebb and there are strong currents around those rocks inshore. I know of no man who could make such a swim. Enter him in the log as "lost at sea", then forget all about him. A dead convict need be of no concern to anyone.'

Six days after *Perseus* sailed into Falmouth harbour, two men were walking on lonely Porthluney Beach, not three miles from Mevagissey, when they saw a body floating face downwards in the surf at the edge of the sand. Wading into the water they pulled the body ashore and searched through its clothing in search of something of value. There was nothing.

One of the men was in favour of leaving the body where it lay, but his companion's Christian compassion prevailed. Borrowing two spades from the gatekeeper at the nearby Caerhayes estate, they buried the unidentified body in a shallow grave in the sand of the foreshore.

Neither man recognised the strange garb worn by the dead man as a convict's uniform. Nor did they recognise Walter Dunn, although both men had regularly attended his reform meetings in the past. The year in the convict-hulk had left his face sunken and lined, aging Walter beyond his years.

The anonymous and unmarked grave on the foreshore was one Walter might well have chosen for himself. All about him the waters he had fished for so many years whispered through the sand to him and renewed the seaweed garlands on his grave each day. For his headstone, he had a tall Cornish cliff, carved by God himself.

Walter Dunn had come home to Cornwall, and he was at peace.

Chapter Twenty-Seven

Ben returned to Mevagissey on 8 May 1822. He arrived during the afternoon of one of the busiest days the fishing-village had known for many years. A huge and unseasonable shoal of pilchards had been sighted in the bay that morning and every boat that would float had put out to net them. The fish were brought ashore in tens of thousands and the fisherwomen worked non-stop in the fish-cellars, salting and stacking the fish and making preparations to extract the valuable oil.

As Ben came down the hill towards the village he saw hundreds of gulls, wheeling and shrieking noisily above the teeming harbour.

Martha Retallick was at work in the Dunn fish-cellar with the wives of Billy and Mark, and a number of other women. They and numerous children were all elbow deep in pilchards. Martha Retallick was chattering and laughing as she worked, as excited as anyone at the good fortune that had come to Mevagissey.

Ben stood in the wide doorway of the fish-cellar for some minutes, and every fisherwoman there saw him before his mother. It was their sudden silence that finally made her look up and seek its cause.

The smile froze on her face when she saw Ben. For long unbelieving moments she looked at him as though she were seeing a ghost. He had been gone for two years, and many times she had doubted if she would ever see him again. Now he was standing here before her.

Of a sudden, she swayed towards the woman standing beside her. Thinking Martha Retallick was about to faint, the other woman reached out a hand to support her.

As suddenly as it had left, the blood rushed back to Martha Retallick's face and she ran across the room to Ben's arms and burst into tears. For many minutes she could only sob uncontrollably in a show of emotion such as Ben had never before seen from her, not even at the time of his father's death. He held her tightly to him while the other women looked on sympathetically.

When Martha Retallick had regained some of her composure, Ben led her away from the fish-cellar to Grandma Dunn's house. Along the way she apologised for the way in which she was behaving.

'It was looking up and seeing you just standing there watching me, Ben. I never had time to prepare myself.'

She began crying softly again, and Ben's arm tightened about her shoulders. Outside the door of Grandma Dunn's house, Martha Retallick paused. Taking out a handkerchief, she blew her nose noisily.

Giving Ben a watery smile, she said, 'I'm weeping like a foolish young girl . . . but you have only yourself to blame. You went from here believing you'd killed Reuben Holyoak, and I thought you must have fled the country. Until that preacher friend of yours came calling, I never expected to see you again. You should have let me know what you were doing . . .'

Ben's surprise at her admonition was genuine. 'I sent as much news as I dared . . . with two men. The first was a miner who left the Tamar valley for Pentuan. The other was a sea-faring man on his way from Plymouth to join a ship at Falmouth. I gave him half a week's pay to call here. I told him if he couldn't find you he should call at Pengrugla. I felt sure Jesse would pass on a message – whatever her situation.'

Ben hesitated, reluctant to ask the question that was burning a hole in his tongue. He searched for words that would not betray his eagerness. 'Is Jesse . . . is she keeping well?'

'She was well enough when I last saw her. But if your message was left at Pengrugla it's not surprising it never reached me. There's no one there with any time for the Retallicks – or for any one else but Reuben Holyoak himself.'

'Jesse didn't marry Reuben Holyoak?'

An overwhelming sense of relief flooded over Ben. He had tried not to build up any hopes after receiving Wrightwick Roberts's news. Now he felt ridiculously happy.

'Marry Reuben Holyoak?' Martha Retallick snorted her

ridicule. 'Jesse wouldn't marry him if he were the last man left alive in England. No, Reuben Holyoak was as responsible as anyone for the death of her mother . . .'

She saw that Ben knew nothing of Maude Henna's death. 'You'd better come inside, Ben. There is a whole lot of news you should be given – and by the look of you a good meal inside your belly won't come amiss.'

Inside the house, Ben had to submit to the combined fussing of his mother and Grandma Dunn, while his grandfather fired questions at him whenever the two women paused to draw breath.

Not until he was sitting down at the kitchen table with a heaped plate in front of him could Ben satisfy his own thirst for knowledge.

'What did Jesse say when you gave her Wrightwick's news – that I was alive and well, and in Cornwall?'

This was the question Martha Retallick had known would come – and for which she had no answer. She had seen little of Jesse in recent months. The Dunn family resented Jesse's interference in the matter of Walter's arrest and trial. They would not be convinced that Jesse had done anything but harm in asking Eulaliah Vincent for assistance. Consequently, Jesse had been made less than welcome whenever she called at the house to see Martha Retallick. It was hardly surprising that Jesse soon stopped coming. Martha Retallick *had* intended going to Pentuan to see the girl, but she had not.

'Jesse doesn't know.'

Ben looked at his mother sharply and waited for her to explain. He would have expected her to be eager to pass on the good news to Jesse.

It was Grandma Dunn who made any explanation unnecessary.

'I don't want to hear that girl's name in this house, thank you! The Dunn family has little to thank her for, and our Walter in particular. He might be here now but for her interference. After all he did for her when she was living under this roof, too . . .'

'Where is Jesse now?' Ben interrupted Grandma Dunn's tirade.

'I don't know,' Martha Retallick admitted unhappily. 'When I last met her she was talking of leaving.'

Ben lowered his knife to the plate slowly. 'Leaving? Where would she go? What did she intend doing?'

'She spoke of finding work on a farm. After you left she went to work at the Happy Union stream-works, thinking to hear news of you there. But none ever came. I think she has given up hope of finding you. She waited long enough for you, Ben, I can vouch for that. It wasn't for the want of suitors, either. Our Walter wanted to marry her, for one.'

'Huh! A lot of good it did him,' snorted Grandma Dunn.

Ben ignored her. There were so many things he needed to know. Most would have to wait for now.

'Where has Jesse been living?'

'At Pentuan, with Captain Ustick and his wife. I doubt if she's still there, Ben.'

'I will need to find out before I do, or hear, any more.'

Ben pushed back his chair and stood up from the table.

'But you have only just arrived home. We have so much to talk about . . .'

Ben had a moment of conscience when he saw his mother's distress, but if he stayed here listening to Grandma Dunn's remarks there would be an argument to upset her even more.

'I won't settle until I learn something of Jesse. I'll be back later this evening. We'll talk then.'

When Ben arrived at the Usticks' home he was let into the house by Fanny Ustick. The big mine captain, newly home from the stream-workings, sat in a chair by the kitchen fire, baby Nathaniel cradled in his massive arms. This was a much gentler Loveday Ustick than Ben remembered. Marriage and the birth of his child had mellowed him.

His first words when he saw Ben were: 'You've grown some, boy. You only need a paunch and you'll pass for Loveday Ustick on a dark night.'

It was a blatant exaggeration, but it was the big mine captain's way of acknowledging that Ben had become a man. The good humour of Fanny and Loveday Ustick quickly changed to distress when they learned that Ben had come looking for Jesse. Fanny in particular was most upset.

266

'Seeing you're here so soon after she left us, I felt sure you were coming with good news. She waited so long for you Ben. She questioned every miner who passed through the Happy Union, in the hope that they might have met with you. Once she met a man who had seen you at the Luscombe mine. I wrote to the captain asking after you, and for weeks Jesse waited for a reply, but we heard nothing.'

'The captain of the Luscombe mine was killed along with five of his men only three months after I left. The boiler burst at the change of shift. The mine was closed down shortly afterwards.'

'We didn't know that.' Fanny Ustick made a helpless gesture with her hands. 'Oh, Ben! If only you had returned three days earlier.'

'There are many things I *should* have done,' said Ben bitterly. 'But I'm not going to spend the rest of my life regretting what *might* have been. I intend finding Jesse as quickly as I can and marrying her. Do you know where she might have gone?'

'No – only that she and Judy were taking the Truro road . . .' Fanny Ustick explained about Judy Lean.

'I'll head for Truro at sunrise,' declared Ben. 'I need to make up for two wasted years – if Jesse will have me.'

Fanny Ustick looked at the determined young man standing before her.

'She'll have you, Ben Retallick. Of that I am quite sure.'

'Bring Jesse back here when you catch up with her, Ben,' said Loveday Ustick. 'Without her I doubt whether my son would be alive to bring me such pleasure today. There is a home for both of you here – and work at the Happy Union should you have need of it.'

Loveday Ustick reached out his hand, trying not to disturb the contented baby sleeping in his arms. 'We wish you luck, Ben. Our prayers go with you.'

Ben left the house warmed by the sincerity of the Usticks and envious of the happiness they had found together.

That night, Ben and his mother sat up until very late, doing their best to fill in the details of the two-year gap in their lives.

Despite his late night, Ben left the house when dawn was

no more than a faint glimmer in the east. He had little idea of where he was going, but he headed for Truro because that was the way Jesse had gone.

The sun rose slowly, reluctant to throw off the pale-grey mist that spread inland from the sea, but once it had broken through it held out the promise of a fine warm day.

Ben trudged along high-banked lanes, occasionally stumbling over a hard-baked ridge of earth that only a few weeks before had been buried beneath inches of snow. When he reached the top of a long hill, Ben paused to look about him and ponder on the task he had set himself. Cornwall was a vast patchwork of tiny farms, many of them tucked away in hollows and valleys, unseen from the road. Jesse might have found work on any one of them.

The narrow twisting lane joined the turnpike road to Truro two miles farther on. Ben had intended resting here for a while, but he found, much to his annoyance, that a young man was already there, seated on the rough-hewn granite milestone.

As Ben approached, the young man turned his face towards him and reached down for a fiddle that leaned against the milestone. Tucking the instrument beneath his chin, he drew from it the first bars of a jig, then paused to call to Ben.

'A tune for you, young sir? One to set your feet dancing along the King's highway?'

Ben was feeling hot and irritable, annoyed that this itinerant fiddler had deprived him of the rest he had been anticipating for the last couple of miles. He made no reply.

Before Ben had taken many more paces, the fiddler struck up a solemn dirge and called after him, 'Since the sun and a merry tune have failed to cheer you, I offer a tune to match your thoughts. It will make the miles seem longer, but for a man who wallows in his own misery the road is already overly long. Give me twopence, my fine young friend, and I will sing you words to match my music.'

Scowling, Ben would have gone on his way without speaking had he not noticed the ashes of a fire set back against the hedgerow. Around it were scattered the balladeer's belongings.

Ben stopped and called, 'Are you often at this spot?'

'Often? No, young sir. I have never been here before. However, I arrived here a week ago and have not left since then. Is that the answer you seek?'

'Then you'll have seen everyone who passed this way during that week?' Ben put the question eagerly.

'Alas, no!' the balladeer smiled sadly, 'I have seen nothing since Napoleon's case-shot took my sight at Waterloo. However, my ears have learned to work doubly hard. They tell me now that you are anxiously seeking someone. From the manner of your asking, it can only be a lady. Your wife, perhaps?'

'No . . . but she will be as soon as I find her. We've been parted for a very long time. I returned yesterday only to learn that she had left three days ago.'

'Three days since was fair-day at Grampound. Many young girls passed this way. Some stopped to listen to a tune . . . a few did not. Would she have been travelling alone?'

'No, she has another girl with her.'

'Ah! Then things are not as hopeless as they at first seemed. Many young girls passed by, riding on farm-wagons, or walking in large groups chiding the young men who walked close on their heels. But only two pairs of women came by that day. The first were early and heavily laden. Farm-women, carrying produce to market. Then, when the sun stood where it is now, two young girls came along. By their step I would put their ages at twenty years, or perhaps a year younger. I remember them well because their walks were so dissimilar. One girl was light on her feet, alert to everything about her. The other was slow of thought and of movement . . . but a kindly girl, for all that. It was she who placed a penny in my hand and thanked me for the tune I played her. Yes, she was a kind girl with a pleasant voice . . . and one who has known much unhappiness, unless I am mistaken.'

The balladeer's description exactly fitted that given Ben of Judy Lean.

'Did they say where they were going? Anything at all that might help me to find them?'

'Nothing at all, young sir – but will you set aside your

269

quest for a few minutes and gather enough twigs for a fire to boil a kettle ? I believe I still have a pinch of tea in my bundle.'

'I can do better than that. I have a pie, and some good French brandy to wash it down.'

'God bless you, young sir! You offer me a feast. Accept the hand of Alan Colborne in friendship. You have a name ?'

The introductions over, the two men settled down to eat. Alan Colborne ate ravenously. It was evident that balladeering in Cornwall had not kept him well fed.

When they had consumed more than half of the food Martha Retallick had confidently expected to last her son for three days, Alan Colborne leaned back against the grassy roadside bank and savoured the night-traded brandy. It had been a present to Ben from Grandfather Dunn. The balladeer sighed in deep contentment.

'It was a happy chance that brought you my way today, Ben. Tell me, why are you out scouring the countryside for your lady love instead of wedding her in some cool and peaceful village church ?'

Warming to the brandy and Alan Colborne's easy companionship, Ben gave the balladeer an outline of the events of the past two years.

By the time he had finished talking he had Alan Colborne's rapt attention, the brandy temporarily forgotten on the ground between them.

'Upon my life, Ben! From such tales as this were the songs of the minstrels of old composed. If I don't make a song of it myself, I do not deserve to call myself a balladeer. But such a quest as yours is not going to be easy.'

Ben's shrug was wasted on the blind man. 'Perhaps not, but by asking at farms and in villages I'll find Jesse one day.'

'You need help, my friend – and you have it! I'll come with you. Between us we will find her. You have my word.'

Ben was not certain he wanted Alan Colborne's company. Guiding a blind man through the narrow lanes of the county would inevitably slow him down. He saw no way in which Alan Colborne could help the search for Jesse.

Alan Colborne spoke as though Ben had voiced his thoughts aloud.

'You doubt my ability to help, Ben? Then listen to me carefully. When did you last see Jesse? Two years ago? Is your memory of her so clear that you could instantly recognise her in the middle of a crowd? No, of course it's not – but mine is! She called out a "Good day!" to me and I heard her speaking in conversation with her friend. I could distinguish her voice from the babble of a hundred others. Then there is her companion – Judy, I believe you said was her name. You would not know her if she stood before you. I certainly would. I know her voice, her walk – even the sweet smell of her hair. I would recognise her if she passed by on the darkest night.'

Alan Colborne paused to take a sip of brandy. 'Such means of recognition may be essential, Ben. Farmers are not doing well at the moment; they will delay taking on workers for as long as possible – until grass-cutting time, perhaps. Your Jesse must attend hiring-fairs, trusting her looks and manners will raise her above the others who seek work. The hiring-fairs are packed with young men and girls, but it is there we must look for her, Ben. Be it Grampound, Truro, Wadebridge – or any one of a dozen other fairs.'

Ben looked at Alan Colborne with a new respect. 'Can you really pick out a single voice from the din of a crowd?'

'That, and much more beside. For instance, I can tell you that approaching us from the direction of St Austell is a gentleman's light carriage.' Alan Colborne paused briefly. 'What's more, it is being pulled by a pair of well-matched horses.'

Ben listened, but could hear nothing. Not until the light open carriage rounded a bend half a minute later did the sounds from it reach Ben's own ears. As Alan Colborne had stated, it was pulled by two high-stepping horses.

'I'll be pleased to have your company, Alan Colborne – if you are quite certain you have nothing else to do.'

The balladeer smiled ruefully. 'I have sat upon this milestone growing ever thinner for a full week, and my enquiring fingers have told me we are but nine miles from Truro Town. On the way we pass through Probus, where there is a small fair today. There I will have the opportunity to earn a shilling or two and return your generosity, while you search for Jesse.'

Feeling about him on the ground, Alan Colborne located his scattered belongings and began tying them in a bundle, talking all the while.

'We must waste no time, Ben. If we step out, we can reach Probus in time for the evening's frolics. Tomorrow we will see the fair out and move on to St Columb and Wadebridge and a few other villages, returning to Truro for the big fair in two weeks' time. I have friends in all those places. We *will* find Jesse, Ben. Be assured of that.'

Already, Ben felt better for having met up with the blind balladeer. Finding Jesse would be only a matter of days – perhaps only hours!

By the time the two men reached Probus the serious business of the fair was over. A few men and girls who had been unsuccessful in hiring themselves out still wandered disconsolately about the fair, but Jesse and Judy Lean were not among their number. After asking a few questions, it was clear they had never been there.

Alan Colborne told Ben he must not be disappointed at this first failure. This was one of the smallest fairs in the county, not known to many outside the immediate area.

But, if trading and hiring had ended for the day, the fun was only just beginning. More than a hundred young people were gathered to enjoy such diverse entertainments as juggling, badger-baiting and Cornish wrestling.

Alan Colborne asked Ben to lead him to a quiet spot where he had an open space for a crowd to gather. When Ben found a suitable place, Alan Colborne leaned against a wall, drew the bow across the strings of his fiddle and began to play and sing a tuneful ballad. He had a clear melodic voice, and it was not long before he had wooed many people from the other attractions. When he ended his song, the crowd applauded loudly and called for more.

As coins were flung on the kerchief spread on the ground before Alan Colborne, Ben left him to his work. His audience would not allow him to move from the spot for an hour or two.

272

Ben wandered about the village for a while. Outside of the fair there was little to interest him. When he saw an ale-house he went inside for a drink.

Before the drink arrived, a frightening din broke out above Ben's head. The ceiling trembled and shook, and clouds of dust drifted down among the customers of the ale-house. Placing a tankard of ale in front of Ben, the landlord smiled at his apprehension. 'Don't you worry, sir. It's only some of they ranters at a meeting upstairs. They don't approve of the goings-on in Probus on fair-day. They're up there telling the Lord of their disapproval.'

The 'ranters' – also known as 'Bryanites' – to whom the landlord had referred, were a Methodist sect which had recently excited some interest by using young women as preachers. Led by a local man, the 'ranters' were notoriously noisy in their particular form of worship.

They were certainly in good voice this night. Their shouts of 'Hallelujah!' and the stamping of their feet made conversation in the ale-house impossible. Before long the dust from the trembling beams and joists formed a choking cloud in the tap-room.

Ben found the noise and the dust intolerable and carried his drink to one of the benches outside the inn door. It was fortunate that most of the other drinkers had already done the same. Ben had just set down his tankard when there was a sudden alarming splintering of timbers. With a mighty crash, the floor of the upstairs room collapsed into the tap-room. The joyous shouts of the 'ranters' quickly changed to screams of terror as they were pitched down through the floor together with tumbling beams, floorboards and fellow-worshippers.

The din attracted a great many revellers from the fair. As each 'ranter' staggered through the doorway, blue serge suit or best Sunday dress torn and covered in dust and plaster, he or she was greeted with ribald howls of derision.

Above the hilarity of the crowd, Ben could hear cries of pain coming from within the collapsed interior of the ale-house. Calling on a couple of men to follow him, he went back inside. On his way he pushed aside a screaming woman and an equally hysterical man blocking the doorway.

The late-evening light was barely strong enough to penetrate the choking dust inside the building, but it was sufficient for Ben to appreciate the extent of the devastation. Wooden joists had snapped off where they slotted into the damp west wall of the ale-house. Half the floor had fallen into the taproom; the remainder was hanging down at a crazy angle.

The cries Ben had heard came from a tangle of wood and masonry at the back of the room, and he and his helpers made their way there. A number of men and women were trapped beneath a pile of rubble. As they were dug out each of them was able to stagger to the door. Only one man was seriously hurt; he had suffered a badly broken arm. It hung painfully by his side as Ben helped him out to the street and sat him down on one of the benches.

The crowd of onlookers, disappointed that no one had been killed, or noticeably mangled, soon drifted back to the amusements of the fair. Ben ripped the shirt from the arm of the man who had been the last to be rescued. The break was serious, with white bone protruding through the skin. There was nothing Ben could do to help the man. He needed the attentions of a surgeon. When Ben called for one he was told that a surgeon would have to be brought from Truro.

Ben had seen a great many mine accidents. He was in no doubt that the arm would have to be amputated above the elbow. After expressing his thoughts to the landlord, he suggested that the injured man be kept liberally supplied with strong brandy.

When Ben turned away to go to where he had left Alan Colborne, the injured man called after him. 'Ben! . . . It is Ben Retallick?'

'Yes.' Ben peered at the man's dust-stained face. It was vaguely familiar, but recognition was slow in coming to him. 'You know me?'

'We worked together more than a year since. At the Luscombe mine. My name is Matthew Bolitho.'

This was the man who had worked at the Happy Union mine briefly and had given Jesse the news that Ben had not left the country. Loveday Ustick had told Ben the miner's name.

Ben returned to Matthew Bolitho and clasped his good hand warmly, looking down at him with renewed sympathy. 'I'm sorry to find you in such a sorry state, Matthew. I owe you my gratitude . . . but no mind. What were you doing at a "ranters" meeting? I don't remember you as being a religious man.'

'Today I'm anybody's man, Ben. For a shilling I'll break ore with the maids, and for a free meal I will gladly shout "Allelujah!" with Wesleyan, Protestant, or Papist. I have more breath for praying than for mining, these days. Besides, there was a young girl preaching today. I believe that if a man needs to pray he might as well be looking upon a fair face as on that of a grey-whiskered old man.'

For the first time, Ben noticed the round-shouldered slightness of Matthew Bolitho and saw how the skin was tightly stretched over the bones of his dust-stained face.

'You should have stayed at the Happy Union for a while. Captain Ustick is a good man. He would have kept you on for as long as you were able to hold a shovel.'

Matthew Bolitho's broken left arm was paining him. Unable to disguise his discomfiture, he used his right hand to shift it to a more comfortable position. This done, he leaned back with his eyes closed for so long that Ben thought he had lost consciousness. Then his eyes flickered open, and the pain in them went far deeper than the shattered arm.

It was a look Ben had seen before . . . in his father's eyes.

'I couldn't have stayed at the Happy Union, or anywhere else, Ben. Not for long enough to keep a job. There are too many days when I *can't* hold a shovel. All I can do then is find a hole and crawl inside where no one will find me. One day I'll fail to come out again, I know that. Perhaps I should be thankful I have no one to grieve for me.'

'This is foolish talk, Matthew. If the surgeon hears you, he'll swear the fall has broken your head as well as your arm. You'll feel better when he's tended you.'

Ben hoped he sounded more confident than he felt. In his heart he knew it would not be long before Matthew Bolitho died, unmourned by the world about him. No one cared about a sick and aged miner. Unless he had a family, he rarely

275

remained in one place long enough to qualify for parish relief. He was doomed to spend his useless latter days begging around the mines of Cornwall, an unwanted reminder of the only certain reward to come from underground mining.

Matthew Bolitho was aware of the emptiness of Ben's words.

'When the surgeon has finished with me I'll be good for nothing, Ben. He'll not save this arm.'

The miner gave Ben a weak smile. 'Mind you, it will help me as a beggar. I can claim to be an old soldier who lost an arm in the war with the French.'

Matthew Bolitho gave a short throaty laugh and spat in the dust at his feet. 'Be off with you, Ben. You don't want to be here wasting time on me. You should be down in Falmouth with that girl of yours – the one who asked me about you when I was at the Happy Union. I would have thought you'd have wed her by now. Had her at home looking after your children.'

'You've seen Jesse . . . at Falmouth?'

'If that's her name, I have. Two days ago at Falmouth Fair. She was with another maid. I wished her "Good day", but I could see she hadn't recognised me. Why should she? We met for only a few minutes at Cap'n Ustick's house. I've grown a deal older since then.'

Matthew Bolitho looked very tired. Reaching out his right hand, he gripped Ben's arm. 'You marry her quickly, Ben. Get yourself a family and something worthwhile to live for. Don't end up like me.'

The miner's hand dropped away and he shifted his injured arm yet again.

Ben dropped three bright new guineas into Matthew Bolitho's lap. 'Here, take these. They might be of some help to you. I'll come back and see you when I return from Falmouth.'

Ben hurried away, and Matthew Bolitho called his thanks after him. Although neither man knew it, Ben had just saved the old miner from a pauper's grave.

Chapter Twenty-Eight

Falmouth Fair was much larger than the one at Probus and lasted for a full week. It was the last day of the fair when Ben and Alan Colborne arrived, but the crowds were still big enough to make a search for Jesse difficult. Twice they pushed their way from end to end of the fair. Then Ben made some enquiries of a tall-hatted constable and learned that all the hirings had taken place on the first day of the fair. There had been none since then.

The news came as a great disappointment to Ben. He had believed he would find Jesse here. Now he was more confused than ever. Had Jesse been hired on the first day? Or had she and Judy Lean moved on to some other town? There was, of course, the possibility that Matthew Bolitho had been mistaken. After all, he had met Jesse only once.

Alan Colborne tried to cheer Ben, telling him they had to expect many such disappointments. He repeated his belief that they would find her in the end. Philosophically, he suggested they put their visit to Falmouth to some advantage.

'Find us an inn with a congenial landlord, Ben. One who will offer room and board to a fiddler who knows how to bring in customers. This is a seafarer's town, and there are no more sentimental men than sailors. They are generous, too. Give them a song or two about far-off places and the girls they left behind there and we'll make more money than a week of playing the fairs. I know that is not our reason for being here, Ben, but with full pockets we can search farther and longer than with empty ones.'

Alan Colborne finally settled for a waterfront inn, the Lord Cornwallis. It was named after the old admiral who had once sheltered his fleet in Falmouth harbour during a violent storm, many years before.

Ben had observed before that Alan Colborne had a fine voice. During their evening at the Lord Cornwallis, he learned that the balladeer also had an incredibly wide repertoire. He sang sentimental ballads, stirring songs of brave deeds at sea, and sea-shanties composed to help along such mundane activities as raising an anchor. Alan Colborne knew them all.

Soon, the inn was crowded to over-capacity, the windows rattling to the roar of the singing. Ben was gradually edged into a corner seat. Facing him across a heavy plank table was one of the few unhappy-looking men in the room.

Ben did not join in the singing, because he knew few sea-shanties, but the man across the table thought that Ben disliked singing as much as he did himself. He pulled a face to express his understanding. Afterwards, Ben saw the other man watching him whenever he looked across the table.

'Are you a sailing man?'

The stranger's voice was thick from years of heavy drinking, with an accent that had its origins in East Anglia. Ben shook his head, not eager to make conversation.

'Then what are you doing here in Falmouth Town?'

The stranger banged his tankard down on the table so hard that the dregs shot into the air and speckled his unbearded face.

Ben said nothing. He hoped the angry stranger would get up from the table to refill his tankard. But he was in the company of an experienced drinker. Used to the slow service offered in crowded waterfront taverns, the man facing Ben bought his drinks in pairs. Sliding the empty tankard from him, he reached for its companion.

'I thought this was supposed to be a sailor's town. Sailors ...? Ha!'

The snort came when his mouth was only inches from the brimming tankard, and once again the stranger's face was liberally spattered with ale.

'For five days I've been trying to take on hands for a ship as stout as any on the Australian run. So far I haven't found a single one! There's not a seaman here ready to go farther south than Lisbon – and not then unless he has a soft berth on a fast packet. In all my years as a boatswain I've never known anything like it.'

The boatswain sucked in a mouthful of ale and looked

speculatively across the table at Ben. 'Are you *sure* you're not a seaman?'

Ben grinned, remembering his brief and inglorious career as a fisherman. 'I'm quite certain.'

The boatswain sighed. 'Then the skipper will have no option but to let some of the convicts up out of the hold to help again. If he doesn't, we'll be anchored in the harbour until most of them have served out their time.'

'Convicts? You've got a shipload of convicts out there in the harbour?'

'Shh! Not so loud, lad. Folk around here would get a mite fidgety if they knew there was a cargo of felons anchored not two hundred yards from their town. They think we'll let them jump over the side during the night and come ashore to murder every one of them in their beds.'

The boatswain wiped ale from his chin. 'I've been on transports for more years than I care to recall, and the only convicts I've seen go over the side are dead ones.'

The boatswain frowned suddenly. 'Until that young fool jumped overboard last Sunday. I still think the skipper should have searched until we found him. For my money he's sitting in front of his own hearth in Mevagissey at this very moment, laughing at us for being as simple as we thought he was. He was no more drowned than I am – and I don't like no convict making a fool of me.'

Ben's interest quickened at the mention of Mevagissey. He was remembering the late-night conversation with his mother the night he arrived there. She had said a great deal about Walter.

'Mevagissey, you say? I have family there. What's the name of this convict?'

'Dunn – though what his first name is I don't know.' The sailor saw the shock on Ben's face. 'You know him?'

Ben nodded. It was a few minutes before he trusted himself to speak. Pushing away his half-finished drink, he rose to his feet. 'Yes, I know Walter Dunn. At least, I did. It seems a great many years ago now.'

As Ben pushed his way through the noisy crowd in the

Lord Cornwallis, the boatswain called after him.
'If you see Dunn, you tell him he didn't fool me. I know he's alive.'

Ben knew different. He had left the Dunn house in Meva-gissey only thirty-six hours ago. That was four days after Walter had dived over the side of the convict-transport.

Only a dead man would have delayed his homecoming for that long.

From Falmouth, Ben and Alan Colborne went to the market at nearby Penryn . . . and then they moved on. St Columb, Wadebridge, Bodmin . . . and many small village markets along the way. Finally, they turned their footsteps towards Truro.

It was two weeks since Ben had left his mother at Meva-gissey. He now knew how difficult was his self-appointed task. Over the years every market in the country had become a hiring-place for labour. It was carried out on an informal and casual basis. Men and women seeking work would gather in a self-conscious but conspicuous group, close to the ring where the cattle were gathered for sale. The farmers spent much of their time here and had the opportunity to eye prospective employees for as long as they wished. It took only a few words to assure themselves that the man or woman had the experience the farmer needed, and a nod of the head concluded the arrangement.

Only rarely were references offered or asked for. If a hire-ling proved unsuitable, he or she would be dismissed without notice and a new worker taken on next market-day. There was a considerable army of work-seekers among farm-workers in the county, and Ben saw the same faces at market after market.

On their way back to Truro, Ben stopped at Probus to enquire after Matthew Bolitho. The repairs to the inside of the inn had already been completed, and when Ben spoke to the busy landlord it was a moment or two before the inn-keeper could even bring the injured man to mind.

'Oh! You mean the man who had his arm taken off? Yes,

I remember you now, sir. You'd met him before, I believe. Very sad it was. He died while the surgeon was taking off his arm. His breathing was bad, I heard it said. Spent too long working in a mine. Never do know when they are too old to go underground, these miners. Here, have a drink on me, sir – and, if your friend can play that fiddle he has tucked beneath his arm, you are both welcome to as much ale as you can sup.'

Alan Colborne played well that evening, but Ben drank the free ale in a dejected silence. The news of Matthew Bolitho's death, coming as it did after days spent fruitlessly searching for Jesse, depressed him greatly. There had been much about the miner and his illness to remind Ben of his father.

The next morning Ben and Alan Colborne walked into Truro. It was not much of a town, being little larger than Mevagissey, and a whole lot smaller than Bodmin, or the sprawling mining-towns farther west. Yet Truro was a town of which its inhabitants were inordinately proud. Well laid out, and with many fine buildings, its residents boasted that it was the finest in the county. It could do no less than have the greatest fair.

The fair was held in the wide central street, but was so well subscribed that it overflowed into every adjoining lane and alleyway. The crowds were thick in every direction, and Ben felt quite sure the whole of the county must be here.

It was difficult for Alan Colborne to make his way through the densely packed streets. The fair-goers neither knew nor cared that he was blind, so intent were they on their own pleasures.

Eventually Ben found a quiet spot for Alan Colborne, close to the river. Here he sat down with his back to a tree and began to play. When Ben looked back at him before plunging into the mêlée once more, Alan Colborne was already beginning to attract an appreciative crowd of his own.

All that day Ben walked the streets of Truro. He found the place where the young men and girls were offering themselves for hire, but quickly learned that this was not primarily a hiring-fair for farm-workers. Those here were not seeking farm work. They were hoping to be hired as servants in the households of the county gentry, Truro being the centre of Cornwall's society.

By the time dusk fell, Ben had almost seen enough of Truro Fair. Constantly jostled by the huge crowd, carried along with them from one entertainment to the next, he would have liked to leave the overcrowded town behind him. Twice he went to the place where he had left Alan Colborne, but each time he was told by the balladeer that he was not yet ready to leave.

'Give me another hour, Ben,' Alan Colborne pleaded on the last occasion, his face glistening from his musical exertions. Showing Ben the weighty bag of coins tucked beneath his coat, he added, 'I have never known a day like this. Another hour and we'll have enough money to keep us searching for Jesse for a full month. The warm weather and the joys of Truro Fair have turned the heads of your fellow-Cornishmen. They are throwing coins into my hat as though it were a wishing-well.'

Driven from Alan Colborne's riverside concert by the clamour of his audience calling for their favourite ballads, Ben wandered along the still-crowded streets. For twenty minutes he watched two heavily perspiring men wrestling. Stripped to the waist, they grappled and slipped, gouged and swore, while a man with a rasping voice called the crowd's attention to the bout that was to decide who was the 'Champion of Cornwall'. As Ben had seen the same men fighting on at least three occasions that day, it appeared to be a long-disputed title.

Farther along the same road, Ben stopped to listen to a barker inviting the passing crowd to a show in a nearby hall. It was, he shouted, 'The most incredible exhibition to be seen anywhere in the world. Inside, ladies and gentlemen, you will see the *amazing* Monsieur Chabert and his sister, Mademoiselle Chabert, only recently arrived from far-away Russia. Before your eyes they will drink boiling oils and lead, eat flaming torches and perform other, equally impossible feats.'

The barker further declared that the *amazing* Monsieur Chabert could actually remain inside an oven with a joint of meat until it was wholly cooked. Unfortunately for the populace of Truro, it had been impossible to obtain an oven of sufficient size to accommodate him here, in the west of England.

Ben had passed the hall where the show was being held before. On each occasion he had been intrigued by the smoke pouring from the open windows, adding considerable weight to the claims of the promoter. Acting on an impulse, Ben fished in his pocket for the threepence entry-fee and passed into the building.

Many late visitors to the fair shared Ben's curiosity. The hall was well-filled. At the far end of the room curtains separated stage from audience. They were half-drawn, giving the audience a tantalising glimpse of a stage and the many wonders to be seen there.

It was like peeping into Dante's kitchen. Great iron cauldrons sat upon charcoal burners, sending steam swirling about the stage. On a long wooden table were laid out a variety of partly burned torches. Occupying the centre of the stage was a frame made up of thin metal. About six feet square, it had shackles for securing a man's arms and legs. Tied all around the frame were a wide variety of fireworks.

Very soon the hall was filled to capacity and the doors were locked by the barker. This loud-voiced showman appeared to be the only other member of the Chaberts' entourage. He attracted the crowd, took their money, and was now busily preparing the show.

Some minutes later the two stars of the show appeared and the performance began.

Monsieur Chabert was a small bald-headed man with a pointed beard and thin waxed moustache. With many flourishes he sampled the contents of the various cauldrons, grimacing painfully as he held 'boiling oil' and 'hot wax' in his mouth. Then he took a sip from the cauldron of 'molten lead'. After rolling it around on his tongue, he drew from his mouth a piece of solid lead, the size of a musket-ball. Upon completion of this 'amazing' feat, a few of Monsieur Chabert's watchers gasped in astonishment. Others laughed derisively.

The plump Mademoiselle Chabert was a little more impressive, biting off the ends of large flaming torches to extinguish them. Smaller torches were dealt with in an even more contemptuous manner. Mademoiselle Chabert devoured them entirely and earned the applause of the whole audience.

Then it was time for the grand finale of the show.

Striding pompously to the centre of the stage, Monsieur Chabert stepped upon the firework-adorned frame. Adopting a dramatic pose, he allowed himself to be secured to the frame with chains and ropes.

For the first time, Ben noticed that the frame was designed to revolve. With her brother firmly secured, Mademoiselle Chabert gave the wheel a couple of slow, practice revolutions.

Satisfied the apparatus was in working order, Mademoiselle Chabert took a blazing torch from the indispensable barker and ran it around the edge of the frame. The fireworks ignited haphazardly and commenced spitting smoke and flames, whereupon she gripped the frame and spun it with a great deal more vigour than expertise.

The results were spectacular beyond all expectations. A great deal of sulphur had gone into the manufacture of the fireworks and thick pungent yellow smoke belched from them. It was sufficient to overcome the most hostile of audiences. On this occasion, the fireworks did far more. Those on one outside edge of the revolving frame had been secured carelessly and a number of them broke loose.

As the frame revolved the fireworks were flung everywhere, but it was some time before the broadly smiling Mademoiselle Chabert realised the shouts and screams were not the reactions of an unusually appreciative audience. By the time she was able to bring the whirling frame to a halt, flames were climbing high up the colourful curtains and licking at the wooden ceiling of the hall.

With commendable presence of mind, Mademoiselle Chabert raised a cauldron of 'boiling oil' from a charcoal burner and threw its contents over one of the curtains. Most of the lower flames were immediately extinguished, but the flames higher up the curtain were not affected.

While she stood back wondering what to do next, the screams of her brother joined those of the crowd. The oaths he shrieked were no more foreign than those of a Cornish miner. In stopping the wheel, Mademoiselle Chabert had left a broken string of fireworks dangling against the star of the act and his clothing had caught alight.

By now choking smoke filled the whole room, and as pieces of burning curtain and ceiling began to fall among them the audience panicked and surged towards the entrance. They hammered futilely against the locked door, and someone smashed one of the two small windows and screamed for help from outside.

Ben fought his way to the door and, with the help of another man, kicked at it until the lock gave way and the doors crashed open.

Ben stood back, his eyes smarting, as the audience scrambled into the street outside. It did not escape his notice that the still smouldering 'Monsieur Chabert' and his 'sister' were by no means the last to leave the hall.

By the time the last of the audience had fled to safety, the roof of the building was well alight, the flames from it leaping high above the roofs of the town houses.

Ben was the last to leave, but when he stumbled outside into the street his choking was as much from mirth as from the acrid smoke he had breathed into his lungs. It had been a truly memorable show. Ben could not remember when he had ever received better value for his money.

Once clear of the building, he paused to look at the huge crowd that had gathered to view the fire. In the distance the town's fire-bell clanged noisily. Ben knew there would be no shortage of helpers when the engine arrived at the fire and already he was relishing the thought of telling Alan Colborne of the Chaberts' extraordinary performance.

As the crowd closed in about him, Ben heard a shrill voice raised above the hubbub. It called his name.

'Ben! Ben Retallick!' It was a frantic, almost hysterical cry as the owner of the voice fought desperately against the crowd to reach him. Ben turned in stunned disbelief. Then he, too, was fighting the crowd.

Moments later he reached out his arms – and Jesse stumbled into them.

Chapter Twenty-Nine

When the initial shock of the long-anticipated reunion had passed, Ben held Jesse at arm's length from him and they both spoke at once.

'What are you doing—?'

'How did you—?'

They laughed together until a sudden unwonted shyness overcame them. When Ben had left Jesse, two years before, there had still been a girlish ungainliness about her. Now he looked at her and saw a very beautiful young woman. Only the sudden trembling of her lower lip gave Ben a hint of the turmoil inside her. As his arms dropped away from her, she took hold of one of his hands and gripped it fiercely.

'Tell me you are real, Ben. Tell me I won't wake in a few minutes and find I've been dreaming.'

'I'm real, Jesse. I arrived at Mevagissey only three days after you left. I've been searching for you ever since.'

As Ben was talking, he became aware of another girl who had moved up to stand silently behind Jesse. Seeing the direction of his glance, Jesse introduced Judy Lean.

Ben was reminded that he, too, had a friend. Quickly explaining about Alan Colborne, he led Jesse and Judy Lean away from the fiercely burning hall to the ill-lit clearing beside the river. On the way he crushed Jesse's hand in his, afraid that even now she might slip away from him.

Alan Colborne was alone, patiently playing a soft air on his fiddle. In the cover of the trees and bushes beyond the clearing, those courting couples who had not left to look at the fire took full advantage of the darkness and Alan Colborne's romantic music.

As they approached, the music died away. Ben, who had come to know the blind fiddler's mannerisms well, knew he was listening intently. When they were still a few paces from him, Alan Colborne's face lit up in a delighted smile. 'Congratulations, Ben! Your quest is ended. Jesse, Judy, I am

286

delighted to meet you.'

When the introductions and explanations were over, Ben asked Jesse where she and Judy Lean were staying.

Jesse looked nonplussed. 'I haven't had time to think about it. Until this evening Judy and I were working on a farm not more than a mile from here. We took work there while the farmer's wife was a-bed, having a baby. The farmer employed the two of us for the wages of one, but he begrudged us the food we ate. His wife had the baby only a week ago, but this morning he had her out of bed milking the cows before she fed the baby. I feel sorry for her.'

'It's a *lovely* baby,' declared Judy Lean wistfully. 'She deserves a better father.'

These were the first words Ben had heard Judy Lean utter. He did not miss the gentle smile Jesse gave her as she explained, 'Judy is a stout defender of the weak and helpless. She adores all babies.'

'If I don't soon get some food inside me, I will be one of the world's weak and helpless myself,' complained Alan Colborne. 'Judy, take my arm. We are going to a quiet little inn owned by a friend of mine. There we will celebrate the reunion of Ben and Jesse and raise a glass or two for the ending of two years of loneliness and misunderstanding.'

The White Swan Inn was by no means as quiet as Alan Colborne had predicted, but after greeting Alan Colborne with great delight the landlord led them all to a small private room. Here they would be able to eat in comfort.

When Alan Colborne told the landlord that they had not yet arranged accommodation for the night, he promised there would be two rooms available by the time they finished eating. Two travellers would be turned out of their room to make way for Ben and Alan Colborne. Jesse and Judy Lean could share a room with the landlord's two daughters.

When Ben expressed his gratitude, the landlord brushed them aside.

'I have no need of thanks for doing something for Alan Colborne. But for him I wouldn't be here serving you today. Neither would I be enjoying as fine a life as any man I know. Not seven years ago I was lying sorely wounded on the hillside at Waterloo, with my company cut to ribbons and the French still firing at me. I had given up all hope when Alan came out of the smoke and din of battle to my rescue. He slung me across his shoulders and carried me back to our own lines. When he put me down he took no more than ten paces towards the battle when over came a French shell. It exploded, and Alan staggered back with blood pouring from his face. He hasn't seen a thing since that day. He gave his sight for me, and I owe him my life. In my opinion, Alan Colborne is one of the true heroes of Waterloo.'

'Only old men remember past battles,' joked Alan Colborne. 'Waterloo is now no more than a name. Even the songs that were written about the battle are forgotten – but the songs I sang today were well received.'

He pulled a heavy bag of coins from beneath his coat and handed it to the landlord. 'Will you take these and exchange them for gold coins to tuck inside my belt? And a bottle of your best brandy, if you please. We are going to have a party.'

The four sat down to the finest meal Ben had ever enjoyed, although, seated across the table from Jesse, he found it difficult to keep his mind on food. She was undoubtedly far more beautiful than he remembered. He could hardly believe his good fortune that she had waited so long for him.

Ben and Jesse had little opportunity to discuss personal matters during the meal. Alan Colborne was at his charming and amusing best, and as the brandy brought a ruddy glow to Judy Lean's cheeks she forgot her natural shyness.

Later in the evening they became aware of raised voices in the main bar of the inn. When the hot and harassed landlord looked in upon them, he apologised for the din. It was, he explained, a meeting of the local parliamentary reform committee.

Ben was taken by surprise by Jesse's immediate interest.

'I thought the reform movement was dead in Cornwall,' she commented.

Mopping his brow, the landlord said, 'I wish it were. It went quiet for a while, but since Robert Peel took over the Home Office many of the measures taken against the reformers have been relaxed. They are up to their old tricks again.'

'You mean they are *talking* loudly again,' retorted Jesse scornfully. 'There's not a man among them with the courage to do more.'

'You are more knowledgeable about reform affairs than you were the day we went to the Crinnis mine,' said Ben, his curiosity aroused. 'I seem to remember that you couldn't leave the meeting fast enough.'

'That was before I experienced the need for reform and had Walter Dunn to explain it to me,' replied Jesse. 'No man has done more for reform in Cornwall than Walter. He lived for reform. Perhaps one day he'll be given the justice he deserves.'

Ben was reminded of his conversation with the boatswain of the *Perseus*. Walter had not only lived for reform – he had *died* for it. There would be no justice for Walter Dunn now. But Ben said nothing to Jesse. Grandma Dunn had accused her of being responsible for Walter's transportation. Ben did not want her to feel she was in any way to blame for his death.

When the noise from the reformers showed no sign of abating, Ben suggested to Jesse that they take a walk outside, and she agreed.

Once outside, Jesse took his arm quite naturally. Ben was so absurdly pleased he wished it was daylight, wanting those who passed by to see the beauty of the girl who clung to his arm.

But the darkness had its own compensations. They walked through the town until they reached a tree-lined path by the river. Here, Ben took Jesse in his arms and kissed her. She did not resist him, but there was none of the fiery response that Ben remembered so well and had thought about during many long and lonely nights.

When he reluctantly released her, she whispered, 'Did you mean that, Ben?'

His voice in reply was as husky as her own.

'Then everything will be all right . . . but give me time, Ben. Please!' She kissed him quickly. Then, taking his hand, she set off along the footpath.

It was Ben who broke the long silence that came upon them.

'You and Walter . . . Ma said he wanted to marry you.'

'Yes.'

Jesse seemed to feel that her reply needed no explanation, but Ben could not leave it there.

'And you? What were your feelings for him?'

'I was – and still am – very fond of Walter. He was kind to me when I had no other person with whom I could share my troubles. I told him I couldn't marry him because I was waiting for you. It wasn't easy for me, Ben – especially after the first year. I had no way of knowing whether you would ever come back; whether you *wanted* to come back.'

'I wanted it desperately, Jesse – but whichever way I looked at it, Reuben Holyoak was in the way. At first I was quite certain I'd killed him. I didn't know how he could have lived after the beating I'd given him. I was so mad with him that I *wanted* to kill him. It was frightening! Then – when I realised he must still be alive – I thought you would have been forced to marry him, for the sake of your mother. That was even worse than believing I was a hunted man. The thought of you living with Reuben Holyoak.'

'Poor Ben!' Jesse's own unhappy two years were forgotten in her concern for Ben. Then, softly, she asked, 'Has there been no one else for you, Ben? You must have met a great many girls during your travels.'

Ben hesitated. Guiltily, he wondered if he should tell her about Aileen Brenahan . . .

'No. No one who really meant anything to me.'

His initial hesitation and oblique answer told Jesse much. She did not press him for an explanation now. One day she would know everything that had happened to Ben during the two years he had been away. For now it was enough that he had returned to her.

They stayed in Truro for a full week. During that time neither Ben nor Jesse mentioned the future. Each was fearful that the other's feelings might have changed. Neither wanted to be the first to risk the happiness they now felt.

It was Alan Colborne who brought the matter into the open. He had done his best to give them as much time together as was possible, making Judy Lean take him out walking for most of every day, whatever the weather.

The four of them were finishing off a quieter-than-usual meal one evening, when the balladeer suddenly downed his knife and turned his sightless eyes in Ben's direction.

'We've been here a whole week now.'

'Yes.'

Ben guessed what was coming and squirmed in his seat.

'Where do we all go from here, Ben? I think the main decision is yours to take.'

Ben took a quick look around the table. Judy Lean was waiting for his reply with undisguised interest, but Jesse had her gaze fixed firmly upon her plate as her knife mounted a half-hearted attack on an unresisting slice of choice ham.

Ben took a deep breath before speaking what was in his heart. 'If Jesse will marry me, I would like to return to mining at Sharptor. I believe the mines there have a great future. As they go deeper they'll find more and more copper. I want to—'

'Ben Retallick!' Jesse's voice was pitched low, but the sound of it stopped Ben short. 'Are you asking me to marry you? Or are you giving us a description of the mines of Sharptor?'

'I'm asking you to marry me, Jesse.'

Alan Colborne stood up quickly. His belt caught the edge of his plate and spilled what remained of his dinner across the table. Reaching out, his fingers touched Judy and he felt for her arm. 'Come, Judy. A man doesn't need an audience when he proposes marriage.'

'Sit down, Judy. You too, Alan,' Jesse said unexpectedly.

As the balladeer sat down obediently, Jesse saw Ben's consternation and she smiled at him. 'I might need witnesses to Ben's proposal should he decide to go away again. Besides, I don't care who hears me say "Yes". Of course I will marry you, Ben, and I will go with you anywhere in the world.'

Judy Lean clapped her hands in delight and Alan Colborne let out a yell that was heard in every corner of the inn.

'Well said, Jesse. As pretty a speech of acceptance as any man will have heard.'

Ben felt so relieved and emotional, he was unable to say

anything. He reached across the table, and when Jesse put her hand in his he gripped it so hard he almost crushed her fingers.

The landlord came running into the room, alarmed by Alan Colborne's gleeful shout, and was told the news by his jubilant friend. Before many minutes had passed the room was invaded by well-wishers from the landlord's family and his staff, all of whom knew the story of Ben and Jesse. Soon a very noisy party was in progress in the room.

At its height, Judy Lean guided Alan Colborne to the corner of the room where Ben and Jesse stood together, both slightly bemused by their popularity. Gripping Ben's sleeve, Alan Colborne drew him away from the others. When they were out of hearing, Alan Colborne said very quietly, 'Now you and Jesse are to be married, what will become of Judy?'

Ben looked across the room to where Judy Lean gazed at Jesse, her devotion plain for all to see. 'She'll be all right, Alan. Jesse and I will take her with us to Sharptor. We'll find a house there and she'll live with us, working on the surface at one of the mines.'

Alan Colborne gnawed his lip nervously. 'I'm going to miss her, Ben. She is a simple good-natured girl, and I have enjoyed her company this last week.'

Ben saw the indecision on the face of his friend. 'What are you trying to say, Alan?'

'Damn it Ben! I want Judy to stay with me. To marry me. But I have no right to ask her. I am a man with no eyes.'

'You are as much of a man as any I have ever met – and more than most. You can also earn a good living. But are you certain of this, Alan? You know very little about Judy.'

'I know she is a simple and honest girl. Far too honest to keep a secret for long. She told me about her baby.'

Ben said nothing, ashamed of even thinking that he should tell Alan Colborne about the birth of Judy's baby. Alan Colborne probably knew Judy Lean better than either he or Jesse did.

'I have tried to say something to her about my feelings, Ben, but the words stick in my throat. I have no right to ask any girl to marry me. None. Please forget I've said anything to you. Take Judy with you and Jesse. Look after her as she deserves . . . '

Over Alan Colborne's head, Ben caught Jesse's eye and signalled for her to bring Judy Lean across the room. Alan Colborne heard them coming and tried to make off. In his confusion he went the wrong way. Had Ben not moved quickly, the blind balladeer would have walked into a wall.

'Jesse, Alan has something to ask Judy. It's of great importance to both of them, but for some ridiculous reason he feels he has no right to speak his mind. I think we should lock them in a room together until he comes to his senses.'

Looking at Alan Colborne's consternation, a delighted smile spread across Jesse's face. 'Well, if it's any help to him, I can give him Judy's answer in advance. Since she met Alan she has kept me awake night after night talking about him. Perhaps if he says what's on his mind she'll give me some peace tonight.'

It was enough for Ben. Disregarding Alan Colborne's protests and the startled looks of the landlord and his family, Ben ushered his friend and Judy Lean from the room and took them to the landlord's own sitting-room where he left them together.

It was fifteen minutes before they returned. One look at their faces was enough to tell Ben and Jesse that another wedding was in the offing.

It was a night the customers of the White Swan Inn would remember for a very long time. The night when the landlord supplied free ale, and a blind ex-soldier entertained them with singing such as they had never heard before.

It was also the night Ben Retallick and Jesse Henna came to one another as they had when they were hardly more than children. They confirmed that the only thing they had lost together was time.

Chapter Thirty

When Ben and Jesse set off for Mevagissey, they left Alan
Colborne and Judy Lean planning a journey to Plymouth to
find Judy's mother and tell her about their wedding plans.
The day was oppressively hot, and before Ben and Jesse were
half way to the coast they saw heavy black clouds banking up
over the English Channel. Hurrying along narrow lanes as
the cloud rapidly filled more and more of the sky, they soon
realised they had no hope of reaching Mevagissey before the
storm broke. It was sweeping inland at a frightening speed.

They were still many miles from the fishing-village when,
on a nearby hill-top, they saw the upper branches of a line
of giant elms suddenly bow before a ferocious wind. Rain,
accompanied by thunder and lightning, moved in behind the
wind, and Ben and Jesse sprinted for the shelter of an open-
doored barn.

Out of breath, they gained the entrance just as the first
heavy raindrops spattered like musket-shots against the barn
roof. Inside, a number of heifers had anticipated the storm
and sought shelter in a more leisurely fashion. The barn was
not large, and Ben did not fancy sharing it with nervous
cattle during a thunderstorm. Fortunately, the barn had a
hay-loft. Clambering up the ladder first, Ben pulled Jesse up
after him and they collapsed on a pile of musty hay as the
storm battered the outside of the building.

It was the worst summer storm either of them had ever
experienced. As they lay in each other's arms, the wind
pummelled the stone walls of the aged barn and tore at the
roof. Twice they heard slates scurry down the sloping roof
and smash on the ground outside. Water began to leak into
the barn in a dozen places, and the beams and joists creaked
in protest at the abuse to which they were being subjected.

But it was the thunder and lightning that was most frightening of all. As the heart of the storm came overhead, lightning

spat at the trees about the barn with a spiteful sibilance that hung on the air for long seconds, bathing the landscape in an intense white light. Each new flash of lightning was accompanied by a deafening crack of thunder that made the earth tremble and sent the cattle in the barn milling around, snorting in terror. All the time this frightening cacophony was going on, the rain beat against the slate-tiled roof with the noise of a million tiny hammers.

It seemed an age before the wind decreased and the unnatural gloom outside lightened as the storm moved northwards. In fact, the storm had raged for hardly more than an hour.

With the passing of the storm, a stunned hush fell upon the land. Ben and Jesse climbed down the ladder from the loft and went out into a steaming world. At the field-gate they met an anxious farmer hurrying from his home to check his livestock.

'We sheltered in your barn from the storm,' explained Ben. 'We are on' our way to Mevagissey.'

The farmer nodded his acceptance of Ben's story. 'It was no weather to be outside. There are three trees down between here and the farmhouse. I reckon the storm took them by surprise. One minute it was miles away, the next it was upon us. If you have friends in Mevagissey, I hope they had more warning than we. There hasn't been a fishing-boat made that could have stayed afloat in such a storm.'

The farmer's gloomy words weighed heavily on Ben's mind until he and Jesse topped the hill above Mevagissey and looked down upon the sheltered little village.

His relief was short-lived. The surrounding hills sheltered the village from all but a south-easterly wind – and the storm had arrived from the south-east.

Coming in behind a high tide, the wind had whipped the sea to a frenzy. All but two of the fishing-boats had returned safely to the tiny harbour, only to be smashed to matchwood by gigantic waves that poured over the harbour wall and flung the boats against the stone quay. Of the two boats that failed to beat the storm, and the seven men aboard them, not a trace was ever found.

295

Martha Retallick was at the harbour where every able-bodied inhabitant of the village was helping to drag repairable fishing-boats from a mass of shattered wreckage. This was no time for her to express her joy at seeing Ben reunited with Jesse. The storm had been an unprecedented disaster for the fishing community.

Looking about her at the scene of devastation, she raised her hands helplessly. 'What a homecoming! Mevagissey can never recover from this . . .'

'Where are the Dunn boats?'

'Who knows? Mark and Billy brought them in safely, but we haven't found a piece of either boat yet.'

Ben stepped forward to help a group of men heaving at a rope that disappeared beneath the surface of the debris-littered water. More men and women came to help, and gradually a large fishing-boat was hauled from the depths of the harbour. As they hauled it through the mud to dry land, water poured from a hole the size of a man's head, punched through the boat's planking.

With the others, Ben and Jesse worked until the light began to fade. The falling tide had failed to reveal any more boats in a repairable condition. The destruction of the Mevagissey fishing-fleet was well-nigh complete.

After trudging despondently to Grandma Dunn's house, Ben and Jesse listened to the family gloomily discussing the bleak future that stretched ahead of them now. It would take months, perhaps years, for the fishing-village to recover from the ravages of this June storm.

So wrapped up were the Dunns in their troubles that the presence of Ben and Jesse passed almost unnoticed. Eventually, the two slipped from the house and set off for Pentuan. Jesse hoped to be able to stay with the Usticks until she and Ben went to Sharptor.

The welcome given to them by the Happy Union captain and his wife was as warm as the Dunns' had been indifferent. The night was half gone before Ben left the house to return along the dark road to Mevagissey.

*

It had been Ben's intention to leave for Sharptor within a day or two, but the problems caused by the storm delayed his departure. There was no work for anyone in Mevagissey. With not a single boat fit to put to sea and hardly a serviceable net along the whole coast, there was no fishing – and no smuggling.

Eventually, after much discussion, Mark Dunn collected every penny the family possessed and went to nearby Fowey, a fishing-town that had missed the worst of the storm. Here he bought a secondhand fishing-boat at a price that only a week before would have seemed ridiculous. Now there was such a demand for boats that customers could be found for anything that would float.

Others in Mevagissey followed the Dunns' example. Any family unable to raise enough money by itself, went into partnership with others and they bought a boat between them.

In church on Sunday, the parson prayed for a fruitful and extended pilchard season. Only this would enable the Mevagissey men to pay off their debts and survive to fish for another season. It might have been better had a prayer been directed to Sir Colman Vincent.

The baronet did not attend their church and he neither knew nor cared about their problems. Only a week after the storm, a lawyer employed by Sir Colman rode on to the quay at Mevagissey, escorted by a large number of militiamen. While the part-time soldiers held back the curious crowd, he posted a notice.

When the fishermen swarmed forward to read it, such a howl went up that it might have been heard in Lamorrack House. They were summarily informed that the tithes had been increased to four guineas for each boat, with an additional two guineas for each seine-net a man possessed. It was more than double the increase successfully resisted by Walter Dunn – and it was payable in advance. Sir Colman Vincent had once again chosen the worst possible moment to increase the tithes of the fishermen.

It was fortunate for the lawyer that he had the forethought

to bring the men of the Cornwall Militia with him. They saved him from a severe manhandling – but not from angry abuse. The fishermen and women of Mevagissey called him every name in their wide vocabulary. They rushed to block his escape from the village, and for a time it seemed that anger might overcome common sense. Then the militiamen closed ranks and slowly, but determinedly, eased their way out of Mevagissey.

When they were gone, the villagers split into tight knots of angry gesticulating men and women, all demanding immediate action. Nobody seemed to have any idea what form the action should take, but word soon went round that a meeting was to be called on the quay to discuss the new tithe rates.

For many – and the Dunns were among their number – Sir Colman Vincent's latest action spelled ruin. They had spent every penny they could raise to buy their new boat, and borrowed more to equip it for fishing. They needed another boat urgently. One would earn no more than enough to feed the numerous members of their family and provide them with essential food and clothing – and then only if it was a good season. Until there was another boat they would be unable to pay off their debt. There could also be no thought of paying wages to Martha Retallick. She would be working solely for her keep, and that might not always be forthcoming. Mark and Billy Dunn had a great many mouths to feed.

Grandma Dunn hinted that it might be better for everyone if Martha Retallick went to Sharptor with Ben and Jesse. It was a suggestion that filled Martha with dismay. She hated mining communities.

Ben and Jesse went to the meeting on the quay, but it soon became apparent to both of them that it would provide no solutions to the problems of the village. No one felt inclined to take command of the meeting. After a great deal of argument, an old fisherman was elected to address his fellow-villagers. The choice was a bad one. The old fisherman rambled on about the effects of the storm and the new tithes, concluding with the defeatist observation, 'We shall have to pay the new tithes, be sure of that. Although where the money is to come from, I am sure I don't know.'

298

'Perhaps Sir Colman will give us time to find the money, if we asked him,' called a voice from the crowd.

Unable to contain her impatience any longer Jesse shouted in a loud voice, 'Have you all forgotten how Walter Dunn dealt with increased tithes, the last time they were raised? Is he the only Mevagissey man with any courage?'

Some of the younger fishermen murmured their agreement with Jesse, but, stung by her words, the old fisherman retorted, 'Would you have the whole village transported along with Walter Dunn? Is that your idea of "winning" an argument with Sir Colman Vincent?'

'Do nothing and you'll find the tithes raised again next year,' called Ben. 'Jesse is right. You have to fight Sir Colman Vincent – and fight to win. Give up now and in a year or two you'll be fishing for him. He'll own your boats, your houses – and you as well.'

'It's easy enough for you to call for action, Ben Retallick,' shouted a voice from the crowd behind Ben. He recognised it as belonging to one of the men who had crewed Walter's boat during Ben's brief fishing career. 'You're not a fisherman. When things get too tough here you can walk out and go off to some mine to earn a living. We must stay and live with whatever decision is reached here today.'

'*If* any decision is reached,' commented Jesse, her voice heavy with sarcasm. 'So far this meeting has been a waste of everyone's time. You might as well have made a collection to pay the tithes to Sir Colman's man when he came here with the militia.'

This time her words stung the fishermen to anger.

'Then why don't you do something to help us?' cried Mark Dunn. 'No doubt Walter taught you some of his tricks, and you have more influence with Sir Colman Vincent than anyone else in Mevagissey.'

Someone in the crowd laughed and others joined in. As Jesse showed her anger, Ben took her arm. 'Come along, Jesse. Leave them to fight their own battles. As they were quick to remind us, there is nothing to keep *us* here.'

White-faced, Jesse shook off his hand and scanned the crowd until she located Mark Dunn. 'All right, I'll go to the big house and speak to Sir Colman. It's what Walter would have done – and I would rather follow his example than the one you have set today.'

Jesse reached for Ben's hand and they walked together from the quay. There was no laughter now. Only the silence of embarrassed men, each too shamefaced to meet the eyes of his neighbour.

Chapter Thirty-One

Time and time again Ben told himself it was foolish to become involved in the problems of the Mevagissey fishermen. Yet there was a nagging voice at the back of his mind that kept reminding him of Walter Dunn. Walter had never allowed expediency to deter him when something really needed to be done – and Ben owed a debt to his late uncle.

Walter Dunn had looked after Ben well when he arrived in Mevagissey as a young boy, fresh from the mines of St Just. He alone of the Dunn family had shown any real concern for Pearson Retallick – and Walter had taken care of Jesse when she desperately needed a friend.

Now Walter Dunn was dead. Sir Colman Vincent was as responsible for his death as surely as if he had ordered his execution. Ben owed it to Walter to do everything in his power to foil the schemes of the baronet and bring about his downfall. He would stay in Mevagissey for a while.

But first Ben needed to find work. The money he had brought with him from Sharptor was almost gone.

This problem was easily solved. Captain Ustick took him on at the Happy Union stream-works. If Ben thought it incongruous that he should accept Sir Colman Vincent's wages whilst plotting his downfall, he never allowed the matter to trouble his conscience.

Ben had reckoned without Reuben Holyoak. Sir Colman Vincent's agent was now involved in every one of the baronet's Cornish interests, and this included his mining ventures.

On Ben's second day at the stream-workings, Reuben Holyoak arrived to collect the account-books while Ben was checking the quality of the tin ore being loaded on the pack-horses. When he saw Ben, Reuben Holyoak's face reddened and Ben thought he was about to burst a blood vessel. Then the agent stormed into Captain Ustick's office, demanding to know why the mine captain had taken on Ben Retallick.

Loveday Ustick lolled behind his desk, the huge bulk of his body overfilling the chair, his hands placed flat on the desk-top, fingers splayed.

'Are you telling me how to run the Happy Union now, Reuben Holyoak?'

'I'm telling you to get rid of Ben Retallick. I don't want to see him anywhere near Sir Colman's property.'

'Stay away from the Happy Union and you won't need to look at him.' Loveday Ustick leaned forward, supporting his great weight on the desk as he glared belligerently at the agent.

For a full minute Reuben Holyoak fought to bring his anger under control. 'I'll go wherever I please on Sir Colman's property,' he said eventually.

'I don't doubt it. But come here telling me how I should operate my stream-workings and you'll leave on the toe of my boot. Now, get out. I have work to do.'

For a moment it looked as though Reuben Holyoak might stay to argue, but when Loveday Ustick stood up, towering above him, the agent retreated hurriedly to the door.

'You'll hear more of this, Ustick.'

Captain Loveday Ustick slammed the door of his office and went back to his desk, leaving Reuben Holyoak to ride angrily to Lamorrack House – without the account-books.

That Sunday, Ben went to Pengony, the village which had elected Sir Colman Vincent to Parliament. He went alone. It was likely he would need to do some drinking, and women were not allowed in many of the county's ale-houses.

Ben's purpose in going to Pengony was to confirm the story Walter Dunn had told to Jesse shortly before his arrest, about vote-purchasing on the part of Sir Colman Vincent.

There were only two ale-houses in Pengony, and Ben found the man he had hoped to meet in the second. He was certain it was the right man when he heard the landlord sarcastically address the bulbous-nosed customer as 'Your worship'.

Ben carried his drink across the room to the man and sat opposite him.

'I believe you were once the mayor of Pengony?' Ben said when the man looked up at him.

'What's that to you?'

'A friend of yours said that if ever I came here I was to buy you a drink.'

'A friend? What friend? I had plenty of so-called friends when I was mayor, but I can't think of one worthy of the name now.'

'Well . . . perhaps he was not so much a friend of yours as an enemy of Reuben Holyoak.'

The ex-mayor of Pengony scowled. 'Don't mention that name to me. He deprived me of land that is rightfully mine.'

'Rightfully yours?' Ben prodded. 'I heard it belonged to Sir Colman Vincent.'

'Did you, now?' The ex-mayor raised his tankard, spilling some of the contents down his coat. He had already drunk more than was good for him. 'His land it might have been, but Sir Colman gave it to me for my use. He owed it to me, he acknowledged that. It was me who bought the votes that put him in Parliament. Fifty pounds apiece, they cost. Cheap at that, they was. They might have cost him three times as much.'

'From what I have heard since, they probably did.' The landlord had been listening to the conversation; now he came across the room and began swabbing down the already clean table. 'There was more money stuck to your fingers than was ever passed on, I am certain of that.'

Other men in the room were listening to the conversation at Ben's table and one of them chuckled. The landlord did not share in the amusement. 'You'll tell that story once too often, one of these days.'

'Why should you worry?' retorted the drunken ex-mayor. 'It was the easiest fifty pounds you've ever earned. You wait and see how much you are offered next time. You'll see who cheated you then.'

'Next time I might be persuaded to vote for someone else, for less than Sir Colman Vincent has to offer. He does little to help the likes of me.'

Ben listened to the exchanges between the landlord and the

ex-mayor of Pengony with a great deal of satisfaction. Downing the last of his drink, he stood up.

'Many men would agree with you, Landlord. The sooner this county gets rid of Sir Colman Vincent, the better it will be for all of us.'

With that, Ben walked out of the ale-house, leaving the landlord and his customers to speculate on what interest he had in Sir Colman Vincent. Ben's visit to Pengony had been successful. The ex-mayor's resentment at his treatment by the Lamorrack agent still rankled. Reuben might well have laid the foundation of his employer's downfall.

But the day of reckoning seemed a long way off when Sir Colman Vincent and his agent rode up to the Happy Union mine a few days after Ben's visit to Pengony.

Ben was called to the mine captain's office. There he found Sir Colman Vincent in a mood of cold anger. Without any preliminaries, the baronet snapped at him, 'You are dismissed, Retallick. Get off the mine immediately. I suggest you take the opportunity to leave the district. Whether or not you take my advice, I do not wish to see you again.'

This was neither the time nor the place for a showdown with the baronet. Ben turned to go without making any reply.

'Wait a minute, Ben.' Loveday Ustick's voice stopped him. As Ben stood in the doorway, the mine captain addressed Sir Colman Vincent.

'Your father appointed me captain of this stream-works, Sir Colman. I've run it well, both for him and for you. I've made a good profit when similar mines were showing a loss. Leave me to run the mine my way and that is how things will continue. I hire the men I want – and dismiss those I don't. Ben Retallick is a good worker. I want him to stay.'

'If you feel so strongly about the matter, perhaps you had better leave with him, Captain Ustick.'

Sir Colman Vincent gave the ultimatum to Loveday Ustick almost casually, then waited for him to climb down from the ridiculous stand he was making.

Ben knew the mine captain better than did his employer. 'Don't make an issue of this, Loveday. I'll go.'

304

'Not by yourself, you won't, Ben. This has come about through Reuben Holyoak's interference. I won't tolerate that. If I am to be captain here, I must run the Happy Union the way I think best. I'll not stay if it's to be otherwise. Do I stay or go, Sir Colman?'

For the first time, Sir Colman Vincent realised he had made an error of judgement, but he could not – and would not – be seen to back down before an employee. Not even the man in charge of the only profit-making venture he owned.

'You heard me, Captain Ustick . . .'

'That's what I thought you would say. Come, Ben.'

The big mine captain clapped a heavy hand on Ben's shoulder and together they walked from the office. Ben was appalled at the consequences Loveday Ustick's action would have for his wife and child. When they were clear of the office he protested strongly to him.

Loveday Ustick's hand tightened on Ben's shoulder. 'Don't take all the blame upon yourself, Ben. Reuben Holyoak has been breathing down my neck for months. He's never forgiven me for taking on Judy Lean after she lost her child. Had you not happened along he'd have found some other way to get rid of me. You mustn't fret. This is Sir Colman's loss, not mine . . . as he'll soon realise. I can walk into any stream-working in Cornwall as a captain. I am the best in the county, and others know it if Sir Colman doesn't.'

Behind them in the mine office, Sir Colman Vincent was seething with anger. He *did* know that Loveday Ustick was the best stream-works captain in Cornwall. He had not wanted to lose him. He could not *afford* to lose him. His financial resources were currently under considerable strain. His income from the Happy Union mine was more important than he would dare to admit to any man.

'Who is the senior man on these workings now?' he snapped at Reuben Holyoak.

'I don't know.'

'Then find out. I want to see him here – immediately!'

Reuben Holyoak hurried from the office and found the tin-streamers gathering together in puzzled groups, looking after their late captain as he walked from the workings with Ben.

'Who usually looks after the mine when Captain Ustick isn't here?' Reuben Holyoak addressed the group of miners nearest him.

'Well, now, that depends . . .' A small bow-legged tin-streamer with a face as knotted as a walnut shell stroked his grey-tinged beard and looked speculatively at the agent. 'How long is Cap'n Ustick likely to be away?'

'For good. Sir Colman Vincent has just dismissed him.'

At Reuben Holyoak's words, a rapidly increasing buzz of anger arose from the listening men. The grizzled tin-streamer stopped stroking his beard.

'Then that leaves me the senior man on the stream-works, but I'll not step into Loveday Ustick's boots. You can go back and tell Sir Colman Vincent he'll need to work the Happy Union himself – with you to help him. I don't know of any man or woman who will stay now Cap'n Ustick has gone. I'll bid you good day and be getting on home now, Mr Holyoak.'

Those men within hearing shouted their agreement with the old tin-streamworker's words. As news of what was happening went around the workings, men and women put down their tools and walked from the mine.

As one man passed Reuben Holyoak, he paused to say, 'I've left the engine running, but you'll need to look at it before an hour has gone by. If it stops, the workings will flood and you won't be taking out any ore for a week or two.'

Thoroughly dismayed, Reuben Holyoak looked on help-lessly as the Happy Union tin-streamers moved away along the road in the wake of Loveday Ustick.

'What the devil is going on?' Sir Colman Vincent stormed from the mine office and confronted his agitated agent.

Long before Reuben Holyoak had reached the end of his garbled explanation, Sir Colman Vincent was so enraged that the agent thought he would strike him.

'You fool! This is all your doing. Damn you for involving me in your own petty quarrel with Ustick.' Sir Colman con-

306

veniently forgot that he had been as keen as Reuben Holyoak to have Ben dismissed. 'If things are not back to normal by the end of the day, I do not want to see your face at Lamorrack again.'

'But . . . Captain Ustick?'

'Get him back. I don't care if you have to go down on your knees to him. Remember, Holyoak, I can do without you, but I need the Happy Union.'

Reuben Holyoak first practised his persuasive powers on the stream-workers, in a final attempt to get them back to work. They jeered at his words and laughed him down. He was left with no choice but to swallow his pride and seek out Captain Ustick at his home.

The door was opened by Fanny Ustick. Tight-faced, she curtly invited him into the house. Although concerned for the future of young Nathaniel Ustick, she had supported her husband's stand against the interference of Reuben Holyoak and Sir Colman Vincent. She knew how proud Loveday was of his tin-streaming expertise. It was not conceit. It was the pride of a man who had put his God-given talents to their best use.

Reuben Holyoak began hesitantly, suggesting that Sir Colman might be persuaded to take Loveday Ustick back as captain of the Happy Union, if Loveday would make certain concessions.

Loveday Ustick was in no mood to make 'concessions'. He opened the door and ordered Reuben Holyoak from the house. Only then did the agent break down and beg the big man to resume work as captain of the Happy Union mine.

Loveday Ustick's own inclination was to disregard Reuben Holyoak's pleading. He was confident of his ability to find a well-paid post elsewhere. It was Fanny Ustick who eventually stepped in to urge her husband to reconsider his decision.

She liked living at Pentuan and believed she and Loveday were performing a valuable service to God and the Methodist Church there. It was this argument that eventually won her husband over. But Loveday Ustick left Reuben Holyoak in no doubt about the terms on which he would be returning to the stream-workings.

'I'll come back to the Happy Union . . . and so will Ben. Furthermore, I'll have no more interference from you. Keep away from the mine or I will personally heave you in the river.'

Reuben Holyoak agreed to Loveday Ustick's conditions with abject eagerness and hurriedly left the house. He had saved the Happy Union stream-works – and his own position as Sir Colman Vincent's agent. In future Loveday Ustick would be left to run the Happy Union stream-workings in his own way.

Chapter Thirty-Two

True to the promise she had made to the Mevagissey fisher-men, Jesse went to Lamorrack House to speak to Sir Colman Vincent. It was the day after the incident at the Happy Union. In spite of her earlier bravado, she was not looking forward to the meeting. It came as a relief to learn that the baronet had left for his Devon estates earlier that very morning. Neverthe-less, the issue of the increased tithes would not await his return.

She thought about the matter all that day. When Ben finished work at the Happy Union he found Jesse waiting for him. One look at her was enough to tell him that she had something on her mind. He did not have to wait long to learn what it was.

'I went to Lamorrack House to see Sir Colman this morn-ing. He wasn't there.'

'Perhaps it was just as well. He'd have been in no mood to listen to you. Not after what happened yesterday. When is he expected back?'

'That doesn't matter now. I am going to see Eulaliah Vincent instead. I want you to come with me, this evening.'

'Wearing these clothes?' Dismayed, Ben looked from his dirty working-clothes to Jesse's neat waist-pinching dress.

'No. You'll need to wear your Sunday best. That's why I came to meet you. I want you to tell Eulaliah Vincent every-thing you have learned about Sir Colman's election to Parlia-ment.'

Ben had not yet made up his mind what to do with the information he had – and today was not a good day to think about anything. He had been working very hard at the stream-works. Because of Loveday Ustick's stand on his behalf, he had felt obliged to work twice as hard as usual. Then Jesse took his hand and smiled up at him, and Ben knew he would do whatever she asked.

When they arrived at Mevagissey together, the Dunn

family showed all their earlier cold hostility towards Jesse. Ben bristled with anger. In view of what he and Jesse were doing to help the Mevagissey fishermen, he felt the Dunns might at least behave civilly towards her.

Martha Retallick recognised his anger and hurriedly bundled him from the room, leaving the others sitting around in gloomy silence.

'Go about your business and take no notice of them, Ben,' said his mother when they were outside. 'They haven't got the boat fitted out yet and they are not used to doing nothing all day.'

'Then why don't they get up off their backsides and do something about it . . . as Jesse and I are doing?' Ben retorted angrily. 'It's little wonder that men like Sir Colman Vincent can walk all over the fishermen of Mevagissey. They take everything that is thrown at them and expect someone else to do their dirty work.'

'That's not true, Ben. They are used to fighting. Every one of them has been fighting the sea for a living since he was old enough to sit in a boat, but this tithe business is something they don't understand.

'They lack a leader. Give them one and they'll follow him no matter where he takes them. Walter was such a man; but I want you to remember what happened to him. Don't get any notion of taking his place. The fishermen's troubles are not yours. Marry Jesse and get out of Mevagissey. You're a miner, not a fisherman – you've told me so yourself, many times. I wish to God it were otherwise, but I wasted half a lifetime trying to make your father something he could never be. I'll not waste the other half seeking to change you.'

'If I leave with Jesse, will you come, too?'

'To live on a mine again?' Martha Retallick shook her head emphatically. 'No, Ben. I can think of nothing worse. Mevagissey is my home. I'll stay here.'

'Then the fishermen's battle with Sir Colman Vincent has to be my battle, too. I can't leave until something has been done about the threat he poses to you. Besides, the Dunns and Retallicks have a number of scores to settle with Sir Colman Vincent and Reuben Holyoak. Now I must get washed and changed. Jesse and I are going to see Eulaliah Vincent.'

Martha Retallick looked nervous. 'Say nothing of where you are going to anyone else in this house. They don't trust Sir John's sister. And be careful what you say to her; they may be right.'

It was the first time Ben had seen the new house built on the site of his former home. It was most impressive. The old barn where his father had committed suicide had been pulled down to make way for the sweeping lawns.

Eulaliah Vincent was in the garden of the house. When she saw her visitors she greeted them warmly, her bright eyes alert and full of a lively inquisitiveness.

'So this is your young man,' she said, when Jesse had introduced him. 'You have been away far too long, Ben Retallick. You are lucky to have found her here waiting for you. Now I suppose you will be rushing her off to be married. Where is the wedding to be ?'

'Somewhere near Henwood.' Seeing her blank look, Ben added, 'It's a village on the edge of Bodmin Moor. A friend of mine is the preacher there.'

'Hah! No doubt you will have a meaningless wedding in church before rushing off to a service in some scrubbed and whitewashed chapel, with no flowers or stained-glass windows to look at. It is as well the law does not allow chapel weddings. If it did, some people would never see inside the churches that have been warmed and beautified by centuries of faith.'

'I'm a miner, Miss Vincent. The chapel in Henwood is a miners' chapel. We'll remember our wedding with as much warmth as any that has taken place in church – or cathedral.'

Eulaliah Vincent stared hard at Ben for a moment or two.

'H'm! No doubt you are right. We all have to live our lives in our own way.'

She turned to Jesse. 'What would you like from me as a wedding gift ?'

'If you could persuade Sir Colman to withdraw his demand for higher fishing tithes, it would be the best possible wedding present anyone could give us,' Ben said, before Jesse could reply.

'What have fishing tithes to do with either of *you*?' Eulaliah Vincent demanded.

'My mother went to live in Mevagissey, after Sir Colman turned us out of Tregassick,' explained Ben. 'Now she has no work because of the big storm – and Sir Colman's increased tithes. She doesn't want to leave Mevagissey, but unless something happens very soon she'll have to come with Jesse and me when we are married.'

'Is this why you have come to see me?' Eulaliah Vincent had a disconcerting stare, but Ben met it squarely before he inclined his head.

'I see. Then we had better discuss it inside the house. That Holyoak man has a tread like a cat. If we are to discuss my nephew, it needs to be in private.'

Eulaliah Vincent led them to a sitting-room from which they looked out upon a small enclosed garden, richly coloured with rhododendron bushes. After both Ben and Jesse had declined an offer of a drink, Eulaliah Vincent said, 'Now, tell me what this is about. How do you think I can help you? I have very little influence over Sir Colman. He has rarely listened to me in the past; I can think of no reason why he should begin now.'

Ben told Eulaliah Vincent the story of the storm and its disastrous consequences to the fishermen of Mevagissey. Then he told her how Sir Colman's increased tithes had dashed any chance they had of recouping their losses.

After listening very carefully, Eulaliah Vincent commented, 'Sir Colman has chosen a most unfortunate time to raise fishing tithes – but, if I try to tell him so, he will no doubt inform me it is a business matter and nothing to do with me.' She shrugged. 'He would be quite right, of course.'

Then Eulaliah Vincent revealed some of her shrewdness. 'But I feel there is more to this than you have told me. What is it?'

Ben was still not convinced he should tell this aristocratic old woman the details of his conversation with the ex-mayor of Pengony, but at Jesse's insistence he did so.

Eulaliah Vincent listened in silence until he had completed his story. Then she said quietly, 'These are serious allegations, young man. Be very careful to whom you repeat them. Sir Colman has much to lose.'

'So have the fishermen of Mevagissey. The future of Mevagissey as a fishing-village is at stake – and with it their livelihood.'

'Perhaps. But how many of these fishermen will stand with you and fight for their future? The answer is none! They did not support Walter Dunn, and they will fail you in the same way. Tell me, how do you intend to use this information?'

'To have Sir Colman thrown out of Parliament,' replied Ben defiantly.

Eulaliah Vincent looked at him thoughtfully. 'I believe you will . . . and you may well succeed. If you do, you will bring shame upon a family that has served Cornwall well for a great many years. I will not pretend to like my nephew, but I was very fond of his father – and I am myself a Vincent. Can I persuade you to change your mind?'

Ben shook his head slowly, 'No. Too many people have suffered at Sir Colman's hands. He claims to represent Cornwall in Parliament, but ordinary people mean nothing to him because they have no vote and can't help to elect him. I intend to prove that we *can* have him removed.'

'Are you certain this is *all* you want, Ben Retallick? To remove my nephew from the House of Commons? Or are you seeking lasting fame for yourself as the "ordinary" man who brought a baronet to justice?'

'I want only to stop Sir Colman from making life impossible for the Mevagissey fishermen.'

While he was talking, Eulaliah Vincent did not take her eyes from Ben's face. Now she nodded, apparently satisfied.

'Very well, Ben Retallick. I will trust you. In return you will need to put your faith in me. David Howell is High Sheriff of Cornwall. He is also a close friend. I will give you a letter for him. Tell him everything you know – then say nothing more to anyone. Leave him to take whatever action he feels may be necessary. Your name need never be mentioned. It will be better so – for all of us.'

Ben could not believe that he had succeeded in gaining Eulaliah Vincent's support. It had been too easy.

His puzzlement showed as he said, 'Thank you . . . but why should you help me against your own nephew?'

'I am trying to avert a major scandal,' came the surprising reply. 'My nephew has made a great many enemies, some of them men of influence. One day one of them will learn about Sir Colman's blatant vote-buying and press criminal charges against him. Every man in the country who clamours for parliamentary reform will point to him as an example of all that is wrong with our electoral system. They will raise such a hullabaloo that the Prime Minister will be forced to make an example of Sir Colman. He would go to prison, and the whole Vincent family would share his shame. By doing things my way I hope Sir Colman will fade quickly out of your lives. Is that not what you seek?'

'Yes, but what if he persists in his tithe demands, from sheer spite.'

'David Howell will attend to that. No doubt he will point out to Sir Colman the folly of increasing his unpopularity at such a time.'

Ben tried hard to hide his elation at the thought that Sir Colman Vincent finally stood on the brink of disaster. He began to thank Eulaliah Vincent, but she silenced him brusquely.

'The last thing I want is gratitude for what I am doing. I will need to keep telling myself that this is for the good of the family. Already the name "Judas" springs unwanted to my mind. Go now, both of you, and come back tomorrow for my letter to David Howell.'

When Ben returned to collect the letter, he learned that the High Sheriff had his estate in east Cornwall, not more than six miles from the slopes of Sharptor. It was all the excuse Ben needed to return to the mines on the moor. He told Jesse he would deliver the letter to Mr Howell, then go on to Sharptor to seek work and a cottage for them.

Jesse had other ideas.

'You are not returning to Sharptor without me,' she declared emphatically. 'The last time you left me you were away for two years. I am not going to let that happen again. I'm coming with you.'

Ben did not argue. He could think of nothing he would enjoy more than to have Jesse accompany him on a journey halfway across the breadth of Cornwall.

Martha Retallick did not share his pleasure. With Jesse nearby, she knew he would always return to the district. If Jesse went with him, there was little to bring him back to Mevagissey.

Ben was eventually able to reassure her that he *would* come back. Then he set off to the harbour. He found Mark Dunn sitting on the quay, repairing a storm-damaged seine-net recently recovered from rocks outside the harbour. The shortage of long seine-nets was almost as serious to the fishermen as the loss of their boats.

Mark Dunn acknowledged Ben's presence with a grunt and a barely perceptible nod of his head. 'Have you come to tell me that girl of yours has seen Sir Colman Vincent? Has he agreed to waive all our tithes?' The fisherman snorted derisively. 'He's more likely to raise them again because we've been tardy in paying up.'

'Sir Colman is out of Cornwall, so Jesse hasn't been able to see him. But it means he'll be making no new decisions for a while. That doesn't mean nothing is being done. I am going to east Cornwall to see the High Sheriff. I want you to tell the other fishermen not to pay any increased tithes. They will be reduced again very soon.'

Mark Dunn lowered the seine-net to the ground and stared hard at Ben. 'What nonsense is this? Can you work miracles now?'

'I can't tell you more at the moment.'

'You'll need to do better than that! If you think I am going to tell Mevagissey fishermen to break the law on your say-so, you'd better think again, Ben. You tell them yourself if you want to.'

Mark Dunn's attitude was not unexpected. He was no leader of men as his brother Walter had been. He would follow the example of the others readily enough. He could not be called upon to show them the way.

'All right, I'll speak to them, but it will have to be tonight. I intend leaving in the morning. Will you put out the word

315

that I'll be at the end of the harbour wall shortly before sunset ?'

Mark Dunn shrugged. 'I'll tell any man I see. I make no promises about how many will be there.'

Mark Dunn's pessimism proved to be unfounded. The tithe issue was of great importance to the Mevagissey fishermen. They were ready to listen to any one who had something to say.

Ben repeated the message he had given to Mark Dunn, adding that he had something of importance to say to the High Sheriff and was quite sure the demand for higher tithes would not be pursued.

Once again it was Mark Dunn who was sceptical. He asked Ben how he was going to force Sir Colman to change his mind.

'I have told you as much as I can,' replied Ben patiently, 'I can only add that *I* am convinced I'll succeed. Others who are in a position to know feel the same. All I'm asking is that you all hold out a while longer against the tithe increases.'

'It's an easy enough thing for you to ask.' This time the dissenter was Billy Dunn. 'You run no risk of a constable coming to arrest you for debt, seizing everything for which you've worked for years.'

'Would you rather give it all up without a fight ?' retorted Ben. 'Is that what Walter would have done ?'

'What is there to argue about ?' asked another fisherman. 'I doubt whether there are more than two fishermen in the village with the money to pay their tithes. No one is going to pay anything to Sir Colman Vincent. We'll hold out against him for as long as we can. Mind you, when the arrests start, things might be different.'

'Sir Colman Vincent will have dropped his demands long before there are any arrests,' declared Ben confidently. He fervently hoped he would not be proved wrong. 'If justice is done, it will be a very long time before Sir Colman and his agent trouble us again.'

'Amen to that,' said a fisherman who was standing close to Ben. 'But we'll believe it when it comes about.'

Chapter Thirty-Three

David Howell, gentleman and High Sheriff of Cornwall, had his home in a quiet valley through which flowed the River Inny. Walking with Jesse along the long drive leading to the house, Ben was reminded of Lamorrack House. David Howell's house was not as large, but it gave Ben the same feeling in the pit of his stomach. The sensation was heightened when, after handing Eulaliah Vincent's letter to a footman, they were left to wait in a modest inner hallway.

Ben was glad to have Jesse with him, and when he smiled at her she whispered, 'Do you remember when we waited together like this to go in and see Sir John?'

'That was a whole lifetime ago!' There was something about the atmosphere here in the hallway that caused them both to whisper. 'We were only children then.'

Jesse took his hand and squeezed it, releasing it again quickly when a door opened and the footman re-entered the hallway.

'Come with me, please.'

He led them along a narrow corridor and up a half-flight of stairs to an oak-panelled door set in an angle of the house. Opening the door, the footman motioned for them to go inside.

Once through the doorway, they found themselves in a small and comfortable study. Standing in the centre of the room, David Howell was frowning as he read Eulaliah Vincent's letter for the second time.

Cornwall's High Sheriff was a short, rotund, well-dressed man of middle-age and he was greatly perturbed by what he was reading. Finally, he peered at Ben and Jesse over the top of the pince-nez, balanced halfway down his nose.

'What is all this?' He waved the letter in the air and glared at Ben. 'I gather the accusations are yours? Do you realise their seriousness?'

'I do . . . But they happen to be true.'

'You *believe* them to be true, which is not quite the same thing. Do you mind telling me why you are pursuing these charges against Sir Colman Vincent ?'

Ben's hopes had sunk the moment David Howell began to speak. He had the same arrogant manner as Sir Colman Vincent himself. Ben felt he had little chance of a sympathetic hearing from this man. Nevertheless, it was important to try to persuade the High Sheriff to take action against Pengony's Member of Parliament.

'I could give you many reasons. He had my mother put out of her house and took away the farm Sir John Vincent had promised to Jesse and myself – but that is all in the past. The important thing at the moment is to get him to drop the increase in tithes imposed upon the fishermen of Mevagissey. Every boat in the village was smashed by the great storm, and the fishermen are facing ruin. Sir Colman's new tithe rates will take away my mother's livelihood and that of most of Mevagissey's men and women.'

'Are you a member of this Parliamentary Reform Party ?'

'No. I belong to no reform movement – yet I must agree with their aims. There is urgent need for reform when men like Sir Colman Vincent can buy their way into Parliament.'

David Howell frowned, but he said nothing for a while. Then suddenly he turned his attention to Jesse.

'Your face is uncommonly familiar. What is your name ?'

'Jesse Henna. I have lived all my life at Pengrugla. I don't think we've met before.'

'Probably not. And yet . . . But never mind.'

To Ben he said, 'Why should Eulaliah Vincent be helping you in this matter ? I must confess I find all this very difficult to understand.'

'Miss Vincent thinks my information might lead to serious trouble for Sir Colman if it found its way into other hands. She said it might even mean prison for him.'

David Howell nodded non-committally. 'How is it you know Eulaliah Vincent ?'

'My mother was her personal maid, and Ben and I are to be married . . .' Jesse's explanation faltered and then stopped as enlightenment came to David Howell.

318

'*Now* I know why you look so familiar! You are the image of your mother when she was your age. By heaven, but she was a handsome girl.'

Suddenly the High Sheriff's whole attitude towards them changed, his air of suspicion gone.

'Now I understand why Eulaliah is doing all this for you. She looked upon your mother more as a daughter than as a servant. Ah, yes! Eulaliah Vincent has bided her time well . . . All right, Retallick, I will do what I can. It may take a while but, if what you have said is true, I can assure you that Sir Colman Vincent will lose his seat in the House of Commons. No doubt Lord Liverpool will disfranchise Pengony at the same time. Not that it will matter very much to anyone except Sir Colman and his fellow Pengony Member of Parliament. Pengony's need for representation disappeared a great many years ago.'

David Howell showed Ben and Jesse from the house himself and watched from the doorway as they walked hand-in-hand down the long driveway.

When they were almost out of sight, he whispered to himself, 'By God, Colman, be sure your sins are seeking you out now. You sowed the seeds of your own destruction when you bedded Eulaliah's maid all those years ago!'

Ben and Jesse arrived at Henwood weary from a long day's travelling, but it did not prevent Ben from pausing on the road before Henwood village to point out to Jesse the mines, dotted along the slopes of the moor, and clustered together in the valley beyond.

Jesse looked from the vast emptiness of the moor beyond the slopes of Sharptor, to the smoking chimneys and torn turf of the valley bottom.

'Where will we live, Ben?'

'I don't know yet. It will depend on where I find work.'

'I hope it's somewhere up there.' Jesse pointed upwards, to where the rocky mass that was Sharptor towered above the village. 'I don't think I would enjoy living among the smoke and noise of the valley.'

Ben remembered the view across the Tamar valley from

his lean-to hut on the moor. He, too, hoped he could find a cottage where he could share the sheer breathtaking beauty of such a view with Jesse.

They walked on in silence until they reached Henwood village, where Ben took Jesse to the Kelynack house. He had already told Jesse of the mining accident that had robbed Mary Kelynack of her husband and every one of her sons. He had mentioned nothing of her daughters.

The door was opened to them by Holly, the youngest of the Kelynack girls. When she saw Ben, she leaped forward and flung her arms about him in a manner that caused Jesse's eyebrows to rise in sharp surprise.

Clutching Ben's hand, Holly Kelynack pulled him in through the doorway, not even noticing Jesse.

'Ma! Ma! Come quickly. It's Ben. Ben's come back.'

Mary Kelynack hurried to the door with Jenny, the second Kelynack daughter, behind her. She did not overlook Jesse, standing silently behind Ben as he hauled back on Holly's arm and halted her eager progress.

'Ben! It's good to see you . . and you, too.' She reached past Ben and took Jesse by the hand. 'You will be Jesse, of course. We've heard all about you. I wondered if Ben would bring you to see us one day.'

As Mary Kelynack looked quickly at the fingers of Jesse's hand to see if she wore a wedding-ring, Jesse saw the surprise on the faces of the two girls. Mrs Kelynack might have known *all* about her. Her daughters certainly knew far less.

'I was hoping you might be able to put Jesse up for a while,' Ben was saying to Mrs Kelynack. 'I want to find work here, somewhere with a cottage to go along with it. Then Jesse and I will be married.'

'You can *both* stay here. The house seems even emptier since Kate left. I am thinking of looking for a smaller place myself. This house is too large for a widow woman and two girls.'

'Kate's gone? Where?'

Mary Kelynack jerked her head in the direction of Sharptor. 'Up there . . . with Moses Trago.'

Seeing Ben's shocked surprise, she answered his unasked

question. 'Oh, she married him properly. Wrightwick Roberts saw to that. I was against the marriage from the start. Kate knew it, but she took no notice of me, nor did she have to. She was a widow and able to choose her own future. For all that, I would be happier if she and Moses had moved into a proper house and not that . . . that *place* on the moor. They say the old men used to bury their dead there, years ago. What sort of home is that for a young girl?'

'If Kate doesn't like it, she might persuade Moses to move down into the village.'

Mary Kelynack let out a loud and meaningful snort. 'Our Kate persuade Moses Trago to do something? They haven't been married much more than a month and she can't keep him at home. He's gone back to his old habits of drinking and fighting in the ale-houses. I feel sorry for our Kate, but I'm not going to interfere. There was a time when I hoped Ah! It is no use talking about it now. Kate knew you wouldn't be coming back – at least, not as a single man. Now sit yourself down, the pair of you. You must be tired out from tramping around the countryside on a day like this. Wait until Wrightwick hears you are back! He's been talking of going to Mevagissey again to find out what happened to you. But he is kept busy around here, although there are still more funerals than weddings ' or baptisms. It's always the way where there are mines. There were four killed at the Marke Valley mine only last week . . .'

Jesse listened to Mary Kelynack's chatter in silence. Later, when she and Ben were eating with the others, at the table, she answered the questions put to her by the Kelynacks readily enough, but she said little to Ben.

He thought she was probably tired; it had been a long day. However, when she had been taken up to the room that was to be hers during her stay, Ben looked in to see if she was comfortable – and he learned there was another reason for her silence.

After making certain none of the Kelynack family had come upstairs with Ben, Jesse closed the door to her room and rounded on him so suddenly he was taken by surprise.

'What did Mrs Kelynack mean when she said that Kate

321

knew you wouldn't come back as a single man? She good as suggested that Kate might have waited for you had I not been around. What went on between the two of you?'

Ben was astonished. He had never before experienced such jealousy. Coming from Jesse, he found it doubly confusing.

'There was never anything between Kate and myself. When I first visited this house she hadn't long been widowed. She broke down and cried and I comforted her. That was all there ever was. I swear it.'

'Did Kate realise that?'

'Of course she did. Why do you think she married Moses Trago so soon after I'd gone?'

Ben had begun to perspire. Whilst protesting his innocence he had suddenly remembered Aileen Brenahan. What Jesse would do if ever she learned about that episode did not bear thinking about.

'Girls are liable to do some funny things when the man they love is going to marry someone else,' said Jesse darkly. Then her face cleared and she kissed him long and lovingly. 'It's all right, Ben Retallick. I love you – but it will do you no harm to know you are marrying a jealous woman.'

Her words did nothing to help Ben's peace of mind. Gulping down his misgivings, he said, 'I need to find Moses and learn where I might find work and a cottage. I'll take you to meet him and Kate tomorrow evening.'

Ben spent the next day showing Jesse around Henwood and the moors above the village. It was now August, one of the finest months of the year to see the moor, with the fern at its luxuriant best, standing tall and dark green on the lower slopes of Sharptor. Above the fern level, where the heather clung to the granite-grey rock-face, it was a subtle blend of pink and grey.

On the summit of the tor, Jesse leaned back in Ben's arms and held her breath at the sheer beauty of the view laid out before her. The distant tors and slopes of Dartmoor dominated the horizon. Between the two moors was Kit Hill, surrounded by woodland, with here and there a church-tower standing sentinel over a crumpled patchwork of multicoloured fields.

'I don't think I have ever seen anywhere quite so lovely as this place, Ben,' Jesse breathed happily.

Ben tightened his arms about her. 'Then you won't mind living here?'

'It will be a wonderful place to bring up a family. A boy could play some marvellous games up here . . .'

'Steady! Saying things like that could put a man off marriage.'

'No, Ben Retallick. Not you. I'll give you a son you'll be proud of – and he will be equally proud of you. But you must promise to bring him up here often. I want him to grow up with the knowledge that there is more to life than a hole in the ground and a mountain of mine-waste.'

'I promise.'

Ben turned Jesse to him and they came together on the moorland tor, surrounded by their future.

When Ben and Jesse arrived at Moses and Kate Trago's moorland home, the sun had moved on beyond the ridge, leaving the ancient cromlech in deep shadow. Jesse was unable to control a shudder as they approached the stone-slab dwelling. She did not know whether it was because they had passed from the sunlight, or whether the sudden chill sprang from a more sinister source. Instinctively, she knew there had been much unhappiness here.

Smoke was pouring from a hole in the stone, indicating that someone was at home, and Ben put his head around the odd-shaped door, built to fit into a gap between the rocks. He called a loud 'Hello', and heard a sound from within. Then the door was pulled wide open and Kate Trago looked out at them.

When she saw Ben, her face showed a mixture of joy and dismay that might have been amusing under different circumstances. Then she saw Jesse, and Kate Trago's hand went instinctively to her hair. It dangled untidily about her face, but neither Jesse nor Ben had eyes for her hair. They were both looking at the ugly bruise that discoloured Kate Trago's left eye and spread over most of her cheek-bone.

'I'm sorry.' Kate Trago took control of herself. 'Won't you

come inside? It's not much at the moment . . . but me and Moses will soon get it fixed up. There's been no one to look after the place for so long . . .'

Ben stepped awkwardly through the strange-shaped doorway and helped Jesse in after him. When he turned back to Kate she had tied her long hair hastily into a knot behind her head and was placing a pot of water on the hot ashes of the fire.

'You'll have tea? We've got some. I bought it only yesterday. I'm not so sure about cups. You are my first visitors.'

Kate Trago laughed nervously. It was a sad uncertain sound. When Ben introduced Jesse, Kate gave her a quick smile, trying hard to keep the bruised side of her face away from the other woman.

Eventually, Kate Trago located two cups. With her hand shaking nervously, she poured a weak sugarless brew of tea from the pot and handed the cups to her visitors.

'Where is Moses? I want to talk to him about the mines in the area. I thought he'd be home by now.'

'He . . . he'll be in the ale-house. He's taken to drinking again, this last week or two. He and brother John will be home when they are ready . . . but it probably won't be until late.'

'Ben, you finish your tea and go down to the ale-house for your talk with Moses. I'll stay up here for a while and chat to Kate.' Jesse's manner was unusually brisk. 'There is no need to come back again. I'll see you at Kate's mother's house.'

Ben had not yet finished his tea, but Jesse took the cup from his hands and shooed him towards the door. Looking over Jesse's shoulder, Ben hardly had time to call 'Goodbye!' to Kate Trago before he was outside. He glimpsed her seated on the far side of the fire, an unhappy forlorn figure. She raised her face to him and then he was gone.

On his way to the village, Ben wondered why Jesse had been so anxious for him to leave the Trago home. He thought about it until the village came into view, then shrugged it away. He accepted that he would never fully understand the workings of Jesse's mind.

Moses was seated in a corner of the ale-house with his

brother John when Ben entered. He did not look up until a couple of men from the Wheal Slade greeted Ben and asked him what he was doing back in Henwood. Moses Trago's face lit up in a brief greeting, but it had returned to its customary scowl by the time Ben called for three drinks and sat down opposite the Trago brothers.

'Hello, Moses . . . John. I've just taken Jesse up to your place to see Kate.'

'Oh? Then I expect you've heard all about me blacking her eye?'

'No. Kate said nothing. But as she did her best to hide it from us I knew it must be your doing. Why, Moses? Kate is a good girl.'

Ben spoke quietly, anxious not to anger Moses. He knew that, if he did, Kate would be the one to suffer.

'I didn't mean to hit her. You can believe that, or not.' Moses glared at Ben belligerently.

'I believe you.'

Moses Trago relaxed slightly. 'I'd been drinking,' he admitted. 'She was nagging at me and I meant to push her away. She must have moved.'

Moses gave a gesture of helplessness, then was angry with himself for showing his feelings. He took the drink that was slid in front of him by the landlord and quaffed half of it in one long movement.

'She should have married you, not me. No, don't argue with me. I'm *telling* you. She only took me because she needed a man . . . any man. It was you she really wanted. Between you and that damned dead husband of hers, I don't stand a chance. I work away at her in bed and know she's thinking of you . . . or maybe it's him. I don't know any more – and I don't care.'

'You're wrong, Moses. Kate married you; it's you that she wants. Why don't you get off home and find out for yourself?'

Moses downed the remainder of his ale and bellowed for the landlord to bring more. Snapping his fingers only inches from Ben's nose, he said, 'I don't give *that* whether I am right or wrong! She married me and she'll treat me as a husband and do as I tell her, or I'll know the reason why. She'll have

325

food for me when I get home and I'll take her whenever I want her. For the rest of it, I'll go my own way, just as I have always done. Now forget about Kate. You didn't come all this way just to talk about her – or did you ?'

Ben finished his drink slowly and deliberately, then set the empty pot down upon the table.

'No, I didn't come here to talk about your wife, although I doubt if she has anyone else to take her part. Bring her down from the moor, Moses. Move out of that tomb and into a proper house. Give Kate something in which she can take a pride. She'll show you she is a good wife.'

Moses Trago's scowl deepened. 'There's nothing wrong with the place we have now. I am not coming down to the village so Kate can tell every nosey biddy my business, while her mother keeps an eye on us every minute of the day. No, we'll stay up on the moor, out of the way.'

'Then I have nothing more to say, Moses. Jesse and I will be wed soon. I hope you'll not object to Jesse calling on Kate sometimes ?'

Moses shrugged impassively. 'As long as Kate is there when I want her she can see whoever she pleases.'

There was nothing more to be said. Ben could not discuss the prospect of work with Moses Trago while his treatment of Kate stood between them.

Ben looked back from the ale-house doorway and saw Moses shaking his head at something his brother was saying to him. Ben wondered whether John Trago ever took Kate's part during the arguments in the cromlech home. He doubted it very much. Ben had never heard John Trago express any opinion of his own. He was no more than a large, silent, brooding shadow at his brother's side.

When Ben reached the Kelynack house, Jesse had not yet returned. He sat talking to Mary Kelynack while he waited for her. He mentioned seeing Kate, but said nothing about her bruised face.

'Was that husband of hers up there ?' Mary Kelynack clattered the dishes for the evening meal.

'No, I met him later in the ale-house.'

Mary Kelynack sniffed. 'He'll no doubt spend all his pay in there – half of Kate's, too, if she isn't careful.'

'I wanted to talk to Moses about finding a mine that could offer me a cottage along with a job.' Ben steered the conversation away from Kate.

'What makes you think Moses would know anything about that? He would probably suggest you make do with a cave, the same as him and my Kate. Anyway, the mines hereabouts will offer you nothing but a low wage. There are more miners seeking work than there are places to be filled. The only way you'll get a cottage is to wait for a man to be killed, then turn out his widow. Even then, you'll find more than one miner ahead of you.'

Mary Kelynack suddenly paused. 'Mind you, now you've mentioned it, I remember Wrightwick saying something about a new mine opening up on Sharptor. He says they are going to work tin when it first opens, but are really after copper. They'll need to build cottages if it is to be any sort of mine at all. It might be worth a try, especially as it doesn't seem to be common knowledge yet.'

'Who is to be the captain? I'll go and see him.' Ben was excited at the news. He had worked for copper in the Tamar valley and stood a good chance of being given work on the new mine.

'I don't think things have gone far enough for the mine to have a captain yet. I do know there will be no adventurers. The mine is to have only one owner – Theophilus Strike. He lives over by Launceston. His family is well known in these parts. Why don't you go to Launceston and speak to him?'

'I will, first thing tomorrow. Thank you for telling me.'

For the next half-hour Ben discussed mining with Mary Kelynack. She declared that the character of the whole area was changing as the mines expanded and took on new men. It had once been possible to walk for five miles in any direction and know every man, woman and child with whom one met. Now, Mary Kelynack said, half the population of Henwood were strangers, all of them bringing strangers' ways to the village with them.

'Before you know it, they'll be complaining about us doing the things we've done here for as along as anyone can remember. Why, only the other day—'

What it was that had happened the other day, Ben never knew. At that moment Jesse came in, and Mary Kelynack called her two daughters in from the garden and began to dish out the meal.

Only the lively chatter of Jenny and Holly Kelynack prevented the meal from being an unusually serious affair. Ben said little for fear the conversation would return to Kate and Moses. Jesse, too, was strangely silent. It was a relief when the meal was over and Ben and Jesse were able to make an excuse to leave the house and go for a walk together in the late-summer twilight.

They walked along the track that clung precariously to the steep moorland hillside, but it was too dark to see the view. There were only the stars, and the dull red glow from the valley bottom as a furnace door was flung open and coal from the Welsh quarries shovelled inside.

Ben told Jesse what Mary Kelynack had said about the new mine on Sharptor. They tried to imagine what it would be like to live upon the tor on such a night as this with the stars peppering the sky and a bloated moon rising over Bodmin Moor.

As they walked they planned their house and garden, family and future. Then, returning along a different track, they passed close to the home of Kate and Moses Trago and they both fell silent.

Not until they were well beyond all possible hearing did Ben say, 'I wish Moses and Kate had dreams for the future. As things are, I think poor Kate can look forward to nothing but trouble.'

'Far more than we realised,' agreed Jesse quietly. 'Kate is pregnant.'

Chapter Thirty-Four

Theophilus Strike was a large man with a florid complexion and a manner that was blunt to the point of rudeness. When Ben explained his reason for calling upon the mine-owner, Strike frowned. 'Who told you about the Sharptor mine?'

'A widow with whom I lodge. Word gets around quickly when a new mine is to open.'

'Does it, be damned! Then I had better get myself a mine captain quickly, or every out-of-work miner in Cornwall will be banging on my door and begging for work. What do *you* know about copper?'

Ben told Theophilus Strike in some detail, confident he knew more about copper mining than the man standing before him.

Theophilus Strike listened for many minutes before impatiently waving Ben to silence. 'All right! All right! I don't want to learn how to mine copper myself. I just want to be sure the men I employ know what they're doing. No doubt you've mined tin, too?'

'Since I was ten,' Ben declared.

'Very well, I'll employ you. Do you know Tom Shovell, of Henwood?'

Ben's face lit up. 'I know him well. We worked together at the Wheal Slade.'

'You'll be working with him again. He is to be one of my shift captains. Tell him I'm making him responsible for taking on all the men we'll need to open the mine. He can decide for himself how many that should be. I don't want him to bother me until everything is arranged. Right, Retallick, you may go now.'

Ben hesitated, and Theophilus Strike looked at him impatiently. 'What are you waiting for? If it's an advance of pay, you can forget it. I will pay a fair wage for work done, but I'll not give a penny on promises.'

'It's not money, but a cottage. I'm to be married soon . . . as soon as I have a house.'

Theophilus Strike came close to a smile as he looked at Ben's anxious expression. He knew his reply would decide Ben's whole future, yet Ben was doing his utmost not to allow his feelings to show.

Strike liked the look of the serious young man standing before him. He was just the type of miner he hoped to attract to the Wheal Sharptor. Once he was married and settled in a mine-cottage, Ben Retallick would constitute a lifetime's investment.

'You can have your cottage, Retallick. Tell Tom Shovell we will have eight cottages up on the tor, close to the mine. He can build another twelve on the piece of land I own in Henwood village. Let your future bride choose where she wants to live – that should please her. The terms of occupancy will be the usual ones. You build the house yourself from mine materials, and it will remain yours during the lifetimes of three named tenants.'

Ben nodded his agreement. His joy was so overwhelming he would not trust himself to speak. Theophilus Strike had given him all he wanted. Now there was nothing to prevent him and Jesse from marrying – and they would have their home on Sharptor.

Although it was nine long miles to Henwood from Launceston, it was as much as Ben could do to stop himself running all the way. When he was still more than a mile from the village, a turn in the road brought the grey granite tor into view and Ben could control himself no longer.

He arrived at the Kelynack house too breathless to say anything. Picking up the startled Jesse, he swung her round and round the kitchen until they both collapsed in a laughing giddy tangle on the wooden bench set against the table.

'You've got the job, Ben? Theophilus Strike gave it to you?'

'Yes ... and much more besides. I can build a house for us. He said you must choose whether it will be up on the tor, or down here in the village.'

Jesse caught Ben's excitement. As she hugged him, she said, 'I can't believe this is really happening, Ben! It's exactly what we were dreaming about when we were up on the tor the other day. How long will a house take to build?'

'That depends how long Tom Shovell takes to find all the miners he needs. There are twenty houses to be built, and the miners will share in their building. Ours will be the first. We can find Wrightwick Roberts and have him arrange a wedding date as soon as you like.'

Tom Shovell was pleased to learn that Ben would be one of his miners at Wheal Sharptor, and he accompanied Ben and Jesse to the site of the mine that same evening.

With Tom Shovell's help, Jesse chose the exact site of the house she and Ben would have. From its windows it would have an uninterrupted view over the wide valley to the east. Behind the cottage, the contours of the moor would not only protect it from the prevailing west wind, but also hide the mine-buildings from view. Ben and Jesse could have found no finer site for a house had they been able to choose anywhere on the eastern moor.

Locating Wrightwick Roberts was more difficult. His Methodist circuit covered a very wide area, his parishioners spread thinly over many miles of moorland. It took in mining communities and farms, Wrightwick's little chapels being dotted here and there around the countryside. After two days of fruitless searching, Ben gave up his quest. He and Jesse would have to wait until the preacher's circuit-riding brought him back to Henwood.

Wrightwick Roberts arrived on the last Sunday of August and joyfully embraced Jesse in his big arms when the happy couple told him they wanted to discuss a wedding.

'I feel I can take some credit for this marriage,' he boomed happily to Jesse. 'It was my news from Mevagissey that sent him scurrying off to find you again – and not before time. He has been wandering Cornwall like a lost soul for far too long. Now, tell me when you would like the wedding to be and I will speak to the vicar at Linkinhorne.'

The Methodist church was in its infancy and the laws of the land did not yet permit Methodist preachers to conduct weddings. Ben and Jesse would have to marry in the parish

331

church, at Linkinhorne. Afterwards, they would return to the tiny Henwood chapel where Wrightwick Roberts would conduct a special service in honour of the occasion.

It was decided that Ben and Jesse would marry when the cottage at Wheal Sharptor was ready to be roofed. Although the first stone had yet to be laid, the time was not as far off as it seemed at the moment.

As soon as Tom Shovell began taking on men, news went around so swiftly that before two days had passed he had a full work-force, drawn from the type of men Theophilus Strike wanted. They, too, were keen on bringing their families to live near the mine and would waste no time in building the cottages. All the stone taken from the ground as they dug the main mine-shaft would be trimmed and utilised in the construction of a cottage that would be built in a month, yet last for two hundred years.

Then, when the Wheal Sharptor shaft had reached a depth of thirty fathoms, and the cottage being built for Ben and Jesse was at bedroom-window height, something happened that threatened to prejudice the secure future they believed was theirs.

A man with a severe limp and an accent that had never before been heard in the area came to Henwood asking for Ben Retallick. He was directed to the Wheal Sharptor.

Ben climbed the ladder at the end of a long shift spent driving the first level at ten fathoms, to find the stranger waiting for him. He introduced himself to Ben as Charles Swindles, from Manchester. A member of the Midlands Parliamentary Reform Party, Swindles' career as a reformer had been assured when he was cut down by a militiaman's sword. It had happened at the great meeting at St Peter's Field, in Manchester, in the year 1819. This was the so-called 'massacre', referred to by the reform militants forever afterwards as 'Peterloo'.

Much to Ben's surprise, Swindles greeted him enthusiastically, pumping his hand and offering his congratulations. 'It's a great honour to meet you, Ben. You've done more for the reform movement by your single-handed action than the rest of us put together. Congratulations!'

Ben was baffled. 'Are you sure you are talking to the right person? What is it I'm supposed to have done?'

'If you're Ben Retallick, then you are the man I've been looking for. Not only have you exposed the sort of vote-buying we know is going on but, with the disfranchisement of Sir Colman Vincent's borough, Manchester and Bradford have gained seats in the House of Commons. We in the Midlands are deeply in your debt.'

'Sir Colman has been thrown out of Parliament? Already?'

'Are you telling me you haven't heard?' Now it was the turn of Charles Swindles to show his astonishment. 'Good Lord, man! This has happened right here in Cornwall, not so many miles from you, yet we in Manchester know about it before you! What sort of an organisation do you have here?'

'I belong to no organisation. I did only what needed to be done. Sir Colman Vincent didn't deserve to be an elected Member of Parliament.'

Even as he replied to the Midlands reformer, Ben wondered how Swindles had learned who had toppled Sir Colman Vincent. David Howell had promised Ben it would remain a secret.

'Sir Colman Vincent can consider himself lucky that our Reform Party didn't learn about him before you. We'd have crucified him. Nailed him to the cross of his own greed and corruption. But what do you intend doing now?'

'Intend doing? I'll finish building my house on Sharptor and be married. Then I hope to work here at the Wheal Sharptor for a great many happy years.'

'You'll spend your life mining, after what you've achieved? That would be a stupid bloody waste – both for you and for the Movement. Stay here by all means, if that's what you really want, but at least take over the leadership of the Parliamentary Reform Movement in Cornwall. Bring it into the National movement. Better still, come back to the Midlands with me and contest one of the parliamentary seats you've given to us. You'll be voted in with an overwhelming majority – the first of a long line of worker-members. It's the chance of a lifetime for you, Ben. You're being given the opportunity to shake this country as though it were an appletree. In the shaking, a lot of rotten apples like Sir Colman Vincent will fall. Parliamentary reform is coming, be assured of that. What's more, it will be a far-reaching reform. Men like you and I, and all the poor miners climbing out of that hole in the ground, will have the right to send our own men to speak for us in Parliament. Men of *our* choice. That's what the Parliamentary Reform Party is working for, Ben. You can be a part of it. Tell men what you did – and how you did it. We'll raise such a hullabaloo throughout the land that Lord Liverpool won't dare hold out any longer. He'll have to give us our rights – or we'll take them for ourselves.'

Charles Swindles' words were spoken with a passionate fervour that shone from him like a madness. He made Ben feel uncomfortable. Beliefs meant more to such men than religion – or even life itself. If Ben threw in his lot with Charles Swindles, he would be swept along on an inexorable tide of fanaticism that would eventually overwhelm him. Ben's gaze went from the wide undulating valley laid out before him to the buildings going up about the Sharptor shaft.

'Politics and reform parties are not for me, Mr Swindles. You pursue your dreams wherever they take you. I'll follow tin and copper lodes. They are familiar things to me. I know what they will bring.'

The fire shining from Charles Swindles' eyes burned away as suddenly as it had flared into life. 'I knew you were going to say something like that to me, Ben. As I toiled up here and looked over my shoulder I realised I had little chance of winning you over.'

He swept an arm in an arc that encompassed the whole valley. 'Such beauty as this kills a man's ambition. He needs to be hemmed in by brick walls, surrounded by misery and degradation; the stench of death and disease in his nostrils. That's what makes a man stand up and fight for his rights. He either climbs above everyone else . . . or they climb upon him.'

Charles Swindles gave Ben a rueful smile. 'A radical in Cornwall is crushed to death between John Wesley's teachings and God's own works. However, I'm a man who is used to doing his best with what he has to hand. Will you at least

334

help me to organise a reform meeting, Ben ?'
'No, but I'll introduce you to those who will . . . '

Charles Swindles held his meeting the next evening, high on
the moor above the mines. If he mourned for the lack of
revolutionary enthusiasm, he was, nevertheless, well pleased
with the numbers attending his meeting. There must have
been four thousand men and women gathered to hear him
speak. It was a tremendous crowd for such an isolated spot.

Ben and Jesse went along to hear the Manchester reformer
remind his listeners of the aims of his party, and its part in
the politics of the new industrial towns of the Midlands.
Since the end of the war with France, the working masses
had been frequently stirred into violent action against their
living and working conditions. The days of wilfully damaging
new machinery were past, but when a hostile mob went on the
rampage most mill-owners were quick to agree to the demands
made upon them. New workers in the industrial areas were
immediately drawn into 'societies' or 'unions'.

Then Charles Swindles spoke of the Parliamentary Reform
Party's hopes for the future, and told of Ben's part in having
Sir Colman Vincent removed from the House of Commons.
Swindles went far beyond the true facts of the matter, and
Ben edged out of the crowd with Jesse, fearful that the
reformer would call him forward and involve him in the
meeting against his wishes.

Ben was unable to prevent men from repeating what the
Midland reformer had said, and it was not long before news
of Ben's accomplishment reached the ears of Theophilus
Strike.

Ben was called to grass from the advancing ten-fathom
level of the Wheal Sharptor late one afternoon. He entered
the mine office to find Theophilus Strike waiting impatiently
for him. The blunt mine-owner wasted no time in coming
straight to the point of his visit.

'Word has reached me that you've been involved in depos-
ing the Member of Parliament for Pengony. Is this correct,
Retallick ?'

'Yes,' Ben replied quietly. His heart sank at the thought of

335

being made to leave Sharptor now, when his cottage was so near to completion. He and Jesse had so much of their future tied up here.

Theophilus Strike waited for Ben to explain. When nothing was forthcoming, he said, 'You are a good miner, Retallick. I have no complaints about your work, but I am starting a new mine here – with my own money. I have taken a big gamble. The last thing I need is to have a troublemaker working for me. If you have any explanation to give, I am ready to listen. If not, you can leave the mine now.'

Theophilus Strike was showing uncharacteristic restraint, and Ben realised he was being given an unexpected opportunity to justify his actions. He also realised he owed Theophilus Strike an explanation.

He began his story with the disaster of the Money Box mine and told of the move to Mevagissey and Pearson Retallick's tragic death at Tregassick. He went on to speak of Sir Colman Vincent's failure to honour Sir John's promise, turning the Retallicks out of their house and attempting to force Jesse to marry Reuben Holyoak. Ben mentioned the two years he had been away from Jesse, during which time Sir Colman had been responsible for having Walter Dunn transported. He concluded by describing the effects of the storm and Sir Colman's increased tithes on the fishermen of Mevagissey, explaining what it meant to his mother and the Dunn family.

Theophilus Strike listened to Ben's lengthy story without interruption. Feeling a shade more hopeful, Ben added, 'All I wanted was to have Sir Colman Vincent drop his increased tithe charges. Had he not, I would have had to support my mother as well as Jesse and wouldn't have been able to get my marriage off to the start I feel Jesse deserves. I went to see Miss Eulaliah Vincent and she gave me a letter for Mr Howell, the High Sheriff of Cornwall. He did the rest.'

'Eulaliah Vincent? Sir Colman's aunt? She helped you?' Theophilus Strike was incredulous.

Ben repeated Eulaliah Vincent's reason for helping, and Theophilus Strike looked at Ben with a new respect, but he had one more question to ask.

336

'What about this man from Manchester? The rabblerouser who has been trying to stir up the countryside?'

'He came to me and asked me to join the reform movement. He promised a great future with them and said I might even become a Member of Parliament myself.'

'Oh? And what was your reply to this promise of fame and fortune?'

Ben looked straight at the mine-owner. 'I told him I enjoy my work here. The roof will be on my cottage next week, then Jesse and I will be married. I am a miner, nothing more – and nothing less. I've no wish to involve myself with any reform movement.'

A long silence hung in the room. Abruptly, Theophilus Strike stood up from the corner of the desk upon which he had been seated.

'How is that ten-fathom level coming along, Retallick? When do you think you'll be sending up first-quality ore?'

Only then did Ben realise how tensed he had been. His short fingernails had dug deep grooves in the palms of his hands.

He began to tell Theophilus Strike about the prospects of the ten-fathom level, but the mine-owner did not really want to know. Minutes later Ben was descending the ladder on his way back to work. He had never been so happy to be going down a mine-shaft in all his life.

Chapter Thirty-Five

Ben and Jesse arranged their wedding for Sunday, 10 November 1822. The house was finished and wedding gifts in the form of unwanted pieces of furniture arrived daily, donated by friends who worked on the mine. The furniture helped to take away the bareness of newly whitewashed walls and curtainless windows.

A fortnight before the wedding, Ben went to Mevagissey to inform his mother of the wedding date. On this occasion he did not have to walk. Wrightwick Roberts loaned him his old circuit hack for the journey.

On his arrival in Mevagissey, Ben learned to his great embarrassment that he had become a hero in the eyes of the fishermen. He was greeted with deference by men who had been no more than familiar faces until now. But not until he reached the Dunn house was he told the whole reason for their respect.

Martha Retallick was at home with Grandma Dunn. After they had both hugged him and said how well he was looking, they fussed over him and brought him up to date on the many things that had been happening in Mevagissey.

Sir Colman Vincent's latest tithe demand had been dropped within a fortnight of Ben's visit to the High Sheriff of Cornwall. It was quickly followed by the news that Sir Colman had resigned as Member of Parliament for Pengony. Then Pengony's two seats in the House of Commons had been taken away from the village and given to the industrial Midlands.

All this Ben already knew from his conversation with Charles Swindles. What he had *not* known was that Sir Colman Vincent had sold the whole of his Cornish estates and was withdrawing to his lands in Devon. Ben's victory over the baronet had become a rout! Now he knew why the villagers of Mevagissey had saluted him so respectfully.

No sooner had Martha Retallick finished giving her son

the astonishing news than Grandpa Dunn, accompanied by Mark and Billy, arrived home. Ben had to listen to the same news over again. This time it was accompanied by much back-slapping and a familiarity he had never before experienced in the Dunn house.

When there was a quieter moment, Ben asked, 'Does this mean Reuben Holyoak is now without work?'

'No,' replied Martha Retallick regretfully. 'He was. Sir Colman dismissed him before news of the sale came out, but the new owner has taken him back – as a gamekeeper. He's still living up at Pengrugla, by all accounts. He hasn't dared show himself in Mevagissey for many months. Nor will he, if he has any sense left in his head.'

'Is the new owner already in Lamorrack House?' Ben was taken aback by the speed with which things had been happening.

'Yes, and one of the first things he did was to come to Mevagissey to speak to us. He stood on the quay one evening with his young family about him and introduced himself to every fisherman who sailed into the harbour. He said he'd heard of the terrible storm we'd suffered in the summer, and promised he would not be looking for tithes until we were back on our feet again. That's the kind of gentleman we need up at Lamorrack, Ben. We haven't seen the likes of him hereabouts since old Sir John died.'

Mark Dunn had replied to Ben's question and the others all nodded their agreement with his words. It was apparent that the new squire of Lamorrack had made a good first impression upon the fishermen of Mevagissey.

'Don't you be forgetting it was Ben who brought it all about,' said Grandpa Dunn proudly. 'He's a Dunn, and no mistake.'

'It was another Dunn who first obtained the information that finally toppled Sir Colman Vincent,' said Ben. 'If it hadn't been for Walter, none of this might have happened. He has finally been avenged.'

For a moment, Ben wondered if he had made a mistake mentioning Walter. The family might have heard news of his fate. Billy's next words reassured him.

'Walter is on the other side of the world. You are here with us in Mevagissey. Come on down to the Ship Inn, Ben. There's many a fisherman who'd feel honoured to buy you a drink. Things are better now, and no mistake. One more good catch of pilchards and we'll be able to buy our second boat for the next season.'

Ben declined his uncle's invitation, pleading that he needed to make an early start the following day. In spite of their protests he did not weaken. He was going to Tregassick to speak to Eulaliah Vincent, then on to Truro to invite Alan Colborne and Judy Lean to the wedding.

The Dunn family kept Ben talking until late in the night, and he was bleary-eyed when he dismounted from the old circuit horse at the gates of Tregassick House. Eulaliah Vincent was having breakfast and insisted upon Ben joining her at the table.

Ben had expected to find this meeting difficult in view of all that had happened to her nephew and the changes going on about her, but the elderly lady was in high spirits. When Ben told her of the forthcoming wedding, she expressed her satisfaction.

'You will make a handsome couple. Jesse is one of the finest-looking girls in the county, and I can think of no young girl who would not jump at the opportunity of standing at your side before an altar. Now, Ben Retallick, what would you like me to bring for a wedding present ?'

'You are coming to the wedding . . . to Henwood ?'

'I most certainly am! I would not miss Jesse's wedding if you were marrying her in America. Why ? Will I not be welcome ?'

'After all you've done for us ? We will both be very happy to have you there. But you'll need to stay the night and we have little furniture in the house.'

'You need not worry about me. I will stay with David Howell. I want to thank him for the manner in which he handled your "problem". I will send him a letter today.'

Now the subject had been broached, Ben was able to ask the question that had been troubling him.

'You don't mind that Sir Colman has gone from Lamorrack House and left you here, alone?'

'Mind? My dear young man, I am overjoyed! After all these years I am able to go about my business with no interference. There is no one to tell me what I must or must not do. For the first time in my life I am free to do what I will, without having some member of my family express his disapproval. My only regret is that I am not young enough to enjoy my new-found freedom even more.'

Ben left the house marvelling that Sir Colman Vincent should have such an aunt as Eulaliah Vincent.

Ben reached the White Swan Inn in Truro at noon on a quiet Sunday. It was a very different town from the one he and Alan Colborne had entered on the May fair-day earlier in the year. On that occasion its streets had been crowded with noisy country folk from miles around. Today there was hardly a man, woman or child to be seen, for all that it was a fine autumn day. Even the White Swan Inn had only a few customers, and the landlord sat at a table with a tankard of his own ale before him.

He recognised Ben and greeted him warmly, drawing him an ale from the huge barrel at the back of the room and setting a chair at his own table.

'You've chosen a good day to come visiting, Ben. Today I have time to speak with my friends and nothing to do but sit here and drink the best ale to be had in the town.'

'Where is everyone?' asked Ben. 'I've seen no more than five persons since I rode in. Is something wrong? Has cholera struck the town?'

'No, everyone has gone to Falmouth. My own wife and daughter with them. A ship bound for Holland with a cargo of strange creatures from Africa put into Falmouth to repair storm damage. The animals are being transferred to another ship today, and everyone has gone along to watch. I would have gone myself had I been able to find someone to look after the inn. They do say there are monkeys on board that are almost human. As large as you and I, and nearly as clever.

341

Aye, and creatures as heavy as four farm-wagons, with horns on their noses sharp enough to pierce the side of a ship. There will be talk of nothing else in this part of Cornwall for weeks to come.'

There was a note of deep disappointment in the landlord's voice.

'No doubt Alan and Judy have gone with them?'

The landlord looked startled. 'Alan and Judy? They left for Plymouth three months ago. I thought perhaps you might have news of them. They were going to find Judy's mother and then return to Mevagissey to visit you.'

Ben frowned. 'We're no longer at Mevagissey, but I was there only this morning. I would have been told had anyone been enquiring for me.'

Ben was disappointed. He had hoped that Alan Colborne and Judy Lean would be able to attend the wedding at Sharptor. He had meant it to be a happy surprise for Jesse. After telling the landlord of his wedding plans, to pass on to them, should they return in time, Ben set off on the long return journey to Sharptor.

Chapter Thirty-Six

Alan Colborne and Judy Lean travelled to Plymouth by sea from the quay at Truro. Judy dearly wanted to tell her mother of her forthcoming marriage and receive her approval. Alan Colborne had grave misgivings about the mission, but there had been few pleasures in Judy's young life and he fell in with her wishes.

It was the first time Judy had ever been on a ship. She found the experience exciting, yet at the same time terrifying. There was a favourable wind, and the voyage took ten hours. Along the way Alan Colborne asked Judy to describe the coastline to him. Her excitement when she recognised Mevagissey, tucked between its surrounding hills, delighted Alan Colborne and brought amused smiles from the other passengers.

Eventually, the ship heeled over to pass through a small armada of dusty barges. From them, stone and rubble tumbled into the water at the mouth of Plymouth harbour, forming the foundations of a new breakwater. The short voyage was over.

With Alan Colborne holding her arm as they walked from the docks, Judy Lean looked back wistfully at the ship they had just left. It had been a magic voyage for her, a time to be happy with Alan without anyone expecting anything more from her.

Judy knew she was not as clever as other girls. She had always known it, but it had never before mattered quite so much. Sometimes, she had even found her simple ways to be an advantage. When she did things for which other girls would have been punished, people merely shrugged their shoulders and turned away. It was 'that simple Judy again'.

Now Judy Lean had Alan Colborne. What he thought of her mattered more than anything else in her life. She wanted him to be proud of her, not forced to make excuses for her. Judy loved Alan Colborne with a depth of feeling she had never before experienced.

'Where do we start looking?' Alan Colborne broke in upon Judy's thoughts as they came to a street that was filled with the noises of a busy sea-port.

'I don't know,' Judy confessed. 'Ma came to Plymouth to marry a sailor. He used to come to Pentuan on the boats that loaded china-clay. That's all I know.'

'It's enough for a start.' Alan Colborne made it sound more hopeful than he really felt. Finding an unknown and unnamed sailor in a large port such as this was well-nigh impossible. However, they would try, and they were in no great hurry.

The first thing they had to do was find a place to stay. Alan told Judy to look for a boarding-house, far enough away from the docks to keep them from being disturbed all night by the noisy arrival of seamen and their waterfront women, but not so far that a landlord would ask too many questions.

They eventually found a quiet room in a house above the jumbled streets of the Barbican. It was a fortunate choice. The landlady had once had a blind son who reached the age of twelve before he was knocked down and killed by a reckless and intoxicated chaise-driver. The driver was the younger son of one of Devon's richest noblemen. The house where she now lived had been a gift to compensate the widow for her tragic loss. Alan Colborne and Judy Lean could have found no more suitable lodgings.

Locating the dock used by the boats engaged in the carriage of china-clay was equally successful. Indeed, it would have been difficult to miss. Spillages in the streets around the dock stained the cobblestones white. Inside the dock, a choking white cloud hung over the ships and drifted on the air to the sensitive nose of the balladeer.

But here the luck of the two seekers ended. For weeks they hung around the docks and adjacent inns, questioning seamen from every boat that tied up at the quay, hoping to find someone who knew of the seaman who had married Nellie Lean from Mevagissey village.

In the evenings, Alan Colborne played his fiddle in a harbourside inn. It was a rough place, and he would not allow Judy to wait for him there. She took him to the door of the inn early every evening, then returned to collect him again at midnight.

It was an arrangement that worked well for a while. Then, one evening, as Judy led Alan Colborne along the uneven Barbican street, there came the noise of running feet behind them. A man shouted, and in the dark doorway of a nearby house a woman began to scream hysterically.

Judy Lean did not know what was happening, but she took hold of Alan Colborne's arm and ran with him towards a dark and narrow alleyway only a couple of dozen paces away. They would have made it to safety had there not been an iron bollard set into the cobbles in the centre of the alleyway opening.

Alan Colborne stumbled over the bollard and fell full length on the ground. In an instant, two uniformed men pounced upon him and dragged him away, ignoring Judy's screams. The press-gangs were out, recruiting seamen for the men-of-war of His Majesty King George IV's navy.

Alan Colborne was hauled to the water's edge and flung into a boat in which a number of other impressed men cowered. Two of them were badly bruised and one was bleeding from a gash on his forehead. At the top of the steps where the boat was moored, the girl Judy and Alan had heard screaming earlier pleaded hysterically for her man to be released. She was noticeably pregnant.

Every time the press-gang returned to the boat with another unfortunate captive, Judy Lean tried to speak to one of the men, but the wails and shrieks of the pregnant girl drowned her own efforts.

When there were a dozen men in the boat, it was evident that the press-gang would soon have as many 'recruits' as they could safely carry. The hysterical pregnant woman realised it, too. When Judy Lean begged her to be silent for a moment, she wailed the louder. Then Judy saw the officer in charge of the press-gang returning with the remainder of his men, two impressed seamen struggling between them.

Judy had to make herself heard now or it would be too late. The pregnant woman still showed no sign of moderating her noise and, in a moment of sheer desperation, Judy lunged at her, pushing her over the edge of the quay into the water. The pregnant woman landed with a mighty splash, her screams cut short as the dirty waters of the harbour closed over her head.

Instantly, there was pandemonium in the press-gang's boat. Flinging aside the man who tried to hold him, the husband of the pregnant woman leaped over the side, quickly followed by another of the impressed men.

The officer in charge of the press-gang, a limping lieutenant, hobbled to the water's edge and looked down upon the scene of confusion. Rounding on Judy Lean, he said angrily, 'Why did you do that?'

'She wouldn't be quiet. No one could hear me. You must let Alan go – he's blind.'

'Blind? Blind?' The officer looked at Judy Lean suspiciously. 'Are you telling me the truth?'

'Yes. He was blinded in the war, at Waterloo.'

It was some minutes before the officer received any answer to his shouts, such was the noise in the boat. The pregnant woman and her husband had surfaced and were swimming in the wake of the second man to leap from the boat. Heading away from the boat to the far harbour wall, the heavy stomach of the woman was proving no handicap to her swimming.

'Leave them!' the officer ordered. 'We have a good haul this evening. They'll keep for another time. Is there a blind man down there in the boat?'

'There is, sir.' Alan Colborne turned his face up towards the speaker.

'Then why haven't you spoken up before?' As he called out the question, the officer nodded his head almost imperceptibly at his coxswain.

Alan Colborne grinned. 'To whom should I have addressed myself in this floating bedlam, Captain?'

The lieutenant scowled. At that moment, the boat's coxswain, who had been working his way to Alan Colborne's side from the stern of the boat, swung a beefy fist. It stopped only half an inch from the balladeer's nose. Alan Colborne did not flinch.

The lieutenant and his coxswain had operated a press-gang together for many years. This was not the first occasion on which a man had attempted to avoid service to his king and country by pleading blindness.

'Yes, I recognise him now,' called another member of the press-gang. 'He's a blind fiddler who plays in the Mermaid Inn on the Barbican.'

'Then get him up here quickly,' ordered the officer. 'And get the rest of them out to the ship. Hurry, now, or every one of them will have someone swearing that he's an apprentice or an honourably discharged seaman.'

The officer passed Alan Colborne on the quay steps and growled, 'Think yourself lucky, fiddler. Had we not learned you were blind before we reached the ship, you would have been thrown overboard and left to swim ashore – eyes or no.'

With that, the lieutenant put his foot against the bow of the press-gang boat and pushed it angrily away from the steps.

Judy Lean helped Alan Colborne up the last few steps and hurried away with him, fearful that the officer in charge of the press-gang might yet change his mind and decide there was a place in a man-of-war for a blind fiddler.

She was trembling so much that, before they arrived at the inn, Alan Colborne made her stop. In an effort to calm her down, he asked what had happened to cause such a disturbance at the quayside.

By the time Judy had ended her story, Alan Colborne was laughing merrily. Reaching for her face, he cupped it in his hands and kissed her long and hard upon her lips.

'Judy, I will hear no man call you simple again. You were as quick-witted back there as any woman or man I have ever known. I am proud of you. I'll not be content until we are married and no one can take you from me.'

Judy made her way back to their lodgings with so much happiness inside her at Alan's words that she felt she must burst. The happiness shone from her like spring sunshine, and the men and women she passed along the narrow streets found themselves returning her smile and bidding the happy girl 'Good evening'.

*

A few nights later, when Judy Lean arrived at the Mermaid Inn to take Alan Colborne home, she found him waiting for her beside the open doorway. She kissed him and took an arm to lead him away. Instead of going with her, he held her back.

'Wait, Judy. I don't want to build up your hopes unnecessarily, but I would like you to put your head inside the doorway and look at a woman sitting close to the fire. I heard her called "Nellie" and she speaks with the accent of south Cornwall. She is with a man, but he's not a seaman.'

Filled with excitement, Judy slipped from Alan Colborne's grasp and leaned in through the doorway.

The tobacco smoke hanging in the room stung her eyes and for a few moments she could not see through the blue haze. Then a group of men standing in the middle of the room parted to allow a serving-girl through.

Behind them, seated by the fire, Judy Lean saw her mother.

'It's her, Alan. It *is* my ma!'

Alan Colborne made no answer. He had hoped he might be mistaken. He knew something of the man who was with Nellie Lean. He was one of the ragged band of men who haunted dockside taverns, seizing upon any opportunity to earn a dishonest shilling.

Alan Colborne had also been listening to the conversation of Nellie Lean and her companion. It was apparent to him that the two were living together in something less than harmony.

It was too late for regrets now. Judy Lean had taken his hand and was dragging him behind her across the room, careless of his limitations, so eager was she to reach her mother.

'Ma . . . ! Ma, it's me. Judy.'

Judy Lean came to a halt before her mother, quivering with the emotion of seeing her again after so long. Judy had never considered that her mother might not share her own joy at the reunion. She hardly noticed that her reception was decidedly cool.

In truth, Nellie Lean was both shocked and dismayed to be suddenly confronted with her daughter. Her romance with the sailor she had met at Pentuan had been a brief and violent affair. When it came to an end, Nellie Lean had taken to the tavern life, accepting all it entailed for a woman. After a while, she met up with Aaron Yeo and became deeply infatuated with him. She knew all about his dishonest ways, but he beat her less often than had her former sailor lover. Aaron Yeo was some years younger than Nellie Lean, and the last thing she needed was to have a hitherto unmentioned grown-up daughter arrive and give Aaron Yeo cause to question her age.

Eventually, the absence of a welcome did register with Judy. She looked at her mother in deep distress, and Alan Colborne felt the grip on his hand tighten painfully.

'Aren't you pleased to see me, Ma? I've been looking for you for weeks. I wanted you to meet Alan. Me and him are going to be married. I thought you'd want to know . . .'

'Of course she wants to know . . . don't you, Nellie?'

Aaron Yeo elbowed Nellie Lean in the ribs. Startled, she looked at him and he gave her a sly wink.

'We're both pleased to meet you and your intended . . . ain't we, Nellie?'

Leaning towards Nellie Lean, he whispered, 'Don't you recognise him? It's the fiddler, the blind man who sits in here and plays every evening.'

Nellie Lean was surprised by Aaron Yeo's unexpected acceptance of Judy, but she took her cue from him.

'Why, yes . . . of course we're pleased to see you, Judy. I'm at a loss for words, that's all, my dear.'

'Well said, Nellie. There, can't you see how pleased your ma is, Judy? Why, unless I'm mistaken, them's tears in her eyes. I'm happy, too. My name is Aaron Yeo. I'm a close friend of your ma . . . a *very* close friend.'

Aaron Yeo gave Nellie Lean another wink and a dig in the ribs.

Taking Judy's hand, Aaron Yeo squeezed it and leered at her, secure in the knowledge that Alan Colborne could not see him.

Judy was too happy to notice anything amiss and she did not attempt to withdraw her hand from Aaron Yeo. Nellie

349

Lean did not miss Yeo's attentions and she became more anxious than ever for her unwanted daughter to leave Plymouth.

'You and your ma must have lots to talk about.' Aaron Yeo relinquished Judy's hand after giving it a final squeeze. 'I'll have some more gin brought here. I'll fetch your fiddle from the landlord, too, Alan. This is a happy occasion. One we must celebrate. No, don't you argue with me. This will be an evening you'll not forget in a hurry.'

When his fiddle had been brought to him, Alan Colborne had no alternative but to play. Aaron Yeo's loud voice ensured that everyone in the tavern knew of their 'celebration' – and many of the customers contributed to the gin that appeared on the table before them.

In between tunes, Alan Colborne could hear that the conversation between Judy and her mother was as one-sided as ever, but it seemed not to matter to Judy. She chattered away happily, as though everything in her life was now perfect.

Then Nellie Lean suggested that Alan was being neglected, and Judy came to kneel on the floor beside his chair as he played and sang.

When he ended his ballad, and the applause was at its height, Judy said happily to him, 'You were very clever to find my ma for me, Alan. Do you like her? Is she what you expected?'

'My thoughts are far too occupied with her daughter,' replied Alan Colborne, avoiding a direct answer to her question. 'But if she approves of me perhaps we can set the date for our wedding?'

Judy Lean frowned. She was having difficulty in concentrating on a reply. Aaron Yeo had kept her glass well filled tonight. 'I . . . I think she likes you, Alan. She hasn't said very much. I know it doesn't really matter, but I would like her to say she'll be happy to have you as her son-in-law. I want her to come to our wedding.'

Judy would have continued her indecisive chatter had Alan Colborne not reached down quickly and laid a finger across her lips, 'Shh! I am listening.'

His remarkable hearing had picked up a fragment of Nellie

Lean's whispered conversation. Now he strained to hear more, doing his best to ignore the noise all about them.

'I don't want to have Judy stay here in Plymouth. I didn't want her in the first place. I left her working for Reuben Holyoak and thought I'd seen the last of her. All my life she's been in the way of everything I wanted to do. Let her go off with her blind fiddler; she can go as far away as he can take her. I don't want her bothering me *ever* again.'

Nellie Lean's words were slurred, distorted by gin and thick with self-pity. Her voice began to rise above a whisper, but Aaron Yeo was quick to silence her.

'Don't be so hasty, Nellie. Judy's a handsome girl. She could prove a great comfort to you . . . to us both!'

'I knew it! I knew it, Aaron Yeo! You've taken a fancy to my daughter. Now I don't matter to you. I saw the way you were looking at her. Well, let me tell you . . . You'd soon be sick to the craw of her simple ways . . .'

'Shut up, Nellie!' Aaron Yeo's voice rose to a hoarse whisper that Alan Colborne found easier to hear. ' 'Tis you and me I'm thinking about, not me and your daughter. I'd be lying to you if I didn't say she was handsome. Haven't you seen the way the sailors in here are looking at her? She's simple, you say? Well, so much the better. She'll do exactly what you tell her. Persuade her to be kind to sea-faring men, Nellie. Some of them have been months at sea without seeing a woman and they are in here with pockets filled with money. Judy can take them off to some room and we'll empty their pockets while she keeps them busy. We'll make ourselves a packet, Nellie. Enough for you and me to move away from Plymouth and make a new start together.'

Judy Lean fidgeted and reached a hand up to Alan Colborne's finger, wanting to speak. He pressed his finger tighter to her lips. He had to hear what was said next.

Nellie Lean began snivelling. 'What are you asking me to do, Aaron? She's my own daughter . . .'

'She *owes* it to you, Nellie. You've said yourself how much you've sacrificed for her. She'll do it; she's a simple girl and I can see she's very fond of you. Tell her you're in desperate straits. That unless you get the money to pay off some bad debts you'll be carried off to prison. Say she need only do it once or twice. She'll believe you; you know she will.'

There was such a long silence that Alan Colborne thought the scheming couple might have moved away. Then, just before one of a large party of seamen cracked a joke that received a noisy reception, he heard Nellie Lean sniff. 'All right. But what about the fiddler? What do we do with him?'

The noise of the seamen destroyed any chance Alan Colborne had of hearing more. He removed his finger from Judy's lips and turned her face up towards his.

'Where are they now, Judy? Your mother and Aaron Yeo? Are they looking at us?'

Judy did not understand the urgency in his voice, but she answered him quickly, 'No. They are talking together. They're not looking.'

'Then take me out of here. *Now!* Hurry, Judy, before anyone can stop us. Move, girl.'

He had never before bullied Judy in this fashion, but it worked. She was hurrying from the tavern with Alan Colborne clutching her hand before she even paused to think.

Once outside, he asked, 'Did you tell your mother where we are lodging?'

'No. Why?'

Judy Lean was a very confused girl.

'It doesn't matter now. Get us back to the lodgings as quickly as you can.'

Out here in the darkness, Alan Colborne's lack of sight was no disadvantage. He hurried Judy away from the tavern, his feet more sure than hers on the cobbled surface.

'But my ma? She'll wonder what's happened to me.'

They turned a corner and Alan pulled Judy to face him. She could just make out his strained face in the light from a nearby bedroom window.

'Judy, do you love me enough to trust me absolutely?'

Judy hesitated, then nodded. Remembering he could not see, she whispered, 'Yes.'

'Then you must believe me when I say we need to get away from here without your mother knowing where we are going. Aaron Yeo has evil plans for you. I heard him persuading your mother to use you to help him to rob seamen. He said there would be no lasting harm in it for you, and your mother believed him. We have to leave Plymouth quickly. You found your mother, and told her we are to be married. Now you must forget her and entrust your future to me. Do you feel able to do that?'

'Yes.'

The sound was forced from Judy Lean's throat.

'Then take us to our lodgings. Hurry, now!'

Alan Colborne had caught the sound of Aaron Yeo's excited voice in the distance. It would not do for him to catch them in this dark and narrow street.

Judy heard the voice, too. Taking Alan's arm she hurried him along narrow alleyways and up steep slippery flights of steps to arrive finally at the house where they were staying.

When they reached the safety of their room, Alan Colborne took Judy in his arms and did his best to soothe away the tears that overwhelmed the desperately unhappy girl.

That day had seen her most cherished dream taken from her and smashed into fragments that could never be put together again.

Chapter Thirty-Seven

Alan Colborne and Judy Lean set off from Plymouth early the next morning. It was grey and cheerless, with a desultory wind blowing through the narrow streets of the port, ruffling the hair of scavenging dogs and sending brittle brown leaves scurrying over the cobblestones.

There was already much movement at the water's edge. The fishing-fleet and a great many merchantmen had ridden in on the early-morning tide. Although it was much too early to expect Aaron Yeo to be abroad, Alan Colborne took no chances. He and Judy made a wide detour round the quays and jetties of the harbour, not approaching the waterfront until they reached the navy yards. Here the River Tamar flowed into the natural harbour of the Sound and they found a ferryman to take them across the river to Cremyll.

When they again set foot on land they were in Cornwall, and Alan Colborne breathed more easily as they set off for Truro. It was his intention that he and Judy should be married there without any more delay.

The weather along the journey was wet and cold, and they made very slow time, staying at a number of inns and taverns where Alan Colborne and his singing and fiddle-playing were welcomed.

Eventually they arrived at St Austell. When Judy mentioned to Alan Colborne that Mevagissey was only a few miles distant, he suggested they pay a surprise visit to Ben and Jesse, believing them to be still in the area.

At first, Judy did not share Alan's enthusiasm for a visit to Mevagissey. Too many unhappy things had happened to her there. Then she thought of the people she knew, servants at Lamorrack House. She could introduce Alan to them; it would compensate her for the heartbreak she had suffered at her mother's hands.

It was already mid-afternoon, but Alan Colborne was so keen to carry his idea into effect that he insisted they set off immediately.

Judy's worry was that darkness would catch up with them before they reached Mevagissey. Her anxiety seemed justified when heavy clouds began to build up overhead, hastening the dusk. Because of this, when they were still a couple of miles from the village, she guided Alan Colborne off the track, on to a path that cut across the shoulder of a steep hill. It passed close to Pengrugla, the place about which she still had occasional nightmares, but it was a quicker route to Mevagissey. She did not wish to lead Alan along a slippery wagon-rutted road in the darkness.

At the top of the hill, they passed through the copse surrounding the house where Judy had lived with Reuben Holyoak, and Judy fell silent, grateful for Alan Colborne's hand in hers.

They were only a matter of yards from the house when Alan pulled Judy to a halt.

'There is someone coming along the path.'

Judy immediately flew into a panic. 'Quick, we must hide.'

'Why? We are hurting no one. It's all right, Judy. I am with you now.'

In spite of Alan Colborne's assurance, Judy stood trembling in the centre of the path, praying that the footsteps did not belong to the man she feared more than anyone else in the world.

Her prayers were offered up too late. Moments later she saw Reuben Holyoak striding along the path towards them, a fowling-piece crooked in his arm. The light was not good beneath the trees and it was evident that Reuben Holyoak had not yet recognised Judy Lean.

'What are you doing here?' he demanded. 'This is private land. You are trespassing.'

From the painful grip of Judy's hand, Alan Colborne realised that she knew and feared this man. Instinctively, he knew that the man now talking to them had been the father of Judy's stillborn child.

'We are on our way to Mevagissey village from St Austell. We came this way in order to reach the village before darkness falls.'

'That alters nothing. You should have set out earlier . . . along the road.'

Reuben Holyoak spoke to Alan Colborne, but he was looking at Judy. There was something familiar about her. He moved closer to see her better.

Alan Colborne smelled the fear that emanated from Judy and he pulled her to him to reassure her. To Reuben Holyoak he said, 'I apologise if we have disturbed you, but we'll not damage any of your property along the way . . .'

'Not so fast. That's Judy, isn't it? Judy Lean?'

Judy nodded with difficulty. Her body was as paralysed with fear as a rabbit confronted by a weasel.

'It's Judy Lean at the moment,' said Alan Colborne, successfully concealing his own unease. 'But it will soon be Judy Colborne. She is marrying me before the month is out.'

'Is that so?' Reuben Holyoak had been watching the way Alan Colborne stood, how he turned his head to hear after he spoke. He realised Alan Colborne was blind – and he immediately dismissed him as being of no account.

'You know you shouldn't use this path, Judy. You'll get into trouble wandering around on other folk's land.'

'We aren't doing no harm, Mr Holyoak. Honest, we aren't.'

Alan Colborne hardly recognised Judy's voice. All the confidence she had gained since leaving Pengrugla had fled from her. She was once again the simple browbeaten girl she had been for all her earlier years.

'We'd better talk about this. You come on into the house with me. You remember Pengrugla, don't you, Judy? The things we did there?'

'Judy is on her way to Mevagissey with me. If you want to discuss anything, you can come down there to do it – although from what I have heard of you, I doubt if you have the courage to show your face to Mevagissey men.'

Reuben Holyoak frowned, then gave a short derisive laugh. 'You have a loose tongue for a man with no sight. Use it as much as you wish, blind man, there is no one to hear you at Pengrugla. Just you sit down on the bank and listen to the birds for a while. When I've finished with Judy I'll let her come back and lead you on your way – like a dog. But don't be too impatient; I want to be sure she's forgotten none of the tricks I taught her.'

Judy was shaking so much Alan Colborne feared she would have a fit. He tightened his grip on her hand and said quietly, 'Move on along the path, Judy, but keep me between yourself and Holyoak.'

Under his prompting, Judy began to move forward slowly, and Alan Colborne went with her. When they were almost level with Reuben Holyoak, Alan Colborne heard him make a move towards Judy. Arms outstretched, he flung himself forward and managed to grip the gamekeeper's coat.

The suddenness of Alan Colborne's move took Reuben Holyoak by surprise. He stumbled and fell to his knees, the fowling-piece slipping from his grasp.

Keeping a tight grip of the gamekeeper, Alan Colborne shouted, 'Run, Judy! Run to Mevagissey and get help from Ben and the fishermen. Tell them Holyoak attacked us—'

A heavy fist caught Alan Colborne in the mouth, splitting his lips and cutting his words short. Releasing one of his hands, Alan Colborne struck out towards Reuben Holyoak's face. The blow struck the gamekeeper in the eye, drawing a sharp grunt of pain from him.

Now Reuben Holyoak became a mad thing. He struck at Alan Colborne again and again, beating him to the ground. Then he knelt over him, punching him in the face, oblivious of the screams of Judy Lean as she saw Alan battered into insensibility.

Judy rushed at the gamekeeper, crying hysterically, and her fingernails raked his face. Cursing, he flung her violently from him. As she fell to the ground, her outflung arm touched the cold steel of the fowling-piece.

Scrambling to her feet, Judy picked up the weapon and pointed the long barrel at Reuben Holyoak. It was one of the new percussion sporting-guns – a weapon she remembered well. Reuben Holyoak had purchased the gun when he was first appointed as Sir Colman Vincent's agent. It had been his most treasured possession. He had cleaned and polished it every night, explaining details of its action to Judy. She had even fired the gun. On the first occasion it had been the result of a generous impulse on Reuben Holyoak's part, but the loud report had terrified her. After that, he had forced her to fire the gun for no other reason than to laugh at her fear.

Terror was in her now, but it had nothing to do with the gun she was holding. Judy Lean's fear was for the life of Alan Colborne, who no longer stirred beneath Reuben Holyoak's blows.

Reuben Holyoak looked up in time to see Judy Lean's finger tighten on the trigger of the gun. He threw up an arm in a vain attempt to ward off the shot and died with a scream in his throat as the charge took him full in the face.

Throwing down the gun, Judy dragged the gamekeeper off Alan Colborne, trying not to look at the ghastly mess that had been Reuben Holyoak's face.

The blind balladeer lay quite still, covered in blood. How much was his own, and how much had come from Reuben Holyoak, Judy did not know.

She tried everything she knew to rouse Alan, but he did not move. He did not even groan, and Judy knew he needed the attentions of a doctor.

Alan Colborne was not a large man, and Judy Lean was a strong girl, accustomed to coping with situations that called for physical strength. After a brief struggle, she lifted him in her arms and set off with him across the fields – away from Reuben Holyoak. She was taking him to a place where he would be certain to receive the best care possible. Lamorrack House.

The arrival of the exhausted bloodstained girl with her unconscious burden caused consternation at the great house. The servant girl who answered the hammering at the kitchen door fled into the house, screaming. Within minutes, the new owner and most of his staff were at the scene.

Judy was immediately recognised, and as she gasped out her story servants were sent running in all directions. One man hurried to Mevagissey to fetch the doctor. Two more were sent to find Reuben Holyoak – and another rode to St Austell for the magistrate.

The two men who had been to Pengrugla returned first.

They were pale and shaken after seeing the result of the violent death meted out to Reuben Holyoak. They avoided looking at Judy Lean. Not until the owner of Lamorrack House drew them outside the room did they give an account of their grisly find. They told him other things, too: of the time Judy had lived at Pengrugla and worked for Reuben Holyoak; of the suspicious circumstances surrounding the birth and death of her child. They also explained that Judy Lean had a limited intelligence.

The two servants exaggerated in the manner of all gossips, leaving the new squire of Lamorrack with the impression that Judy Lean's mental state was akin to madness. He immediately ordered them to lock the door on her and left the two servants to guard the room where she waited by Alan Colborne's side.

The door was unlocked to admit the doctor, and he was still in the room examining the cuts and bruises of the now semi-conscious Alan Colborne when the magistrate arrived.

The Reverend Hawkins was hot from his fast ride and full of the importance of his office. He listened impatiently as the servants who had been to Pengrugla told of finding Reuben Holyoak's body. The magistrate's thoughts were already leap-frogging ahead of their words.

'I remember this girl well,' he told the owner of Lamorrack House. 'I protested that she should have been charged with murder when the inquest upon her child was held. It has taken the death of an innocent man to vindicate my judgement. Mr Holyoak gave evidence against her then. No doubt she has brooded on the matter all this time, and returned with an accomplice to seek revenge.'

The squire of Lamorrack had been thinking along similar lines, but he was surprised at the alacrity with which the St Austell magistrate leaped to such a positive conclusion.

'I must admit there are suspicious circumstances surrounding Holyoak's death. An investigation must be carried out,' he said. 'But had the girl come here bent upon revenge she would hardly have brought her accomplice to my house.'

The Reverend Hawkins shrugged his shoulders, his mind closed to any argument against his theory. 'Who can follow the tortuous workings of a simple mind? I will be obliged if you will keep the girl and her accomplice under guard until my constable arrives, sir. Meanwhile I must return to St Austell and make the arrangements for an early hearing. The Assizes commence before the month's end, and there are no cases of note to be heard. A murder trial should ensure that His Majesty's Judges do not waste their time in Cornwall. I thank you for your help, sir.'

The Reverend Hawkins carried out his promise with almost indecent haste. Judy Lean and Alan Colborne appeared before his bench only two days after their arrest and were swiftly committed to Bodmin Gaol, there to await trial at the forthcoming Assizes.

It would not be a case to excite any great interest or controversy. It was nothing more complicated than the murder of a gamekeeper by a wandering balladeer and his woman. It would not merit even a single paragraph in the national newspapers of the day.

Chapter Thirty-Eight

The wedding of Ben and Jesse was the little mining community's event of the year. Jesse was the envy of every future bride in Henwood. Not only did Martha Retallick attend from Mevagissey, accompanied by her two brothers and their large families, but Fanny and Loveday Ustick came, too, as did Theophilus Strike – and Eulaliah Vincent.

Eulaliah Vincent's carriage was the first light vehicle seen in the village. The roads in the mining area were not suited to the frail wheels and sophisticated springing of a town vehicle.

Waiting in Linkinhorne church for Jesse, Ben felt strange and uncomfortable in a new serge suit and a shirt of stiff cotton. It proved to be particularly difficult when Ben tried to turn his head against the tight collar to get his first glimpse of Jesse in the white wedding dress she had kept a secret from him.

Then she was by his side, with the young Kelynack girls in attendance, looking more beautiful than he had ever seen her.

When the vicar told them to kneel, Ben's boots, new from a Liskeard shoemaker only the day before, were reluctant to bend, creaking with all the noise of a ungreased door. Ben cast an embarrassed sidelong glance at Jesse and was mortified to see that she was smiling. Then she looked up at him and shared her smile, and Ben relaxed.

The vicar of Linkinhorne did not prolong the ceremony. Neither Ben nor Jesse belonged to his church. The ceremony was necessary only to satisfy the letter of the law. Twenty minutes after entering the church, Ben and Jesse left it as Mr and Mrs Retallick and returned to Henwood for a service in Wrightwick Roberts's small chapel.

Eulaliah Vincent had spoken disparagingly to Jesse of a chapel wedding service, but she found little to fault here. The interior had been newly whitewashed, and there was no shortage of flowers to provide a splendid splash of bright colour. Most of the flowers had been gathered from the moorland shrubs, but there were also a few precious late-autumn blooms, picked from the gardens of the miners' wives.

Wrightwick Roberts was not a preacher to give short measure at a church service, whether it celebrated a baptism, a marriage or a funeral. He made quite certain that no one in his chapel was in any doubt about Ben and Jesse Retallick being well and truly married.

Outside the chapel, the young couple faced a barrage of congratulations from friends and wellwishers, many of whom had been unable to make the journey to Linkinhorne or crowd into the tiny chapel.

The greetings over, Ben and Jesse were sent on their way to the new house on Sharptor in Theophilus Strike's small gig.

At the house, a veritable feast was laid out for family and friends, all the food having been provided by neighbours and guests. Theophilus Strike, in particular, had dipped deep into his own pocket to celebrate both the wedding and the completion of the first house on the Wheal Sharptor. The celebrations went on until late afternoon, when Eulaliah Vincent was the first to say her farewells to the newly wed couple.

'I wish you every happiness for your future together,' she said. 'And I expect you to bring your firstborn to visit me. Not that you need wait until then to come to Mevagissey. With Reuben Holyoak dead there are no bad memories left and no reason why you should not come to see me as often as it pleases you.'

'Reuben Holyoak dead?' Jesse was startled.

'Why, yes, dear. I thought you must have known. He was shot by a young girl whose mother once worked at Lamorrack House. Judy Lean. You must have known her. She was a little – well, simple. She and her lover are to be tried at next week's Assizes in Bodmin. Mrs Retallick will tell you all about it. I must leave before it is too dark. My coachman is not certain of his way, and these lanes will surely shake out whatever sense of direction he has.'

Eulaliah Vincent left the house and climbed into her carriage. As it pulled away, she waved her handkerchief gaily from the window, unaware of the furore she had left behind her.

Jesse was dumbfounded at the news of Reuben Holyoak's death and Ben immediately sought out his mother, taxing her with keeping the news of Judy's arrest from him and Jesse.

'You mustn't blame your mother, Ben.' Loveday Ustick had seen the expression upon Ben's face when he went in search of his mother. Guessing the reason, he had tried unsuccessfully to head him off. 'We all knew about it, but no one wanted to say anything until after the wedding.'

'Judy and Alan wouldn't kill anyone, not even Reuben Holyoak – and, God knows, Judy had just cause for that.'

'The news is true enough,' declared Loveday Ustick. 'One of the maids from Lamorrack House told Fanny about it. Judy arrived at the big house covered in blood after killing Holyoak.'

'But why?' Jesse asked. 'Why should she kill him? What was she doing anywhere near Lamorrack House?'

Loveday Ustick would have given anything not to have told Ben and Jesse why Judy Lean and Alan Colborne were near Mevagissey, but he was unable to lie. Dropping his glance to the toes of his dusty boots, he said 'She and the young man were on their way to look for you at Mevagissey. That's all I know about the matter. Fanny went to see her in St Austell lock-up before she was sent off to Bodmin Gaol, but she didn't get much sense from the poor girl.'

'Ben, we must go to Bodmin to see them,' Jesse said to Ben.

'You'll need to be quick,' said Mark Dunn, who had been listening to the conversation. 'The Assizes begin this week.'

Ben nodded. It was customary on the mines for a man to be given a week off work when he was married. Ben had intended using the time to improve the cottage. That would now have to wait. 'We'll go to Bodmin tomorrow.'

The news of the arrest of Judy Lean and Alan Colborne brought a swift end to the wedding celebrations and, that night, the bed-talk of the newly married couple was concerned not with their own future, but rather with the present predicament of their friends.

*

Ben and Jesse's arrival in Bodmin coincided with the ceremonial entry of His Majesty's Judges of Assize. The two judges, resplendent in long red cloaks and wearing shoulder-length, powdered wigs, rode into Bodmin Town in an ornate coach, escorted by a mounted troop of the Cornwall Militia. The judges were met by all the dignitaries of the district, led by the mayor in his robes and with the chain of office about his neck. Behind him, various other officials made up the welcoming committee, each carrying the insignia of his particular office.

This scene of ancient splendour was in sharp contrast to the squalor Ben and Jesse found within the high grey walls of Bodmin's gaol.

The gaol, although not yet fifty years old, was ill-maintained and hopelessly overcrowded. Judy Lean and Alan Colborne were imprisoned in separate parts of the building, and it was only by parting with a hard-earned gold sovereign that Ben was able to persuade a wheezing old turnkey to bring both prisoners together to meet their visitors. It was doubtful whether the single gold coin would have proved sufficient encouragement had the gaoler not been a miner in earlier, healthier years.

The reunion between Alan Colborne and Judy Lean was highly emotional. Judy clung to Alan Colborne and wept as though her heart would break. It was many minutes before she recovered sufficiently to talk. Even then, she clung to Alan Colborne's hand in the manner of a pathetic frightened child.

Alan Colborne told Ben and Jesse the story of their encounter with Reuben Holyoak. There was no doubt in his mind that, had Judy not shot the gamekeeper, Reuben Holyoak would have been in Bodmin Gaol awaiting trial on a murder charge.

Ben was incredulous. 'How can you and Judy possibly be charged with murder? This whole business is absurd!'

'I wish it were, Ben. We are charged with murder, and the magistrate who committed us is determined to prove his case. He was overheard to say that Judy will not escape justice twice.'

364

'Oh, no!' Jesse let out an involuntary cry of anguish. 'Not the Reverend Hawkins?'

'He said I killed my baby,' Judy Lean suddenly cried. 'I didn't, did I, Jesse? You know it isn't true.'

'Of course it isn't true, Judy. The Reverend Hawkins is a vengeful old man. No one will take any notice of him; you just wait and see.'

Jesse spoke without conviction. The Reverend Hawkins was a magistrate, and a persuasive and passionate speaker. Given the opportunity he might well sway a jury. Judy Lean's present appearance would be on his side. She was wearing the bloody dress in which she had been arrested, and it was doubtful whether she had washed since being thrown into Bodmin Gaol. Far from arousing the sympathy she so desperately needed, Judy looked every inch the murderess the Crown claimed her to be.

Clutching another of Ben's guineas, Jesse hurried from the gaol and returned within the hour carrying a dress and a cardigan, both of which fitted Judy Lean tolerably well. Then Jesse demanded that the turnkey fetch soap and water. When it was grudgingly brought by the grumbling old gaoler, Jesse embarrassed Judy Lean by making her strip off her old dress, wash all the parts of her body that were visible to the eye, then put on the new dress she had just purchased for her.

The transformation from dirty drab to demure young girl was quite dramatic. Even the ill-humoured old turnkey now looked at Judy with a modicum of respect. While they talked, Jesse also tidied up Judy's hair. When she and Ben left the gaol, Jesse was satisfied that the simple girl could now stand before a jury and not be convicted on her appearance alone.

The trial was due to be held in the Assize Court the next day and, on the way from the gaol, Jesse asked Ben whether he thought Judy and Alan stood any chance of gaining an acquittal.

'I would like to think so,' replied Ben unhappily. 'But the only fact that cannot be disputed is that Judy killed Reuben Holyoak. *We* know she is telling the truth about what happened. Whether she can convince a judge and jury is another matter. We will just have to wait and see.'

Ben and Jesse spent that night at the White Hart Inn, in the centre of Bodmin Town. Every inn and lodging-house was crowded with court officials and witnesses, brought in from the four corners of the county. Ben and Jesse were obliged to share a room with an asthmatic old man and his wife. The ancient couple had been called to the Assizes to give evidence in a hotly contested tithe dispute between a farmer and the vicar of his parish. They smelled strongly of pigs, and their snoring was reminiscent of the same animal.

Ben and Jesse spent a sleepless night and rose in the morning with an unreasonable hatred for the old couple whose faces beamed amiably at them above the blankets of the bed across the room.

It proved to be a bright and clear late-autumnal day, making the inside of the Assize Court seem even more gloomy than it was. Ben and Jesse arrived there early, to be sure they would not miss the case against Alan and Judy.

It was the first time Ben had been in a court-room, and he found it difficult to adapt to the ritualistic unreality of the proceedings. The judge, barristers and court officers addressed each other with the exaggerated courtesy of the medieval age of chivalry. Ben had the feeling that he was watching stage characters playing out parts they had all carefully rehearsed beforehand.

This feeling was heightened by the atmosphere in the public gallery. Crowded together, shoulder to shoulder, the spectators pronounced their own verdicts on cases still being heard and commented loudly on the physical attributes and mental prowess of all those holding the stage in the well of the court.

So convincing was this air of the theatre that, when the first case was brought to an abrupt conclusion and the judge placed a small square of black cloth upon his head, it was a few moments before Ben understood its implications. It came as a deep shock when he realised that by this simple – almost comic – gesture the Judge of Assize was ordering the execution of the weeping man in the dock.

The charge on which the poor unfortunate had been convicted was stealing a gentleman's purse containing twenty guineas.

366

The next case on the list received an even briefer hearing than had the first. A woman had broken into the house of her sister-in-law during her absence and stolen two shillings she found on the mantelshelf.

The jury announced their verdict of 'guilty', without retiring – but their foreman added a strong plea for clemency. The convicted woman had been in dire straits. Deserted by her husband, the brother of the robbed woman, she had been left with two young children to feed.

Ignoring the plea of the foreman of the jury, the stern-faced judge awarded the convicted woman the same sentence as the previous prisoner. Donning his 'black cap', he ordered her to be taken away and legally put to death. When the woman was dragged away, screaming for mercy for the sake of her children, the judge drew his lips together in a tight thin line of disapproval.

As the screams died away, Ben thought grimly that Judy Lean could expect little understanding from the man who would try her for her life.

This view was strengthened when the next prisoner, a boy of eleven, was brought up from the cells. Hardly able to see over the edge of the dock, the small boy pleaded guilty in a tremulous voice to the charge of stealing a handful of candles from a mine-store. When the judge was informed that the boy had been convicted of a similar offence two years before, he promptly sentenced him to fourteen years' transportation. On this occasion, the judge explained that the sentence was being passed in the hope of saving the boy from pursuing a useless and criminal way of life.

This sentence brought a brief outbreak of angry murmurs from the spectators in the public gallery, but the sound was swiftly silenced by a stern glance from the judge.

Then it was time for the hearing of the murder charge against Judy Lean and Alan Colborne.

When the two were escorted into the prisoners' dock, chained and manacled, Jesse's hopes sank. The night had undone much of her work. Judy Lean's long hair straggled untidily in front of her face, and she had managed to get the front of her new dress grubby.

367

Ben was watching the judge and saw the frown of annoyance which crossed his face when both prisoners pleaded not guilty to murdering Reuben Holyoak.

The prosecution's case unfolded rapidly, and the evidence took Ben and Jesse by surprise. It was obvious from Alan Colborne's manner that he, too, had no prior knowledge of the case now being made out against himself and Judy.

It was alleged that Alan Colborne and Judy Lean were on the Lamorrack estate as trespassers on the day of the murder. Their reason for being there, said the prosecuting barrister, was to break into Reuben Holyoak's house and steal whatever they might find. He went on to suggest that Reuben Holyoak had caught them in the act and, after a fight, had been killed in defence of his property.

One of the servants from Lamorrack House gave halting but honest evidence of finding the body of the gamekeeper on the path, only yards from his house at Pengrugla, clearly killed by a shot from his own gun.

Next, the prosecution called the doctor who had examined Alan Colborne. His report, supported by the bruising still to be seen on Alan Colborne's face, conjured up a picture of a desperate fight.

Then it was the turn of the Reverend Hawkins to give evidence – and his story was the most damning of all. He described Judy Lean as a girl of loose morals, whom he had once arrested for the murder of her bastard child. She had escaped justice on that occasion, he told the court, only because of an irresponsible verdict by a coroner's jury, drawn from men of her home village. Now she had enlisted the aid of an itinerant musician to help her wilfully kill an honourable and respected man . . .

At this point, Jesse could contain her seething indignation no longer. Before Ben could stop her, she had sprung to her feet and called the magistrate a liar.

'Reuben Holyoak was no honourable man,' she shouted angrily. '*He* was the father of Judy Lean's bastard child. He took advantage of a simple-minded girl when she was working for him as a servant . . .'

Jesse had made a similar outburst once before, on Judy

Lean's behalf, but this was no coroner's court being held in a village inn. As Ben tried to pull Jesse down to the wooden seat the judge demanded fiercely that she be silent.

'If I have any more of such conduct in my court, I will have you committed to prison until these Assizes are over, and then you will be publicly whipped,' he declared. 'If you have something to say that is relevant to this case, you will wait for the appropriate time. Is that quite clear?'

After staring back at the judge defiantly for some moments, Jesse nodded her head, once. Sitting down heavily, she turned to Ben and in an angry whisper hissed, 'I'll have something to say, all right. That magistrate is not going to destroy Judy with his lies.'

'You'll say nothing,' said Ben firmly. 'If one of us needs to give evidence for Judy and Alan, I'll do it. You will only get angry and make things worse for them – and for yourself.'

Jesse opened her mouth with a ready retort, but she left it unspoken. Ben was right. She was far too upset to make a useful contribution to Judy's defence.

'All right, Ben. But don't allow the Reverend Hawkins to get away with any one of his lies.'

Ben was relieved that Jesse had given in so easily. Had she insisted on giving evidence, he had no doubt that he and his bride of a few days would have spent the duration of the Assizes separated by a high stone wall.

The Reverend Hawkins continued with his evidence. Whenever he praised Reuben Holyoak, or attacked Judy Lean's character, Jesse writhed with indignation, but she managed to remain silent.

There was little more prosecution evidence and, after an adjournment for lunch, it was the turn of Judy Lean and Alan Colborne to speak on their own behalf.

Judy Lean did not help her cause in any way. She had understood little of the proceedings and was not certain of what she was expected to say. She brought a smile of satisfaction to the face of the prosecuting barrister when she admitted picking up the gun and shooting Reuben Holyoak with it.

Much to Ben's surprise, Alan Colborne showed up little

better when his turn came to address the court. The time he had already spent in custody had sapped his confidence. In a hesitant voice, at times barely audible above the noise of the court-room, he told how he and Judy had headed for Mevagissey and taken a short cut through the Lamorrack estate. When he gave his version of the violent confrontation with Reuben Holyoak, Judy Lean began crying in the dock beside him, making his story even more difficult to follow.

Twice the judge curtly ordered Alan Colborne to speak up. His words brought only momentary improvement. Eventually, the judge sat back in his chair, displaying boredom, his thoughts elsewhere.

When Alan Colborne ended his evidence, he had said nothing to influence the jury in any way.

Peering sternly at the public gallery, the judge sought out Jesse. When he found her, he said, 'Now, young lady. Is there something you wish to say to this court?'

Ben stood up quickly, before Jesse could change her mind.

'I am her husband, my Lord. I would like to speak in her stead.'

'A wise decision,' said the judge. 'Step forward, if you please. I wish to conclude this trial today.'

Ben pushed his way to the front of the court and climbed the steps to the witness-box. He looked at the sea of faces turned towards him. Every man and woman in the court was waiting to hear whether he had any dramatic evidence that would alter the inevitable verdict of the jury.

Looking at the two unfortunates in the dock, Ben wished desperately that he had. Then he began to address the court in a firm and determined manner, telling them something of Judy's background.

He had not been talking for more than two minutes when the judge called him to a halt.

'I am waiting to hear *evidence* from you, Mr Retallick. Character references and excuses may be permitted *after* the jury has reached a verdict.'

Ben was left in some confusion. He wanted to tell the court the true version of the magistrate's story; to inform the judge and jury that Alan Colborne and Judy Lean were neither murderers nor thieves; to explain that Reuben Holyoak was a bully – and worse. It needed to be said *before* the jury arrived at a verdict. He tried again, telling them about Reuben Holyoak; that he had been the father of Judy Lean's stillborn child.

Once again the judge called him to order, banging the wooden bench in front of him angrily.

'Such allegations directed against a dead man are neither admissible nor viewed with anything but distaste by this court. Is that all you have to offer by way of "evidence", Mr Retallick?'

'I am trying to tell you the kind of man Reuben Holyoak really was. Why, he once attacked my wife . . .!'

'The matter was reported?' The judge looked at Ben from beneath lowered brows.

'No.'

'I expected as much.' The judge leaned back in his chair with a sigh. 'Mr Retallick, you will kindly leave the witness-box. If you wish, you may return to speak for the prisoners after a verdict has been reached.'

Ben hesitated. He thought of his own fights with Reuben Holyoak and of the man's attempts to collect higher tithes and have Ben dismissed from the Happy Union mine. Told here, in this court, it would sound as though Reuben Holyoak had been doing no more than his duty. It would not help Alan Colborne and Judy Lean at all.

Reluctantly, Ben left the witness-box and made his way back to Jesse. He did not look towards the dock when he sat down, totally dejected.

Jesse reached for his hand and squeezed it comfortingly. 'He did not *want* to hear anything said in Judy and Alan's favour,' she hissed angrily. 'He listened readily enough when the Reverend Hawkins spoke *for* Reuben Holyoak.'

The verdict of the jury was never in doubt. In their eyes, Judy Lean was exactly what the magistrate had said she was – an immoral girl. She had given birth to a bastard child and been lucky to escape trial for murder when it died. Since then she had been travelling the country in the company of a wandering musician – and she had admitted shooting Reuben Holyoak.

Alan Colborne and Judy Lean were found guilty of murder.

Once again, Ben was asked if he wished to say anything on behalf of the newly convicted couple.

White-faced at the verdict, Ben returned to the witness-box and made an impassioned plea on behalf of his friends. He spoke of Judy Lean as a simple but truthful girl, who had known little happiness in life until she met Alan Colborne. He spoke of her until he saw the judge showing signs of impatience. Then he told the judge what he knew about Alan Colborne. How he had been blinded by cannon-fire after saving the life of the man who was now landlord of the White Swan Inn, at Truro.

Ben might as well have said nothing. No sooner had he finished talking than the impatient judge reached for the square of black cloth and solemnly sentenced Alan Colborne and Judy Lean to be hanged.

In the cells beneath the court, Ben and Jesse found their friends in a state of shock. Neither of them could believe they were to die at the end of a hangman's rope.

When the tragic pair were taken back to the prison, Ben and Jesse left Bodmin determined to fight for the lives of Alan Colborne and Judy Lean.

First they went to Tregassick to see Eulaliah Vincent and ask yet again for her help. The elderly lady promised to write to her friends in London, but she doubted whether they would be able to set aside the ruling of an Assize Court Judge.

On their return to Sharptor, Ben saw Theophilus Strike and asked for his advice. At first, the mine-owner refused to involve himself in such a matter, but after Ben had told him the full story he promised to do whatever he could.

Next, Ben approached David Howell, only to learn that the High Sheriff of Cornwall had already received a letter from Eulaliah Vincent and had agréed to intercede on behalf of the convicted couple.

Having done all they could, there was nothing for Ben and Jesse to do but wait – and this was the hardest part of all.

The date of the double execution was set for the thirteenth day of December. When the hanging was only a week away and no news of a reprieve had been received, the uncertainty became unbearable.

Then Theophilus Strike rode to the Sharptor mine late one afternoon and sent for Ben.

Ben climbed the ladder to the surface and shivered as the cold air chilled the perspiration that clung to his body beneath the thin working-shirt.

'I have news for you, Ben,' said the grim-faced mine-owner. 'It is not entirely good. Alan Colborne's sentence has been reduced to transportation for life. For that he has to thank the Duke of Wellington, who personally interceded for his life.'

Ben's delight at the news quickly died away as he waited in vain for Theophilus Strike to tell him of a reprieve for Judy Lean.

'You are still waiting for news about Judy...?' Theophilus Strike shook his head. 'The Home Secretary felt unable to make any recommendation on her behalf. She must hang. I am sorry, Ben.'

Chapter Thirty-Nine

On 12 December 1822, Judy Lean was married to Alan Colborne. The ceremony took place in the small prison chapel at Bodmin Gaol. Both prisoners were allowed to wear their own clothing in place of the red and brown patched prison garb.

The prison governor gave the bride away, and Ben and Jesse were witnesses to the ceremony. The prison chaplain was an old man, more used to burying his wretched flock than conducting weddings. He kept forgetting the circumstances of the couple he was marrying and repeatedly alluded to the 'long and fruitful life' they would have together. It caused great embarrassment to everyone except the bride.

Even at this late date, Judy seemed unaware that her life had only a matter of hours to run. She was so happy to be marrying Alan that the hearts of everyone except the confused old chaplain went out to her. After the ceremony, the prison governor gave a small party for the newly-weds in his own house, in the prison grounds, supplying food and drink he had purchased from outside the prison.

Before long, the strain of maintaining an outward show of cheerfulness in the shadow of what the morrow was to bring proved too much for Jesse. She managed to maintain her composure during the harrowing farewell with Judy, but once outside the governor's house, she broke down and wept as though her heart would break.

Ben and Jesse returned to the gaol early the next morning and already the streets of Bodmin were seething with excited sightseers, in town for the hanging. A few were disappointed. They had arrived expecting a double hanging. Their only consolation was that it was the man who had been pardoned and not the woman. The hanging of a woman was always a popular spectacle. Only two other women had been hanged in the preceding fifty years' history of Bodmin Gaol.

The gallows were erected on a platform above the gate of the gaol, and many people were already gathered there to be sure of getting a close view of the hanging. Jesse was incensed to see two house-servants from Lamorrack House among them. They would both have known Judy Lean well.

Prisoners were not usually allowed visitors on execution days, but the understanding governor had given Ben and Jesse special permission to remain with Alan Colborne until after the hangman had earned his fee.

The blind balladeer was seated on his hard wooden bed, his head clutched in his hands, when they entered the cell. He raised his face to them and they saw the haggard look of a man who was suffering mental anguish such as few men had known. More than once during the long terrible night that had just ended, he had prayed that his own reprieve might prove to be a mistake and he be allowed to die on the scaffold beside Judy.

He pleaded with the turnkey who let Ben and Jesse into the cell to be allowed to visit Judy, but the turnkey had his orders. No one must visit her but the furtive hangman, who would look through the bars of her cell to obtain a rough estimate of her height and weight, and adjust his rope accordingly.

All that morning, Ben and Jesse sat in the cell with Alan Colborne, trying hard to find things to say. Through the barred window, the noise of the crowd gathering outside the prison could be plainly heard. Alan Colborne became increasingly restless. Finally, he stood up and paced the cell with a skill that bespoke many unsleeping hours.

When there were less than fifteen minutes left before the execution-hour of noon, the door of the cell swung open on heavy complaining hinges and the prison governor entered.

Ben and Jesse started to their feet, convinced he had arrived with news of a reprieve to put an end to this nightmare.

There was to be no reprieve. The governor had come to suggest that Ben, Jesse and Alan Colborne spend the remaining minutes of Judy's life in the chapel. There they might pray for Judy's departing soul – and the thick chapel walls would keep out the triumphant roar of the huge crowd when the trapdoor dropped from beneath her feet.

The governor had been in charge of the prison for much of his life, but the hanging of Judy Colborne was the unhappiest task that had ever come his way. It was not only because he had been caught up in the pathos of her tragically short marriage. The governor of Bodmin Gaol believed in the innocence of the convicted girl.

Alan Colborne realised why the prison governor had made his suggestion, but he declined the well-intentioned offer.

'Thank you, no. If there is a God, He will take Judy to him without my prayers. Though why He should allow her to suffer so is beyond my meagre understanding. For myself, I want to know the moment this unjust deed is committed. It is more surely a murder than anything Judy has committed. She is no more guilty than I, Governor. I should be with her on the scaffold, standing by her side. At least allow me to see her once more . . . please!'

Deeply distressed, the governor shook his head. 'It is too late. She is prepared for what is to come. It would be cruel to upset her now. It may be a comfort to you to know she is standing up to her ordeal well. She is a brave girl.'

Alan Colborne banged his fists against the stone wall. 'How can that be a comfort to me? How can anyone find comfort when they know an innocent girl is to die? She killed Holyoak to save my life. If it were not for me . . .'

Ben took Alan Colborne's arm. After a desperate struggle to regain control of himself, the distraught man shook himself free. 'I . . . I am all right now.'

The prison governor pulled a watch self-consciously from his pocket. 'I have to go.' His discomfiture was evident. He had to be present at every execution carried out in his gaol.

'Go!' whispered Alan Colborne fiercely. 'Would that I were going, too. My thoughts are there before you.'

The heavy door slammed shut behind the governor, and his footsteps could be heard hurrying along the stone-flagged corridor towards the condemned cell.

In the cell, nobody spoke for some minutes. Then they heard a murmur of interest rise from ten thousand throats beyond the prison wall.

Alan Colborne turned from the window. 'They have taken Judy to the scaffold . . . Oh, God!'

376

Jesse was very close to tears but she took his hand. 'Be brave, Alan! Be brave!'

Even from this distance it was possible to feel the excitement of the vast crowd. Their voices buzzed with all the menace of a monstrous swarm of bees.

Suddenly the gaol bell began to toll. It was a deep melancholy sound that reverberated around the stone courtyards and granite buildings. It went on until those in the cell heard a sound that chilled their blood. It was a long-drawn-out muffled scream. The terrified scream of a girl having a dark hood pulled over her head.

The sound was cut off abruptly in the moment that the bell stopped tolling. For long seconds the whole world held its breath at the deed that had been committed in the name of justice.

Then the crowd found its voice with a roar that sent pigeons in panic-stricken flight from trees half a mile beyond the town.

Alan Colborne sank to his knees, his face contorting in agony.

'Judy . . .! Judy . . .!'

Jesse held his head to her, and Alan Colborne's sightless eyes wept for the wife they had never seen.

Chapter Forty

Alan Colborne was transported in the early spring of 1823, taken direct to a transport-ship waiting out the worst of the winter storms in Falmouth's Carrick Roads.

The prison governor sent word of the impending move to Ben, and he and Jesse went to bid farewell to their friend. It was a distressing experience. Alan Colborne was no longer the cheerful balladeer who had always made light of his blindness. His fiddle, recovered by Ben from the St Austell constables remained untouched in a corner of his cell.

Alan Colborne behaved almost as though they were strangers, and spent the whole of their visit complaining that a blind man should not be sent to an unknown country where he would be unable to fend for himself. It was as the governor had told them when they arrived for their visit: Alan Colborne had surrendered to his blindness.

There was little Ben and Jesse could do for him. Ben gave him all the money he could spare, but it was accepted with little gratitude. Only when it was time for them to leave the gaol did Alan Colborne show any sign of emotion. For a moment it seemed he would beg them to remain a while longer – but then he turned away and said nothing as the impatient jangling of the gaoler's keys drove them away.

Not until Alan Colborne had gone from Bodmin Gaol did Jesse really recover from the deep shock of Judy's execution. It would have taken longer had not another event occurred to give her something new to think about.

Ben and Jesse were awakened in the darkness of the night by a heavy and persistent banging on the door of their Sharptor cottage. When Ben threw open the window and called to ask who was there, the voice of Moses Trago came up to him from the moonless darkness.

'It's Kate . . . The child is coming, and she's having a hard time. Will Jesse come up and help?'

'Surely! Wait there a moment. I'll be down with a light.'

'Ask Jesse to hurry, Ben. I've left Kate up there with only brother John for company. He is more frightened than she is of what is going on.'

When Ben withdrew his head from the window, Jesse was already dressing. He went down to let Moses Trago into the cottage.

By the time Jesse came downstairs, Moses was pacing the floor impatiently. Ben had not expected him to be in such a state. There had been no noticeable improvement in the relationship between Moses Trago and his wife in recent months.

On the way to the strange home, some of the reason for Moses Trago's concern became apparent. He spoke as though Kate had already given birth to a son. When Jesse suggested the child might be a daughter, Moses fell silent while he thought about it. Then he said, 'No, it will be a son. It has to be. A man needs a son.'

The facilities offered by Moses Trago's moorland home had not improved since Ben and Jesse's first visit. On the contrary, they had deteriorated considerably over the last month. Kate Trago had suffered an uncomfortable pregnancy and been forced to give up work during the eighth month. With no money of her own, and none forthcoming from Moses, household items such as soap had become luxuries that were out of her reach. For the last couple of weeks, Kate had spent much of the day lying on her bed, her aching legs swollen to twice their normal size.

One look at Kate told Jesse that this would not be a simple birth. She was panting uncontrollably, and the eyes she turned up to Jesse were filled with pain. Brushing back perspiration-soaked hair from Kate's face, Jesse knew she must have been in labour for some time, yet there was no sign of the baby arriving yet.

'I need help here,' Jesse said to Moses Trago. 'Is there any-one in Henwood village skilled in delivering a baby?'

Moses looked startled. 'Yes, Mary Crabbe. But she's never been needed for a birth in this house before. My mother—'

'— has gone! And small wonder,' snapped Jesse. 'We kept pigs in a better house than this at Pengrugla, as you know full well. Mary Crabbe is needed here. What's more, Kate needs her mother, too.'

Moses opened his mouth to protest, but Jesse was in no mood for argument.

'If you are too proud to fetch her because you have had words, then Ben can do it for you. I need both Mary Crabbe and Mrs Kelynack to help me, and I need them here – now!'

As both Ben and Moses Trago turned to leave, Jesse called, 'Wait!'

She pointed to where John Trago sat huddled in a corner, a dark blanket wrapped about him. 'You can take him with you. Then stay away yourself until this is all over, Moses. No man is needed here tonight. Your hour of glory will come when everyone else has done the work. Then you can go to the inn at Henwood and have everyone tell you what a great man you are – for doing something to which you gave little thought at the time, and contributed nothing since.'

Kate Trago groaned from her mattress of heather, and Jesse turned to her, leaving the men to file silently out into the dark night.

'You are welcome to your woman, Ben Retallick,' growled Moses Trago. 'I am damned if I'd let my wife speak like that to any man.'

'She was not speaking to *any* man, Moses,' replied Ben quietly. 'She was speaking to *you* – and she is right. From what I hear, you've put little enough into your marriage since we last spoke together.'

'Hold your tongue,' Moses said angrily. 'Had I wanted such talk I would have fetched the preacher, not you and Jesse. What I do is my own business. You go and do your wife's bidding – but tell Kate's mother I want her out of the house an hour after the baby is born. I'll not put up with *her* tongue wagging at me, too. I'll knock up Mary Crabbe.'

Moses Trago stamped off, with the brooding John Trago following silently behind him.

Mary Kelynack dressed as quickly as she could. After telling her two girls where she was going, she hurried up the hill by Ben's side.

380

'Did Kate ask for me ?' she asked eagerly, when they cleared the village.

'Kate is not well enough to do any asking,' admitted Ben. 'Jesse sent Moses and me out to fetch you and Mary Crabbe.'

'Good for Jesse,' declared Mary Kelynack. 'With Mary Crabbe up there with us we'll manage well enough.'

Ben was working day shift at the Wheal Sharptor. He was ready to leave for work before Jesse returned home to the cottage. Mary Kelynack was with her, and both women looked thoroughly weary.

'Moses has his son,' Jesse managed a weak smile. 'He is a boy of whom Moses can be proud. He arrived fighting the whole world.'

Mary Kelynack snorted. 'He'll need to be able to fight the world with a name like "Morwen"! I have never heard such a name in these parts. But he is his father's son, all right. Not a cry could we raise from him, and he was born with a black scowl on his face that I have seen Moses wear too many times. I feel sorry for the child. What chance does he have in life, being brought up in that cave ?'

Mary Kelynack looked about her at Ben and Jesse's home. 'Why can't Moses find my Kate a nice little place like this ? Kate has not had an easy time this last year. She deserves more than life has given her. Even her firstborn chose to come into this world backwards.'

'I don't think Moses would settle to a house,' said Ben. 'He prides himself on being different from other men.'

'Pride ? Where does that enter the matter ? Living in a hovel is no cause for pride!'

'Perhaps he'll change now he has the son he wanted so much.'

'Moses Trago does not *know* what he wants,' said Mary Kelynack bitterly. 'He thought he wanted to leave Sharptor but, after a couple of years away, he ran back here again. He wanted to marry my Kate, but within a month it was plain for everyone to see he'd made a mistake. Now Kate has given him the son he *thinks* he wants. He'll soon learn there is more to being a father than having a son grow up and call you "Pa".

381

A son is the greatest responsibility that God ever gave to a man – and responsibility is the last thing Moses Trago wants. I tremble for my daughter when I think what he'll do when he learns that bitter lesson.'

Mary Kelynack wrung her hands together in despair. She had never before commented on Kate's marriage, but the long fight to bring her first grandchild into the world had breached the wall of her reticence.

'We are Kate's nearest neighbours,' said Jesse gently. 'We'll do what we can for her. She knows she can always call upon us for help.'

'Knowing and calling are two very different things to Kate,' commented Mary Kelynack with much bitterness. 'But it makes me feel better to know you are close to her.'

Mary Kelynack's harsh criticism of Moses Trago was justified before many months had passed. Moses refused to accept that the needs of the baby had to be satisfied before his own. Kate, for her part, made few concessions to her husband's pride. The baby came first with her in all things. This uncompromising attitude earned her a great many beatings.

As soon as Kate Trago recovered from the ordeal of child-birth, she returned to work at the Wheal Sharptor with Jesse. Whilst they and the other bal-maidens worked, breaking down the ore for the stamps, baby Morwen nestled in a wooden box nearby. Wrapped in an old woollen blanket, he lay watching the high and low clouds passing overhead in an unequal race, until he was lulled to sleep by the ringing rhythm of hammer on stone.

On days when the weather was exceptionally bad, Morwen was placed in the shelter of the sorting-sheds. The noise of hammering in such an enclosed space occasionally caused him to blink in sudden alarm. For the remainder of the time, he viewed the underside of the roof above him with as much interest as he gave to the sky outside.

The Wheal Sharptor was proving to be a pleasant and profitable little mine. The miners were fortunate enough to have cut into good tin lodes at shallow levels. This meant that the ladders did not yet need to go down to any great depth. Theophilus Strike was not over-generous to his miners, but neither was he a greedy man. It was not his policy to tear as much ore from the ground as could be brought out in the shortest possible time. By keeping his mine relatively small and shallow, he was making a very useful profit. He would continue to do so when the roofless buildings of many of the larger mines stood in desolation amidst mountains of mine-waste: mute memorials to blood and sweat . . . and avarice.

The miners who worked for Theophilus Strike reflected his attitude in their own work. Almost every one of them was a married man, content to have a steady job for as many years as he dared to look ahead. They were all experienced miners who knew every aspect of mining – and they did it well.

The Wheal Sharptor was a happy mine.

Such a state of affairs was exceptional in the confused and discontented years of the early 1820s. Throughout the country men were clamouring for unprecedented changes in the accepted pattern of life. Paradoxically, many of those who resisted these demands most strongly were the very ones who had brought about the need for change.

Almost unnoticed during the wars of the early nineteenth century, Britain had become the greatest manufacturing country in the world. Men were drawn from the land in their thousands and moved to hurriedly constructed industrial towns. There, in dingy unsanitary conditions, they worked the new machines in huge factories, going home at night to spawn ever-growing families to add to the gross overcrowding and fuel future discontent.

England's glut of cheap labour that utilised husbands, wives and children soon put her years ahead of all her foreign competitors. Huge fortunes were made and remade; but the money was distributed among very few men and, as the country's manufacturing prowess increased, so Britain's agriculture fell behind.

In spite of the momentous switch from agriculture to industry, those who ran the country from Parliament were either landowners, or representatives of landowners. Protecting their landed interests came as naturally to them as drawing breath. Foreign produce coming into the country was taxed to the point where it became hopelessly expensive and beyond the reach of the vast mass of the rapidly increasing population.

Even when the Government was made aware of the problem, it did nothing to alleviate the hunger of the people. Instead, it passed a series of unwise Poor Laws, throwing the burden of feeding the swollen ranks of the poor on to the parish in which they lived. By these means, the Goverment succeeded in antagonising yet another section of the country's society: all those men who were wealthy enough to pay rates and taxes.

The clamour for reform gathered strength as men of substance called their own meetings. They sent petitions to the Prime Minister calling for an end to the heavy burden of taxation, rates and tithes, under which they reeled. They, too, now demanded the right to elect men to Parliament who had *their* interests at heart.

The mood of these latest recruits to the reform movement was made known to Ben one evening in the late summer of 1823. He was working in the garden of his cottage, stripped to the waist, when a horse and rider turned off the main track to Henwood and headed up the hill towards the Wheal Sharptor. The horse stepped carefully. The mine-track was torn and scarred by the hoofs of the Wheal Sharptor pack-horses which daily slipped and slithered down the hill, laden with ore for the smelting-house. The rider looked up the hill at the group of cottages. Seeing Ben in his garden, he headed in his direction.

When he drew closer, Ben sank the blade of his pointed shovel deep into the earth and leaned upon the long handle, eyeing the horseman. It was rarely that one saw a saddled horse in these parts. Ben was quite sure Sharptor had never seen a more elegant rider. Wearing a coat of soft blue velvet and long black riding-boots, the approaching man reminded Ben of some sleek well-fed mole.

Easing his horse to a halt on the other side of the wall, the rider called, 'I am seeking Ben Retallick. Would you tell me where I might find him?'

'You have,' replied Ben curtly. 'Have we met before? I don't recall you, sir.'

'We have not met before, Mr Retallick, and I doubt if you will have heard my name, but I have heard much of you and am pleased to make your acquaintance.'

Swinging down from his horse, the rider looped the reins over the unpainted gate-post and entered the garden. Extending his hand to Ben, he said, 'I am Richard Hoblyn, of Liskeard.'

Ben shook the outstretched hand, but he had no idea why this well-dressed stranger should have sought him out.

Seeing his puzzlement, Richard Hoblyn explained, 'I have been anxious to meet with you since I first heard of your part in having Sir Colman Vincent's parliamentary seat taken away from him – but may we discuss this matter inside your house?'

Ben frowned. It appeared that the whole of Cornwall was now aware he had been responsible for the downfall of Sir Colman Vincent. Slipping his shirt over his head he tucked it inside his trousers and led the way inside the cottage. Ahead of him he heard Jesse running upstairs to the bedroom. She had been at the open window watching Ben when Richard Hoblyn came up the hill. She now hurried to change from her working-clothes.

Inviting Richard Hoblyn to take a seat in the best room, Ben said, 'Such stories tend to become exaggerated to suit the mood of the teller, Mr Hoblyn. You mustn't believe all you have heard.'

Carefully adjusting his velvet coat about him on the chair, Richard Hoblyn said quietly, 'Nevertheless, Sir Colman is no longer a Member of the House of Commons. You are wise to be cautious, of course. You have set a dangerous precedent; but it is one I hope to emulate. I am a merchant in Liskeard. I, and many of my friends, are most dissatisfied with the two Members of Parliament who currently represent our borough. Indeed, I stood against them in the last election on the reform issue. As they are both from a titled family I had little chance of success. However, I now have reason to believe

385

that a large sum of money was distributed to buy the votes of men who might otherwise have voted for me.'

'You are probably right, Mr Hoblyn – but what has this to do with me?'

Richard Hoblyn leaned forward in his chair. 'I am here to recruit your aid, Mr Retallick. Certain of my friends in the reform movement are reluctant to take action against our present Members of Parliament. They fear certain . . . retribution? I would like you to attend our next meeting and speak to them. Tell them how you tackled a similar case of electoral bribery – and won!'

Ben shook his head. 'I'm sorry, Mr Hoblyn. I have already refused a similar request, made by a man who travelled all the way here from the Midlands. In Sir Colman's case I became involved because his actions were affecting me and my family. I have no wish to be caught up in the reform issue, or anything else that doesn't concern me.'

Richard Hoblyn looked at Ben in some surprise. Without giving the matter too much thought, he had assumed Ben must be a supporter of the reform movement. Before he could say more, Jesse entered the room. She had put on her best cotton dress and hastily brushed her long black hair down about her shoulders. The transformation from untidy bal-maiden to beautiful woman was astonishing.

Richard Hoblyn sprang to his feet, his expression one of frank admiration as Ben introduced Jesse.

An awkward silence fell upon the room, until Richard Hoblyn began explaining his presence to Jesse, in an attempt to win her support. 'I had hoped to persuade your husband to address a reform meeting in Liskeard, but it seems the idea is not entirely to his liking.'

Jesse glanced quickly at Ben before replying. 'Ben probably knows better than anyone that talking at meetings is a waste of everyone's time. When it comes to making a decision, it takes ten men ten times as long as one.'

Richard Hoblyn conceded that Jesse might have a valid point, but added, 'I already know the course of action *I* must take, but my opponents wield great influence in the county. I need the wholehearted support of my own townsmen. By telling them of his success in the action against Sir Colman Vincent I sincerely believe your husband might win such support for me. The majority of the voters feel as strongly as I about the matter of blatant vote-purchasing, but they are frightened. If we attempt to remove our present Members of Parliament and fail, it could have dire consequences for us all.'

To Ben, Richard Hoblyn said, 'I am prepared to pay you well for your time.'

Ben's pride bridled at the merchant's offer. 'The man from the Midlands promised me a seat in the House of Commons; that, too, failed to tempt me. No, Mr Hoblyn. I sympathise with you, but this is not my quarrel. I want no part of it. I suggest you do as I did last year. Go to see David Howell. He is no longer High Sheriff of Cornwall, but I'm sure he'll be ready to advise you.'

'You know David Howell?' Richard Hoblyn looked at Ben incredulously. His manner towards Ben had so far been condescending. Now he felt he might have underestimated this quiet young man.

'I had a letter of introduction to him. He was most helpful to me. I'm sure he'll know what you should do.'

'He might at that. I believe he is a recent convert to the reform movement. I am obliged to you, Mr Retallick. Perhaps my journey here has not been wasted after all.'

Richard Hoblyn took his leave after casting a final admiring glance at Jesse. At the door, he paused and turned back into the room.

'You will be coming to Liskeard Fair, next week, of course?'

The annual fair was held in Liskeard, to celebrate a saint's day. All the mines in the area ceased operation for the occasion. Ben and Jesse, in common with the other miners and their families from Wheal Sharptor, would be attending.

'Yes, we'll be there.'

'Good! I am keeping open house at my home in Dean Street. I will expect to have the pleasure of welcoming you there.'

Chapter Forty-One

Ben woke before the sun rose, on the day of the fair. Slipping quietly from the bed, he opened the window to check upon the weather. To his great relief, it was dry. A look at the stars, rapidly fading into the grey of morning, told him it was likely to remain so. He and Jesse would be walking to Liskeard, a distance of almost six miles. Rain on a normal fair-day was bad enough. Today it would have proved calamitous. They would be dressing up not only for the annual fair, but also for a visit to the Hoblyn house.

Ben and Jesse took a long time making themselves ready and were still eating breakfast when Wrightwick Roberts came to the door. He had spent the night at Tom Shovell's house and would walk to Liskeard with Ben and Jesse. The big preacher was not given to paying compliments, but so impressed was he with Jesse's appearance that he assured her he would see no more handsome woman at Liskeard Fair.

Jesse dropped him a mock curtsy. 'Thank you, Wrightwick – but don't tell me you are going to Liskeard Fair to look at young women.'

The serious-minded preacher frowned, unaware that Jesse was joking. 'I am not going to the fair to enjoy any sinful pleasures, Jesse. I am going as a dedicated servant of the Lord. My duty is to protect the souls of simple miners. My attentions may not be welcomed by those I seek to save, but that will not turn me aside from my duty. Now, I suggest we hurry, or the fair will be well under way before we arrive.'

When Wrightwick Roberts turned away, Jesse pulled a wry face at Ben behind the preacher's back. Ben grinned in reply. 'We'll be there in plenty of time for you to save souls, Wrightwick. I doubt if any miner will give you a hearing until his money has run out.'

'I'll not wait to be given a hearing, Ben. Rather than see a good man lost to the Devil, I'll give him a drubbing first. He will feel all the better for it tomorrow morning.'

Ben's grin widened. 'Then there will be more than one miner going down from grass tomorrow with sore bones but a happy heart. This should be a fair-day to remember.'

Despite Wrightwick Roberts's anxiety about their tardiness in setting out, it was still early when the trio left Sharptor and headed across the moor to Liskeard.

Soon they met with men from other mines and their families. Some Ben knew, others he did not, but such was the cameraderie among miners that they all walked on together. While the men talked of mines and mining, the women discussed births, marriages and deaths and the children boasted of what they intended doing at the fair.

There was another, less altruistic reason for banding together in a large group. As they drew closer to the town, they met with crowds of farm-workers, also heading for the delights of the fair. With the advantage of numbers on the side of the miners, there was less chance of the farm-workers picking a fight.

Such caution had only been gained by years of hard-won experience. The farmers and their workers resented the men who tore the heart out of the soil, spoiling good farmland with thousands of tons of useless and unsightly mine-waste. In a similar fashion, the townsmen looked down upon both miners and farm-workers as lacking social graces the townsmen believed came with the refinements of town life.

The sun was still climbing into the sky when Ben, Jesse and Wrightwick Roberts reached Liskeard. Here Wrightwick Roberts took his leave of them. He had matters of religious business to discuss with the local Wesleyan preacher before he could give the fair the full benefit of his disapproval.

Already the streets of the market-town were teeming with miners and farm-workers from outlying communities. Tall-hatted town constables worked valiantly to prevent stalls from blocking the narrow streets, trying in vain to leave room for the noon coach to pass through.

Ben and Jesse moved through the crowd, pausing to express sympathy for an old mangy bear with sore watering eyes. The bear shuffled and swayed at the end of a chain in unrhythmic time to the music of a fife, played by its tinker owner.

They met with more music farther along the road. A small monkey, dressed in red coat and hat, turned somersaults to the tune of a penny whistle played by an ex-sailor.

All around, tempting aromas rose from the food-stalls, and a wide miscellany of goods was offered for sale.

This was the section of the fair that catered for the rag, tag and bobtail of fair-goers. Amongst them, the pickpockets who followed the fair around the countryside carried out their nefarious activities. These pickpockets were an ever-changing band. As petty thieves graduated to their ranks, so others were caught and transported – or occasionally hanged.

In the market-place at the other end of town, the serious business of the fair was conducted. Here were sheep, pigs and cows, brought to the fair for sale or exhibition. Few miners found their way here, and Ben felt out of place among men whose conversation centred around prime beef, milk yields and the size of a prize cow's udder.

Eventually, Ben and Jesse left the fair behind and made their way to the comparative quiet of Dean Street. They were going to take up Richard Hoblyn's invitation, although Ben was not at all certain the merchant would remember extending it to them.

When they arrived at the house, Ben and Jesse saw it was one of the finest in an area of imposing new residences. The house and gardens were crowded with people. Most of the women were over-dressed and ostentatiously bedecked with jewellery. The men wore a variety of styles. Some were dressed as befitted solid prosperous merchants. Others sported the flamboyant fashion favoured by King George IV when he was Prince Regent.

This was the new 'élite' of the country's society: England's middle class; the moneyed ranks of merchants and shop-keepers; men of trade.

In the garden were tables laden with foodstuffs of every description, many of which had never before been seen by the urchins who crowded outside the gate, begging pennies from those who went inside.

Ben and Jesse were stopped inside the gate by a servant

who evidently thought they had entered by mistake. Ben was explaining that Richard Hoblyn had invited them, when the host himself came hurrying across the lawns, closely followed by a young man in his late twenties, dressed even more elegantly than Richard Hoblyn.

'Mr and Mrs Retallick! How nice of you to come.'

Turning to the elegant younger man, Richard Hoblyn said, 'May I introduce you to my younger brother, Crispin?'

Crispin Hoblyn took Jesse's hand. Bowing low, he raised it to his lips, 'I am honoured, ma'am. My brother returned from Sharptor singing your praises, but your beauty far surpasses his meagre description.'

Releasing Jesse's hand with exaggerated reluctance, Crispin Hoblyn switched his attentions to Ben and proved he had a surprisingly firm grasp. 'You can be proud of your wife today, sir. She is the fairest flower in this garden.'

Ben was not sure he approved of this foppish young man admiring Jesse so openly, but Crispin Hoblyn had a disarming manner. It was difficult to take lasting offence at him.

Then Ben and Jesse were taken to meet the other guests. Although the Hoblyn brothers had given them a warm welcome, neither Jesse nor Ben felt entirely at ease in such a gathering.

Jesse was fully aware of the lack of quality of her clothes. She had a very attractive slim figure, and her tight-fitting bodice attracted more than one admiring glance from the men, but their wives were fully aware that the dress was home-made, of a cheap cloth.

Ben, too, felt clumsy in his heavy boots and rough serge suit among these men of fashion, but he soon forgot his self-consciousness when he listened to their conversations. By now he had been separated from Jesse and, on the occasions when his host left him for a few minutes, Ben found that the other guests ignored him. They talked together as though he were not within hearing.

It very soon became apparent that the 'reform' sought by these men was not the same as that fought for by the men of the Midlands – or even that of the men of Mevagissey. These men expected to achieve considerable personal gain from an extended franchise. For them it meant no less than the passing of power from the landed gentry to themselves. They had no thought of giving the vote to *all* men. A vote given to a fisherman, a miner or a farm-worker would be a vote wasted. More, it would be downright dangerous! Tantamount to handing power to the masses. From such foolish ideas were revolutions born.

It was more than an hour before Ben was able to make his escape from Richard Hoblyn, and then not until he had given his promise to attend the reform meeting being held in a field at the edge of the town. Ben realised this was the real reason he had been invited to the house, but he would have preferred to stay away from the meeting.

Ben had not seen Jesse for some time and he was becoming anxious about her. Eventually, he found her, bright-eyed and sparkling, seated on a chair inside the house, surrounded by a number of young men. Of Crispin Hoblyn there was no sign.

Ben plucked Jesse from her admirers with a curt apology to them. Not until they were on their way back to the fair and well clear of the house did he begin to relax.

He grinned at Jesse. 'I would rather spend a day working down a mine than chatting with folk like those at Hoblyn's house. They are not our kind of people, Jesse.'

Jesse gave Ben a sidelong glance. 'You speak for yourself, Ben. Crispin Hoblyn thought otherwise. He even hinted he would like to make me his mistress!'

Ben stopped, his jaw dropping in disbelief. 'He did what!'

Jesse took his arm and hugged him to her. 'There's nothing for you to be angry about, Ben. He put it in such a gentlemanly way that he might have been asking me to stitch a button on his coat.'

'I . . . I'll break his scented neck . . .!'

Jesse looked up at him happily. 'Do you know, this is the first time I've given you cause to be jealous? You needn't worry, Ben. I gave Crispin Hoblyn no encouragement. I'm quite certain he makes a similar approach to every woman he meets . . . In fact, I would have been quite disappointed had he made me an exception!'

Ben looked at Jesse in bewilderment. There were times when he felt he did not know her at all. This was one of them.

Everyone in Liskeard knew of the reform meeting, and most of them attended. The meeting began quietly enough. From a small platform set up at one end of the field, Richard Hoblyn and some of his friends, made long dull speeches about the need to slash taxes and review the voting laws of the land.

For perhaps half an hour the meeting followed its predictable path before a number of men elbowed their way through to the front of the listening crowd. With a start of surprise, Ben saw that one of them was Charles Swindles. With him was another man Ben thought he had seen before.

When they and their friends were immediately in front of the platform, they began heckling. At first, the speaker ignored their interruptions. Then he broke the cardinal rule of any speaker. He tried to reply to some of the questions they hurled at him.

Finally, in sheer exasperation, Richard Hoblyn stood up and shouted, 'I don't know who you are, but if you have something to say on the subject of reform one of you may come up here and say his piece. Then perhaps you will allow this meeting to proceed without interruption . . .'

Before Richard Hoblyn had finished talking, the man Ben had seen before was being helped on to the platform amidst noisy applause from his supporters. He was a stout red-faced man with long grey hair turning to white.

'Gentlemen – and ladies – of Cornwall. You may have heard of me. My name is William Cobbett . . .'

An excited murmur went through the crowd, and suddenly Ben remembered where he had seen the man. He had been addressing the huge gathering at the Crinnis mine, years before, when Ben and Jesse had attended their first reform meeting with Walter Dunn.

Cobbett was a well-known reformer and political dissident, and Ben saw Richard Hoblyn's discomfiture. The merchant could not have anticipated that his meeting would attract the attentions of such a man. He would certainly not welcome his presence. Both men claimed to speak for the ideals of 'reform', but they had little in common.

Speaking with a powerful voice, rich with the rustic accent of Anglia, William Cobbett had none of the rambling ineptitude of Richard Hoblyn's reformers. His voice was heard by every man and woman in the five-thousand-strong crowd, his words blunt, spoken without regard for his listeners' sensitivities.

William Cobbett's views went far beyond the reform of Parliament. He called for the abolition of the House of Lords and all the privileges that sprang from the possession of land and wealth. Pointing to the heavens, he roared, 'All men are equal in the sight of God! Is that not a Christian precept? Yes, it is . . . and Wesley did his fellow-men a disservice by urging them to accept their lot in this world in exchange for a vague promise to improve their status in the next. There is nothing in the Bible that says a man must stay poor and work twice as hard as he should – just to make another Christian rich!'

Cornwall was a staunch stronghold of Wesleyan Methodism. Cobbett's criticism of the founder of the Methodist Church provoked an angry outburst from many of his listeners. Immediately, the men who had pushed their way to the front with Cobbett closed in on the platform and turned to face the crowd. They were neither miners nor Cornishmen. Ben guessed correctly that William Cobbett travelled with an escort of men of his own convictions – and they all looked tough.

The crowd's displeasure did not bother Cobbett. Still in full flow, he castigated all forms of authority and urged the miners of Cornwall to join together in a 'Union of Miners'. He told them their labour was a powerful weapon in the fight against all that was wrong with the country's parliamentary system. The miners in the North of England had already set the precedent. Now Cornwall was being given the opportunity to join the national fight.

394

William Cobbett knew how to rouse the miners of the North, and he could whip the industrial workers of the Midlands into a frenzy – but he knew nothing of the Cornish miner, neither his method of working nor his stubborn independent nature.

The vast majority of the miners here were 'tributers'. Tributing was a traditional method of mining that made each man virtually self-employed. They bid against each other for a particular working-area in a mine, after which the miner's own skill and hard work determined how much he earned.

Some mine captains paid lower rates than others, and a few mines skimped on the matters for which they were responsible. Inadequate shaft work and poor maintenance were the cause of too many deaths, but the miners usually managed to set things to rights without any outside help.

Suddenly, a hand gripped Ben's arm and a voice shouted, 'Here is someone who can tell you how to topple authority. One of your own kind. Ben Retallick – a miner.'

Charles Swindles had recognised Ben in the crowd and, unnoticed by him, had made his way from the platform to Ben's side. Now he pushed him towards the platform while the crowd gave him an uncertain reception and Jesse stood tight-lipped and disapproving behind him.

Ben began to struggle against Charles Swindles' grip, but then he looked about him at the miners in the crowd. He had seen many of them emerging from a mine shaft, filthy and exhausted at the end of a shift. Others he had watched giving away their hard-won money to the landlord of an inn or beer-house.

On the platform in front of them now were men who were prepared to use the miners and take just as much from them, but in a more subtle and dishonest way. Neither Hoblyn nor Cobbett cared about those to whom they were appealing. The miners and farm-workers would be used, and then discarded, as expediency and ambition dictated.

'All right, I'll speak.'

Ben shook off the hand of Charles Swindles and made his way to the platform. He ignored the proffered hand of William

Cobbett and sprang on to the wooden platform.

His arrival brought a few genuine cheers from miners in the crowd who knew Ben, or had seen him in their district.

Standing on the platform, looking out over the sea of faces extending over the full length and breadth of the field, Ben experienced a moment of panic. Then he remembered some of the snippets of conversation he had overheard at Richard Hoblyn's house, and he began to speak to the crowd.

'As Charles Swindles has just told you, I am a miner, as are most of you here.' Ben drew in a deep breath and said firmly, 'They are the only true words I've heard spoken today.'

A startled hush fell upon the huge crowd and Ben was quick to follow up his initial impact.

'This meeting has been called to discuss parliamentary reform. There cannot be anyone here who doubts that reform is needed. It's not right for a few landowners to control the lives of thousands of men and women from the day they are born to the moment they die; to tell them where they must live, what work they will do – even who they are allowed to marry. In a moment of anger, one of these landowners can dismiss a man and turn his family out to starve to death. He can bring pressure to bear on the adventurers and close any mine in the country. Not one of us is safe from men with such power.'

The applause that greeted these words was led by the men on the platform. Alarmed by Ben's opening words, they were now convinced Ben had used them only to gain the attention of the restless crowd.

Ben swiftly disillusioned them.

'Yes, we all want reform. But what exactly is this "reform"? What will it give *us*, the miners and farm-workers of Cornwall? Richard Hoblyn and his friends see it as a chance to put *themselves* into Parliament; to have bills passed to ease *their* taxes and make life better for the merchants and shop-keepers of the country . . .'

'Well said, Ben!' cried Charles Swindles gleefully. He had hardly got the words out before Ben switched his attack to include the Midlands' Chartist and his travelling companion.

'William Cobbett is no better. He wants to lead us to a revolution, with himself standing behind us as an English Napoleon. He says we must all stand up and fight . . . but for what? For William Cobbett? He has no knowledge of the way we Cornish miners work and is interested only in the trouble we can stir up to help *his* cause.'

From the corner of his eye, Ben saw William Cobbett signalling to some of his men. A couple of them moved hurriedly towards the platform.

'Yes, we need reform – but not just for the sake of change.'

One of William Cobbett's men reached on to the platform and grasped Ben's ankle. Shaking him off, Ben shouted his final words to the crowd, who were now cheering him wildly.

'My advice to you is to refuse to be pushed into doing something you'll all regret. Do nothing until a man comes along who knows our ways. Our problems . . .'

Two of William Cobbett's men gained the platform and rushed Ben in an attempt to throw him off. Ben's fist dropped the first of them to his knees. The second man swung a punch which caught Ben on the side of his head and made him stagger. He recovered quickly and, taking his attacker by the collar, dumped him unceremoniously in the lap of William Cobbett.

Ben leaped from the platform to the ground and was immediately surrounded by Cobbett's men. For a few minutes he fought valiantly to defend himself before Wrightwick Roberts's voice roared, 'I'm with you, Ben,' and the preacher fought his way to Ben's side. At the same time, a figure leaped from the platform, knocking two of Ben's assailants to the ground.

It was Crispin Hoblyn. Scrambling to his feet, the elegant young man adopted the exaggerated stance of a prizefighter. Exaggerated or not, he swung a beautiful right hook to down another of Cobbett's men. Now many of the miners in the crowd surged forward and the odds swung overwhelmingly in Ben's favour. The men from the Midlands were chased from the field.

397

Ben grinned as Wrightwick Roberts dabbed his bloody nose, looking indignantly at the blood staining his handkerchief.

'You were right, Ben,' the preacher said nasally. 'No God-fearing Cornishman could possibly follow a man who insults John Wesley and is ready to spill the blood of a servant of the Lord.'

Jesse fought her way through the excited crowd to Ben's side and looked anxiously at the graze along his cheekbone. Over her head, Ben met Crispin Hoblyn's eyes.

'I'm obliged to you,' Ben said stiffly, remembering his advances to Jesse.

'The pleasure is all mine,' Crispin Hoblyn produced his infectious grin once more. 'Though I doubt if my brother will agree with me. He certainly did *not* agree with you.'

Crispin Hoblyn rubbed his knuckles proudly. 'Tom Cribb, the prizefighter, taught me his art. This is the first opportunity I have had to put his teaching to the test.' He looked down at one of William Cobbett's followers who knelt on the ground with bowed head, groaning loudly. 'I owe Tom a night out when next we meet.'

Crispin Hoblyn looked beyond the crowd to where a large body of bright-coated horsemen rode down the track to the field. 'I think we had all better leave now. It would seem the magistrate has called out the militia. It would be a sad end to a wonderful day to spend it sharing a cell with some of Cobbett's rabble.'

Ben and Jesse arrived within sight of Sharptor when the sun was sinking low behind the high moor, sending long fingers of shadow far out across the valley.

There had been little opportunity to talk on their way home from Liskeard. Many miners walked the same rough roads, full of excitement at the eventful meeting they had attended. They attached themselves to Jesse and Ben, talking all the while of what had occurred at the Liskeard Fair reform meeting.

Some miners who had left the meeting after Ben and Jesse

overtook them along the way, passing on the disturbing news that a few of the young hot-headed miners had stoned the militia. They said there had been a number of arrests. Minutes later, another miner caught up with them. He had later news. The disturbance had been caused by a small group of drunken farm-workers. Only two arrests had been made, both by the constables, and both for drunkenness.

Shortly before Sharptor was reached, the track divided. The upper route went to the Wheal Sharptor, the lower to the Marke Valley mines. Here the last of Ben and Jesse's companions left them. They were alone for the first time since leaving Liskeard.

Rounding a shoulder of the hill, they paused to gaze eastwards, to where the patchwork of tiny fields and spinneys blended with the mauve haze of distance. Ben looked at Jesse, but she was seeking something in the valley.

'There's Linkinhorne church steeple . . . in among those trees.'

'I'm sorry, Jesse.'

'Sorry?' she turned to face him. 'Sorry for what?'

'For breaking up the reform meeting. I'm not a reformer at heart – and I don't like people using me. Hoblyn, Cobbett and Charles Swindles are not reformers, either. Each of them uses the reform cause to achieve his own ends. Walter must have been the only honest man in the whole of the reform movement. It really meant something to him. It would break his heart if he could see what has happened to the cause for which he gave so much.'

'It broke his heart soon after his arrest,' said Jesse huskily. 'Not one of the many men Walter helped had the courage to raise his voice in protest on Walter's behalf. Had you spoken in favour of reform today you would have been setting out on the same road that Walter took – a road to unhappiness and broken promises. No, Ben, you told the men at that meeting how you felt, and I'm proud of you for doing it. Besides, I don't want a husband who thinks more of an ideal than of me. I love you, Ben. I want you to love me . . . with all your heart.'

Ben kissed Jesse and as they walked slowly along the path

with their arms about each other. Ben looked up the hill to their little grey cottage, tucked in a fold of the moor.

'This is what I want from life, Jesse. I have a job I enjoy, a home in one of the most beautiful spots in the land . . . and a wife who is fancied by the gentlemen of the county.'

Ben grinned happily at Jesse. 'One day we'll have a family of our own. Then I'll have all that any man could need.'

Jesse stopped suddenly. When Ben looked down at her he saw she was smiling at him in delight.

'You couldn't have said anything to make me happier, Ben. I've been waiting for the right moment to tell you my news. Now you've given it to me. Ben Retallick, you are going to be a father. Soon both our lives will be complete. May God give us many years to enjoy them – together.'